"WHAT IF PATTON HAD...?"

"There's an atomic bomb right here in Bavaria," Gerda said, getting up from the couch and putting her arms around Lowel.

"What do you mean? You're not making sense!"

"A bomb. A thousand times more deadly than the one dropped on Hiroshima. It's got a warhead that can penetrate all the way to Moscow and blow sky high all your dreams of peace. A bomb with a shiny helmet and a brain, and its name is Patton. What if they succeed in detonating him, Lowel?"

But Lowel was gone. He was already running, down the stairs and into the street where his jeep was parked...

BLOOD
★★★★ AND ★★★★
GUTS
★ IS GOING NUTS ★
CHRISTOPHER LEOPOLD

A BERKLEY BOOK
published by
BERKLEY PUBLISHING CORPORATION

History records that the day after his disastrous press conference which led to his dismissal from command of the U.S. Third Army, General George S. Patton, Jr., went chamois hunting. This book is a novel, not a verifiable historical account. It suggests, as a novel just might, that General Patton in fact went hunting for bigger game in September 1945: namely the Russian bear. Now any real historian knows this is a lousy goddamn lie. There's no evidence to suggest that the real reason for Patton's dismissal was an itchy trigger finger, rather than an unguarded remark about Nazis being no different from Republicans and Democrats. However, the documents do suggest that if Old Blood and Guts had been allowed one last trial of strength, he might even have given up swearing.

CHRISTOPHER LEOPOLD

Principal Characters

The Americans

General George S. Patton, Jr.

Major General Hobart R. Gay
Major General Regis Halleck
Colonel Bob Miller
Major Lowel Packer
Major Wallis Du Camp
Major Al Kopp

General of the Army Dwight Eisenhower
Captain Kay Summersby
Lieutenant General Walter Bedell Smith

Staff Sergeant Offenbach
Pfc. Brewer
Private Maggio
Private Cohn

The Germans

Major General Klaus von Ritter
Herr Martin Sauber
Herr Frolich

Gerda Gettler
Eric Weber
Rudi Frolich
Johan

The Russians

Marshal Tolbukhin
Major Bogamov

Abbreviations Used in the Novel

SHAEF	Supreme Headquarters Allied Expeditionary Force
USFET	United States Forces European Theater
USAAC	United States Army Air Corps
CP	Command post
POW	Prisoner of war
PFC.	Private first class
PX	U. S. Army Post exchange
DP	Displaced person
GI	U. S. Army serviceman, derived from term "Government Issue"
PATTON 75	"A suicidal highball of champagne, brandy, and possibly other disastrous mixtures," Kay Summersby
FRAGEBOGEN	Questionnaire every German citizen was required to complete by Allied occupation authorities
MUSS-NAZI	German who joined the Nazi Party for career reasons
G-1	U. S. Army Personnel Staff
G-2	U. S. Army Intelligence Staff
G-3	U. S. Army Operations Staff
G-4	U. S. Army Supply Staff
G-5	U. S. Army Civil Affairs Staff

Contents

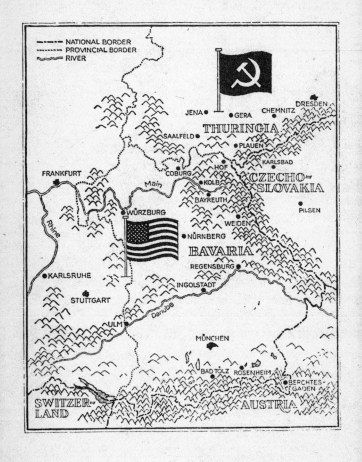

NATIONAL BORDER
PROVINCIAL BORDER
RIVER

DRESDEN
JENA • GERA • CHEMNITZ
THURINGIA
SAALFELD
PLAUEN
KARLSBAD
FRANKFURT
COBURG • HOF
CZECHO-
Main
KOLB • SLOVAKIA
BAYREUTH
WÜRZBURG
PILSEN
WEIDEN
Rhine
NÜRNBERG
BAVARIA
KARLSRUHE
REGENSBURG
INGOLSTADT
STUTTGART
Danube
ULM
MÜNCHEN
BAD TÖLZ • ROSENHEIM • BERCHTES-
SWITZER-
GADEN
LAND
AUSTRIA

"In time of peace, prepare for war."

From an address to returning U.S. combat men, July 13, 1945, by General George Patton, Jr.

Winners and Losers Late May 1945

"What else is new today, Hap?" General George S. Patton, Jr., inquired of his faithful watchdog chief staff man.

"Just a few comings and goings," General Hobart Gay informed him. "Sorry, George, but we've finally lost control of the 7th Armored. The switch is to Luke Clay in Berlin. But the news isn't all stop. You'll be glad to know we're clawing back General Halleck. They've definitely assigned him to command VII Corps."

Patton contorted his face into a crooked-toothed grimace. Was it just six weeks ago that he was hammering against the Czech frontier with the finest body of brawling instinctive fighters ever conjured together in the history of warfare? Half a million rootin' tootin' hard-swearing bastards who had joyfully ridden their way from the Normandy *bocage* to the gates of Prague with a kind of instinctual touch-feel just six weeks ago. And with them he, George Patton, soaring to the ultimate Valhalla of military glory, with press panegyrics that must have bought an extra shade of bilious green to the faces of

1

Eisenhower and Bedell Smith. Goddamnit, he hadn't just won the fighting war almost singlehanded. He'd beaten them to the punch in the headline scramble too. From the *Colorado Courier* to the Chicago *Herald Tribune* the story was all "Old Blood and Guts." (Next month he would have to shyly slide around America, dodging a barrage of ticker tape and trying not to open his big blurting mouth.)

"Sure, it had to be Halleck. They just know how I rate that guy. But at least now I've got time to make up my mind. Was Halleck the unluckiest guy I commanded or just the goddamn thickest . . . ?"

There was nothing you could actually put your hand on and scream bloody murder; on the face of it George Patton could be seen to have received his just deserts. They'd graciously donated him that extra fourth star to hang on his helmet (along with a prize collection of no-talent goddamn baboons). They'd confirmed him in his Third Army command (only to take it back in ever-growing dribs and drabs). They'd given him a stately pleasure dome to disport himself in—Max Amann's country residence in the alpine sap resort of Bad Tölz, slap against the mountains in Upper Bavaria. A supreme example of Thousand Year Reich kitsch. Still, one of the best houses he'd ever seen, with a bowling alley, swimming pool, boathouse and two boats—the whole thing a vast mausoleum to the ill-gotten gains Amann had made by virtue of being Hitler's World War I sergeant and the publisher of *Mein Kampf.*

They had even made him Military Governor of Bavaria, probably from a shrewd instinct that Old Georgie might feel particularly ill at ease behind an office desk.

And now they'd given him Halleck, the most exasperating sonofabitch who had ever served under him, the one guy that really stuck in his gullet. Yeah, those sly guys at USFET, the Frankfurt Mafia, he sometimes called them, were really picking up the points now.

"There's just one other thing," Gay was saying. "That is

if it's not too irksome to don your gubernatorial hat. We haven't yet pitched on a guy to run Kolb for us. It's a small enough joint but you might think it was pretty key. It's bang against the Russian occupied zone."

"Aren't there any cleaned-up Nazis?" asked Patton with his crooked smile.

"Sorry, can't do. They're getting hot on those new de-Nazification clauses. Seems there's only one guy with no Nazi affinities. It's funny really. He couldn't stomach the Nazis because he thought they were too right wing. His name's Frolich."

"Welcome to the Court, General," said the very pleasant, very smiling, fresh-faced Major Wallis Du Camp. "Sorry I couldn't be present to meet you at friendly old München, but we've had a little trouble over what you might call proconsular etiquette. General Patton is minded to have a new mess uniform designed for staff officers of the Third Army now that the war's over. And he wanted my aesthetic advice."

"I can't quite figure . . ." slurred General Regis Halleck as he stood before the massive structure that the fortunate publisher of *Mein Kampf* had erected for himself in the old-fashioned spa town of Bad Tölz.

"Yeah. I forgot to mention my name's Du Camp. I'm aide-de-camp, bottle washer, strong-armed man, and cultural adviser around here. But proudest of all, I'm wine taster extraordinary to General Patton. I add tone and culture to the brutal proceedings. Guess I slid in just after you slid out."

"I read about you," recollected Halleck. "You're the playboy from Monte Carlo."

"Yeah," drawled Wallis, "I have been known in the balmy days of peace to frequent that frowzy old dump. I'm also great with duchesses and marchionesses. I know Cocteau and Sartre. I've written poems to Edwige Feuillère and most recently managed to stop a horde of bucolic GIs from cutting loose in Baron Mumm's *très privées* caves. Without me, warfare would be a very vulgar affair. And now I'm adding tone to Bad Tölz, not that it needs that much help. Gee, don't you think the scenery's fantastic, General?"

"Where's Berchtesgaden?" asked Halleck as he surveyed a familiar scene of pine forests and towering Alps. This was myth land, Nazi land, Niebelung land, home of a lonely monomaniac genius.

"Don't let the past impress you, General," said Du Camp lightly. "All the action right now is at Bad Tölz. One because it has the world's greatest general permanently resident within its spa contours. Second because it constitutes a court, I guess a bit like Bonaparte in Lombardy or Caesar in Gaul. Third because we have all the brightest Nazis here from Rundstedt downwards. Fourth because we have the smartest uniforms. Fifth because all the sights are laid on. When you're tired of boar skewering in the hills or trout fishing in Lake Tegernsee, there's always a touch of the real macabre, close at hand in the lovely old folksy town of Dachau. Seeing old Georgie take the SS by the ears and lead them through the gas chambers is a pretty memorable exercise in theatrical guilt."

Two GI guards saluted stiffly as their boots rang on the steps that led into Max Amann's pleasure dome, the perfect publisher's weekend retreat.

"Not bad for rookies," commented Du Camp. "Most guys here are newly enlisted men. But it doesn't take us long to hone them down into soldiers."

Halleck had the uneasy feeling he was being taken over. From the earliest days at West Point he had gained notice, and even praise, for a studied taciturnity. He had simple beliefs. A soldier was there to feel out the situation and then solve it. It was just a question of coming to terms with it. So if in the early days to a superficial onlooker he might have lost points on sheer communication against a MacArthur or a Stilwell, he came to be respected in other circles precisely because he was not like the above-mentioned generals. "One thing about Halleck," wrote an early report, "he gives you 120 per cent. No. 150 per cent. He is all action. He doesn't waste words." And again,

"Halleck is strictly a no bullshit merchant. But deep down he studies the all-time greats and, it must be assumed, assimilates their lessons. Whatever Halleck may blow, it won't be his mouth!" But this guy Du Camp was beginning to ring bells, dissonant, ugly bells in Halleck's not too picturesque mind. Yeah, he'd heard about Du Camp. He was one of the slimies, oozing his way up the military ladder with a gladsome manner and a toothy smile.

"Would you mind waiting here, sir?" said Du Camp with more respect as they halted in some vestibule and a group of young officers peered toward them. "You might care to take a look at some back numbers of *Yank* magazine while I go and locate General Gay. But don't mention George Baker and those Sad Sack cartoons when you meet General Patton. Old Georgie throws up pretty bad at the very mention of Baker. Swears there ain't one single sad sack in the whole Third Army."

General Halleck's sturdy butt sank reluctantly onto one of Hitler's publisher's chintzy sofas. He tried to memorize the command breakdown in Third Army. "G-1 personnel, G-2 intelligence, G-3 operations, G-4 supply, G-5 civil government, G-1 personnel, G-2 intelligence . . ." And then he had to fix faces to the groupings. One thing was for sure. The Third Army had moved some since the Fécamp fiasco. To be precise it had moved over more ground faster than any army in history. For Halleck it was like catching up with a high-combustion legend. Then his heart warmed as at last he saw a face he knew.

"Hi, Hap," he said as Chief of Staff Hobart R. Gay gave him his outstretched hand. "Guess I've just about finally caught up with you guys."

"You look in good condition, Regis," said Gay appraisingly. "Only trouble is," and Hobart's voice sank to a whisper, "the old man's gone nuts on etiquette since we got peace, and I notice you're not wearing your Third Army shoulder patch."

This was a different Gay, thought Halleck. Not the smiling diplomat who smoothed the troubled waters on every conceivable occasion, but a man seared for months in intense heat. A young yet tired man. A weary man, maybe a homesick man. A man who suddenly longed for his wife and kids way back in the States. Certainly the old Hobart Gay would not have got het up about a shoulder patch.

"You know the score, Regis. The shoulder insignia reads White A on blue background circled by Red O. I was figuring you'd know how hot the old guy is on matters of detail. He's got an eye for that kind of thing. Especially now. It's as if he was trying almost to screw up the peace we've won."

"Yeah, you're right, Hap," ruminated Halleck. "I've gone and put my stupid foot into it again. Suppose there's one chance in heck he won't notice?"

The sun was beginning to slip away behind the spectacular mountains. A benevolent amber light was filtering into the room in Bad Tölz where two elderly men were talking. One was a German in his late sixties, a distinguished gray-haired man with a military mustache wearing a baggy prewar double-breasted suit.

The other man was balder but more robust in complexion. He had the tanned face of a company president with a lot of time to spend on his yacht. In fact he was wearing a tailored uniform and there were four rows of ribbons over his left breast pocket. There were also four gold stars on his shoulders. Ex-Wehrmacht Major General Klaus von Ritter was being received in audience by General George S. Patton, Jr., Military Governor of Bavaria and commander of the U.S. Third Army.

"We understand the hostility of your American peoples," the German was saying. "We understand that there are those among us who have done many wrong things. There are even, I am regretting deeply, comrades in arms who are forgetting the conduct of honor that is expected of officers. I have not come here today, Herr General, to plead for your friendship, I have come to ask only for mercy on my townspeople."

"Go on," said Patton encouragingly.

"General, we are a mountain folk. Our rock fields cannot produce the foods we are needing to keep our children alive. And now our population is swollen by wretched peoples who must escape the Bolshevik savages. I understand how it is necessary to have your 'pass' system for German citizens. You are naturally not anxious for our peoples to move in large mass about the country. You are nervous to keep us under your thumbs; but if no soul in our township can travel more than three kilometers, not even the mayor and I myself his counselor, how are we to purchase the foods we must obtain to save our people from starvation?"

The German veteran looked at his legendary enemy who seemed to be smiling either in sympathy or at his discomfiture. He could not be sure. General Patton's bull terrier Willie was lying curled at his feet, a symbol of unexpected humanity, or latent menace. Again the old Wehrmacht officer was uncertain.

He said, "The request I am making is not easy for me, my General. But it would be harder if I did not know, having had the privilege to oppose you in warfare, that you are not only a supreme commander but also, sir, a chivalrous knight, generous to worthy adversaries your sword is striking down."

General Patton opened his mouth to reveal a set of gray teeth. He said, "If you were up against the Third Army, General, you've got my sympathy. Refresh my mind—where did we meet?"

"I have had the honor to oppose you as divisional commander with Army Group B on the Seine at La Roche Guyon."

Patton grinned. "I can't say you guys over there lost me too much sleep. As I remember, General Haislip caught the goddamn bunch of you with your pants down."

A look of infinite sadness crept into the eyes of the down-at-the-heel German general. "I can only tell you, sir, we had nothing. They called us an Army Gruppen. We were not hardly a division. And half of these were non-German troops and old men..." He paused. He had noticed how fast Patton's eyes were narrowing. As a general he was quick to remind himself that no victor likes to be robbed of the magnitude of his victories. "But when we are realizing the threat your army is posing to our Seine River line, we concentrate all our resources. We bring in 88-mm. artillery, *Nebelwerfers,* and new infantry. My General, we smash your pontoon craft, we destroy your regiments as they muster on the opposing bank; but still you come at us like wildcats. I do not know how you penetrate our carefully prepared dispositions, but I know a captain is ringing me on the command phone and shouting, 'Herr General, these Americans are not human, they are walking on the water'!"

George Patton leaned back in his velvet armchair all chuckles. "Gene found a small dam you guys seemed to overlook. I told him to get the hell over it, in single file if necessary. Jesus Christ, you're damned right, General, that army of mine did walk on the water!"

"We left many wounded on the field," Von Ritter sighed, "but my information is that they were treated with honor. I know this could not have happened on the Russian front, I would not even like to leave my wounded to the English as they behave now."

"Or some of your SS buddies." Patton smiled grayly. "Those guys didn't rock anybody to sleep!"

Von Ritter hung his head in remorseful agreement. "I ask only for my townspeople the honorable treatment for which your Third Army is famous."

Patton slowly raised himself from his armchair and walked a little stiffly toward a large mahogany desk. He asked, "Who's our military governor over there in Garmisch?"

"He is Brigadier General Leibling, Herr General. Yes, he is a Jew. I can understand how he could feel about us, but we have surrendered all our Nazis, all those who have known," Von Ritter's voice sank, "of those terrible things. Yet he has ransacked every homestead perhaps three times, and his soldiers are terrifying our women and children. I do not wish to criticize an American officer, General, but we are in despair for our town."

Meanwhile Patton had been speaking quietly over the telephone. Suddenly the great man's voice shrilled into one of those outbursts for which he was famous—or notorious. "Is that Leibling! This is Patton. Now you listen to me, you're going to get off your big slimy ass down there and feed that goddamn town you're goddamn starving to death. Don't say 'but' to me, you stinking bastard! Get wheat into those goddamn bakeries, get fresh vegetables into the stores, and give out candies to every kid in town—or you no longer have a job with Third Army. Another thing, I want blue travel passes issued to the Mayor and my friend Major General von Ritter. Do you hear me? Whadaya mean the Mayor's a Muss-Nazi? I don't care if he's goddamn Mussolini—he's got to go get food for those Kraut kids you're fuckin' murdering! Have you got my message, Leibling? I'm not having any sonofabitch Hebrew going around like some goddamn Herod slaughtering holy innocents in my goddamn command!"

Major Lowel Packer had a number of problems. One of them was that he was not a soldier. A year ago he had been one of Harvard's brightest young professors with a secure corner in group psychology. Early in 1944, Scribner's had published his provocative series of lectures entitled *The Challenge of Victory*. While the popular imagination was still obsessed with the day-to-day struggle against Germany and Japan, Professor Packer had turned a penetrating eye on the future problems of victory and occupation. In view of the Allies' declared policy of "unconditional surrender," he had forecast they would be taking over countries where normal social and economic patterns had completely broken down. "There is a danger," Lowel Packer had warned, "that we shall be responsible for populations suffering from acute group psychosis."

For an academic treatise, Packer's book had pulled off a remarkable sales success. It had been synopsized in *Reader's Digest* and talked about by thirsting book club subscribers. Perhaps more significantly, it had reached the attention of the Pentagon, where its contents had been noted, and filed. Three days after the Allied victory in Normandy, Professor Packer had been astonished to find himself drafted.

"Look," he had told his examining board, "I'm thirty-six, I'm shortsighted and maybe even color blind. Also I've got three kids to support."

The Army hadn't shared his misgivings. They'd put him straight into uniform with the rank of captain. Then in November 1944 they'd posted him to SHAEF's Continental base section at Rheims as a major to await the final conquest of Germany.

It had been a difficult time for an intellectual who so far, at least, could see no valid reason why he should have been torn away from his wife and young kids and the pleasant evenings with compatible friends in Cambridge, Mass. The very impressiveness of his rank had helped the Major to feel out of place that long, drafty winter in the ruined old town of Rheims. At the best his gold leaves drew disbelieving stares from fellow officers. Once or twice when the PX Bourbon was circulating freely he had been offered purple-fisted violence by war-scarred majors who believed they'd earned their insignia.

The collapse of the Third Reich still found Major Lowel Packer in Rheims, by this time actually beginning to hate the superb rose window of that jewel of a cathedral.

Then Major Packer received orders to report to U.S. Forces European Theater Headquarters at Frankfurt. A brief interview with a G-5 colonel had been immediately followed by a friendly talk with an attentive brigadier general.

"Maybe I've just been wasting my time, sir," Packer suggested hopefully. "Could be that it's all been one big mistake. If the Army doesn't need me, there won't be any rehabilitation problems. They're keeping my seat warm at Harvard."

"You couldn't be more wrong, Major," the General had comforted him. "It may have taken a little time. But now we've got a mission, a confidential mission, I should stress, that's really going to help you earn your pay."

A few minutes later he was in an elevator to the sixth floor of the huge I.G. Farben building. A breathtaking glimpse of the ruined city of Frankfurt, an aide tapping on a polished door with three gold stars; then he was in the presence of a man he recognized from the background of a hundred war conference pictures, even though his head was bowed over his desk. Lieutenant General Walter Bedell Smith, Eisenhower's famous Chief of Staff, was inviting him to be seated.

Some seconds of silence were filled with the scratching of "Beetle's" pen. Then a sudden question.

"You're the guy who wants to give therapy to the Germans—is that right?"

"Sir?"

"You wrote this book, didn't you? Guess I saw it in *Reader's Digest.* How we've got to nurse the Germans back to sanity."

"It was just a thesis, sir," Lowel Packer said humbly. "I didn't expect it to lead me where it did."

Bedell Smith looked up, the pale face of a man who for four years had had to struggle with illness as well as his country's enemies. "I guess your credentials have impressed quite a few people here. What's holding you up from getting onto the ground in Germany?"

Major Packer briefly related his frustrating history in military government.

"Anyway, your problems are over, Professor—I should say Major, shouldn't I? I'm transferring you as from Thursday."

"Could I ask where, sir?"

"To General Patton's headquarters at Bad Tölz."

Major Packer must have winced behind his horn-rimmed spectacles.

"Don't worry," a smile to be replaced even faster by the familiar gray expression, "George won't eat you, at least not whole. Officially you'll be attached to the Third Army, reporting to General Patton, but unofficially you'll be reporting directly to me."

Bedell Smith returned to his writing. It looked as if the interview was over, which put Packer in the position of having to ask lamely, "What will I be reporting, sir?"

"Everything that happens to you," Ike's Chief of Staff told him without looking up, "how much encouragement you get, and how much you don't, where you're allowed to participate and where you're told to keep out. I will welcome your impressions of Army morale and the civilian situation in Bavaria and I would appreciate any statistics you may care to give me on the rate of war criminal prosecutions in the zone. Also as a psychologist," the pen paused like the General's words over his writing pad, ". . . as a psychologist I would be interested in any confidential views you may have on General Patton's mental health."

Major Al Kopp had had a lot of experience with Germans. In the first place there were his aunts, uncles, and cousins back home where he was born in a well-heeled suburb of Houston, Texas. These kinds of Germans, his kith and kin, were basically as American as blueberry pie, recognized, however grudgingly, by every Pole and Italian and nigger in the state as second only to Anglo-Saxons in true Americanness. Some of his aunts and uncles were unsatisfied even with this amount of respect. They talked of the exciting things that were going on back "home" in Germany, about the new evidence that was coming to light regarding the biological superiority of the Aryan race. It seemed this mad Adolf Hitler really was on the ball, and later you had to admit that golly he'd certainly knocked the hell out of those lousy French Latins and just about twisted the goddamn tail off the scrofulous British lion. Then suddenly the United States was at war. Overnight Hitler became a character destined to "live in infamy" along with the stinking, yellow Jap bastards who'd sneaked up on Pearl Harbor. And Al Kopp, riding hell-for-leather with Patton's Third Army, was meeting a new kind of German that hid by day and killed by night.

A little later he'd met them face to face, if this was the way you could describe an encounter with corpses.

It was the afternoon that Old Blood and Guts finally got Bradley's permission to advance through Argentan and close the Falaise gap, a feat which had proved beyond the resources of British 21st Army Group. Major Al Kopp was a tough, sharp-shooting officer, prized by George Patton as such—the one man on Third Army staff who recklessly sought daredevil front-line combat duty. But what he had seen that afternoon had very nearly made him vomit. So many young German kids dead in so many differently gruesome ways. The RAF Typhoons and USAC Mustangs had sure made shit of the Germans who were trying to get out. He saw an officer with precisely the same shade of hair and skin pigmentation as himself with half his face turned into a purple feast for flies. He'd seen a kid ten years younger than he was gripping a stomach that spilled all over a Normandy meadow. He had thought if it hadn't been for an accident of immigration, that legless torso could have been him lying there. But, being a good soldier, he said to himself, "Shucks, let's get on with this lousy war!"

Nine months later he had met a lot more Germans, some of them more dead than alive, but all of them alive. These were the endless streams of prisoners who had shuffled into Third Army cages as the war closed, so many you couldn't run up the barbed wire fast enough. By this time Major Kopp had gotten to hate Germans, especially Nazi Germans. Now he found what he hated most of all about them was the servile way they were creeping into captivity, almost as if it was a betrayal of his own red, German blood. So when a Wehrmacht general smiled gratefully at discovering an American staff officer who could speak German fluently, Kopp killed the budding cordiality with a snarl.

Gerda was an exception. He had found her among a group of high-ranking Luftwaffe officers who had surrendered to a Third Army patrol near Karlsbad in Czechoslovakia. The Colonel on the spot had called up for someone at Patton's CP to come over and have a look at them, and Kopp had been assigned the job. He found them sitting on a bench outside an Army field kitchen, guys in snazzy peak caps, loaded with gold braid bending over to slurp up their coffee like so many bums at a soup kitchen. Only she had held her head high.

That really wasn't so surprising, considering she was quite something to look at. The rich, sleek fair hair. Large brown eyes that looked right back at you. Firm breasts underneath the blue-gray officer's jacket. (One of the GIs who had brought them said she'd tried to pass as a man. Boy, she had to be kidding!)

These were crazy times when a guy could get away with crazy orders. "Send the rest back to the POW cages. I'm taking the girl to General Patton's CP for further interrogation." What a ride, he and this fairy-tale Fräulein in the back of a jeep, passing the time of day and a bottle of Bourbon between them while he slowly worked his hands between her Luftwaffe officer's jacket and Luftwaffe officer's pants! In fact he didn't realize quite what a hot property he was handling. According to Colonel Koch's people (Patton's G-2 intelligence section) the dame was none other than the legendary Nazi woman pilot, Gerda Gettler, one of Hitler's most decorative protégées. For a few days it looked as if he was going to have to surrender his prize to the gray, earnest de-Nazifiers of General Eisenhower's military intelligence. Luckily the Old Man had agreed with him that it would have been a shocking crime to offer a neck like Gerda's to Eisenhower's hangmen.

Well, it had been a long war, and if you couldn't get home to all those girls it would be so nice to come home to, what was wrong with Gerda? The truth was that Gerda was all the different girls Major Al Kopp had dreamed about on that long road into the Reich. Submissive, arrogant, sweet, cruel, compliant, cold, hot, torrid, tender, teasing, and tempestuous; a girl like he had always half suspected only a German girl could be. In a way Major Kopp often regretted he had to spend so much time drinking with fellow officers that could have been spent at home with Gerda in their little apartment in Bad Tölz. An officer and a gentleman could honorably spend all the time in the world screwing the ass off a girl like Gerda Gettler.

The boys were coming home. Under the point system, mustering out had become a stampede. To fill the emptying ranks, the War Department sent rookies direct from their six weeks of basic training in the States to the formations in Germany. One of them was Pfc. Perry Brewer from Kentucky. Three days ago Pfc. Brewer had been sunning himself on the decks of the *Queen Mary* as she steamed in her wartime battleship gray toward St. Nazaire. Today he was on parade in full equipment on a bleak parade ground in Rosenheim surrounded by a seemingly endless landscape of trucks, olive-green barracks, and barbed wire. The mountains of Bavaria were visible in the distance, but it was a pretty far distance.

"You guys think you're here on a vacation, don't you?" a staff sergeant with a chest broad enough to take a load of battle honors was bawling at them.

"You think you're here to see Europe, screw a few Fräuleins, spend your Chesterfields on a Kraut Mercedes and sneak home to Mom. Well if that's what you lousy creeps are thinking you're real dumb. You poor, chicken-bellied, bed-wetting bastards just happen to have joined the greatest fighting outfit the world has ever known. You're not in the Army now, you're in General Patton's Third Army, and boy that's one helluva difference. You're going to wish you'd joined the fucking Foreign Legion before we're through with you shits! You think you're unlucky? How do you think I feel, how do you think General Patton feels with a bunch of goddamn stinking fairies like you in the Third! Want to know something? You and I ought to get down on our knees and thank Jesus Christ we licked the Krauts before you got here— they'd have goddamn eaten your balls."

A titter of nervous laughter ran through the swaying ranks. In basic training they had been permitted to drill in helmet liners and fatigues. Now Perry Brewer and the other draftees had heavy steel on their heads and full packs on their uniformed backs, and they had been standing at attention for twenty minutes.

"You think that's funny?" Sergeant Offenbach hollered. "Well, I've got news for you. I'm worse than the Krauts. I'm going to eat your balls and have your creepy little pricks too!"

A rookie named Private Maggio at the back of the squad collapsed.

"Take that coward's name, Corporal Danziger," screamed the Sergeant, "and tell him when he wakes up he's charged with insubordination to a noncommissioned officer!"

Now Offenbach approached the squad with an expression of molten hate. Brewer thought he was going to knock down the recruit he had come face to face with. Instead, he thrust a thick finger at his own shoulder patch. "You see this—it's the proud insignia of the Third Army—the insignia you punks are disgracing by wearing. You want to know what this means?" He indicated the white letter "A" and the red letter "O." "It stands for Army of Occupation on account of the fact that the Third occupied Germany in the First World War. Now we're here again and this time we're goddamn going to stay. You hear that, you stinking bunch of creepy little fags? You're Third Army. You're never going home!"

From the bedroom window of his apartment on the outskirts of Rosenheim, Martin Sauber had a fine view of the Austrian mountains where Mozart's Salzburg nestled. Cataracts and age had dimmed his sight, but his memory supplied an accurate picture of their blue contours.

The living-room window opened on a less picturesque scene: the badly bombed town of Rosenheim, which in any case had been defaced long before the war by the smokestacks and warehouses of its thriving chemical and textile industries. In the foreground, just within range of

Martin Sauber's shadowy vision, was a military barracks. In his time he had seen a host of different formations drilling there: pickelhaubered infantry of the Imperial German Army, heavy-helmeted boys, earmarked for Ludendorff's desperate 1918 offensives; the assorted uniforms of Bavaria's revolutionary red army, the flower-decked alpine hats of the Freikorps liberators, brown shirts, black-tunicked Waffen SS, Wehrmacht battalions, the ragged up and down lines of the Volksturm levies, and finally, perhaps least military of all, these strangers from halfway across the world.

He could not see them very clearly as they musterd this daybreak on the field gray parade ground. But he could hear how unevenly they came to attention, and he thought he could discern a wild flurry of rifles as the detachment presented arms and the Stars and Stripes climbed the flagpole. Even the bugle sounded strangely unmartial. The flag was solemnly being hoisted to a syncopated lilt suggestive of Negro jazz rhythms.

"Jesus Christ," Sergeant Offenbach hollered, "maybe I haven't always been perfect, maybe once or twice in this man's army I haven't exactly abided by the Good Book, but what the hell did I do to deserve a bunch of lousy, stinking pukes like you? You know, I'm a kindhearted fella, I love kids and animals; but you guys are gonna turn me into a goddamn homicidal maniac. We're going up to Kolb. That's frontiersville. So you're going to be drilling right under the goddamn eyes of these bastard Russians. And I warn you if I catch you presenting arms like a lot of bedwetting, juvenile epileptics, I'm gonna kick your stinking asses off!"

All the same Martin Sauber was too old and too wise to take a patronizing view of the new army under his window. It had been fashionable when they first came into the war to make jokes about the American's fighting abilities. Goebbels' radio had found it particularly difficult to take decadent America's mobilization seriously. But Martin Sauber, as a practical businessman, had seen nothing particularly amusing about making enemies with the world's most powerful economy. He had also

noted that no amount of parade-ground discipline had
been able to prevent these "degenerate" hordes from
overrunning Bavaria in a matter of days. No, they did not
look or bear themselves like soldiers, but their technology
was formidable and they had proved themselves reliable
fighters. Besides, once they had smashed their way to
victory, they had respected private property. For all their
faults, they represented a welcome barrier against the chill
winds from the east. In any case there was no other
barrier. They would have to do.

"It is going to be a fine day, Lisa," Herr Sauber called
to his wife in the bedroom, a shrunken figure under a rose-
patterned duvet, sleepless and in pain from the cancer
which was a secret between Sauber and the doctor.

"Gentlemen!" said General Patton as he beamed over
the assembled company in the general dining quarters of
Third Army staff, in a room in which the publisher of
Mein Kampf had dined, if not wined, a certain talented
new author on his list.

"Gentlemen, tonight the Third Army has achieved one
of the most arduous of the wartime directives I set it. For a
long time I had my eye on a certain general, sorry SS
Obergruppenfuehrer, Ernst Hart. Hell, I had the
goddamn bastard breathing down the neck of XX Corps
with his crack 57th Panzers when we tried to close the
Falaise pocket. Then if the same guy doesn't turn up at
Saarbrücken. So I said to General Walker 'bring him back
alive. And that's an order. I'd like to ask the bastard a few
pointed questions.' At that time he was commanding the
best goddamn panzer division the Huns had in the West.
He drove in a few pickets and soon they started calling the
sonofabitch the German answer to Patton, and it became
an affair of honor. Now, gentlemen, we have General, I
mean Obergruppenfuehrer, Hart as a valued guest at our
table, so I think we may take it honor is satisfied. And as
the evening hots up I'll hope to pitch a few questions to the
guy, but first I'd like each man around this table to
introduce himself to General, hell yes! General Hart,
starting with you, Gay."

Major Du Camp's popping eyes were recording the whole scene, and maybe he was the only man there with the necessary balance to estimate exactly how wild it was. Here was the solid phalanx, which had geared Patton to victory, that much-maligned transmission system that had somehow co-ordinated the Third Army and produced the most spectacular land victories of World War II. There was Hobart Gay, Chief of Staff. Oscar Koch, possessor of a high IQ, master planner of the war room. And then there was entertainment in the shape of Major Al Kopp, the pistol-packin' Texan who could wow up any ball.

But the yawning gaps were there. Like the legendary Colonel Codman, who had returned to the States. And with him the roll call of Patton's finest corps and divisional commanders: General Eddy, General Grow, General Wood, General Walker—all departed. The new senior officers coming in had very little experience in active combat. Hence Halleck: a bull-necked-looking guy with a crew cut and very little evidence of brain or *savoir vivre*. But a stubborn bastard and a fighter through and through. But who gave a damn while the star was still there?

As a man who had lived through most of General Patton's more recent cafardes, and done an honest job in trying to smokescreen or even explain them, Major Du Camp had that slightly *déjà vu* feeling in a precipitated form. The case of the GI, whom Patton had slapped in the 93rd Evacuation Hospital in a fraught moment during the Sicilian campaign. The case of the slurs against the noble Russian ally at a pre-D-Day speech to the good people of Knutsford in Northern England. But that was kid stuff compared with what was happening here and now before Du Camp's wide-open eager, staring eyes.

There was a funny thing called de-Nazification, which explicitly forbade any kind of social contact with the beaten Germans. Then there was a small matter of war crimes. As an SS general, Hart came not just from one of the elitest groups of Nazi Germany, but one of the most criminal. Waffen SS contingents had committed countless war crimes and atrocities on the Eastern Front, where Hart had won his spurs. There generals had in many cases been found to have co-operated with the vicious SS and SD units in shootings, hangings, torturings, transportings, and a whole load of similar barbarous goings-on. Hart's place was in a Munich jail, not here at Patton's table. So much was clear. In inviting him, Patton was guilty of prima-facie disobedience to the whole spirit of the control government and the directions of General Eisenhower.

"All right, gentlemen," Patton was saying, "I refer everyone back to Third Army briefing, January 21, 1945. I read from my notes. 'It's that guy again. He's trying to block us out of Saarbrücken, as he held us at bay at Metz for six weeks. But we're gonna weave around him. We're gonna hold him by the nose and kick his pants.' Any comments?"

"Pardon me, General," said Hart as he sipped his Jesuitgarten wine, "you are still fighting yesterday's war. Pardon me again, but we do agree you won the campaign in the Palatinate."

"Not so fast," said Al Kopp, who was getting fidgety. "Wasn't it you, General, who referred to the men of the Third Army as an ill-assorted horde, and to some of the gentlemen around this table as bad and timid leadership?"

"And that was true," said Hart, a blond, sensitive-looking and surprisingly youthful film-star-type German. "But you read Rommel's book. You mastered the principles of Guderian. You understood that tactical and strategic, offensive and defensive are just so many claptrap words used by unimaginative staff officers. For that, at least, I salute you."

"Okay," said Hap Gay. "And sure Guderian invented it—the whole principle of inventive attack. The total rejection of shibboleths. The ultimate war of movement. Just curling around obstacles and kind of stretching out your arm with no mental preconditions, just figuring how far you could go. Now that was warfare. But hell, you just didn't do it. Bob Grow or John Wood, they'd have taken Moscow in '41, or Stalingrad. You panzer guys weren't even loyal to your own principles. Isn't that true, George?"

"Goddamnit, Hap," murmured Patton, "you're too close to me for comfort. Among you gentlemen I can talk freely, and I must admit that, like most of you, I have my own private fantasies. And I'd like to take out just a little time among friends to explain one of them. Briefly, it's the Moscow situation. We're into late November, early December. Hitler's mounted his make-or-break panzer offensive. The scenario includes Von Kluge's Fourth Army, Guderian's Panzer Corps, plus substantial independent panzer forces commanded by Von Hoth and Sepp Dietrich. The only trouble is that the whole scene is a predictable replay of that time-honored German General Staff concept called Cannae. We had it at Tannenberg, they tried it on in 1918. Then they gave it wings and wheels. So we had speeded-up Cannaes in Poland, France, Greece, then on the Russian borders and, most prior to Moscow, down in the Ukraine where Marshal Budenny had his balls singed off."

"You are referring, mein General, to the battle role of our glorious Wehrmacht. Can any army except Napoleon's match such victories?" put in Hart.

"I agree. Sure they were triumphs. But man, the methodical railroad-track-bound march of these triumphs sticks out like a sore thumb. It's like Joe Louis taking five minutes to land you with his right. And that's what went wrong with Moscow. Just another goddamn Cannae. Pincers to the right of them, pincers to the left of them—volleyed and thundered!"

"I was there with Guderian," said Obergruppenfuehrer Hart. "The glass showed minus thirty degrees. We had to light fires under our tanks to start them in the morning. The panzer thrust wasn't repulsed. It was literally frozen in its tracks."

"Yeah," dismissed Patton, "you had your difficulties. What cavalry commander doesn't? When we were racing up to the Siegfried Line, we suddenly discovered that the Limeys had gotten hold of our gasoline supplies. So what did we do, Koch?"

"Put all the available gasoline into just one third of our Shermans," answered the administrative brain behind Patton's victories.

"A device, incidentally, that I'd tried on in 1917 with the Renault tanks I commanded at St. Mihiel."

"But ice is different," insisted Hart.

"Goddamnit, man. Didn't one of Kluge's units come in sight of the Kremlin towers? You weren't that far off. It was just that Zhukov read your goddamn predictable unimaginative stuck-in-the-ice book. Look, if I'd been Guderian, I'd have been sitting in the Kremlin, like Napoleon, by mid-December. Guess I'd even have had roast turkey and cranberry sauce there for Christmas, cooked by Sergeant Phu Lee. Who, I'm glad to announce, is doing the honors today with this delicious wurstbraten or whatever you Krauts call it. Yeah, I'd have just busted my way through, by instinct more than planning."

"Even with the German Army, General?" mischievously asked Du Camp.

"The German Army is a fine body of men. I never criticized them. Yeah, I could have led them into Moscow. Zhukov's more a gorilla than a leader."

There was a silence around the candlelit table, broken only by the steps of an orderly coming in with a written message for Patton. After a second Patton rose and left the room.

"Evening, ma'am," said Pfc. Brewer in a broad Kentucky accent. "I guess it's great to know you, but I want you to understand it ain't exactly my idea to come here. Fact is, left to ourselves most of us would be drinking a Coke in the canteen or listening to Carmen Miranda on the radio. Or just writing a letter to folks back home. I come from Kentucky, ma'am. But I guess you never heard of Kentucky."

The lady didn't seem to understand; you could even say she didn't want to understand. In the old days she had run a superior boardinghouse in Kolb with a regular and faithful clientele, and she had run it well. Now her fifty-

five-year-old husband was dead, knocked out in the
defense of Königsberg by a T-34, a *Panzerfaust* frozen to
his hand. Her two sons had been swallowed when the
Allies almost closed the Avranches pocket, and were now
temporary lumbermen in Canada. Her boardinghouse
had been requisitioned. A large, bosomy lady in her mid-
forties, she had always in a discreet kind of way provided
services to some of her regular guests. She was now in the
business for real—for whiskey, Coke, Spam and a pack of
Camels.

"As I was saying, ma'am," continued Brewer, "would
you mind if I sat down for a bit? It's sure been a heavy day.
It ain't that much fun being a raw recruit in peacetime
Germany. Looks like if you missed the war, you've really
got to prove something." Frau Muller had been at her new
job for just three weeks. She wasn't very young, and she
wasn't very pretty, but she enjoyed her job and she was
beginning to perform it with a certain professionalism.
She was that rare thing: a natural whore.

"As I was saying, ma'am," continued Private Brewer,
"for some of us rookies, peace isn't that hot. We ain't got a
chance to be heroes. But they won't let us rest, either."

In three hard-working weeks Frau Berta Muller had
come to know and classify them all, but when it came
down to it, Homo sapiens wasn't that complex. There
were the hard professionals, the guys who screwed and
screwed and then screwed again. Men who had been
hardened and toned up by the fighting; for these men she
had somehow by sheer technique to counteract hang-ups
about her age. And then there were the drunks, the
paranoiacs. And there were the problem boys, the brash
showoffs who went obstinately limp even beneath Berta
Muller's practiced soft fingers (her touch was perhaps her
greatest asset). And then there were the simple homely
rookies, boys like Pfc. Brewer, who had to be skillfully,
gently raped, lovingly seduced, led tremulously down the
red path of sin—away from Mom with her pumpkin pies
and from the little stringy loving sixteen-year-old girl next
door, her hair done up in a Shirley Temple bow. Berta

Muller was not often given the choice, but there was no doubt where her heart and body lay. She was a natural seducer of innocents.

It would take her just four or five minutes to break down Pfc. Brewer's bashfulness.

The Jesuitgarten, followed by kirsch and *Sachertorte* flown in from Vienna, had mellowed the company. Then came jugs of Munich beer.

"Gentlemen," said Patton, "the thing about a thinking general is that he never ceases to be a student, a student of war. As you know, I'm a great one for kicking my soldiers hard in the butts to keep their morale up. I guess I'm not much kinder to my staff. In fact I'm an expert in arresting any sign of complacency. As Hap and Koch can testify, the war games and problems I set them would have given Moltke or Ulysses S. Grant a headache. Because you never know when you might become operational, and I'd sure hate them to be caught like the Russkies were at Brest-Litovsk in '41. So despite the *Sachertorte,* I guess, Obergruppenfuehrer Hart, you'll see scant signs of excess flab around here. Tell them about our war games, Koch. Dole them out some Rock Soup."

Koch got up and had the central lights turned off. Then he pulled a cord and a large map came down the wall to the floor.

"Gentlemen," said Koch, "we call this very creative, totally fictitious operation Rock Soup, after a favorite aphorism of the General's which may or may not be familiar to you. Here is the area currently occupied by Third Army. Here are our tank units. And these are our infantry divisions. And here is Bad Tölz. Now, turning to this other map, you get a look at what's on the other side of the border. This is the extreme point of Marshal Tolbukhin's Fourth Guards Army. Here's a hotbed of real crack T34s that can blast the hell out of any group of tanks in the world in a static shooting match war, which they just won't get. Here are big concentrations. And here. Tolbukhin himself sits here, doling out large quantities of top class vodka to visiting VIPs. And here you have what amounts to a strategic or tactical reserve. Now the stimulating problem General Patton has set our planning, intelligence, operations, and statistical sections is this..."

"Ever seen a dick like this?" Private Maggio asked a tall, willowy slim-limbed blonde of about twenty-two, two doors along the corridor in the Rathaus, where the commissioner for land grants had sat in earlier times of peace. "Get that dick, lady. Run your gorgeous peepers all over it. All seven quivering inches of it."

The girl began to take off her skirt, to fold her clothes neatly on the chair beside the camp bed.

"Jeez, lady, you're going to too much trouble. I'm not that ambitious."

The young blonde stared at Maggio in amazement. But already the scene was changing. Maggio's dick, which had jetted out of his service fly like a Mustang on takeoff, was now losing horsepower, curling back over itself as its engines lost momentum.

"It's your fucking fault, you highfalutin goddamn broad," squeaked Maggio. "But I'm gonna be real hard on you."

Bending low over the girl, he forced her face upward until her mouth was rubbing against the wilting object that was sticking out of his GI pants. "Suck," roared Maggio in his high-pitched Bronx squeak. "Suck me, baby, like you've never sucked before—or General Patton himself will want to know the reason why."

The passive touch of the Fräulein's lips did the trick. "Woweeee!" screamed Maggio as he exploded all over her face.

The man at the head of the huge horseshoe-shaped boardroom table in the requisitioned I.G. Farben building actually looked like the chief executive of a major corporation. A youngish fifty-five, he was nevertheless pale and flabby around the jowels from hours of concentrated desk work. In fact it was only the uniform and the medals that identified him as a soldier.

General of the Army Dwight D. Eisenhower was alone in his Frankfurt mausoleum wrestling with the problems of running a quarter of Germany.

Once again the immediate problem was Patton. There was a report on his giant table from Robert D. Murphy, his political adviser, who had just got back from a visit to Bad Tölz. His conversations with Patton were supposed to have been about the problems of de-Nazification, but Murphy had reported "Twice he asked me with a gleam in his eye whether there was any chance of going on to Moscow, which he tells me he can reach in thirty days." In recording his anxiety about the Bavarian situation and its pro-Nazi overtones, Murphy reminded the Supreme Commander of his earlier encounters with Patton when he was Military Governor of Morocco. He didn't need to expand. Ike could remember that crisis only too well.

"Our reports show," Churchill had fulminated, "that the Vichy S.O.L. and kindred fascist organizations continue their activities and victimize our former French sympathizers, some of whom have not yet been released from prison. Well-known German sympathizers who had been ousted have been reinstated. There have been cases of French soldiers being punished for desertion because they tried to support the Allied forces during the landing."

What is it about George that can't seem to accommodate to civil administration? Ike was now bound to keep asking himself.

The phone buzzed discreetly on his mammoth desk. The soothing voice of Kay Summersby, his English secretary and aide, said that General Beetle wanted to see his chief urgently. The implication was that Bedell Smith was in an ulcer-tearing rage, but Kay had this wonderful ability to make even the most irate incoming visitations sound like routine calls.

"Take a seat, Beetle," Ike murmured across the empty canyons of space he had allowed them to call his office.

Lieutenant General Bedell Smith settled grimly into a chair on the right-hand curve of the horseshoe table. Ike glanced around the vast piece of furniture as if he was

looking for the missing members of the I.G. Farben
board (some of them now under arrest for employing
slave labor to its limits). Actually he was looking for
Tedder, Spaatz, General Morgan, Admiral Burroughs
"Pinky Bull," and the other absent friends from that great
loyal SHAEF team now back at home or reporting to
their national occupation zones. Everybody had had to
make adjustments to victory. Ike had had one of the
hardest adjustments to make. His supreme command no
longer embraced any allies and covered only a segment of
Europe stretching from Württemberg to Austria.

"Okay. What's this morning's world crisis?" Ike asked
with a gentle grin and soft voice. He had become sensitive
about the way his voice could echo around this oversized
office if he raised it too much.

"It's Third Army again," Beetle reported without an
answering smile.

"You mean it's George again, don't you?" Eisenhower
sighed.

Beetle nodded.

"What is this thing about George and political
responsibility?" the Supreme Commander asked himself
again, this time out loud. "Does he have to make trouble,
or is he just accident prone? You remember the trouble he
got us into in Morocco with his buddy General Noguès."

"Yes, sir," Bedell Smith repeated unhelpfully.

"Boy, that was some bawling out we took from the
President! I guess if General Marshall hadn't stepped in
with the White House to smooth things over,
well...maybe I wouldn't be, maybe we wouldn't be
sitting here."

Like most intelligent men of ill-health, Bedell Smith
was anxious to get to his point. He said, "Sir, I have a
report that a wanted Waffen SS war criminal was a guest
of honor at General Patton's headquarters last week."

"Who else knows about this?"

"Naturally, my information is confidential, and we're
doing our best to keep it tight."

"There are a helluva lot of Congress people touring
down there in Bavaria."

"At least it hasn't made any newspapers at home yet."

"Look, Beetle," Eisenhower said, grinning bravely, "I've spent the whole morning up to now worrying about George—has he got to wreck our whole day?"

Bedell Smith's smile was thin-lipped in the extreme. "The officer's name is Obergruppenfuehrer Ernst Hart. He is wanted by the Russians for the murder of over five thousand of their civilians and partisans."

"Hell! They'll find out he's been eating with George!" Ike suddenly caught up with what the real fuss was all about.

The Chief of Staff's straight military shoulders imperceptibly shrugged. "Yes, sir, they'll find out sooner or later. Their Intelligence doesn't miss much. When they do find out, there's going to be hell to pay. They're not going to like it in Washington either; they're going to tell us we've handed the Russians another ready-made excuse for getting out of the agreements they made at Potsdam."

General Eisenhower made another row of creases in that once phenomenally boyish brow. "Look, Beetle—you've got to have George publicly issue orders to put this guy—what's his name—under trial for war crimes. And we've got to make sure everyone gets to read about it. I want a maximized p.r. push on this one!"

"I'm afraid it's going to take a direct order from you, Ike. We've already made representations from my office. General Patton takes the view that war crimes in his area are his own responsibility. To quote the General, 'I decide who is and who isn't a goddamn Nazi.'"

Ike's hand started a nervous walk toward the telephone. Then it stopped and his fingers drummed. "Beetle, what's going on down there in Bavaria?"

"Maybe General Patton is getting bored," the Chief of Staff suggested icily.

"I think you're right. We've always had this trouble when George didn't have any fighting to do. But now I have this very disturbing report from Murphy, and you're telling me he's entertaining a notorious mass murderer. I don't think, I pray God, George is disloyal," the Supreme

Commander worried at his thoughts, "but I guess he can be influenced. He's always been open to flattery. Beetle, do you figure—I don't know—there could be some kind of Nazi thing going on down there?"

"If there is, Ike," Bedell Smith said with one of his sudden shifts into intimacy, "you could nail it by relieving George of his command today."

Eisenhower lowered that worrying forehead onto his cupped hands. He said, "You realize he's a hero back in the States now—getting a lot of the plaudits that rightfully belong to Brad. What do you do with a situation like that?"

Beetle had no suggestions. "In the meantime, sir, we're trying to keep a watch on things at Bad Tölz. I've got this man Major Packer on the G-5 staff down there. He's keeping us pretty well informed. At the same time I've got Colonel Bob Miller, one of our best G-2 people, down there taking a discreet look around."

"Well, I want to be kept closely in touch with their progress." Ike looked up, wearing the familiar bulldog expression which had perhaps been borrowed from Churchill. "If you want any more G-2 people or anybody else down there, you just come and ask me. I'm giving this operation maximum priority! You understand?" Ike was feeling more comfortable; he had the sense that he could have made a decision.

Bedell Smith nodded. "And Obergruppenfuehrer Hart, sir. You will presumably be issuing direct orders to General Patton this morning instructing him to place him under arrest."

"You said it, Beetle," Ike agreed firmly. His hand took another wander toward the phone. This time it stopped on the receiver. "But first I guess I better clear this with General Marshall in Washington. I'll phone him as soon as they wake up back there in the States."

Bedell Smith bowed tolerantly and tiptoed out of the cavernous room. He knew that from the sacking of General Fredendall in Tunisia to the weekly reprimand of General Patton in Bavaria, things had always had to be cleared with Eisenhower's ultimate "Chairman" (whom a later Eisenhower would refuse to defend from the smears of Senator Joseph McCarthy).

Sergeant Joe Offenbach sat back in the ex-deputy Gauleiter's leather-bound chair in the Rathaus at Kolb and grinned at his chief aider and abettor in crime and victory, Corporal Danziger.

"How long does a screw take, Wally?" he asked directly. His tall, gangling subordinate and buddy allowed his eyes to roll around the ornamental cupids on the ceiling for a few seconds. "With those guys there, I dunno. Guess it could last all night."

"Don't be hard on the kids, Wally. Sure, they're greenhorns, sure they're rookies. Sure they're shit-scared. Sure they're sad sacks. But I love every man of them, every mother-fucking sister-screwer of them. And that's for true."

"You're certainly showing them life, Joe. The broads look great, but are they clean?"

"Okay, okay, so they get the clap. That's a part of it. Like combat duty. You could call it Third Army basic training. I'm not figuring on leading a lot of pussyfooting virgins against the Russkies. That's why I'm giving them just five minutes."

"Ain't that long, Joe," said Danziger.

Joe Offenbach put a rough brotherly arm around Danziger's thin shoulder. "I know what you're thinking, Wally," he chuckled. "Long enough to get the clap, too short for a good screw. But then who said Joe Offenbach was a charity home for orphans?"

"Poor bastards," pronounced Danziger with some feeling.

"You're right, Danziger. They're poor bastards. And I'm going to change all that. I'm going to turn them into soldiers. Did I say soldiers? Other armies have soldiers. The Third Army prides itself on its brawlers. So here's the plan, Wally. Get those mother-fuckers out of the arms of their clap-ridden lays and back on the road in full gear. Give them just a whiff of real combat. Lead them on a little friendly forage across the frontier. Pay a visit to our great buddy Ivan the Russkie. And who knows, maybe snazzle a few hairs from Uncle Joe Stalin's mustache."

Corporal Danziger smiled laconically. He had an uneasy feeling the night had hardly begun.

"Greetings, Maestro," said Colonel Bob Miller of Army Intelligence to Eric Weber, late of the Berlin police. "It's an honor to meet you." He was talking to a diminutive German of about fifty-five in an American Army raincoat two sizes too large and a pair of Luftwaffe officer's well-tanned boots. "Speaking as a policeman, I'm sure glad we were able to bail you out. The only thing we've got against you is that you seem to suffer from excess modesty. Why the heck did you have to bum around in a Luftwaffe uniform?"

They had picked him up in a DP camp outside Augsburg. A shambling, shuffling figure with four days' growth of beard on his face. Oberleutnant of the Luftwaffe Supply Service. And maybe the disguise would have stuck had it not been for the eagle eyes of Bob Miller, lent to the U. S. Army by Los Angeles Special Investigations, as he flipped through the photos of the inmates.

"A policeman isn't always popular," replied the policeman, "and today there could be a confusion in people's minds."

"Crap," bawled Miller. "Not about you. You're not just a policeman, you're a celebrity. Your use of forensic aids to track down the murderer in the Annie Braun case of '38. A classic, Weber. We've got nothing on you."

"You are kind, Colonel," said the German Inspector, smiling. "Even so, I found it wiser to remain anonymous. Even in your army there are people who confuse the Gestapo with the civil police. And sometimes they don't wait to argue."

"You're clean," Miller told him. "I did a quick flip checkup and there's nothing the most prying anti-Nazi can pin on you. You were just a cop trying to protect law and order. Okay. And don't you dare say anything else."

The Colonel oversimplified, as Weber well knew. The last fifteen years had been a long period of frustration for this able bureaucrat, although in the circumstances he had decided to live with it. Too often in earlier days he had handed over for trial a charming and sophisticated crook only to learn with amazement that the man had been torn apart in the Gestapo cells. At other times he had succeeded in tracking down a dangerous sex criminal only to be warned that he enjoyed the Party's protection. So as the bombs fell and Nazi Germany turned progressively crazier, the plump little cigarette-smoking detective had withdrawn into his private hobby, which was listening to Mozart. While Berlin was being steadily pounded to rubble, he had pondered by his phonograph upon the stellar magnificence of Donna Anna's aria *"Du kennst den Verräter"* from *Don Giovanni;* tried to fathom how much brain in ratio to inexplicable inspiration had produced the second movement of the Clarinet Concerto, and reflected on the motivations of Cherubino in *The Marriage of Figaro.*

If Miller told him he was clean, he wouldn't argue, but there would be others who would be less easy to convince.

"If I had my way," Miller was saying, "I'd whip you straight out of that Charlie Chaplin outfit you're wearing and make you a bona fide member of the American Army, G-2 Special Investigations Division, with license to pry and roam and sniff around. I'd give you U.S. status, a U.S. paycheck, and a brand-new U.S. uniform. But it ain't quite as simple as that. So I'm sending you straight up to the Hotel Edelweiss in Upper Bavaria with instructions to wash, shave, unwind, and generally reorient yourself back into the role of policeman extraordinaire, you beautiful bastard. And then I'm going to subpoena you into the role of special agent working with G-2 to uncover..."

Weber accepted a delicious-smelling Lucky Strike cigarette. "To uncover exactly what, sir?" he asked, blowing out the exquisite, unersatz smoke.

Miller grinned. "It's a complex field of inquiry, Herr Inspektor, but maybe not unfamiliar, to an investigator who's seen service with the Third Reich, even though he does happen to be clean. What we're broadly speaking of undertaking is the surveillance of one military authority by another, like it might be your SS keeping a watching brief on the operations of the Abwehr, or maybe Goering's Luftwaffe keeping up with the news at Himmler's hq. In this case, your client is Lieutenant General Bedell Smith of USFET Hq. here in Frankfurt, and the outfit we're putting tabs on is General Patton's Third Army in Bavaria—just what they're thinking, just who they're meeting, just what they're doing, or not doing, about Nazism in the zone. There could be nothing to it—except a protracted vacation for you and me in picturesque Bavaria. Guess you'll find that quite a refreshing change from Berlin. On the other hand," Miller said, shrugging his huge shoulders, "you never know. They don't usually send me where there's nothing doing."

Not Such a Peaceful Peace

"I saw you, whoever you are," came the deep, welcoming voice of Staff Sergeant Josiah Clay, as it boomed down a cavity of rubble into a dark hole lying beyond the intersection of two shattered boulders.

Josiah was just about the most popular guy in the 4th Indiana, on duty at Ansbach with the Third Army; a strapping six-foot-four-inch Negro, every glistening, cleaned-out, polished inch of him a warrior.

"Come out, baby," he crooned, lifting one dully glowing regulation boot over a crazily twisted stanchion. "I'm comin' in ter git yer so why not start comin' quiet ... like a good boy should," his velvety Paul Robeson tones caressed.

Lowering his U.S. Army regulation cap beneath a charred and twisted main cable, Sergeant Clay flicked on his lighter. A few yards ahead a mass of battered masonry danced in the shadowy light. Some feet ahead something feathered over a rink of broken glass. A sibilant whisper cut the silence. "Come on now, you grand ole creep," joked Josiah Clay; "you ain't scarin' no one. 'Cause I'm gonna getcha, and there ain't a guy livin' who can 'scape Sergeant Clay when he's so minded." And, matching action to words, Clay stepped further into the black hole. Impossible to know whether this had been a cellar or a basement or a ground floor that had been lowered by the sheer gravity of Strategic Air Command's antipersonnel bombs. Impossible to know either if he was crunching into a factory or a slum or a middle-class home or a fire station. This area of Ansbach, the so-called industrial section, had been systematically flattened block by block by General Carl Spaatz's Boeing Forts. A sudden scuddering over glass far to his right brought the now burning-hot lighter crazily swinging in an arc across the Staff Sergeant's face: picking out the big brown eyes now childish and scared.

Then there was more scampering to each side of him. Like rats. In this section of Ansbach the inhabitants were cave dwellers, and the caves were literally sewers: a high-penetration bomb had penetrated deep into the main city sewage works, unleasing a lava of unguent. The only thing that got you were kids. Kids everywhere, covered with scabs and vermin, kids in rags, kids in nothing. Starving kids, scurvied kids, kids pleading, kids cadging, kids sullen, kids in shock, and some kids on crutches without hands and feet, blinded by bomb splinters, scarred for life by incendiaries.

And then it hit him whack across the face, curling around his neck like a lasso, knocking his U.S. Army cap with its gleaming eagle crest skew-wise over the back of his head. A snake of burnished steel, a coiling whip of wires flailing at the end viciously like a cat-o'-nine-tails. As he arched back his neck, his feet were lifted from under him. He was down on the ground and still goggle-eyed when a kick like a mule slammed straight into his crotch. As the nausea rose in the Sergeant's stomach and began its crazy zigzag passage through his body, his last consciousness was of a pygmy figure riding him on the chest, light enough to be borne up and down by Clay's stentorian, panicked breathing. Until a gleaming point of pure steel penetrated his heart with surgical precision and wrote a sudden finis to the brief, popular, and Christian life of Sergeant Josiah Clay.

"Strip him," came the command.

Busy hands dealt with the brass buttons on Sergeant Josiah Clay's tight-fitting, slim-cut jacket with its row of ribbons.

Blood was flooding onto the smart fresh-laundered Army shirt through which the ceremonial jackknife with a brass swastika on its hilt had gone. The same knife was used to sever the Sergeant's tie clean off below the knot. All his equipment starting with the cap was carefully bundled into a sack, ending with his boots and trousers. Inquisitive hands wrenched down Josiah Clay's underpants. There was a stunned silence. The sheer size of the Staff Sergeant's apparatus even in its present pulped and wilted form provoked a whistle from one, a giggle from another, a shrill racial profanity from a third.

The military police discovered the Sergeant's body that night dumped outside the shattered skeleton of the former fifteenth-century Rathaus in Ansbach's center.

On the mahogany desk there was a silver-framed picture of a handsome man, aged about forty-five, wearing a Wehrmacht officer's cap. This was his son Ludovic, promoted in 1943 to the rank of staff general, missing, presumed killed, at Stalingrad.

There was another picture of a smiling, youngish woman posed in prewar sunshine on a doorstep with two flaxen-haired children. This was his daughter Ursula. She had been living widowed and alone in Leipzig when the Russians overran the city. There still hadn't been any word from her.

In effect, Herr Sauber's study was a picture gallery of the past. The wall by his writing desk was covered with framed photographs. A few of them were recent, most of them brown with time. Not all of them were as poignant as the two pictures on his writing desk. There was a picture of himself and Lisa laughing into the camera as happily as a couple of peasants on a mountain pass in some bright Twenties afternoon. Another showed a

younger, more virile self playing deck quoits on the S.S.
Bremen. There was also a photograph of a fine modern
chemical factory; like his daughter it was also in the hands
of the Russians.

One of the browner mementos showed a middle-aged
Herr Sauber got up as if for some surrealist fancy dress
party. In every respect he looked like a bowler-hatted
Munich businessman, except that he was wearing a white
armband and carrying a Mauser rifle. The explanation
was, of course, that Herr Sauber had served for a brief
spell with the civilian militia that had helped the
Reischwehr and Freikorps forces round up the Bolshevik
terrorists who in 1919 had seized Munich. As a Bavarian
who had lived through all forty-five years of the twentieth
century, history was bound to loom large in Herr Sauber's
life.

So along with the wedding picture and the christening
snapshots, there was the old King Ludwig III in
lederhosen at his favorite game of skittles in a Munich
tavern. Some Freikorps officers, one of them a nephew,
jovially linking arms outside a detention camp for
Communist traitors. In another, on a wet afternoon of
civic ceremony in the Ludwigstrasse, Prince Rupprecht of
Bavaria bowing stiffly to shake Herr Sauber's hand. And
in another beer hall, his old friend Anton Drexler,
secretary of the German Workers' Party, looked out of a
passe-partout frame with his fellow committee members.
One of them was a young man with strangely penetrating
eyes, and a gaunt face that had yet to fill out.

"My poor son, my poor son," Herr Sauber murmured,
shaking his head.

"I don't like it, Al," said Regis Halleck to Major Kopp
at about half-past four in the morning as the wrought-
iron elevator crunched its way up to floor 5 in Patton's
seven-hundred-room headquarters.

"What exactly don't you like, Regis?" drawled the
pistol-totin' Texan, as he took a fast plug at a silver pocket
flask filled with Tennessee mash.

"War games, I guess," continued Regis as Staff

Sergeant Joe Flecker led them down a corridor to Room 517. "I don't like theories. I don't like staff creeps and . . ."

"Easy there, Regis," his friend drawlingly admonished him. "Don't forget your ole buddy Al Heck-or-Glory Kopp. He's a staff creep."

"Sure, sure," murmured Regis as the muscular two-hundred-pound two-star general did a bottom flop straight onto the bed. "Sure, you're a staff man, Al. But goddamnit, you're no staff creep. You're about the only ordinary good guy left floating around here."

"Ain't that simple," said Kopp, tucking into the Bourbon. "No staff guy's that simple. Figure that's maybe why they're staff men."

"Not you, Al," his friend reassured him as he stuck out a huge paw into which the Bourbon flask that Kopp had whisked over to him somehow miraculously stuck. "You're like a breath of fresh air. Pure, hundred-per-cent Texan desert air."

"Speakin' of fresh air," drawled Kopp, "guess they've given you the most breathtaking panorama ever to come out of a travel brochure." He stepped out onto the wooden balcony. To one side the lights of the chic little Bavarian spa town still twinkled fitfully; for the rest there were rapidly scudding clouds, half-blanketing ghostly swathes of Teutonic forest, beneath a dazzling full moon. The stars in the sky seemed to bring out a responding twinkle from the white mountaintop.

"Gee, what a sight for sore eyes. Get that panorama, son!"

"Come back here, goddamn you," came Halleck's voice from inside. "You've still got some explaining to do."

"It's simple as potting buffalo: the old guy's gettin' restive. He's an action guy. Give him no action, and he gets all itchy. Wants to start shooting at shadows. And then he's got another problem around his neck. The goddamn Third Army. You've seen it, Regis. Two months ago it was over half a million strong. The most highly mechanized bunch of guys in the whole Western world. Packed full of high-explosive, gasoline and bullshit. The old guy used to rave about bustin' straight through to the Urals and having it out with Ivanovitch, John Wayne style. And you know something, Regis, I guess he could have just about pulled it off."

Halleck didn't need that much filling in. He knew how officers and men were cooking the point system to get home fast. How Patton's top cronies had fled. How the army numbered maybe two hundred fifty thousand—half of them already rookies and replacements.

"Take *you,* Regis," continued the sharp-shooting Major. "He's brought you back from nowhere and given you a corps. 'Cept it ain't a corps, it's a training outfit, though you've still got some nice armor there."

"Why me, goddamnit, Al? I ain't exactly one of Patton's blue-eyed boys."

"Maybe he thinks you're a man at war with yourself," volunteered Kopp. "Maybe he figures you've got a past to live down. Maybe he feels a kind of shame has put some fire into your guts—who knows, or maybe they wished you on him."

"Sure, sure," drawled Halleck as slumber hit him like an HE shell. "Sure, sure. But can you tell me one thing? What the heck, for the love of god, what the Jesus fuck is that thing called rock soup?"

"The guy's going through a kind of biblical phase," said Kopp. "Like he's got his hands on the tablets of gold, like he's communing up there with Jehovah on Sinai. So it's all homely parables and hominy grits. But behind the parables, Regis, there's a kind of golden truth. So Messiah Patton went up onto the mount and said to his disciples, 'There was a guy once and he was a kinda vagrant. And he went to a hacienda in New Mexico. And he said to the woman of the house, gee, I'm sure hungry. Tell you what, I sure could do with some rock soup. And what did the lady say? I'll tell you, my disciples. She said, what the heck is rock soup? And the vagrant said, just bring me a pot of hotted-up water and I'll do the rest. And taking out of his pocket two beautifully rounded white pebbles, he said these will make the tastiest soup in the whole of New Mexico. So the woman went away and when the water was boiled she produced the same, my disciples. And he put the pebbles in and sniffed it. And then he said, do you know what will make it just perfect? Just a few old dried out vegetables. Well, she went and fetched these, and then she added some meat and so forth, till the pot was overflowing with goodly tasty morsels and juices. Here endeth the lesson, brethren,'" stated a white-faced Major Kopp, the veins in his forehead standing out as they tended to after his second or so bottle of Bourbon of an evening. "Understand this parable, my friend Regis, and you've got Patton and the Glorious Third and you and me and the Russkies laid out in it. And all our futures encompassed therein, sayeth Al Kopp the prophet."

"Know one thing about Joe Offenbach," slurred Private Jacoby as he lazily unleased a clutch of darts at a detachable center-page pinup of Betty Grable that hung over Private Maggio's bed. "The guy's gone dumb these last few days. He's climbed off our backs."

"The boredom factor," explained Ned Cohn, immersed in a copy of *Yank* magazine. "Even sergeants can get afflicted. It gets into their gut and rots the whole system. He's the kind of slob who's only really fulfilled when he's skewering a few Krauts or knocking off a nice fat slice of pussy."

"Any of you guys seen this?" asked Pfc. Brewer, and he held aloft a book entitled *How to Get into Bed with Your Wife*. "Some creep dreamed up a whole series of these. Just to help the GI rehabilitate. There's even a chapter here on 'How to Talk to a Civilian.'"

"Don't you worry, man," put in Maggio. "Joe Offenbach says we're never going to see the States again, and sometimes I hope the creep's right. Who wants civilian pussy when you can ram it up the backside right here in Krautland for a couple of Camels. If you ask me, the only danger is the clap. That's why sucking's safer than fucking. They say Sergeant Offenbach's got it. That's why he's keeping so coy lately. Someone ain't exactly been tuning in to the *Voice of America*. You know the slogan."

"Let's hear what's going on in the wide wide world," suggested Jacoby as he fiddled with the dials on the radio. "That preacher cutie has probably stopped sermonizing by now. We might be able to pick up the baseball scores."

"And do not forget," said a voice, "the Lord is indeed now, as always, a very present help in trouble. What a thought to take with you on your journey through the campaign of life."

"Creeperoo!" said Maggio. "I'd like to insert my old Army bayonet straight into the bung-hole of that preacher creep."

"Hang on," said Cohn, "he's winding up."

A new voice came on. "This is Colonel Bob Miller of Third Army Headquarters. You haven't heard of me— I'm new to Third Army. I've got an important announcement to make. As you know, General Eisenhower has issued a Non-Fraternization Order, and just in case anyone doesn't quite understand that many-syllabled word, I'd like to spell it out in further detail. It means precisely this: don't hobnob with any—repeat, ANY— member of the civilian population here in Occupied Germany. That means Nazis and ex-Nazis and ex-members of the Wehrmacht and local authorities and women and young girls and even kids. This is important. Even kids. If any of you feel like a charitable act like giving, as a friendly or sympathetic gesture, a bar of chocolate or a stick of chewing gum, have second thoughts. First, because such an action is strictly illegal and could lead to a charge under the Chief of Staff's directive to United States Forces of Occupation in Germany, No. JCS 1067. Second, because by such an act you could be placing your own life in danger. Some of these kids can say thank you with a shot in the guts or a lethal jab in the general region of the genitals. At the moment I am investigating a series of deaths, which could have been caused by fanatical ex-members of the Hitlerjugend, who just don't seem to be able to erase old scores from their paranoiac minds. Have no doubt that the offenders, of whatever age, will be brought to military justice without compassion. But for the moment, while investigations are in progress, play it easy, play it wise."

"Don't worry, fellas," commented Maggio, "the officer said nothing about pussy, just kids—and who the hell's interested in kids?"

"Good morning, General Halleck. This is Staff Sergeant Flecker wishing you a bright good morning this twenty-ninth day of May 1945. The thermometer is at fifty-six Fahrenheit as of now, but General Patton's up and by all reports hot on the ball. I've got American coffee in the can, and some toast and marmalade. And one other thing—the General's clocked you in for nine-fifteen and he sure hates to be kept waiting. But I don't have to tell you that, sir."

Patton returned his West Point salute with a gray-toothed smile. He said, "Good to have you in the Third again, Regis."

Halleck was no coward. He had never allowed anybody to get that idea into his head, even his own. But a combat command under Patton had always been something different. It could be exhilarating, a heady experience—but it could also be hell on the pit of a man's stomach—like you were an ant on a grassless desert on whom the Almighty God had decided to shower all his rage with creation. Maybe a peacetime command would be different.

"You're looking fine, you old sonofabitch," Patton said, grinning genially. "That's good, because I've got one helluva lousy job for you."

"Trouble seems to be my business, sir," Halleck said, and smiled ruggedly, then flushed a little at the unfortunate truth of his statement. Outside it was a crisp if sunny blue morning in the Bavarian Alps, but a long, hot Sicilian coast road was creeping across his mind.

"Down here it's pretty quiet," Patton was saying. "We got nothing much to worry about except a few million starving Germans and DPs and these goddamn punks our

'Supreme Commander' keeps bringing in to stir up the whole stinking crap heap. But where you're going, Regis, it's different..."

That summer in Sicily the word had gotten around that General Allen was going to get the ax because he was making insufficient speed along the northern coast road to Messina. "Why, Leven's taking such a goddamn time to capture Troina you'd think he was working for that bastard Montgomery," Patton had been heard to storm as he climbed back into Bradley's scout car. Nobody had briefed Halleck that Troina was held by the 15th Panzer Grenadiers when he had decided grimly he'd pull off a copybook Patton stroke on his own initiative and swing his division out of the mountains onto the town.

"The food situation up there is worse than here, if such a goddamn thing's possible, and along forty-five per cent of your territory you'll be facing those Russian bastards. Added to that, supplies of gasoline are down to rock bottom!" Patton was saying.

"Christ, what the hell do you goddamn think you're fucking playing at, Halleck?" he could still, and would forever, hear George Patton bawling at him as his shattered infantry streamed past them like a commuter crowd. "You've not only screwed up your own attack, your goddamn sonofabitch cowards are screwing up General Allen by retreating across his goddamn line of advance! Who gave you orders to put your goddamn face into this battle?"

"I'm giving you one simple directive," an older, softer-voiced Patton said behind a polished feudal desk, "and that's to keep that corps of yours on a mobile footing. Now that's not going to be easy, Regis. We got this goddamn crazy point system which says we've got to ship home all our best men and make do with a lot of mild-swigging high-school kids."

Somehow Halleck had never been able to lay the ghost of that terrible reprimand in the bloody sunshine of Sicily. He had expected daily to be stripped of his division. When General Allen and his second-in-command General Roosevelt were fired two days after capturing Troina, he

*had literally started to sort through his effects. But he was
still in command when the Allied forces rumbled into
Messina. Talking over the campaign the next day, the
American Seventh Army commander had said, "Regis is
no Hannibal; he's more like one of his goddamn
elephants. But at least the old sonofabitch isn't afraid to
walk into those Kraut bastards." This assessment had
reached Halleck through the grapevine, and in the
circumstances he accepted it with gratitude.*

"Another thing you gotta do, Regis, is to keep hold of
the reins in your corps area. You're going to have a lot of
ass-lickers from Frankfurt who are going to creep around
telling you how you got to do this or that on the orders of
General Eisenhower, or that interfering bastard General
C. L. Adcock, 'Over-all G-5 Divisional Theater Commander,' whatever the hell that means. They're going to tell
you how you gotta fire this Kraut who's trying to repair
the goddamn sewage system on account of the fact they've
got a picture of him sieg-heiling in the back row of the
Nürnberg rally. Or they're going to say how you've got to
put this damn pervert Jew captain from the Bronx in
charge of this town because he speaks German and he
hates the Krauts—I've got a lot of them down here, and I
can tell you those incompetent bastards would strangle a
baby in its carriage."

*Sicily had been one thing, Normandy had been
another. Maybe because of what had happened in the
foothills around Troina, Halleck seemed to have lost that
extra spark of spontaneous aggression; so when Bradley
had ordered him to get Bob Grow's race for Brest down
into first gear, he'd obeyed orders and gotten himself sent
back to England as a result of another soul-blasting reprimand from Patton.*

*Next time, Halleck had told himself, as he wandered
on his futile tours of inspection of the tank-packed
English countryside, he'd play it differently. He'd sock the
Krauts with everything he had, whenever and wherever he
could find them. But there had been no next time. Deep
down in his innermost heart, General Regis Halleck had
never been able to decide whether he was deeply*

disappointed or fundamentally relieved.

"You're corps commander, Regis, and that means you're responsible for ever goddamn American, German, DP, Russian, Pole, Lat, Cossack or Croat in your district," the now sixty-year-old Patton said as he took the band off another Havana cigar. "They're going to tell you that half those Germans ought to be behind bars, and you've got to put those Poles, Cossacks, Croats and God knows what else—lots of them great fighting men—back on a train for the east so the Communist bastards can cut their throats. In fact they're going to tell you you've got to run your district down so fast it's just ripe for those filthy Mongol peasants to walk in and take it over." Patton leaned across his big desk and fixed Halleck with the luminous gaze that had sent many men to glory, or disaster. "Well, General Halleck, that's one thing you're *not* going to do."

"I'm reading you, General." Halleck flinched. Why did he feel like a man failing to wake up from a nightmare?

"I want a fighting outfit up there in Kolb, Halleck. And so, if the poor bastards only knew it, does the U.S. of A."

The decision to forbid fraternization between Allied servicemen and German civilians was doubtless honestly motivated, but it was asking for trouble. It soon became obvious that you couldn't run a country without seeking the advice of the locals. As a result, the U.S. Army administrators had to bend the rule fast. On the sexual front, the decision had disastrous consequences. Banned from talking to girls in public, love-starved GIs had to find their creature comforts in dark side streets and seedy brothels. As could have been foreseen, VD swept the ranks of the conquering armies. In an effort to slow the march of syphilis, someone at Frankfurt hit on a compromise. GIs could introduce nice German girls to their PX canteens, but they couldn't buy them food, only liquor. Again, as might have been expected, drunken debauchery became a disciplinary problem to equal unsavory lust.

Perhaps the non-fraternization edict bore hardest on

those U.S. soldiers who had relations in Germany. It was
one of the ironies of the war that the bridge at Remagen
had fallen into American hands, thanks to a large extent
to a U.S. officer who happened to have been born in the
Rhineland town. There were lots of boys of good German
blood who had fought their way home with Eisenhower's
armies. Now that the fighting was over, they felt entitled
to look up their relations. Major Al Kopp was one
German-American who decided on his own initiative to
anticipate Ike's sensible later decision in mid-July to let
the silly restriction drop. Of course, as a member of
General Patton's staff he ran little risk of prosecution.
From the beginning, Old Blood and Guts had indicated
that non-fraternization, like a lot of other edicts
emanating from Frankfurt, didn't necessarily apply to
Third Army.

"Lisa was so hoping she could be up to welcome you,"
Herr Sauber said. "She has talked so much about her
nephew from America. I will take her your flowers, and
perhaps if she is feeling a little better, you can see her later.
In the meantime, Major..."

"Al, please."

"You will take a little schnapps?"

The tall Third Army veteran looked even taller in the
modest, leather-bound armchair of Herr Sauber's limited
living room. Frankly, he had expected a good deal more
splendor, because it was no secret on his side of the family
that Uncle Martin was loaded, one of the richest men in
Bavaria, his Aunt Frieda back in Texas used to boast. He
guessed that the Saubers' clean but humble apartment
was another thing he needed, as a victor, to feel guilty
about.

"Well, sir, I'm glad to see you're looking fine." It wasn't
true. He thought the old guy looked terrible, but of course
he must be about eighty now.

"I manage as best as I can in the circumstances."

"I guess it was pretty tough for you both..." Funny, he
had never said the word before to a German, "...in the
war."

Herr Sauber shrugged his shoulders. "It is over. That is

the important thing. At least let us pray to the gods it is over between us."

Major Kopp wasn't a particularly sensitive or feeling man, but he couldn't get it out of his head that his aunt dying of cancer and this old man's white face and mildewed eyes were somehow his fault, his war guilt.

He said, "You look around the towns here. You see a lot of places bombed that didn't have to be bombed. I guess that's something we wouldn't want to do again."

It was an olive branch to add to the flowers he had brought his Aunt Lisa. It was grasped in a way he didn't expect.

"You airmen were soldiers of your country. You had to do your duty," Herr Sauber told him.

"I never remember how we got to be at war with Germany. I guess if we'd had our way, it wouldn't have happened." Al Kopp smiled bashfully. "You must have hated Third Army when we came busting in here."

"On the contrary, I have the profoundest admiration for your Third Army."

"You're kidding?"

"Particularly for your General Patton."

"Well, sure he's a great guy, but look what he did to you."

Herr Sauber smiled, a fatherly smile. "My boy, you are very young. You must allow me, from my greater experience, to assure you that leaders, real leaders, are rare in this troubled world. They demand to be saluted, no matter from where they come."

They were funny people, Krauts. Kopp couldn't make them out, even though he happened to be half German.

"So you really like the Old Man," he said, grinning. "Guess he'd be really thrilled to hear that."

"You would tell him?"

At first Kopp thought it was a cry of fear, then he realized it was a plea.

"Sure, if you like—George Patton is one helluva general, but he's a sucker for a compliment, particularly when it comes from, well . . . an ex-enemy."

"I can understand that," Herr Sauber said, nodding

thoughtfully. "A great leader is of necessity vain. He cannot be otherwise, knowing how far he towers over ordinary mortals."

Kopp grinned. "That could be George's tragedy. He knows he's the best darned general we have, but he's still got to take orders from a lot of smaller guys."

The old man looked solemn. "You must tell your great commander the governorship of the Kingdom of Bavaria is not a position to be despised. Our country is rich in resources and talents; we were a powerful, civilized nation while the Prussians were still highway robbers. We have survived the assaults of vandalism over many centuries, and where we have not been able to conquer our invaders, we have managed to . . . absorb them. We are, my dear Al, a miraculous nation, and as our protector against the Russian horde your General Patton has a sacred trust. You must assure him that I have the highest confidence in his abilities. I believe he is an exceptional man. Perhaps even a man of destiny."

Kopp was looking a little guiltily at his empty schnapps glass. Victory had conditioned him to the quick swig, the fast drag, and the easy snatch with drink, cigars, and women. Herr Sauber shuffled over to him with an avuncular refill.

"You must tell me more about your great fuehrer Patton," he said, smiling, "and I will tell you more about our country."

The first confidential report from Major Lowel Packer, G-5, U.S. Army Headquarters, Bad Tölz, to Lieutenant General Bedell Smith, USFET, Frankfurt.

May 29, 1945

I regret to report that after two weeks' attachment to U.S. Third Army Hq., Bad Tölz, Bavaria, I have yet to be favored with an audience by General P. I have admittedly caught sight of the General twice. On both occasions it was so to speak just the flash of a highly polished helmet as he sped through the town in his open Mercedes (the rumor is the machine was confiscated from Goering). What surprised me personally was the enthusiasm with which he was hurrahed by the local folk here, many of them in rags and all of them, as we know, limited to 600 calories a day. Not to mention the fact the General is supposed to be our conquering hero, not theirs. A spontaneous demonstration for a great man by any standards? The first time I thought yes, and have to confess to feeling a small lump in my throat. The next time I wasn't so sure. I thought maybe I'd seen this movie before, meaning I seemed to be conscious of an element of stage management. Also they tell me a lot of these cheering burghers were shouting anti-Russian slogans.

Again I must regret that I have not been put sufficiently in the picture to give you accurate statistics about the de-Nazification program as it is being implemented here. I know that there are a total of ten cases pending in the military court. (Certainly ten seems not that many for a big province like Bavaria.) On the other hand at least five of the civil administration in office in this town are alleged to be A-1 category Nazis, one with a grisly reputation for atrocities in the Ukraine.

My apologies for an altogether pretty unsatisfactory report. I hope to supply more factual information next time. My problem is I seem to be the unwanted guest at a party where everyone else is in a huddle. Nobody down here is hurrying to take yours truly into their confidence.

L.R. Packer
Major, U.S. Army

"Get moving, you bastards, or I'll kick your goddamned asses off!" Sergeant Offenbach bawled. In full battle gear with his hand on the magazine of his Thompson .45-caliber submachine gun, he was chasing his helmeted rookies out of their huts like a mad dog in a chicken run.

"Hit those trucks and watch your safety catches—you're carrying live ammo, God help you!" Now he was driving them like scampering fowls toward a line of trucks already revving up.

"Someday I'm going to kill that fat ape," Pfc. Perry Brewer gasped as he put his Garand rifle over the nearest truck's tailboard and hauled himself up.

"Save your ammo. You might need it, you slob!" The Sergeant's voice came back at him as fast as a punch. As always, Offenbach was right behind him, but today there was a difference. He looked as happy as John Wayne in a war movie.

The troubles had started in the British zone earlier that month. On May 20 a displaced persons' camp near Hamburg, containing Poles, Latvians, and Yugoslavs, had erupted into four days of murderous violence that had finally been put down by troops from a local Royal Artillery barracks.

The cause of the mayhem had been a visit to the camp by Russian and Communist Polish and Yugoslav "liaison" officers, one of whom had been lynched. Their purpose had been to persuade the more nervous of their co-nationals that a secure future awaited them in the new Communist world. At the subsequent inquiry a number of DPs alleged that the Communist officers had threatened imprisonment and torture for their families failing a satisfactory response.

By that strange telepathy that exists between barbed wired communities, the news of what had happened in the north had traveled. As a result, every displaced persons' camp throughout Germany was braced for the obligatory visits of "liaison" officers from the east. Sergeant Offenbach and his brood were racing, as fast as a pressed-home accelerator could shove, along the empty Bavarian roads toward DP Camp 16 near Burglengenfeld.

"Okay, get out and fall in," they heard the familiar cry of Corporal Danziger outside the truck. Pfc. Brewer had time to register that for once he didn't add, "You lousy bums!"

Now they could see where all the noise was coming

from. They were forming up outside the wire of an old German Army barracks, and the place was in turmoil. As if it was a day of liberation, hundreds of grimy faces were pressed against the wire shouting: the difference about today was that these liberated DPs were screaming hate.

Captain Robert Hartman of Lafayette, Indiana, came loping down the road with a white-faced MP at his heels. Offenbach called his men to attention; Hartman immediately stood them at ease.

"Okay," Hartman called, "you don't need me to tell you all hell's going on in there. These DPs have got hold of some Communist officers. We've got to get them out. We don't know what they've done to them, but we know they were dragged into the camp office, which is there, the second hut from the left. Make a note of that hut's position, because we can't afford to lose our way."

"You hear what the Captain says!" Sergeant Offenbach hollered.

"Now this is what we're going to do," Hartman told them. "We're going to have our mortars drop some smoke shells to clear those goons off the wire. Then we're going in. You'll fix bayonets as soon as you're in the compound, take your safety catches off and keep on going till you get to that hut. I don't want any of you guys sticking anybody for the hell of it but if they get in your way you've got to keep on going. Any questions?"

"Yes, sir," a voice from the back line. "How do we get over that wire?"

"You fuckin' jump it!" Sergeant Offenbach answered for the Captain.

In the fields behind the road, a mortar battery, manned by veteran pfc.s and noncoms, opened up. Curses and howls started to issue from the faces at the wire, then they disappeared in smoke.

Captain Hartman unslung his carbine and said, "Okay, let's go."

The camp fence was an eight-foot structure of wire mesh. They'd climbed higher obstacles in training, but always as a carefully rehearsed operation—the first man in line supporting the second, and so on. Now they were trying to perform gymnastics in suffocating smoke and every rookie wanted to be the first to get a lift up, instead of the one that got left behind. Perry Brewer involuntarily took five scrambling GIs on his back and when he tried to claw his way up the wire himself, got a savage boot kick in his face. Jacoby got shoved off the top of the wire just as he was trying to decide the best way to jump. As he hit the ground his Garand rifle exploded at his cheek and a bullet hummed off into the crowd behind the smoke. He had taken his safety catch off too early.

"Okay. Fix bayonets now!" a ghostly apparition of Sergeant Offenbach howled.

They picked themselves up groaning and sweating and started to run after him, some of the rookies still wrestling with their bayonets. After about fifty yards the smoke began to clear and the summer sun came out on a mob of DPs screaming with rage and terror. Private Ned Cohn noticed with relief that layers of the crowd were peeling away at their approach. He didn't realize that a battalion of GIs charging with fixed bayonets can be a panicking spectacle however green the GIs behind the bayonets happen to be. All the same, these were desperate people, and some of them stood their ground. Cohn saw Sergeant Offenbach slug down a little man in an oversized peaked cap with the hard part of his submachine gun. The next thing he saw was that he was coming face to face with a DP waving a piece of metal piping. His hair was about the same length as the stubble on his face. His mouth was open to show two yellow teeth. Cohn couldn't understand what he was screaming, but it sounded something like "Ameriki! Ameriki!"

The face came into close-up so fast Cohn didn't have time to think out his options. Instead he kept his bayonet up and found it had sunk itself in the man's throat. The DP tried to shriek but the sound came out differently, an insane sound, like a paraplegic in unbearable pain. Cohn let go of his rifle in horror as the DP grabbed it and fell with it in the dust. Then Cohn felt a blow under his spine and Corporal Danziger was shouting for him to pick it up.

The young private, still less than a year out of high

school, reached down and touched the swaying butt with shaking hands. "He won't let go, Corporal!" he cried.

Corporal Danziger shouted, "You better step on him fast and get your rifle back, or you're behind bars!"

Perry Brewer found himself on the heels of Sergeant Offenbach as he bounded up the timber steps of the camp office hut. "Smash that door in! With your rifle butt, you dumb cluck!"

Brewer was surprised how fast the wood splintered. Offenbach gave the remnants of the door a kick and they were looking at two DPs standing behind a row of trestle tables with their hands up.

"What do we do with them?"

"Leave the bastards! And follow me!" Offenbach shouted. He had already sprung over the trestle-table barrier and had knocked down the DP nearer the inner office door.

Next thing they were looking at four men in funny hats. These were the Communist liaison officers from Poland, the surly, peasant faces of commissars under the proud headgear of Napoleon's elite Polish cavalry. One of them had an open wound running diagonally across his face; another was bleeding at the mouth. They were all bound tight to their chairs. A little gray-haired man in a scarecrow suit was sitting beside them with an automatic that went off seconds after the Americans burst in. He probably had time to see half the nearest Red officer's head come away like a detonated cliff-face before he was tumbled out of his chair by a burst from Offenbach's submachine gun.

There was a big, wild-eyed DP on the other side of the prisoners with a jagged piece of broken glass in his hand. As Offenbach fired, he leaned across the officer closest and began to cut his throat.

"Shoot him!" Offenbach yelled.

Brewer brought his Garand up to his hip. There was no need to take aim at this range. He pulled the trigger. It didn't move. This time it was a case of forgetting to slip the safety catch off. Bullets smashed past Brewer, inches from his helmet, and ripped the DPs chest open. The man fell over scratching his body as if he was looking for fleas.

"Next time remember you've got a safety catch, or brother, I'll gun your heart out too," Sergeant Offenbach muttered with a funny smile on his face.

By this time Captain Hartman and another bunch of riflemen had broken in at the far door. He said, "God, Offenbach, did you have to murder these guys?"

The Sergeant pulled his submachine gun back to his big chest with difficulty as if it was an animate thing. He said, "Take a look at these Commie officers, sir—and the guy whose brains you're standing on."

It took the whole rescue force facing outward to make an exit with three surviving officers to the main gate. Sergeant Offenbach walked beside them with his machine gun cocked, as seemed appropriate, considering he was the man who had more or less saved their lives. All of the Communist officers were now bleeding from wounds. The last to be harmed had a deep gash in his throat, so it was perhaps understandable that he didn't murmur a word of thanks, but the others didn't say anything either.

The Army ambulances were waiting at the main gate. As he was helping the first officer in, Sergeant Offenbach suddenly put his arm out to shake the foreigner's hand, maybe because he had half expected the Pole to do the same. The officer looked blankly at the Sergeant's stubby fingers, then turned his back to enter the ambulance.

"Commie bastards! We should have left the shits in there!" Sergeant Offenbach spat at his men.

Second Confidential report from Major Lowel Packer, G-5, Third Army Headquarters at Bad Tölz USFET Hq., Frankfurt

> *May 30, 1945*
> I have at last made the acquaintance of General Patton. I was fortunate, or maybe not so fortunate, to collide with the General and his retinue as they were descending the steps of our impressively *sturm und drang* headquarters, here at Bad Tölz.
> The General looked at me with his most

belligerent gaze and remarked, "So you're the goddamn absent-minded professor they've dressed up in Army uniform to come and teach us to administer the goddam Krauts. Do you want to know something, Major—your goddamn tie isn't even straight!"

On the other hand I have been able to establish more cordial contacts with Major Wallis Du Camp, a pleasing, informed mondain and, as I understand, a trusted member of the General's inner circle.

Major Du Camp has kindly promised to arrange a series of lectures for me to MG officers here in Bad Tölz and in the main corps centers.

Accurate figures concerning de-Nazification prosecutions in Third Army area are still elusive. I get the impression that most commanders are working by rule of thumb. Certainly I hear nothing of an applied psychological pattern (forgive the unintended pun) in military government here.

The essential work of branding the war criminals ("a defeated society's necessary scapegoats" to quote my own book) can hardly be helped by the example being set at Third Army Headquarters. I understand from my new friend Du Camp that a leading SS general was entertained at General Patton's board the other evening. Major Du Camp spoke breathlessly (and maybe with just a little sense of shock) of the General's notorious record of crimes in Russia of which one can only assume General Patton is ignorant.

I guess once again this is a pretty scrappy kind of report. Maybe I should request a transfer.

> L.R. Packer
> Major, U.S. Army

A convoy of military vehicles was speeding down Neuhauser Strasse with headlights full on. An old lady who came nightly to pick at the ruins of what had once been her fashionable apartment didn't look up. She had seen too many triumphal progresses.

The cavalcade roared into the Max Joseph Platz scattering skinny-limbed kids who ought to have been in bed, if they had had any.

"Hey, where the hell is this Bürgerbraukeller!" an American voice shouted in the warm early June night as over a dozen engines idled.

"All these goddamn ruins look the same!" another Yankee voice hollered the obvious.

A Münicher was dragged from the shadows and placed on the running board of the leading camouflaged Oldsmobile.

"Okay, Fritz," someone else shouted, "take us to the Bürgerbraukeller. Don't tell us you goddamn don't know where it is—it's the cellar your fucking Fuehrer creeped out of."

A few twisting turns later Major Lowel Packer and a mob of drunken U.S. officers tumbled out of staff cars at the foundations of a ruin that was flooded with light.

A sumptuous red carpet led down through the masonry heaps to a scene that could have been a Saturday night at the Waldorf-Astoria, except that there was no roof and that instead of Xavier Cugat and his Latin-American music a band of shirt-sleeved GIs with sweat stains under their arms were giving "People Will Say We're in Love" the full brass treatment.

"Great you made it, Lowel." A grinning Major Wallis Du Camp broke away from a gaggle of dark-brown-jacketed officers to greet yet another of his vast circle of intimate friends. "You know what we're celebrating, don't you?"

"Isn't it a bit early for the Fourth of July?" Packer wondered.

"Boy, Professor, you could sure do with a refresher course in history." Du Camp winked (the other eye signaled a white-coated German waiter to bring his champagne tray over). "Let me remind you, O lofty eminence of our most ancient alma mater, that this is the first anniversary of D-Day. We just had to have a party! Tell me, O sage of the Charles River's sacred waters, can you think of a crazier, nuttier, more historically appropriate address to stage the celebrations than Adolf

Hitler's bombed-to-hell, bourgeois little beer cellar?"

Packer sipped his ice-cold Perrier-Jouet, the best from Goering's cellars, laced with brandy of a similar class. "I didn't know Third Army came ashore on D-Day," he said.

"No wonder General Patton suspected you're an Eisenhower spy," Du Camp chuckled. "That's just why we're throwing the best D-Day party in Germany—to show the world we darned well ought to have been there! In the meantime, Lowel, it's quite a party. Don Ameche's over from Hollywood and just in case you think we're provincial peasants here in Munich, Jimmy Henry's flown in to do a show with Janice Heinz. There's lots of liquor, courtesy of the Third Reich, and if you're tired of talking to your fellow officers, there are some truly incredible German women with whom you have my full permission to fraternize. Why don't you mingle?"

Du Camp was right about the fellow officers; Lowel Packer was tired of trying to mix with them. There were some young lieutenants and captains, fresh from the States with campaign chests as naked as his own; he could sometimes strike up a light-hearted conversation with them, but these conversations never got very far. Sooner or later a sour-faced older man with a blaze of color on his chest would move in to freeze a budding friendship. God how he hoped that his reports were proving so inept they would have to repatriate him to Cambridge, Mass.!

He was not looking for women, but in trying to avoid the snubs of his Third Army's veteran leaders he couldn't help noticing that the woman two uniformed shoulders away seemed like the embodiment of all the sophisticated glamour that had been swept away when the *Blitzkrieg* broke over Poland. She was a breathtaking blonde straight out of a 1939 edition of *Vogue*. Her hair was cut stylishly short. An egret wrap hung loosely over bare shoulders. A low-cut gown carried silken elegance all the way down to her feet.

"Ma'am," Packer said, smiling gingerly. "I hope you'll permit me to say that's a very charming dress you're wearing."

The vision of glamour raised a pair of wide, weary blue eyes. She said, "If you want to sleep with me, it will be five hundred Lucky Strikes. Eight hundred if you wish tricks."

"Hi there, kids," Wallis Du Camp gurgled as Packer stood blinking at the amazing proposal. He threw one arm around Lowel and the other around the German woman's seemingly untouchable shoulders. "In case she hasn't introduced herself, this is Hortense. Cute, isn't she? And every inch a countess. I'm not kidding, Lowel, Hortense here is a genuine Hohenzollern aristocrat. You're talking to the Countess Hortense von der Spegen. Now why don't you two start making small talk? Could end up in something big."

"I have told him my terms. They are the same I offer you," the Countess said, turning away with dignity.

"Why are you looking so goddamn shocked, Lowel?" Du Camp grinned. "I know you come of good New England Puritan stock, but this is Germany 1945. It's like nothing we ever learned in our schoolbooks. What did we do to deserve it?" the young Major asked gleefully, and then became thoughtful at his own question.

"I know it's hard for some of us," he decided finally. "I mean guys like us who couldn't pressure the draft board fast enough to get us into the fighting. We didn't manage to catch up with the heroes who liberated France and captured Germany; so sometimes we think we don't belong here and want to go home."

"Amen to that," said Major Lowel Packer.

"But there, my dear fellow sophisticate, you'd be making one helluva mistake. Have you thought, really thought, what we're going back to? Sure, I know you're married and you've got kids. But that was romance. Stolen embraces while the world plunged into war; smoochy partings at railroad stations while the conductor blew his whistle. But the great tomorrow waiting for us back there in the States is something a helluva lot different. It's pancakes and maple syrup, and *Saturday Evening Post* neighbors sitting on their rocking chairs and wondering why you're late back again from the office. It's ice cream for Sunday dinner and asking yourself how

in Christ's name you're going to pay your home loan
installment on Monday morning. It'll be don't let's listen
to the world news time, because what the hell's the world
got to do with the United States of America. It's there
waiting for us, Lowel. We can't escape it, but we can delay
it."

"I don't want to delay it..." Lowel Packer began.

"In the meantime," Major Wallis Du Camp said,
throwing out his arms, "we've got a party in Adolf Hitler's
beer cellar. Okay, you disapprove. You find it morally
offensive for a beautifully aristocratic woman to offer you
her body for five hundred cigarettes. But maybe one day
when you're mowing the lawn of your oh so *comme il faut*
Cambridge clapboard colonial home, you'll say to
yourself, hey, what are they doing in Germany now? And
by then, Lowel old boy, it'll be too goddamn late. Because
now, and only now, in Germany we have a chance to live
like lords of the Middle Ages. We can take our choice of
castles, hunt anything we like on four feet or two. The
cellars of the country are at our thirsty disposal. We've got
a thriving black market where a guy can earn a helluva lot
more loot than he'd ever make on Wall Street. We are at
liberty to institute a new Renaissance or a new Dark Ages,
depending on our cultural inclinations. And, of course,
over the ruined Reich's fabled womanhood we exercise
the inexorable privilege of *droit du seigneur*. By the way
that's Karen Hennecke you're ogling, Lowel—one of
Goebbels' loveliest movie stars. I wouldn't try anything if
I were you, she's got the clap. But let me introduce you to
the attraction of the evening." He patted them a
bonhomous path through an impasse of American and
French uniforms. "I'm sure you've read about her,
Lowel," he called back over his shoulder. "She was
Germany's greatest woman aviator before the war, and
would you believe, she got a Bronze in the Berlin
Olympics. I guess she really loved Hitler, she's as proud as
a tigress." He had paused near a striking blonde. "Allow
me to present Fräulein Gerda Gettler!"

The woman turned imperiously from a group of signal
officers and examined Packer with cold, searching brown

eyes, particularly taking in Lowel's naked medal chest.

She said, "So you too, Major Packer, are a soldier without battles."

"Lowel here is one of our leading Harvard professors, Gerda," Wallis Du Camp effervesced. Everyone in his enormous circle had to be a leading name in something. "He's a foremost authority on psychology, so better watch it he doesn't try and get you onto a couch."

The woman athlete pointedly didn't smile at this crude sally. "What brings you to Germany, Major? There is not much psychology for you to study in a jungle, and that is what Germany is now—a primitive jungle."

"Hey, now!" Du Camp cried clapping his hands on his sleek, close-cut dark hair. "Don't let's start talking politics. This is party night."

"I asked the Professor what he is doing in Germany."

Packer blushed under the direct, mostly hostile gaze. "I guess I'm here to, well, er—advise on military government."

"There is no military government," Fräulein Gettler assured him. "There are just little men making money on the black market."

"And also," Packer decided to assert himself, "it is my responsibility to check on the prosecution of war criminals in this zone."

Gerda lowered her honey-blond head, then surprised Lowel by raising two elegant white sleeves in the air. "I surrender, Major," she said. "I am guilty of the most wicked crime of loving my Reich. You had better bring me to trail without delay." She had brought her head up. Packer saw it was wreathed in a contemptuous smile. She said, "Do not think I am laughing at you, Major. I am only sorry for you. You will have to prosecute so many million Germans of that crime."

"You gotta admit Gerda's got spirit as well as looks," Du Camp crooned delightedly, and Packer couldn't deny it. With this extraordinarily beautiful German woman there was no question of sordid negotiations over cigarettes, no expression of weary submission at a price. Gerda Gettler put him in mind of some magnificent pagan princess led in defiant captivity into a debauched Roman emperor's court. At last he was fascinated.

"I appreciate how you must feel, ma'am," he said gallantly. "I can only say your loyalty does you credit. But I guess, well—you must have looked around you, you must realize where we are standing now, and you've obviously noticed it's a ruin. Can you really be so proud of the achievements of your glorious Third Reich?"

"Sure, baby, I've noticed the ruins," she said in mock Americanese. "Sometimes I wonder who made them. Do you think it could have been rats?"

"But listen . . ." Packer began, thrilled at the expectation of arguing as an equal with this formidable, glamorous woman. But Wallis was whispering, "Hey, quiet down, you two—Jimmy Henry's starting his show."

The band had struck up the theme tune that weekly beamed Jimmy Henry's show coast to coast. Maybe not at the same Sunday peak hour they liked to keep warm for Hope, Crosby, or Benny, but every Saturday at seven wasn't far off that peak.

A light came on downstage in front of the band, and a stooped figure in a dinner jacket shuffled into it and raised a Hitler mustache to his lip. "*Sieg Heil!* Fellas," he shouted, "it's great to see you all down here in old Adolf Schicklgruber's place!" Now the comedian turned around to examine his ruined surroundings in mock disbelief, then brought a pair of popping eyes back to his expectant audience. "Hey! I thought they told me Adolf Hitler was a house decorator." A burst of laughter, and then the punch line. "No wonder he had to take up dictatorship. This is the lousiest job of home decorating I've ever seen!" A roar of uninhibited male mirth. A German waiter dropped a champagne glass and was ordered to pick up the pieces. Packer saw Gerda Gettler turn pale and quickly light a cigarette. Outside four middle-aged Germans wrestled with a bunch of kids, to empty the contents of a garbage can of crushed oranges.

"You know, I was talking to Bing and Bob on the Paramount lot earlier this week. I told them I was coming over here to Germany to do a few shows and maybe get a look at the famous Third Army." Spontaneous applause. "The boys said, 'You better be careful, Jimmy, if you're going to visit Third Army—they've got a better entertainer than all three of us.' I said don't tell me it's Jack Benny?" Dutiful laughter. "'No, Jimmy, he's a helluva lot better than Jack Benny—though he can be pretty mean too—the name is General George Patton. Boy, can that guy get the critics raving.'" An embarrassed titter. "Well, I've had the privilege of meeting your great General, and I'd like to say I'd hate to share the billing with him on a Monday night in Yonkers. If there's any limelight going, that old trooper's got everything it takes to steal it. Anybody know where I could borrow his scriptwriter? He can get away with language that would give my sponsors kittens. But what character. I guess the only people who didn't find him funny was the Germans." Relieved applause.

Jimmy Henry lit the cigar that was a hallmark of his act and sucked meditatively at its tip. "Matter of fact, I hear they're thinking of teaming up your commander with Bing and Bob in a new road movie. Dorothy's wearing a bearskin sarong in this one 'cause they're calling it *The Road to Moscow*." A gasp from the audience. "They say it's gonna tickle the Red Army pink!" Now the comedian's eyes bulged naturally at his audience's chaotic reaction. There were noisy cheers from some quarters, intermixed with ecstatic cries from some of the German women. From other parts of the dismembered cellar there were groans and catcalls, a good deal more hostile than the puny joke actually seemed to warrant.

"Who the hell's writing this slob's material?" a brigadier general from Seventh Army wanted to know. A decrepit German waiter smiled in his face. Gerda Gettler turned to Lowel Packer with strangely radiant eyes. Major Wallis Du Camp bustled backstage at the urgent instigation of two senior Third Army officers.

But Jimmy Henry had already got the message. "And now I'd like to do a little piece I did with Janice Heinz for the USO in Paris last year. Thank the good Lord the shooting's over, all over the world, but it seems kinda appropriate to do it again tonight."

This was the cue for Janice Heinz to step up onto the boards. Her name was still trailing Joan Leslie and Jinx Falkenburg in poster type size, but as the officers of Third Army could readily appreciate, she had better legs than Joan Leslie and a lot bigger boobs than Jinx Falkenburg. Janice was dressed as every red-blooded American's dream of a Parisian midinette. The sketch that followed produced mainly good, honest, bawdy laughter from the audience. It involved Jimmy Henry, now wearing an outsize GI helmet, and an "oo la la monsieur" Janice in a sequence of hilarious misunderstandings resulting from his innocent request to be shown the sights of Paris. Only a French officer complained, "This charade is offensive."

There was no doubt about Janice Heinz's sex appeal. The posters hadn't exaggerated, or rather hadn't needed to exaggerate, her superb proportions. But even when she stripped to her brassiere it was the electricity of the German woman standing disdainfully next to him that Lowel Packer experienced. He couldn't wait for the show to be over so he could resume their fascinating conversation. In fact he could hardly control his impatience when Don Ameche was invited to clamber up onto the platform to give his impressions of Germany.

At last the lights went down on Jimmy Henry and company and the band swung smoothly into "Laura." "One way or another," Lowel Packer told Gerda, "I guess you and I have a lot of misunderstandings to clear up."

"We understand each other perfectly, Major. We are enemies."

"But you're a guest at our party, you're drinking our champagne."

"Excuse me, Major—it is *our* champagne."

She turned her back on him, and made the gesture even crueler by accepting the offer of an infantry lieutenant to dance.

"Okay," Packer called after her, "you've just demonstrated you haven't got an argument. None of your gang ever had a decent, respectable, intellectual argument, but don't think you can get away as easy as that; I'm going to cut in." He started to wade in among the unloving cheek-to-cheek dancers.

Inspector Eric Weber, formerly of the Berlin police, trod the well-carpeted corridors of the Hotel Edelweiss warily. He was no stranger to the comforts of five-star hotels, but there was something about the Hotel Edelweiss that made him feel like an outcast in his own land. This was partly a matter of appearance: inconspicuous in his plain pinstripe suit, with nothing about him to catch the eye or draw attention, he yet cut an almost ludicrous figure among all these beefy, drawling, smiling officers of the Third Army who were up here to hit the bottle, play the odd game of crap, jaw about the war, and take in the odd lungful of oppressively fresh mountain air. In their midst Eric Weber's moral isolation was total. Dinnertime found him tucking into an *escalope viennoise* with the sudden realization that this was his first good meal since early '44. A bottle of Piesporter Auslese gave him wings somehow to bridge the vacuum of experience that separated him from these loudmouthed groups. At the large round center table in the Winter Garden Restaurant a handful of exuberant Third Army men were reliving the recce to Bastogne.

"Yeah," said one, "Old Georgie did a quick flip about a hundred eighty degrees on his own axis. You should have seen Beetle's face. He'd been calling us the lousiest collection of no-good staff men in the history of the U.S. Army. When Patton told Ike he could move right away, the old smoothie almost shit."

"Herr Ober," roared a beefy-looking officer with a crew cut and major's leaves on his shoulders, "Herr Ober. If that goddamn Kraut doesn't fetch the Moselblümchen mighty fast, I'm gonna lead a recce party right down into the cellars. Any volunteers for the Third Army's most daring exploit to date?"

"Hot dog, Al," said another, "guess if we can't have General John Wood to lead us there, you could be the next likeliest guy."

"The plan of action is mighty simple. Some of us will hold Fritzie by the nose, others will kick him in the balls. The rest will sneak in past his flanks and enfilade the Kellerei."

Eric Weber swallowed a final lump of his *escalope* with unease. Then a waiter told him he was wanted on the phone. In the Winter Garden, as he left, the Keller expedition party was rising shakily to its feet.

"Hi there, Weber baby," came Bob Miller's voice. "I'm sure glad we found you. Things are busting out all over back at home base. I'm coming right up. With all amateurs around, I sure could do with the cool advice of a professional policeman. See you in two hours."

"What do you know about the Werewolves?" asked Bob Miller abruptly in the coziest and most intimate of the Hotel Edelweiss's five bars at two in the morning.

"Nothing," Weber said, smiling bleakly. "They don't exist."

"Sure, I know. Some guy in Goebbels' propaganda department dreamed up a real Hitchcock and made Ike shit in his pants with fright. Yeah, I know. Werewolves Productions, Incorporated. Real scary, the phantoms of Niebelungland, starring Boris Karloff, Bela Lugosi, and Lon Chaney, Jr."

"Even the Germans were never convinced," Weber said. "They knew that Hitler would die in Berlin and without him there would be no further resistance."

"Even so, Bormann kept prattling about them on the radio, didn't he? All those clichés about betraying the Fuehrer's trust, all that crap about the last Nazi Redoubt in Upper Bavaria, around here, I guess. It didn't smell that wrong to us. We thought the thing could just about be on."

"Americans are romantics," said Weber. "You wanted to believe in the Werewolves."

"Well," said Bob Miller, drawing deeply on a cigar, "well, we didn't believe in it. And now we do. That's about the whole of it, Weber. Something down there is bumping off lonely, homesick GIs one by one. And it isn't Uncle Dracula. And it looks like a concerted effort. There's a brain behind it somewhere. We've had about twelve of these little incidents in the last week, and the guys aren't just the pansies, the dope addicts, and the black-market racketeers—though some may be. Others are fine upstanding guys. Well-liked people—the kind you just can't figure anyone bumping off a month or so after the official killing stopped. And the funny thing is that the same kind of thing has been happening a few miles away, on the Russian side of the border. And when they plug them, they invariably whip the uniform. If this kind of thing goes on it's likely to make a lot of our Third Army veterans a heck of a lot more homesick—that's the morale side of it. But mainly we've got to get who's behind it— that's why it's kinda handy to have the best policeman of Germany on my payroll. Which reminds me, Weber, we never did quite come around to figuring out how much you were going to screw us for. Gee, what a noise those guys are making down there!"

The fires were supposed to have gone out all over Europe, even if the lights had only fitfully gone on again. But tonight on the Bavarian mountainside there was as bright a blaze as any Allied incendiary attack could have sparked. The Hotel Edelweiss was burning as merrily as a Fourth-of-July bonfire.

"Don't ask me what happened," Major Al Kopp said, grinning sheepishly. "I guess we just had ourselves a ball." He was standing with Major Wallis Du Camp on the gray morning after at a spot that the day before had been the Winter Garden Restaurant of the Hotel Edelweiss. The local German fire service was still pumping water into the smoldering hot oven around them. U.S. soldiers were sorting through the rubble, trying to salvage what valuables were left.

"But Al," Du Camp said weakly, "it was such a lovely Gemütlich kind of place. You could really stretch your legs in there."

Major Kopp scratched a prickly face that circumstances had prevented him from shaving. "Those guys were too damned slow coming up with the vino," he explained. "I don't know, heck, you gotta show these goons who's boss. All we did was break into the lousy cellars and grab ourselves a bottle or two."

"Sure," Du Camp sighed, "and the whole hotel goes up in smoke. It's just a pity you happened to choose an evening when one of Eisenhower's trusted *espions* was sampling the local hospitality. As a result, General Patton has been favored by a fifteen-minute telephonic bawling out by the Supreme Commander, and General Patton, in turn, has vented his almighty fury on me."

"They shouldn't have left so much vintage hooch lying around in that lousy cellar," Major Kopp muttered, as if this accounted for the steaming ruins at his back.

"It doesn't help matters that the proprietor happens, or should I say happened, to be a Jew," Du Camp reminded him. "They're sensitive about this kind of thing in Frankfurt."

"Shit, you'd have thought we'd raped the little punk's grandmother," Al Kopp protested. "Okay, we brought some bottles upstairs and because we weren't getting any service I started opening them up for myself with my Colt at point-blank range. You know how it is, Wallis. You have a few beers, maybe a few bottles of wine. How was I to know the place was so darned combustible?"

Du Camp offered his brother officer a Turkish cigarette; he was not one for standard PX issues. "At least you could have had the sense to get the hell out of here like the rest of your fellow revelers. What were you waiting for? The Congressional Medal of Honor?"

"You know how I am, Wallis," Kopp said, smiling wistfully, "General Patton's personal hero—the boy stood on the lousy burning deck—that's me! Or shall I confess I was so damned stewed I couldn't run to save my ass?"

A jeep pulled up beside the two men. A smiling colonel with shoulders like a bear called from the front seat, "Major Kopp, maybe I could give you a lift back to Bad Tölz."

"As if I had a choice." Kopp tugged on his cigarette. "That's Colonel Bob Miller of G-2, Frankfurt—the Eisenhower agent you were talking about. Guess what, he's put me under arrest."

Wallis Du Camp, in two minds, watched the pair drive off. Foremost he was trying to figure just how life could go on in the post-Edelweiss era, which was now gloomily unfolding. He'd miss the creature comforts. He'd miss the Bavarian baroque. He'd miss the cupids and the little orchestra and the dance hall and those five legendary bars. But there was one thing that he wouldn't altogether miss, and that was the personal presence of Major Al Kopp—the most mad, wild, and altogether frightening guy ever to creep into a general's favor. You're jealous, you bastard, Du Camp accused himself. You want a larger share of the General's ear; it looks just now as if you're set to grab it.

"I'm going to do something I hardly ever do," Patton told Kopp a few hours later. "I'm going to throw the whole goddamn book at you. I'm going to stop you, Kopp. I'm gonna send you back to the States with so many bad-conduct marks they won't even give you a license to shoot your goddamn Texan peashooter. And then I'm gonna break you as a man. By the time I've finished with you, Kopp, about the only guys who might pick you off the floor might be Hollywood talent scouts scouring the country for goddamn extras for B Westerns."

The Texan stood there, pale but unflinching, his troubled, cloudy sky-blue eyes still seeking out the General's with a kind of quizzical, dog-like devotion. When Patton dismissed him with a flick of the hand, Kopp still remained there, his lips forming words that somehow never quite became articulate.

Patton got up from his desk and moved over to the

Major. And then his eyes suddenly twinkled and he put a fatherly arm across the aide's shoulders.

"Okay, okay," he said. "I guess I can't quite annihilate an officer who's seen me right from Kasserine Pass to the Czech border. But just you tell me, you bastard, what made you fire the goddamn place?"

There was no answer.

"I'm going to do you a favor and put you out of harm's way. Keep you cool and clean for a week or so and then take a rain check. If Ike's still hot on the trail by then, we may have a fight on our hands to keep you."

When he had gone, Patton pressed the buzzer for Hobart Gay. "Hap," he announced, "did you ever discover that morale and discipline were getting a shade slack around here? Tell you what I'm gonna do. Place the whole goddamn Army from the staff downward on a quasi-war footing. As of now. I want the heads of all staff sections from G-1 down in my office in one hour. And I'm keeping Major Kopp in cold storage. He's a helluva lousy bum in peacetime, but you've gotta somehow hang on to your goddamn heroes!"

Letter of instruction to Third Army corps and division commanders from General George S. Patton, Jr.—Bad Tölz, June 1, 1945

Unless we exert ourselves, much of the greatness and efficiency which has marked this Army will be lost. You will therefore pay attention to the following:

1. Discipline... if you their commander cannot enforce discipline in peace, you are useless in war...
2. Sense of obligation! Everything in the Army belongs to the United States—you are part of the United States—the things which you waste, spoil and destroy are things for which you and your children and your children's children will be paying for years to come...
3. Deportment and carriage... You the soldiers of

the greatest Army of the greatest nation in the world wander about like furtive pickpockets with your shoulders slipping, your stomachs sticking out, and your heads hanging down...show the world how great you are. Look like soldiers.

4. Maneuvers. You will immediately initiate and continue a series of maneuvers from the squad to include the reinforced battalion—battles are just a number of battalion fights...

5. Ceremonies: important as a means of impressing our enemies, our allies and our own troops...

I will personally inspect the administrative, tactical, and ceremonial activities listed above.

Three jeeploads of MPs climbed laboriously and noisily up the mountain road to the chalet where Obergruppenfuehrer Ernst Hart was to be surprised and arrested at the direct orders of General Eisenhower. Colonel Bob Miller and Eric Weber had seats in the rear vehicle. "Mind if we come along for the ride?" Miller had casually asked the MP Captain. Now as he puffed at a Tiger tank gun of a cigar, Miller was whistling a tune by Rodgers and Hart. "In that mountain greenery where God paints the scenery, just two crazy people together..." He hadn't got unreasonable expectations about this mission, but at least it was one helluva beautiful summer day up here in the mountains; except for the smoke of his cigar the air was as wholesome as Esther Williams, and then you never knew. If nothing else resulted, Bob Miller could feel pleased with himself that his representations to Frankfurt had born fruit. At last Third Army had orders to put one leading Nazi behind bars. And after the Hotel Edelweiss affair, they weren't even going to try to disobey. At the same time, there was always the chance that Obergruppenfuehrer Hart wouldn't exactly thrill to good old-fashioned American interrogation methods. It could just happen that he would consent to sing sweetly about his old comrades in Bavaria and how they were facing up to defeat.

The small convoy stopped for Captain Ralph Carswell, who was leading the expedition, to ask the way from an aged Bavarian peasant.

"I see now how you won the war," Eric Weber said, smiling shyly, as the Captain's appalling German carried raucously down the idling line of vehicles. "You Americans have this gift for tactical surprise."

"That's enough of that, you Nazy ass-licker," Miller said, grinning savagely. "You want to end up in a cage for suspected Party members?"

"I'm sorry," Eric Weber said, bowing, then slumped under an almighty slap on the back.

"I love you, you cute little German policeman," Miller roared. "Just so long as you keep your nose on your work."

"In that mountain greenery we're gonna have ourselves a beanery..."

The convoy was moving again. After about five more minutes' steady climbing, they came around a sharp bend with a view of an attractive chalet nestling just off the road in a clump of pine trees. Now they started to accelerate. The jeeps raced over the last two hundred yards of road and careered with their famous disregard for potholes up into the chalet's tiny driveway.

Captain Carswell was a heavily built man, but he leaped out of the jeep with surprising agility and, with his driver behind him, started to approach the front door with his Colt drawn. Two more MPs with carbines disappeared around the back of the building. The second jeep plowed into the fir trees on the far side of the chalet, and more MPs spilled out to keep that side of the building covered. Miller's driver swung his jeep around so it blocked the drive. He and his companion also jumped out with carbines.

"You see how we do it in America," Miller told Weber with another staggering slap on the back. "We don't leave any damn thing to chance, 'cause we learned our business in a harder school than you guys ever had." It was at this moment that a Luger bullet passed his cap like an angry bee.

"Holy cow!" Miller shouted, as everybody else hit the ground. "The bum's going to make a fight of it. And to think General Patton was nice enough to ask the louse to dinner!"

A second shot exploded in the dust close to Captain Carswell's bulky torso. He and his driver clambered to their feet and ran to the front door. They stood there under the protection of its awning, like two people taking shelter from a sudden shower of rain. Meanwhile carbine and revolver fire opened up on the three other corners of the chalet.

"Hold it!" Miller bellowed. "I want that baby alive and well!" He flattered his voice in thinking it could be heard over the gunfire that was ripping into the Nazi's home.

It was only when the Luger had stopped firing that he was able to take things into his own hands. "Tell your guys to cut out that god-awful noise," he screamed, "and let's get inside this casa."

He bounded up to the chalet and vaulted in through a window that Captain Carswell hadn't had time to notice was open. He clattered up the polished timber stairs. The MP's fire was still shattering glass and punching holes in the chalet's frame. Kicking open the bedroom door, Colonel Miller was nearly flattened by another impromptu burst from American rifles. He strolled angrily over to the splintered rear window and scowled down the muzzles of two of Carswell's men who were crouching in the firs. "Okay, you guys, you nearly killed a U.S. Army colonel, and that is a capital offense. I'll get both you bastards in front of a firing squad if you don't put those toys away right now. And don't think I won't live to tell the tale."

Then Miller turned around to inspect what was left of the chalet's defenses. The Luger owner was lying against the wall by the opposite window. He turned the bundle over as Carswell, who had now pantingly caught up with him, kicked the Luger out of a stiffening hand.

Miller was looking at the face of a woman who could possibly have been beautiful before the world went to war. Now her face was lined and also smeared with sweat; no milk of human kindness in it. There was blood oozing from her right breast. What momentarily unnerved Miller was when Frau Hart suddenly opened her dead-looking eyes and said, "You are not Third Army...You are Eisenhower killers...Communists...Third Army is with us."

They finally found Ernst Hart in the bathroom with his blond head lolling over the side of the bidet and a pair of Eddie Cantor eyes staring at the ceiling. There were no bullet wounds on his body.

Eventually Eric Weber politely elbowed his way through the jam of gun-toting MPs who were pushing into the bathroom and knelt down over the body. He closed the popping eyes and murmured as if it was a prayer, "That is curious."

"What do you mean it's curious?" Miller demanded. "The guy had a past and he also had a handy tablet of cyanide—that's war, or whatever you call this crazy time!"

Weber looked up meaningfully at his boss. He said, "The Obergruppenfuehrer has been dead for at least three hours."

For a few seconds Miller scratched his cap. Then he said, "Don't be so fucking polite; what you're telling me is the bastard was tipped off!"

Death and Fraternization

General Hobart Gay, Third Army Chief of Staff, had a sixth sense about the telephone that linked him to his commander. He knew when it was going to ring seconds before it actually rang, and he could tell before lifting the receiver how it was going to blow. You got to be as sensitive as this after three years' dedicated service to the most unpredictable commander in World War II. This morning when this phone rang he picked it up as if it could have been an antipersonnel device.

"Hobart, who let that goddamn Russian bear into my officers' mess?"

"You mean Major Bogamov, sir!" Gay sighed, as his hand stretched for a cigarette.

"I don't care what the murdering Mongol bastard is called. You get him out of here this morning, Hobart, or maybe you'd like to nominate your replacement."

"I'm sorry, sir, but..."

Patton's voice roared over General Gay's explanation like a Sherman tank. "I'm not having any slit-eyed assassin in a gentleman's mess, do you hear me, Gay? You know what those goddamn apes did to those Polish officers in Katyn. I've got the pictures here in my office. You ought to take a look at them, Hobart. You'd throw up into your soup every time you had to sit down at the table with a goddamn Russian. I want that sonofabitch kicked straight out of here back into the goddamn sticking mud hut where he belongs. That's an order, Hobart!"

"... by special request of General Eisenhower, sir," Gay at last managed to blurt out. "Apparently it's part of a new Anglo-American initiative, sir; they're anxious the Russians..."

"Don't you talk to me about any goddamn Anglo-American initiatives," the telephone exploded in Gay's hand. "Remember that almighty disaster called Arnhem—that was Anglo-American initiative. Remember that goddamn charade called Monty's Rhine crossing—a month after we had taken a pee in the river—that's another Anglo-American initiative. Whenever I hear those words 'Anglo-American' I feel like I want to puke; because 'Anglo-American' means the lousy British, and the lousy British were the biggest liability we had in the war. Why those bastards couldn't even lick the Italians by themselves. And they had to kill every goddamn living creature in Caen before they could find the guts to take the town. Those bastards don't know how to fight and they don't know how to govern a goddamn country. Do you know what those sonofabitch diplomatic British have done with the Jews in their zone—they've sent 'em back to Belsen, of all goddamn places!"

"Maybe I'll just call it an initiative, then, sir."

"What is this so-called initiative?"

"There's a certain amount of anxiety, sir, that we're losing contact with the Russian area of occupation. USFET is worried about the East-West suspicion that's building up. The idea is, sir, to build confidence by arranging for permanent Russian military representation with every army group."

"And let them sniff around our dispositions and stick their snotty noses in our files so they can see just how little we've got to stop the slit-eyed bastards with when they start moving in! Have they gone crazy up there in Frankfurt, or just soft—soft on Communism!" The tone of voice suddenly changed to that of the cagey military politician who ultimately obeyed his own interpretation of his orders. "This Bogamov thing—is it really a 'special request' or is it a goddamn order?"

"I'm afraid it's an order, sir," General Hobart Gay murmured. He added cautiously, "I guess Frankfurt is getting a little sensitive about their orders."

"Okay, here's what you do. You keep that ogre locked up in his quarters, and if he wants to go out and take a pee, you make goddamn sure he's got a GI escort! You tell him it's an American Army custom for officers to eat in their quarters—I'm not having him anywhere near my officers' mess. Maybe we can let him out if Ike drops in, but otherwise you keep that savage out of my sight."

General Gay reached for another cigarette. "Sir, there could be serious political repercussions."

"I hope there goddamn will be serious political repercussions! I hope it'll drive those Russian bastards so fighting mad they'll goddamn try and ..." General Gay could picture Patton's face now. He saw it creased in deep conflicting lines as he struggled to stop his mouth from giving dangerous words to his ferocious feelings. He seemed to succeed in constructing some kind of dam across the danger area, but the torrent of anger overflowed in another direction. "Christ, doesn't that Sunday-school-reared Kansas kid up there in Frankfurt realize those Russian sonsofbitches don't read the Bible? I'd like to see him try telling those bastards to forgive their enemies! I tell you Hobart, those murderers wouldn't wait till Good Friday to nail our Savior to the cross—they'd goddamn crucify him in the cradle. And the way things have gotten to be now, I guess you'd find the British and our Supreme Commander handing them up the nails. You've heard what the British did to those poor Cossack sonsofbitches in the Drau Valley—shipped them off like suffocating sardines to Siberia. You know what they forced our men to do at the DP camp at Kempten? The same thing, only thank the Lord the GI is more merciful than those British bums! They're trying to make us goddamn hangmen for the sake of those Commie butchers!" A terrible laugh rattled over the wire. "You know I sometimes think it's kinda funny, Hap, that goddamn crusader's sword Ike and his SHAEF gang used to wear on their shoulder patches—the way he kept talking about his 'crusade in Europe' in his damned boring dispatches. Well, if that was a crusade we were fighting, I'd like to know where the hell Jerusalem is? We haven't got there yet, Hobart. It's still four thousand goddamn miles away!"

"Where the Chrissake do you think you're going?" bawled Sergeant Offenbach at the scurrying figure of Private Jacoby.

Eight weeks of Pavlovian feed-in froze the GI's feet to the ground and he slurred from the diagonal to the upright. "Just figuring on going into town," explained the man from Michigan. "If you've no objection, I'm studying German, Joe. Thought I might take a degree when I get out."

"Haven't I told you, you runt," boomed Offenbach, "you'll never get out? Particularly now. It seems we've got a fine new commander for VII Corps. A mean bastard called Halleck. He'd make Stonewall Jackson look mobile."

"All the same, Sarge," reasoned Jacoby, "we GIs do have a Bill of Rights. We've got two years' college education for the asking when we leave the Army. And to be candid—I sure need that education. So I just fixed for a few German lessons from Fräulein Frolich. I pay her in cans of coffee."

"You mean the Bürgermeister's daughter?" asked Offenbach with interest.

"She's really cultured," explained Jacoby. "She's gotten herself some basic schooling in Cologne and a diploma in literature at Munich. She speaks German with a non-Bavarian accent—that's quite something."

"Yeah," sneered the Sergeant. "And she's probably all

of sweet seventeen. She's as clean-pussyed as Deanna
Durbin—so you goddamn well keep your crap-riddled
fingers off her. She happens to be the Bürgermeister's only
daughter."

"You know him, Sarge?" asked Jacoby innocently.

"No one knows Krauts, son. There's a specific order
called Non-Fraternization and Eisenhower will personally chew the hide off any GI who breaks it. But strictly
between you and me, the Third Army can't run this
goddamn country without some communication with the
conquered enemy. And if you had to fraternize,
Bürgermeister Frolich wouldn't be such a bad choice.
He's got an American viewpoint on things. He'll lick your
boots all the way up with his slimy tongue. He'll hold your
prick for you while you urinate. Then do up your fly. He
salivates at the thought of Patton. And that ain't so bad.
All in all he's the kind of Kraut you can do business with.
Just as long as you bawl him out if he doesn't grovel to the
Stars and Stripes three times a day before meals. And
thank God in his prayers for General Patton and the
Third Army, who saved the paunchy Bavarian burghers
from the Red Peril across the hills. But his daughter ain't
for the taking. I've booked her fresh and virginal for
Captain Hartman on Thanksgiving Day."

"Heck, Sarge," complained Jacoby, "that's positively
feudal."

"Okay, run along, kid," said the Sergeant indulgently.
"But remember what I said. If it's a little Kraut learning
you're after, okay. But don't forget there's a great big
brass chastity belt wrapped around Fräulein Frolich's
virginal fanny. And it reads 'For the personal use of Third
Army officers only. All other ranks jerk off.'"

Offenbach pondered a few moments as the upright
figure of Private Jacoby marched out of view. Things
weren't going so badly. In fact if you had to pick anyone
from that group of pussy-willowed rookies, your eye
would lead you straight to Jacoby. Of all that section he
was the smartest, the cleanest cut. He was a serious kid,
too, with a will to improve himself in life. Not so bad. And
then he was obviously in good standing with Bürgermeis-

ter Frolich and his daughter. Not so bad either. Just so
long as he didn't push Frolich off course by screwing his
daughter, Jacoby could be a useful stooge and ally;
someone to drive a truck, outsmart a sentry, or tap a few
German sources of supply with a few literate words in
German. And if he yelped, Offenbach had him—on a
simple violation of Non-Fraternization.

He made a mental note to pitch further into Jacoby
that night.

The slim, girlish form of Herr Frolich's daughter had
indeed turned the young Jacoby's head and even
enfiladed his heart. But though Anny Frolich in a girlish,
blushing kind of way had proffered her cool, slim body to
him in the course of the last two lessons on the poetry of
the Jew Heine, Jacoby had refused to grant her what she
really seemed to be wanting on a point of strict medicine.
He was almost sure he'd contracted the clap. In fact, with
the rest of his unit, he was booked into an inspection at
Third Army General Hospital in Munich the following
week. Meanwhile he had a moral concern about passing a
virulent dose of gonorrhea onto his Gretchen during her
very first spasm of love. His reluctance had had a strange
aftereffect: the Bürgermeister had found his daughter
crying in her room after the lesson and had drawn the
conclusion that the GI had raped his daughter in the
middle of *Faust,* Act One. He was relieved that it was an
American who had taken his daughter's maidenhood, and
resolved to question her no more about it. He found in
Jacoby the kind of lad who'd have made first-rate
material for the Waffen SS, and though the name Jacoby
might do with a little probing, there was no doubting that
the slim, fair-haired, blue-eyed GI had the right physical
credentials.

The demure Fräulein led Harrison Jacoby through the
large reception hall and into the main reception room,
notable for a huge desk, commissioned by the Bürgermeister's grandfather from a local craftsman, and a
general feeling of Biedermeier comfort.

"Where's your father?" asked Jacoby with some concern.

"He is at the Rathaus," explained Anny. "It's just like old times. He's just appointed new deputies, and do you know, Harrison, they're the same guys who served under him last year."

"Why do you use words like guys?"

"It's simple: every German girl wants to speak English, but we prefer it with an American accent. Like our men." She had led him to a well-upholstered sofa into which the GI's strained body gratefully sank. He took off his cap and threw it onto a chair; she passed her hands very lightly across his slightly long fair hair.

"But you are almost un-American," she said. "You do not have—what do you say—crew cut. And look at these fingers. They are long and sensitive—the fingers of a pianist. And you want to learn German. This is a compliment. Very few of your compatriots, Harrison, would admit to such a desire. The language of Streicher and Heydrich."

"The language of Goethe and Thomas Mann," countered Jacoby, reddening.

"Maybe that is all now a little besmirched," reflected the girl. "Maybe the language too has been contaminated by Zyklon B—those amethyst-blue crystals of hydrogen cyanide the SS orderlies poured down the ventholes onto Jewish women and children."

"Germany will rediscover itself," declared Harrison Jacoby, his well-pressed trousers engaging the girl's lower limbs at the point where the simple Bavarian floral peasant skirt folded over the tanslucently fleshed knees.

The girl's hands went around his neck and over his hair. His body wilted on Bürgermeister Frolich's favorite armchair as she stretched over him: her lips came down smack on his in a long, sensual, and imprisoning kiss.

"Why do you resist me, *liebling*?" she breathed, a more sensual odor, the pungent reek of fertility now beginning to emanate from her girlish body.

"Wow! You sure do something for a guy. But heck, this

isn't what we should be doing, Fräulein," said Jacoby. "I mean, you're the Bürgermeister's only child, and besides this is his house and his goddamn sofa. You just can't . . ."

"Who said I'm the Bürgermeister's only child. I have a brother. He was the class of '29. That makes him just sixteen. He was committed by Hitler to a final defense of the Oder bridgeheads outside Berlin. That's his photo on the desk."

In a cap too large, in trousers too baggy, in boots too worn, a small grimace of derision emerged from an unformed wisp of a face.

"Where is he now?"

But Anny Frolich's lips were again on his, her legs parted, pressing tightly into his haunch. The GI came out of a swoony kiss to exclaim, "I s'pose you could call this a kinda lesson in German."

"Let's talk English, *liebling,* good American English. In these times a girl can feel no shame. She will use words. Any words. *Liebling.* Fuck me, fuck me. What do you Yankees say? Screw. Yes, screw." Her fingers were inside the buttons of Jacoby's tailor-made trousers.

"Heck," he said. "I can't. Just can't."

"Why can't, darling?" She imitated the short American "a." "What can't do for a girl? A captive, defeated German girl? A deranged girl. A girl who begs you on her knees for a good American fuck. What could be simpler or easier?"

"Okay. I'll give it to you straight." Wrestling her hands away from his trousers, he pulled himself into an upright position on Bürgermeister Frolich's Biedermeier couch. "Okay. I'll tell you. I got the clap. The goddamn fucking clap, ain't that some joke."

She drew straight back, sitting right on the other side of the sofa now.

"And," he continued, "the joke is it happened about two minutes' walk from here. In the cellars beneath the Rathaus. And it isn't that surprising, Fräulein, they say about half the Third Army's come down with it."

"Are you sure?"

"Sure I'm sure. Would you like to look? After all," he said, offering to unbuckle his belt, "you were just about to help yourself. But joking apart, if you can only wait a month or so there'll be no problem. And here's consolation. The U.S. Army has a Bill of Rights for guys who've contracted the clap. We're booked solid as a troop into Ward 19 of the Third Army General Hospital in gay old München. Come to think of it, you could send me some grapes."

He desisted because tears, genuine tears, were beginning to flow from Anny Frolich's large, hazel, and beautifully unmade-up eyes. "Well," he said, "I must earn my GI Bill of Rights to further education. Get me somehow to old universities of Europe—and you, Fräulein, must earn your quota of special GI high-caffeine coffee. So it's back to Heine, honey."

Neither party had noticed, but the door had slightly moved ajar and then back again on its hinges. A figure of about five foot six inches, looking more like fourteen than sixteen and dressed in lederhosen and a ragged coat, was hunched there, motionless. And tears were in his eyes also. As the GI's broken German started to drawl the immortal verse of Germany's finest Jewish poet, the boy quietly left the house and ran, almost noiselessly on bare feet, away down the street.

Major Lowel Packer fingered the purple envelope nervously and also a little guiltily. It contained a personal letter from Gerda Gettler, the beautiful ex-aviator he had met at the Munich *Braukeller* party. He had just sealed his latest report, which had ended:

> . . . maybe I should add that among the other guests at these fraternal hijinks was the darling of Hitler's air pioneers, Fräulein Gerda Gettler. I am not aware that the lady is a wanted war criminal, but she professes the frankest sympathy with the *ancien régime*. You may feel that someone at USFET should check her out.

• • •

The letter from Gerda was short in comparison. Written in a flamboyant English script, it simply said:

> Greetings, enemy,
>   I should not like you to think I am unwilling to defend my *intellectual* convictions. If you would wish to join battle, I shall be in the Prince Ludwig chocolate house this afternoon at 1600 hours. Come if you wish. But if you are not anxious to risk an embarrassing fraternization, do not worry. I understand how it is with our conquerors.
>   Gerda Gettler

Of course he had to go for a lot of reasons, some of which the Harvard professor had to admit he was scared about. There were just as many reasons for not going, but the note was in essence a challenge to the man in him. There was actually no choice. All the same, as Lowel Packer walked down into midafternoon Bad Tölz when, in happier days, Savile Row-tailored German invalids would be taking the air on sticks or in wheelchairs, he was sorting through his mind for the most respectable explanation for coming. The best he could think of was that hypocritical word "duty."

He found he had arrived five minutes early, perhaps because he was secretly determined not to miss her, or to find that she had got into a tête-à-tête with another officer. The place was in fact filled with American officers and German girls. The Prince Ludwig had provided a means for the more responsible Third Army officers to get around the ban on entertaining German women. Although the patisseries offered were largely based on wood shavings and the hot chocolate was only occasionally supplemented by black-market U.S. Army rations of the real thing, the ambience was typically Bavarian and could be said to offer a more romantic background for a budding affair than a raucous PX bar. Lowel Packer was lucky to find a small table with a free seat to offer her when she strolled into the cafe at the stroke of four.

She said, "Do not trouble to get to your feet. I assure you none of your brother officers find it necessary to stand up for a German woman."

On the way through the little unbombed town of camera-toting GIs, Lowel had figured out one line he might take, and this opening remark provoked him into pursuing it.

"Look, why don't we agree on something here and now—let's agree to cut out all this victor and vanquished crap!"

She smiled unapologetically. "I understood, Major, you were going to overwhelm me with arguments for the superiority of your cause."

"This is your tea party, Fräulein," Packer rapped back.

She opened a silver cigarette case and lit a Chesterfield with a gesture that showed little regard for its worth. As at the party at the Burgerbraukeller she was wearing an open shirt and slacks. She was also wearing a double string of pearls as a choker around her neck which Packer reckoned by this time practically any other German woman would have had to sell.

"In that case, Major, it was gracious of you to come. You must have so many important duties."

Her words were as harsh as tracer bullets, but the expression in her fantastic brown eyes was not totally hostile.

"Okay, you want to tell me what a regular guy Adolf Hitler was." Packer allowed himself to smile. "Why don't you shoot?"

She raised her cigarette to eyelash level, as if she was looking along a pair of sights, and said, "Bang! Bang! Bang!" And then they both laughed.

"I guess we do have a communications problem," Lowel said, grinning. "When we say 'shoot' in the United States it doesn't have to mean you've got to pull a trigger. It's kind of argot for talk."

"Perhaps it is because so many of your 'talks' have been with the gun. 'This gun does my talking'—isn't that what your Wild West heroes say?"

" 'Guns are better than butter'? Don't tell me you don't know who said that. And don't tell me you don't know where he is now."

She tossed her blond hair back. "Goering was a fool and a traitor!"

"And Adolf Hitler?"

"You know it is not permitted to mention his name," she whispered, as a number of bleary, lipsticked faces turned in their direction.

"Tell me something," Lowel demanded, "why do you go on defending that gang of psychopaths? It's not only dangerous, it's crazy. Okay I grant you that before the war you could have had an excuse for thinking they were going to do something purposeful and creative. And right, even at the beginning of the war I guess you could have thought, well, at least they've given us a magnificent army and a whole lot of easy victories for not much blood. But now you've heard what they were doing in Russia, the really nightmare things they were doing to the Jews, you've got to admit . . ."

"You can only say what you know," Gerda told him. "I only know that the Party gave me everything. In my case, as you may have heard, it was the chance to fly—faster and higher than any woman before in the world. They gave me beautiful machines with the hearts of wild animals, made with so much German skill and love and hopefulness. They gave me such speed and such freedom that no other machine could ever touch me. Major Packer, I only know I have come down to earth, and it is not a very pretty place."

"It doesn't always do to have your head in the clouds—even for a beautiful woman like you."

She said, "It is very close and crowded in here."

He thought she was getting up to walk out on him, but she turned back with a surprisingly provocative smile. "Perhaps you would like to take chocolate in my apartment?"

Packer hesitated on the pavement outside the Prince Ludwig as she nonchalantly moved ahead of him along the pavement. Then a couple of GIs turned their heads and wolf-whistled, and he felt bound to accept the prestige of being her escort.

"I didn't know you lived in Bad Tölz. I somehow got the idea you were from München."

"You would like me to fill in another *Fragebogen,* Major? I assure you I have already completed five. No, I have lived in München, but it is not so easy to find accommodation there today." She turned to him with an expression he couldn't see because she was now wearing sunglasses. "So many of its houses seem to have fallen down."

They passed a billboard where two official posters were displayed. The first was a series of shattering pictures of concentration camp victims under the stark heading "Who Is Guilty?" The second showed the same selection of atrocities and stated bleakly "You Are Guilty!"

"You didn't even give them a glance, did you?" Lowel said.

Gerda looked at him through her dark glasses. "I'm sorry, I do not know who you mean."

As he settled on a scarlet upholstered divan in her apartment, she said, "Yes, I know what you are thinking. You are thinking it is strange for a German woman to be living in such comparative comfort; she ought to be living in the cellar of a bomb site and stretching her hands out for cigarettes. By the way, will you have a cigarette?"

"Thank you, I don't smoke."

"I could make you chocolate, but it is possible you may prefer something to drink. Will you have a glass of whiskey? I regret it will have to be Bourbon."

She was right. The surroundings were exceptionally luxurious for an unrepentant Nazi in the summer of 1945. The implication seemed obvious. Gerda was somebody's kept woman, and as far as Lowel knew, the only people with the money to keep a girl like Gerda in this style were officers of the U.S. armed services.

She brought a tall glass of Bourbon on the rocks to him with a secretive smile. She said, "You must promise not to mention this in your reports. They might get ideas—bad ideas—about me."

"What reports?" He sat up with a jolt on the divan.

She joined him on the divan and told him softly, "You are blushing, Major Packer." It was bound to be true. Only this morning he had asked his superiors at USFET to check Gerda Gettler out.

"Just what kind of reports am I supposed to be writing?" he asked, wishing just for once that he did smoke.

"Oh, I don't know. Perhaps about the weather. Perhaps about how is morale in the Third Army, how many of your 'criminals' are employed by General Patton's staff; what is the mood of your great General—I don't know."

"You seem to know an awful lot," Lowel breathed. At least he was grateful to himself to having decided that morning to reroute his reports via a new courier.

"Perhaps I have a woman's intuition," she suggested as Packer's wandering eyes froze on an object on the mantelpiece. It was a silver model of a Sherman tank, one of those he knew had been minted to mark the victory in Europe for Patton's corps commanders and intimate staff. He realized then that Gerda Gettler could have one hell of an intuition.

He turned to try and look her straight in the face, and was dismayed to find it lit up with a seraphic smile. "Okay," he murmured, "suppose I file reports on Army morale—I happen to be hired by the Army as a group psychology specialist."

"And everything that is going on here at your headquarters in Bad Tölz. Is that psychology?" Words like knives. A smile like an angel.

"What does it matter to you anyway? You're a self-confessed Nazi. You don't care...a damn, I guess!"

She got up and walked over to the window where the mountains were turning pink in the afternoon sun; perhaps so he could admire the undulating movement of her hips or perhaps because she simply felt like taking a walk.

Looking out on the serene mountains, she said, "Major Packer, we are both people who are holding certain sincere convictions—that is rare in Germany today, on either side. It is perhaps because we are sincere that we are also both vulnerable."

Lowel leaned back as casually as he could in the hot-colored divan. He said, "I take it you're telling me security at Third Army Headquarters is lousy."

She had turned into profile against the crepuscular mountains. The sun, or its reflection, gave a definite contour to her beautifully proportioned breasts, and played imaginative lighting effects around the outline of her face, a model of Aryan breeding, but far more sensual than any fascist sculptor's dream of womanhood. She said, "American security is always lousy. It is important for you to learn that."

"Listen, I don't know where you get your information..." Lowel began, and then suddenly caught up with what she was saying. "Hey—wait a minute! You're trying to threaten me, aren't you?"

She turned from the window to look at him. The light from the mountains aureoled her fair hair. "How can I threaten you, Major? I belong to the vanquished."

The word "vanquished" was spoken with patent insincerity, and as a result Lowel Packer suddenly felt very scared. There seemed to be a clear threat lurking behind her studied humility. Where was it going to come from? Outside there was shouting, but it was only the shouting of German kids playing in the street below. His eyes raced around the apartment. There were paintings of alpine scenery, a heavy regional clock by the silver Sherman on the mantelpiece, a marble-topped coffee table with gilt legs, thick scarlet curtains to match the upholstery of the divan and chairs—no instruments of death. Then the phone rang in another room and he thought to himself, My God, is this some kind of signal?

She went to answer it, and Packer told himself, No you don't, make a run for it. Half of him still actually wanted to stay. He got up and moved over to the mantelpiece and picked up the silver Sherman (boy, what his young fourteen-year-old wouldn't give for a toy like this!). The inscription read "Third Army Europe July 1944–May 1945—the biggest bunch of bastards that ever went to war." There was no owner's name.

He was still examining the object when Gerda came back into the room. She said, "Don't worry, it doesn't shoot."

"All the same, a Sherman is a funny toy for you to have..." Lowel said mirthlessly. "A Tiger would be more like you."

She came up very close to him. Her perfume smelled a million miles away from the rubble of Germany in "year zero." Was he crazy to look for a knife?

She said without irony, "We don't need to be enemies, you know. We could learn to live in peace."

"Who is he?" Lowel Packer asked, fingering the silver Sherman.

"A gallant enemy."

"I was curious to know his name—maybe I've met him."

She placed her hand on his medalless chest. "Perhaps you have. Perhaps you have not. My security is better than Third Army's."

"What the hell is your angle?" Packer wondered. "Okay. You've got someone high up at Third Army Headquarters who's nuts about you—maybe to the extent of talking in his sleep. If you want a psychologist, all right, I'll take on the job for a fee. Otherwise what's your cozy little setup got to do with me?"

"You mustn't be so hostile," Gerda whispered. "I am proposing a treaty of peace." She had slipped her hand under his jacket. He felt exploring fingers moving down his trim dieted stomach. He was under attack from the corniest gambit in the sex war. But he hadn't seen his wife for twelve months, and this woman was no ordinary German tart putting out hungry fingers for cigarettes.

"What are the terms?" Packer asked. He found he was already kissing her extravagantly scented neck.

"Love," she smiled. "Or if you like, total surrender."

"By me?"

"By both of us."

Her hands had found the region of his body, the basic family man's apparatus which the U.S. Army in its perversity had demobilized for the duration and beyond. At the same time he started to tear at the studied casualness of her too well-tailored casual shirt.

"Any other terms?" He was looking at the naked breasts that half of him had insanely desired from the first encounter in the beer cellar, if only because they belonged to a woman who, whatever the morality of her convictions, bore herself proudly in defeat.

"Only the trust I demand of my victors and victims," she said, smiling. "Darling Major Packer, you have my permission to write wonderful American poetry about me, but no reports. We are both too vulnerable."

Up to now she had been soft and melting. Now she dragged him down savagely to the scarlet divan, helping him to tear off her calculatedly casual slacks with even more savagery than his own.

Lowel Packer sank into the heaven and hell of a wild sexual hunger, backed by a double sense of guilt. Hadn't he already asked USFET to check Gerda out? Like the eager member he thrust into her ravenous body, this was another action that could not be called back.

Corpses were not an uncommon sight in Germany in the summer of 1945. Usually, however, their bones were showing and their skins had the parchmenty look of deprivation. Most corpses, whether that of an emaciated DP, ex-prisoner, or underfed German, looked as if they had a right to be where they were, and how they were. This one, lying at a street corner on a damp Sunday dawn at a crossroads in Regensburg, was different. Naked as a newborn babe, it was also as plump and fleshy as a pampered infant. Its new state of death actually seemed a crime against nature. Similarly the wounds that had been inflicted on it added up to an impression of outrage—an affront against the rounded limbs and corn-fed tissues.

The fact that the late Pfc. Bill Johnson had been stripped of his uniform could not conceal his identity as a member of the U.S. armed forces. The corpse was too healthy-looking to have been anything other than a hundred per cent American. This was one body that truly invited a sense of shock. Even the German policeman looking gloomily down on it couldn't avoid a feeling of disgust at the way such a wholesome body had been subjected to such a brutal, St. Sebastian-like martyrdom.

"Was wollen Sie?" snarled a voice from behind the balcony.

"Is that you, Herr Frolich?" panted Private Ned Cohn.

"You wait down there," commanded the Bürgermeister's voice.

When the heavy portal swung inward, Cohn went with it, like a man in a swing door. "Glad to see you, Herr Frolich," he gasped. "I guess you think this is quite irregular."

"I think you come from Sergeant Offenbach's unit," said Frolich, smiling, his pig-like eyes taking in instantly the state and identity of the GI.

"We've just been ordered out on maneuvers, sir. The whole unit's on alert... It's just that Private Jacoby, sir..." gasped Cohn. "If he misses this, he'll probably be court-martialed."

"And so?" inquired the Bürgermeister, his eyes pinpointing Cohn, whose hand was gesturing at the staircase and beyond.

"It's hard to explain, sir," gulped Cohn, his breath now returning, his heart pumping less erratically, "but if you let me up those stairs I might be able to trace him."

"I see," remarked the Bürgermeister. "You are suggesting that my daughter and the Private are in there together."

"Sorry, sir," piped Cohn, "but there isn't that much time. I mean, we move in three quarters of an hour."

"And if I told you that there is no foundation for your insinuations about Jacoby and my daughter?"

"Gee, Bürgermeister. I don't mean anything, it's just that Sergeant Offenbach's waiting back at camp, bawling his head off. Unless Jacoby makes it, the Sarge is going to pulp the juice out of him." He had a problem. To elude a solid barrier of two hundred twenty-five pounds' worth of heavy Bavarian sausage, girded up in a heavy leather coat from which snatches of baby pink naked body coquettishly peeped. And then he had a brainwave. It wasn't for nothing that Ned Cohn was the official gag guy of the unit, the wisecracking court jester to Monarch Joe Offenbach and his Merry Men. He turned to the door and did a quick James Cagney resigned flip of the mouth and eyebrows. "Okay, okay," he drawled, "if that's the game, I guess you have me on the ropes..."

The German moved to one side to escort him out of the door, as Cohn swung quickly to the left and, head-butting the Bürgermeister in the stomach, made for the oak-paneled staircase. To the gurgled backing of rich Bavarian expletives he made the landing. Three doors, all of solid oak. Behind him the staircase seemed to tremble and give way as the Bürgermeister's body pounded up behind him. Then Cohn found the door. It was locked: it just had to be the one. Thumping on it till his fingers bled, he screamed, "Jacoby, Harrison. You bastard. You've got half an hour to make it, or you're a dead duck. No kidding, Harrison. No kidding."

But the door did not give way. Instead an ox blow on the back of the neck from the Bürgermeister's oversized hands felled him to the ground. Then the door opened. The Bürgermeister's bloodshot eyes blinked and blinked again for one instant as his sixteen-year-old daughter Anny, that little fresh flower of the Alps which, by some quirk of biology, Frolich had somehow procreated, tumbled into his arms: a cascade of now clotted blood suspended like a crimson icicle from her crotch: the swastikaed overcoat of the Deutsche Mädchen hanging limp on her narrow shoulders. Then she was sobbing in his arms and the Bürgermeister's consoling bear hug created a bastion around her.

"Here, Al," Colonel Bob Miller called cheerfully to Major Al Kopp, who was lying on his bed reading an old copy of *Life*. "I brought you a present."

He tossed a bottle of Bourbon through the air. Kopp sat up to catch it and said, "Hell, I got enough of this stuff."

"Me, I can never get enough," Miller said grinning, lighting another of his foul-smelling cheroots. "Why don't we have some, chew the fat? Incidentally, that's the real Old Kentucky, ninety proof."

Major Kopp sat up on his bed, took the cork wrapping off with a yawn. He said, "I know you're a helluva big noise at USFET, Colonel. What's a senior Intelligence guy like you doing with a simple court-martial case like me?"

"I hate to see anyone deprived of their freedom," Miller told him, reaching across for the bottle and taking a large swig, "least of all an American officer of your distinction. Maybe we could talk about that for a little while."

"What the hell is there to talk about? We got bored. We wanted to see a little action. We got a little liquor. And this lousy Kraut hotel burned down. It may be an indictable offense—but it's natural."

"Natural?" Miller smiled charmingly, passing the bottle back to the Major. "I guess they never told you the war is over."

"Maybe that's the trouble." Kopp took a suspicious swig at the Bourbon, and seemed reassured. "I mean...well, in Third Army we got kind of used to fighting—busting places up was what we got paid for."

"What's the matter with you Third Army guys?" Miller seemed to ask innocently.

"As I said, Colonel, we did a helluva lot of fighting."

"I suppose it never occurred to you a lot of other guys did too," Miller suddenly rapped out. "Even guys who didn't happen to wear your lousy Big A shoulder patch."

Kopp jerked to his feet. The Bourbon bottle suddenly became a potential weapon. "Sir, you realize you've insulted the honor of the finest goddamn..."

"Oh, sit down and cut the crap!" Miller beamed. "Don't tell me you're crazy enough to add an assault on a senior officer to your charges."

"We were the finest goddamn army in the whole stinking continent of Europe!" Major Kopp muttered, still looming over the Colonel.

Miller surprised him by taking the bottle out of his hand and helping himself to another swallow. "Sure," he finally agreed. "I guess you *were* about the finest fighting outfit in Europe. But now, if you want my candid opinion, I'd say you were a disgrace to the U.S. Army. You're drunk. You're flabby. You're undisciplined, and you don't have the basic loyalty to carry the responsible duties you're here to do."

"That's a goddamn foul, stinking lie!" Al Kopp shouted.

"Take a look at yourself, Major," Bob Miller said, smiling cheerfully, "and have another drink."

Kopp shook his head and settled back on his crumpled bed.

"Okay, mind if I help myself? Major Kopp, I'd like to tell you a little story, on account of the fact I know you're cooped up in here and maybe have the time to listen. Yesterday I accompanied a patrol of your MPs to arrest a notorious Nazi mass murderer, guy name of Obergruppenfuehrer Ernst Hart I dearly wanted to talk to. You may have met him, he was your sort of guy—he liked burning down property too. Other people's. Anyway, what happens is this. As our top secret mission approaches his chalet, we come under Luger fire. No, that's the surprise, it's not the guy we want—it's his wife going around like a headless chicken. Poor dame gets hit with everything we've got. So that's her. Now you're going to ask where was the guy, and that's the other surprise. He's been lying dead in the bathroom from cyanide poisoning for *three goddamn hours!* Now why do you think that was, Major Kopp?" He lingered over the German name. "Well, do you want to know what I think? I think it was because someone on your creepy staff here gave the lousy bum the tipoff!"

Major Kopp said coldly, "Maybe you're forgetting, Colonel. I'm confined to quarters. I don't see anything. I don't go anywhere."

"Look, I'm not accusing anyone, least of all you, Major—guess you've had enough trouble for one month. No, I just want to talk to someone who has the leisure to listen. And right now, Major, it occurs to me you have the leisure to listen. Besides, it could just be you could fill me in on Obergruppenfuehrer Ernst Hart. You were there, weren't you, when he was entertained with honors here at Third Army Hq. in Bad Tölz?"

"Colonel," Kopp said, grimacing, "shouldn't you go and talk to General Patton—he issues the invitations around here."

"So you're turning disloyal on your commander, too!" Miller snarled.

"I didn't say that. I said . . . hey," Kopp's eyes gleamed with belated realization, "you're trying to get me even deeper in the shit, aren't you?"

"Boy, have you got sensitive in here," Colonel Bob Miller beamed. "Don't worry, I know how it is when you get taken out of your day-to-day duties and into a kind of isolation. You start imagining things. Now let's get back to realities. I've had reports it wasn't just a social occasion—that strictly tuxedo evening when that lovely individual Obergruppenfuehrer Ernst Hart called to pay his respects to your army commander. I've heard—maybe you can deny it—that what you guys were discussing in there were concrete plans for an invasion of Russia."

"I said why the hell don't you go and talk to General Patton? Why don't you take your goddamn Bourbon bottle, too?"

"You're right there," Miller chuckled, "maybe this is a problem for General Patton, and maybe I've got no right trying to chew the fat with a poor, innocent, busted member of his staff. Tell you what we'll do, we'll have one more drink and I'll be on my way. Incidentally, I guess you're not suggesting that General Patton was responsible for what you guys did to the Hotel Edelweiss?"

Major Kopp grabbed the bottle from the Intelligence Colonel and took an angry gulp. "I told you what happened at the Hotel Edelweiss!"

"Yeah," Miller said, nodding, "now I remember you

told me. One thing you didn't tell me though, Major. Maybe you could fill me in. You didn't tell me why you picked on the one hotel in Bavaria that happened to be owned by a Jew, a poor guy name of Kellerman that had only just got up the courage to come out of hiding in Switzerland and try and rebuild a business here in Germany. That was a funny coincidence, wasn't it, Major? Or maybe," Miller added, gleaming, "it was no fucking coincidence at all!"

"Why don't you get your big ass out of here, Colonel, sir?" Major Kopp said grimly. "Otherwise you're going to tempt me to put one helluva an extra offense on my charge."

"Yes," Miller laughed, "I guess that's sensible thinking, Major. I thought maybe we could talk about the charges they're preferring against you, and ask ourselves whether a poor big-assed failure like me could do anything about trying to lighten the load at your court-martial, but I guess we caught each other on a bad day. Incidentally, I'll keep what's left of that Bourbon."

Colonel Bob Miller again relieved the Major of a bottle that was in danger of becoming an offensive weapon. But he ambled very slowly to the door, giving the Major all the time in the world to hit him with anything else he had in mind to throw. "Gee," he murmured, pausing by Major Kopp's inlaid writing desk near the door, "those are lovely kids and that's a mighty fine lady." He was looking at a highly posed photograph of a woman and her kids.

"Yes, that's a proud family you've got there, Major. Guess you must have missed them a lot—still, you're going to be reunited with them soon. Pray the Good Lord you'll all be sitting down together to that Thanksgiving turkey! Hey! That's a lovely-looking woman!" Miller's eye had moved to a snapshot in a small leather frame. "Could that pretty little lady be your elder daughter? No, I guess not, those are the Bavarian mountains behind her." Bob Miller didn't add that the "pretty little lady" was looking dreamily over her shoulder at the camera completely nude.

"Yes, that's some beauty, a real proud beauty...face

seems familiar, somehow. Maybe I'm confusing her with some movie star..."

"That is my private desk and those are my private effects!" Kopp snarled.

"I'll say this for you, Major," Bob Miller said, grinning in the doorway, "you've got some mighty handsome private effects."

"Sit down, Herr Weber," said Bürgermeister Frolich. "As two Germans who have somehow survived, I'd say we owed each other a toast."

Eric Weber sipped the Bürgermeister's plum brandy with interest, but it did little to warm the wintry smile that was playing over his thin lips. The name Frolich rang vague bells, and if it was true that each German had lived a century in the last thirteen years, then it was necessary to dip back even before that—before the march of time with its hysterical crowds cheering the new Chancellor's progress through Hesse and Thuringia. Back still further to a time when the SS bands were unkempt, straggling packs of hooligans, the riffraff whom Ernst Roehm had collected around him, the petty criminals who were not even worth arresting.

"But like me, you never made the fundamental error, Herr Frolich," observed the detective. "Unlike two out of three adult Germans you never quite committed yourself to the Party. For different reasons, I fancy. I was a policeman, and there it finished. I have never been able to be enthusiastic about any man-made crusade or institution. In your case, I think it was more interesting. You were not a Nazi, because you were too much of a Nazi. Do you understand me?"

The Bürgermeister gave a loud guffaw, ham-fisted the policeman hard on the back, and slopped another spirit-raiser of hundred-proof plum brandy into Weber's glass. "Deduction correct, Herr Weber," he chortled. "The Nazi bastards were never quite right-wing enough for me. Even the SS. Lucky in a way, wasn't it? There are, as you know, Inspector, positively no left-wing politicians left in Upper Bavaria. So when the good Americans tried to find some

German or other to run the place, there were remarkably few candidates, outside the Allied de-Nazification code."

A pale smile played over Weber's lips.

"They say that particularly down here, the occupying powers are not so concerned about the record of ex-Nazis. General Patton, our excellent Governor, is flexible. It would seem it's as simple as a man's a Nazi only when I say he is. So we may as well burn our excellent police records. Those, that is, that aren't sunk at the bottom of the Oder."

"General Patton," guffawed Frolich. "The greatest Nazi of us all. A man we Bavarians can understand, like some understood another genius, in those heady days of the Munich Putsch. A man at peace with himself, at war with the world. A jovial predator."

Inspector Weber's eyes narrowed further. Then he leaned forward, his elbow on the table, his gray, blotchy eyes searching out the rubicund pig's scalp that confronted him. "I could spend the evening very pleasantly here, Herr Frolich," he said quietly. "And we might find that we had even more views and persuasions in common. But like you, under the occupying powers, I have a definite area of work to perform. In my case it isn't power politics. But that base, and usually sordid, thing called criminal detection. So for the third time I am compelled to ask you, the fourfold question with which this pleasant, if somewhat early, drinking session began. First, have you any suspicion as to what weapon was wielded, by whom, which caused the slight but painful penetration of your young daughter's vagina? Then there's the case of this young American soldier called Cohn. It seems remarkable that he was found unconscious near your house at the same time as the assault on your daughter. Third, there is the most remarkable query of all. Exactly how the American soldier, now identified as Harrison Jacoby, came to be throttled, stripped of his uniform and found dumped in a heavy armoire in your daughter's bedroom. All this, you must admit, Bürgermeister, is of some slight interest to the professional policeman, or 'cop' as my chief, Colonel Miller, chooses to call it. But all this begs the most interesting question. I did not arrive here to track down a murder or double assault. I came here in search of a man, or rather boy. I must now go through the stupefying, but necessary, formality of showing you a photo and asking you whether you can identify it."

The boy was in camping equipment. To be more precise, he was around a campfire. There were three other short-haired adolescents with him. They had been caught in the middle of something as innocent as singing, because they were linked arm-in-arm. The one whom Weber's nicotine-stained thumb jabbed at was the youngest and the handsomest, or even the prettiest. He looked thirteen to the others' sixteen or seventeen.

The Bürgermeister sank back in his chair with a vague, disdainful shrug. "You know who it is, Inspector, so I can't let myself be obtuse. You are pointing out, unless I mistake it, my young son, Rudi Frolich. And to get the record right I must say that he persevered in Germany's cause a few weeks or months longer than us clever men of the world, eh, Inspector? In fact, he was last heard of manning some impossible bridgehead trying to protect Berlin against the final Russian T34 advance. Stupid little infant. Now, three months after the war, I haven't heard from him. Honestly, Inspector, I frankly do not know if he is alive or dead. All I know is that his mistimed devotion to his country has shown him as a fool, not a hero—and very likely a dead one."

And now for almost the first time, the Inspector smiled. "Herr Frolich," he murmured, "I really must ask for another glass of this very excellent plum brandy. It is very seldom that a policeman brings anyone good news. But on this occasion I hope I bring as much joy to your heart as your brandy does to mine. I must tell you that according to my very up-to-date records your son, Rudi Frolich, is very much alive and kicking. In fact, on the basis of recent reports, collated by the American and German police, I should venture a guess that kicking is a slight understatement."

General Hobart Gay was in an ugly situation. He had just seen Major Bogamov of the Soviet Military Mission to the door of his office. The Russian had clicked his boots and allowed a smile briefly to flicker across his stony Siberian face. Hobart had replied with a casual salute and a friendly nod.

General Gay hated this peace. Hated it for what it was doing to his chief and his army and to each of them individually. From dashing cavalryman to repressive police officer in eight breathtaking weeks. He hated the boredom, he hated the stench of ruins and bodies that hung around everywhere, hated too the gangs of hungry people who shuffled the shattered streets. Those old people who moved aimlessly around like dogs scrounging for a bone—the crippled heroes of the Wehrmacht, shuffling along on crutches and sticks—the kids pestering the GIs for chewing gum and chocolate like kids from the slums of Alexandria. The occasional "accidents" that obliged you to write home deeply consoling letters to proud parents in the States without quite mentioning how some damned fool GI managed to get himself killed in a brothel.

But all this you could justify on the basis of normal administrative problems connected with victory. What got to the General's guts and made him sick with worry and a sense of impotence was this business of repatriation. Sending back good soldiers like the Poles and the Cossacks who quite rightly hated everything that Stalin and Communism stood for. And others who had been forced at gunpoint to put on German uniforms. Amid the misery of the Occupation this forcible repatriation cut through the gloom like a shriek of despair.

"Looks like trouble," said Hobart Gay to Colonel Koch, Third Army's legendary Intelligence chief. "Just seen Bogamov. He requests an urgent meeting with Patton."

Colonel Koch whistled. Then he slowly drummed his fingers on the table. "You know the Old Man hits the roof at the merest mention of Russia. What the heck does Bogamov want anyway?"

"They're asking for their pound of flesh again, Osc. Those poor Cossack bastards we've been trying to hide in

VII Corps sector. If only I could figure some way to bail them out. Seems Uncle Joe's got an attack of bloodlust again and he won't sleep till he's got those two hundred guys nice and snug in quicklime. And as far as Ike and Frankfurt are concerned, he can have them."

"Sure—to put them up against a wall and shoot them."

"Okay, come in, Eric," Bob Miller called from his office back at USFET, Frankfurt, "and have a lousy cigarette." He tossed a pack of Luckies across his desk at the German detective. Eric Weber caught the pack and placed it carefully back on the desk in front of the Colonel.

"Thank you, I have my own," he politely rebutted his master's obvious piece of condescension.

"Okay, then," Miller said, grinning behind his cigar smoke. "I'll show you a picture of a beautiful broad, though you don't deserve it, you surly bastard." He slid a photo blowup across the desk. "Feast your eyes on this honey and tell me where you've seen her face before."

Eric Weber took out a pair of glasses that only his extreme professionalism convinced him he needed. "Ah yes, the lady is Fräulein Gerda Gettler, the distinguished air woman and athlete."

"Right first time as usual, Professor! Now take a look at the snapshot I made this blowup from, and tell me if you recognize the lady's companion."

Eric Weber pushed his glasses up onto his forehead and sighed. "Of course, it is Adolf Hitler."

"You've hit the jackpot, Eric."

"I imagine the photograph was taken at the Berlin Air Review in July 1938."

"And you'd be right again," Miller crowed. "Now, for the big question, maybe you'd like to tell where she is now."

Eric Weber shrugged. "According to your informant, Major Packer, she has been seen at American forces' parties in Munich."

"And where do you reckon she ought to be? I'll tell you

where I reckon she ought to be, Inspector Weber, and that's behind barbed wire."

Weber took a deep pull on his own cigarette from his own pack of Luckies. "I do not know much about the Fräulein's political life, or indeed her sex life. I would call her a specialist, a specialist of the air, I think you could find better game—I mean greater war criminals—closer to the ground."

Colonel Bob Miller lit another cigar. He said, "From where I sit I'm seeing it a little differently, Inspector, but that's maybe because you're a romantic, Mozart-loving Kraut. Maybe you can't face up to the idea of watching your last authentic Aryan angel being dragged down out of the skies." A mighty puff of cigar smoke rolled across Miller's desk obliterating Weber's little Lucky Strike cloud as conclusively as a U.S. Army Air Corps command strike against a handful of Luftwaffe fighters. "But I've been doing a little research, mein lieber Eric, while you've been investigating your goddamn GI murders, and I've got it straight from General Adcock's G-5 office that this delectable piece of Nordic womanhood is indictable under capital war crimes charges."

"Then perhaps we are all guilty," Weber murmured.

"Come clean," Miller chuckled. "Were you ever instrumental in getting a couple of slave laborers shot because they were a few hours late coming up with a spare part for your lousy Messerschmitt 262 jet? No, you weren't, were you, Eric, on account of the fact you didn't happen to be working on that big Nazi jet fighter project. But luscious Gerda Gettler was. Those slave laborers got a couple of bullets in the head as a result of her no doubt technically justifiable complaint. I agree she's one helluva fine-looking frail, but the fact is we've got enough evidence to let her swing—and I don't mean to Tommy Dorsey's orchestra."

"And does that lead us anywhere?" Weber asked.

"I want to show you another picture of this cutie," Miller said, smiling, "and this one's the sexiest of the whole goddamn lot." He pushed across his desk a copy of the photograph he had noticed in Major Al Kopp's quarters. "Guess where I found this, Eric. Don't worry, I'll tell you—among the personal effects of Major Al Kopp, General Patton's formerly indispensable aide. What do you think, Eric? Could it be that the gallant Major is keeping the lady in the style she is accustomed to?"

"She is still an attractive-looking woman," Weber murmured.

"And could it be that the Major has been the recipient of a lot of alluring Nazi pillow talk? You know who the owner of the Edelweiss Hotel was? Guy name of Kellerman, a little Jewish fella who'd just crept back across the Swiss border to what he thought was a better Germany. It looks to me what we got down there was another little Reichstag fire."

Eric Weber said, "On the other hand, Major Kopp and his companions could have had too much to drink."

"Who the hell's side are you on?" Miller demanded nastily. "Maybe after all you're still working for them. A habit can be hard to break."

Weber lit another Lucky Strike. "You employ me to be objective, Colonel Miller," he said tonelessly. "I have always tried to be objective, no matter whom I have served."

Miller pushed back his chair and stalked over to the window of his I.G. Farben building office. It looked down to a chromium fishpond where water lilies floated. At the far end of the pool, near the officers' club, there was a gigantic statue of a female nude, another dream of Aryan beauty. Some GI pranksters had touched up the left nipple with luminous paint.

"Okay," he cried, "maybe you'd like to tell me what the hell it is we're supposed to be investigating? I'm used to nice, easy, simple cases where you get maybe one corpse, one lead, one goddamn criminal. We're getting to have quite a few corpses, a helluva lot of leads: what the hell are we hoping to find?"

"Yes, it would be simpler if the Fuehrer was still alive, and we could prove that he is still directing resistance in the Bavarian redoubt," Weber suggested with a little smile.

"Don't try to be funny, you crooked German. Just tell me what it is we're supposed to find."

"Of course it is that very complex and intangible thing called a 'conspiracy.'"

"Or maybe what we're looking at is just an army with a crazy general and a lot of shagged-silly GIs who are whooping it up in picturesque Bavaria. Maybe what we're really investigating is an army that'd done too much damn fighting and is now going soft around the edges and rotten inside. We could simply be studying a great outfit in the process of disintegration, while the local patriots sit around and cheer. It could be what we've got, Weber, is a job for some goddamn military historian!"

Weber looked across at the tall figure, standing at the window like a big man behind bars. He said, "I think you should not despair altogether, my Colonel—there are some interesting indications."

"Sure! We'll get this flying cutie in, give her a good old-fashioned American interrogation—and maybe she'll lead us to a genuine nest of fighting Werewolves. You never know your luck."

"I was thinking more of these murders of your army personnel, two in the last three days at Regensburg, at Kolb. They are not all of the same pattern, but there are similarities. Perhaps I could read you some statistics." Weber took out a crumpled typed sheet of paper from his wallet. "Last week there were eight murders of U.S. personnel in your zone of Germany. Three occurred in the Seventh Army area, five in the Third Army area. Of the murders in the Seventh Army area, all but one have motives such as a fight over a woman or a dispute over a black-market transaction. This is not the same picture in Third Army's area. Three of the crimes appear to be totally without motive and one is doubtful. There is another interesting feature—in four cases the bodies have been stripped of their uniforms."

"Maybe they're cold down there in Bavaria. Those bastards could be collecting their winter wardrobes."

"The variety of ranks is also interesting, Colonel Miller. They include a colored staff sergeant, two corporals, and two Pfcs."

"Like someone was making a collection?" Miller asked seriously.

"Someone, or some group," Weber nodded. "I find it an interesting theory that this may be a concerted operation, because from my investigations of three of the corpses, I am convinced that the murderers were all children."

General Patton came out of his Bad Tölz office like a Force 5 tornado. "Who made me an appointment with that goddamn gorilla? I thought I made myself clear, Hap. I don't want that goddamn creep from the reptile house hanging around here."

Hobart Gay heaved an inward sigh. He'd done his honest damnedest to block Major Bogamov right out from the metallic blue gaze of his chief, but every time Bogamov bounced it straight back to Russian Fourth Guards Army Hq. across the border, with the inevitable sequence that the plumply affable Marshal Tolbukhin took further occasion to remind his true comrade Ike over in Frankfurt that more down payments were due for that comradeship. From there the ball landed slap back via Bedell Smith's out tray onto Hobart Gay's neatly paperless desk.

"If you're referring to Major Bogamov, General," remarked Gay, "I'd beg to tell you that guy's real heavy. He may be just a major, but he has behind him about two hundred forty pounds of Marshal Tolbukhin's fake friendship. And we all know how he hits it off with Ike. Remember that victory march in Berlin, General. I thought the old bear was going to squeeze the living daylights out of our Supreme Commander with that hug of his." General Gay hated the godless, monotonous, flattening creed of Soviet Communism like a Prohibitionist might loathe liquor. But his chief's all too evident hostility was insufficient to rid the Bad Tölz headquarters of the creeping presence of Major Bogamov, official

Russian liaison officer, with a roving brief to scout out all elements of Joe Stalin's monolithic state which might be hiding in Third Army territories. Particularly and most searingly the Russian's filing-drawer mind was now devoting itself to the Cossack problem—those thousands of acrobatic, quaint-hatted cowboys of the Don Valley who had loathed Stalin and all his works sufficiently to side with Hitler in the war and wear German uniforms. Just a month ago Third Army units had penetrated their camp at Fogelheim to rescue a number of Soviet officers who had sniffed out the Cossack camp and started to argue credos with the fierce Cossack community. Now the Russians were stepping up pressure to get the whole Fogelheim setup rooted out like a wasps' nest—the inhabitants shunted across the border to account for their crimes against the Soviet state.

Which was where friction might start. The Cossacks were simple, brave, horse-loving people with strong religious beliefs: so by chance was the General commanding the U.S. Third Army. And even worse, behind his brusque exterior the General barely concealed a highly emotional sensitivity. He had been known to weep when confronted with his wounded heroes. In fact his overflowing and not always tightly controlled sympathies were perhaps the only feminine facet of his complex persona.

. "You know what that rat Bogamov wants, Hap," the General was musing. "What chance do you reckon we've got of putting out a helping hand toward those poor goddamn Ukrainians?"

"There just isn't, George. You know how heavy the repatriation issue is. It's top line all the way down from Truman and Attlee. And they say Joe's set his heart on welcoming back the prodigals to their fatherland."

"The poor bastards. What will they do with them, do you reckon, Gay? Hang them at the frontier? Refrigerate them to death in Siberia like a carcass in a Chicago packing plant? Or just plug them through the back of the head like they did to those Polish officers at Katyn? But I'll tell you one thing," and the General's expression set grimly, "if I was one of those Cossack bastards, they'd have to tear me out of that camp and I'd make them sweat blood for every inch they moved me. And there's another aspect to this, Hap. It concerns a small thing called soldierly conduct. Some newspapermen are kind enough to claim I got together the finest bunch of brawling, hard-fighting, hard-drinking, tough-swearing, pig-obstinate goddamn beautiful heroes in the history of warfare. And now they want us to use this force as a kind of civil police. That I turn them loose against simple God-fearing women and children. This isn't Third Army business, Hap. That's a job for a parcel of OGPU thugs and murderers!"

"Message received and understood, sir," said Gay, his brow furrowing. "But I find it my duty to tell you that the timepiece says eleven-thirty hours and that you have an appointment with Major Bogamov."

The short, sturdy figure of Major Bogamov stiffened to a textbook Soviet salute as Patton turned to greet his guest.

They paraded in full combat equipment at a chill 04.30 hours. Everyone knew Old Blood and Guts was getting pretty hot about morale, but this was positively inhuman. Hadn't they won the war, well—not exactly their unit, but the heroes they'd replaced?

As they stood there shivering, Captain Bob Hartman moved toward them out of the semidarkness. "Okay, you guys," he snapped, "you've had a few maneuvers at this hour before, and I guess they're not that popular. But this one's different. This one's for real. And I'll tell you straight that it's a dirty job—more a thing for cops than GIs. But that's not your problem. What you guys have to remember is that you're gonna have the top brass breathing down your necks. General Halleck, our new corps commander, is coming down and he's grabbed the best tickets for a grandstand view. Now unless the job's clean he'll bawl us out. Or to put it more plainly, he'll tear a few strips off me, and I'll chastise Sergeant Offenbach. And he'll no doubt dole out to you guys the kind of treatment that would make Auschwitz look like a circus. Now is everyone here, and are we all ready to go?"

The Captain's blood was flowing deliciously: he had that warm feeling on the desultory morning, a feeling of comradeship, of purpose achieved, of challenge accepted. There was only one thing wrong. "Hey, you guys, where the heck is Sergeant Offenbach? He's got the keys to the armory and there's a special issue for this show."

"He's coming now, sir," shouted Maggio. To his buddies he muttered, "Gee, get that old gorilla breaking into a canter. He's probably sold the whole armory to the Krauts and had to buy it back again double quick. He sure looks beat."

It was true. No one who had followed the Sergeant's war-like career would have recognized the holder of the Purple Heart who had marched with Patton through Kasserine Pass and flushed the SS out of Palermo. Sweating lustily, unshaven and with a look of vicious insubordination on his face, the Sergeant emerged through the gloom and gave Captain Hartman a reluctant and desultory salute. "Request permission to issue special firearms, sir," he mechanically jerked. And then led his disheveled unit to the armory to get them.

"Okay, guys, relax. Unwind. World War III ain't bustin' up all over yet," drawled Staff Sergeant Joe Offenbach as he halted his weary company outside the armory. "It's just that some S.O.B. dreamed up a cute little idea of repatriating all those slaphappy Cossacks up at Fogelheim. And entraining them back to Russkieland, where they belong. So all we have to do is a little pushing and shoving. The occasional homer in the direction of the balls. And maybe a rifle butt nicely directed into the eye socket, just to point the sweet way home. Frankly, it's gonna be a bit of a yawn, but as our Captain from Lafayette Military Academy would say: Dooty is dooty."

The company shuffled from attention to at-ease as he spoke. Maggio fished for a Camel in his combat jacket; Cohn volubly farted; Brewer slouched onto his knees and finally squatted redskinwise on the damp ground.

"The only trouble is," continued Offenbach, fiddling with the armory door keys, "some runt's gone and made a general exercise out of it. So I'm gonna hand you guys out rifles and a couple of submachine guns. Each man will

carry six tear-gas grenades. And a pickax and shovel. But
don't get me wrong, buddies. There ain't gonna be no
shooting. Just a little friendly persuasion with the butt of
a Garand."

Three silhouetted figures came out of the gloom at
them. "Who's in command here?" cut in a curt military
voice. "Am I right? Is this Captain Hartman's outfit? I
want to talk personally to the guys who are going to make
the key assault."

Even the rookiest of rookies could clearly make out a
general's two stars shining brightly through the misty
gloom, and beneath it a face that seemed to gleam from
back issues of *Stars and Stripes*. A prominent nose,
glinting gray eyes, a Cromwellian wart on the left cheek.
A martial alertness and intensity that took vibrant form in
the quivering of a muscle just below the right eyelid: a face
carved out of granite, a living, breathing animate slice of
pure American folklore. Some gaped, some climbed
wearily to their feet and offered an apologetic salute. In
the case of Offenbach it was like a drunk hitting a live
power cable. His body ramrodded to attention as he
unfurled before his troop such a salute as had not been
seen this side of VE-Day plus one.

The two-star general's eye twinkled in simulated
friendship as the spirited nerve end took up a still more
spirited rat-tat-tat at the bottom corner of his right eye.
"Steady, Sergeant," cautioned the General. "I never
forget a face, and I certainly haven't forgotten yours. But
what troubles me is . . . where? where? where?"

The General, whom we must now officially identify as
Regis Halleck, looked up at the vanishing night stars,
then down at his well-polished boots. Twisted around a
little, while the quivering eyelid stepped up its dance to the
speed of frenzy.

But Sergeant Offenbach was coming back to life—
slowly the peacetime reason-mutated man was replacing
the war hero, as Halleck floundered.

"Yeah, General Halleck," he finally emitted. "Yeah,
General Regis Halleck, I sure know you. Christ, I can
even remember your name. Mine's Offenbach, by the

way. And I think furthermore we last met face to face at Troina. A small town in Sicily in the heaviest concentration of 88 flak that ever made a company do a collective shit."

"Oh yes, I remember you now," Halleck said softly. "You were a hero, like all the men there. And I guess I let you down. I let you down because somehow, somewhere I just wasn't physically and morally prepared for the highest demands of war," the General confessed with amazing candor. "But don't blame me, Offenbach. I've paid for it. And I've tried to re-equip myself physically, spiritually, and morally for the tasks ahead. And believe you me there are tasks ahead, Offenbach. Tasks that need heroes like you and your men, fresh to war though they may be. Tasks today... and tasks tomorrow."

"Yes, sir," riposted Offenbach, and his motley group of rookies raised a shallow shout. Halleck looked up startled, and then blinked. His puppet arm elevated itself.

"Okay, men," and Halleck's voice changed again to the accustomed clipped tones of command. "You may not have met me before, like Sergeant Offenbach here, but I guess you all know something about me. Like, I like things clean and tidy. I'm a stickler for detail. And I don't and won't stand any kind of goddamn balls-aching nonsense. Okay? We have a good mission on today. Not for us. But for our friends, those gallant Russian Allies who saw the Krauts off at Stalingrad and Moscow. Old Joe Stalin would sure like to get his hands on those slobs who ratted on their country and fought for the enemy. Men, it is our splendid mission to rout out a hornets' nest of Cossack Nazi-lovers—put them in a box and dispatch them all clean and tidy to Russia. Now some of us may know what a heck of a mess the British have been making of this kind of mission. Let's show them what the Third Army can do. Because now you have precision planning, the way old Regis likes to conduct his campaigns. No detail forgotten. That's why we're striking at dawn. That's why I've ordered the Major in command of the camp to soft-soap them for days—heck, some of those guys even think they'll be entraining with their wives and children for Arizona at the expense of Uncle Sam. Do you read me?"

"Loud and clear, sir," the group mumbled rather than shouted.

"In fact they will be shunted toward the west, except that around Nürnberg the train will suddenly switch lines. And I think that a nice little parcel of traitors will be delivered to Uncle Joe's safekeeping before dawn tomorrow. So much for the general strategy, because I always like every man to know exactly how his role fits in, however seemingly insignificant it may be. Now you men here of Captain Hartman's company have been personally recommended to me because of your previous experience of this kind of operation, when you released some very important Polish officers from the grasp of their fellow countrymen. Now I am ordering a repeat performance—with music. It's a fact, men. I've ordered up the band of the Third Army to reassure everyone— Cossacks and Americans alike. And while they play I want to see something gradual occur, as inevitable as clockwork, and goddamnit as flawlessly perfect. I want to see you guys go in and sort them out. Peaceably, for we bring not the sword, but goddamnit if they won't have peace, we'll give them the sword. That's the reason for the special arms' issue this morning. Rifles will do for most purposes, but when the going gets rough it's nice to know we've a few Thompson subs handy. If the scene goes wild, I suggest we liven it up with a little tear gas. If a door's blocked, you batter it down. Axes are part of today's key equipment. One more thing, men. It isn't often that a corps commander personally superintends a matter of this scale. But I guess we all have to start eating out of the same porridge bowl sometime. Thank you, men. See you at Fogelheim."

It was seven in the morning when the convoy hit the encampment. The first truck skidded to a halt inside the courtyard of this former eyrie of the SS Einsatzkommandos, now a DP camp, specializing in Cossack POWs. At low throttle the eight other trucks slid into file beside it.

"Know the creepiest thing about this dump," side-mouthed Brewer to his buddy Maggio as they shambled out of the truck and formed a lethargic line. "Used to be an SS plug-hole. Was reading about a guy called Dr. Sprengle. They say he was trying to construct a kinda Frankenstein monster superman out of spare parts of Jews."

In the center of the drill field General Regis Halleck was conferring with Captain Hartman and the camp commandant. Beside them stood Major Bogamov.

"The jerks, the lousy jerks. They picked us for the real shit," swore Offenbach.

"Who's that Russian guy talking to the General?" Cohn wanted to know.

"He's a creep called Bogamov," Offenbach informed him. "They say he's been bumming around Patton's Hq., swallowing all the dirt old George can deal out to him because his orders are to get those Cossacks within easy range of a Russkie firing squad."

There was no doubt about it, General Halleck was peeved. "What the heck," he was emitting, "what kinda un-American bastard has blown the cover story?"

"You just can't tell how it sprang a leak," the Commandant was nervously telling him. "Maybe some of our men actively sympathized with these traitors, who can tell? All we know is that this time yesterday the Coassacks were convinced they were going to start a new agricultural community in upstate Arizona. Then they suddenly caught on. Most of them have barricaded themselves in the inner courtyard through there. Some of the diehards have locked themselves in the main block. There's no doubt, we're going to have to bring them out man by man."

The General pondered for a moment, his foot drumming on the tarmac, while Major Bogamov tried to read his purpose through tight Mongolian eyes. "Okay, Major Bogamov," he decided, "it's going to get a heck of a lot dirtier than we had bargained for. But you're going to have your traitors in a nice tidy package, come what may. Overnight we laid some extra tracks to the Fogelheim railroad and now we can entrain the prisoners just three hundred yards past the camp gateway. And to keep everyone in the right frame of mind, we've decided on a musical interlude."

From one of the trucks a strange group had been assembling, with oddly bulky cases. But now as the autumn sun pierced the grimness of the courtyard, the band of the U.S. Third Army struck up gallantly in a spirited march by Sousa.

"That's what they did in the SS camps," commented Offenbach. "Those Yids used to dance to their death to the rhythm of a Viennese waltz."

"Okay, men," commanded Captain Hartman, "we're goin' in now. Sergeant, lead your men in through that entrance over there."

They went through an archway in a V-formation. When they emerged into the inner courtyard the whole group lurched to a halt. The square was thronged by a silent crowd. On the outer flanks stood the Cossack soldiers in their field-gray Wehrmacht uniforms, with arms linked. Deeper within there was another cordon of Cossacks, but deeper still, like a Cossack wagon train, were women in shawls and graybeards kneeling in the dust, and children screaming. At the apex, drawing the eye instantly toward it, was a raised dais and on it an altar covered by a deep blue cloth and a giant crucifix. Around it were arranged icons, while religious banners of the Orthodox faith hung limply, to mark the holy ground. And behind was a resplendent army of priests in full Orthodox ceremonial, in glinting red and gold and yellow. As Captain Hartman's contingent hit the inner court, the High Priest raised his hands and the whole congregation burst into a liturgical lament.

"Break them up," commanded Hartman. "Use your rifle butts if you have to." And then they were in among them. Cohn had his rifle butt in the neck of a Cossack, and he went straight down, blood cascading. Maggio went through the gap and had his arms around a pale Cossack girl of about twenty-two, whom he started to drag from the circle. Offenbach stood on the outside, egging his men on with much vocal encouragement.

"Jeez," snarled Brewer, "get that creep Maggio. He's got his hands up the only decent broad in sight."

Then Maggio emerged again on the outside of the circle, clutching his groin and hollering like a maniac.

"Okay," commanded Hartman, "every man get back here behind me. Slap on gas masks and prepare to assault with tear-gas grenades."

The soldiers limped back behind their captain and sergeant and donned their gas masks. Then Offenbach started hurling the tear-gas grenades into the thick of the Cossacks. One burst on the altar and a priest disappeared beneath the blue canopy. The whole congregation began to moan as the smell of the gas punctuated that of the incense. A child screamed, a priest raised his voice in a cacophony of liturgy. Then Hartman found that Halleck had ordered up a supporting company and together they went in. This time men and women and children were floundering. Some were kicked into insensitivity beneath U.S. Army boots, others hauled out and straight through the gates and onto the waiting train. Some joker raised his submachine gun and splattered the crucifix on the altar table. A priest collapsed into it, his white beard liquifying into crimson. Then Brewer got beneath the altar and with one giant heave overturned it, and suddenly the priests were nowhere to be found, just the old one moaning on the concrete with a bullet wound in his neck. As the prisoners were individually escorted off, the strains of the Third Army band emerged through the lamentation.

A canteen truck drove up and distributed coffee and doughnuts to the combatants. An Army band marched solemnly into the inner courtyard, while the bandmaster whipped through a sheaf of music. "Okay, men," he clipped out, "take your cue from the music entitled *Songs of the Soviet Heroes.* General Halleck's orders in honor of Major Bogamov."

As they ate their doughnuts and lit cigarettes, Bogamov himself came into view with General Halleck. The Russian was volubly pointing to a list and gesticulating.

"You've done well, men," Hartman told them, "but it seems the job's unfinished. Some of the senior officers have blockaded themselves inside the main building and we've gotta get them out. Sergeant Offenbach, would you take a pickax to that door."

Offenbach lumbered toward the door and started to batter it down. Then Hartman was leading them down a corridor. Door after door was battered open but with no one inside it. They were joined by the Commandant. "I guess they've gone to the temporary chapel. I'll show you the way."

This time Maggio raised the ax and suddenly, with a lurch, they were inside, rifles at the ready, while Offenbach squirted in a dose of submachine fire for good luck. It took them a few seconds to accustom their eyes to the gloom of this room. And then the shapes solidified. There were perhaps eight or nine men in the former Cossack temporary chapel. One had put his neck through the window, and by wringing it in circular motion against the shattered glass, was in fair way toward decapitating himself. Four were hanging from the ceiling in varying degrees of rigor mortis. One had disemboweled himself on the altar steps. One had simply lain on the altar and inserted a poniard of shattered glass straight into his larynx. One was blundering with a section of rope without getting anywhere. The main impression received by Captain Hartman and his men was of some motionless tableau, suspended in space, suspended in time. The only sound was the gasping of breath from strangled necks and the dripping of blood. It was a morgue to please the soul of the Marquis de Sade.

Maggio started it—that was always in the cards. But it spread like a wildcat strike. When he started to scream GREAT FUCKING JEEEEEEZ till his lungs gave out, Offenbach had the option of clobbering him, knocking him cold with one well-aimed Joe Louis right. Instead he put an arm around Maggio's shoulders and added his voice in high falsetto to the scream. Then Cohn and Brewer gathered around and put their arms around Offenbach and Maggio and together they slayed each other, like they'd heard the greatest crack of Corporal Danziger's lifetime, the greatest gag of them all. And there they stood in the midst of this dying tableau, screaming, whining, slapping each other on the backs in sheer convulsion, holding their stomachs and their mouths. Captain Bob Hartman came toward them, and they broke. They went through the door and out into the corridor and the courtyard and past the band playing *Song of the Volga Boatman* and past the disturbed gray eyes of General Halleck and the interested stare of Major Bogamov. And out through the camp gate and on toward the trucks and the rail line. And smash into a small group of people.

"Christ," roared Brewer, "if it isn't Old Blood and Guts himself." For it was at this moment that General Patton had timed his arrival at Fogelheim.

"I've just been refreshing myself with your record," Patton said to Halleck a little later in the Commandant's office of the DP camp at Fogelheim. "Not that I really needed to. The salient events in it, sir, are seared in my soul and in the collective memory of the Third Army. First there was Troina in Sicily, when you busted one of my key divisions against an impregnable *Panzergrenadier* position at Troina, right?"

"Yes, sir," gulped Regis Halleck.

"And then there was Avranches, when you obliged me to bust you by trying to hold back General Grow on General Bradley's orders. Okay?"

"There were good military precedents behind that decision, sir," gulped the VII Corps commander.

"And now we have Fogelheim. Just name me four things wrong with that operation, General."

"Some of the soldiers were green and untrained, sir. There was a breakdown in morale in the ranks."

"Sure," dryly remarked General Patton. "I have had the misfortune to see that for myself. But I've always been fair, Halleck, haven't I? After all, this is probably the first time you've led your men in action."

"That would be correct, sir," concurred the two-star general.

"Okay, General, here are the charges. First there's the

business of forcing Major Mullen, the camp commandant, to dissimulate with the prisoners with a view to hiding the nature of their intended destination. Some lying bastard gave them the idea that they were being accepted in upstate Arizona. Any fair-minded man who has observed the pathos of these people can only regard such lies as a blot on the honor of the entire Third Army. Then there's a failure to check with the provisions of the Yalta Agreement about repatriation of nationals. Of the senior officers arrested, no less than three were White Russian generals with service records dating back to the Russian Civil War. Two others came from Lithuania and owed no allegiance to the Soviets. Another was a German from East Prussia, who was about as Russian as you are. These men should have been granted asylum in the West, yet you slavishly attempted to hand them over to the tender mercies of Major Bogamov and his pack of gangsters. Third there was the grotesque use of my personal bond. But all of this is a matter of detail. So I ask you a question. You have dined with me and my officers at Bad Tölz. What view do you take of our intentions?"

"To hold the Third Army in a constant state of maximum efficiency and preparedness," snapped Halleck.

"You're right, Halleck. But against what enemy?"

The nerve above Halleck's right eye was beginning to flicker, as Patton came behind his corps commander and put a friendly arm around him. He could have used a drink just then.

"Look, General. This is strictly not a bawling-out session. I would like to assure you, you are still, as of this minute, on the payroll of Third Army. So I'll tell you a few home truths. I've always had a funny gut feel about you that somehow Third Army gave you a raw deal. So I'll be plain with you, Halleck. When we first met, we were fighting Germans. Now I've got news for you, General. We've whipped the Huns. And like all energetic forces, we're now groping for a new Leviathan to compare chest measurements against. When you whine and snivel and ass-lick the Russian bear, I groan in my soul, General Halleck. Because I loathe and abhor that Communist sonofabitch more than any Nazi. But when you hand back to the Communists their most deadly enemies—the finest natural cavalrymen this side of the Alleghenies—I start to sweat all over. Sooner or later, and I'd say sooner, we're gonna holler for those goddamn Cossacks."

General Patton stumped away, saluting Regis Halleck and the shambles of the Fogelheim operation with an assortment of Third Army staff and VII Corps officers at his heels. His driver, Pfc. Woodring, came on the double to help the four-star general into his command car. The General started to hoist himself into the front seat, then froze. One of the staff officers hurried up to see if the General was all right—the thought had crossed his mind that he could have had a stroke. But Patton was looking at a line of Sherman M4 tanks that Halleck had ordered up to stand by "in case of trouble."

The General said, "I don't know what those goddamn Shermans are doing here, but they're always a fine sight."

There was a murmur of agreement from the officers. But no one saw the tears that had sprung into the General's eyes, nor understood the intensity of emotion that lay behind an apparent wisecrack. "Guess if you can't have horses, that Sherman is the next best goddamn thing."

They were wondering why the Old Man was keeping them waiting by refusing to settle down in his command car. Patton was looking at a single column of Sherman tanks and seeing hundreds stretching into the obscurity of their own sun-flecked dust. In fact he was seeing the might of Third Army, mobilized at last, pouring southward into Brittany down the narrow road that defined the breakout from Avranches.

The Krauts had had Panthers and Tigers, the latter possessing a firepower and armor complement that could overwhelm a Sherman in single combat. The difference was the Krauts couldn't make Tigers fast enough, and the very size of the fifty-five-ton monster made it a helluva problem to lug to the front and a mighty inviting target for prowling Allied Typhoons and Mustangs.

The compact, no-nonsense Sherman, on the other hand, was bred in the best traditions of American mass production. You got one blown from under you and you traded it in for a new model—no problems about spares, either. The Sherman after-sales service kept up with Third Army thrusts wherever they went. The only thing a Sherman needed was gas and still more gas. It wasn't the Sherman's fault if at certain crucial moments in the campaign in Europe the supreme gas station attendant, General Eisenhower, decided for the best political motives he wouldn't "fill 'em up."

Now they were going to standardize the Pershing M26, a fine machine undoubtedly—90-mm. cannon, 89-mm. armor thickness, more than a match for the Mark VI Tiger and maybe even the Russian T34. But General Patton couldn't envisage any future campaign or world war without the Sherman. He hadn't been joking when he had said just now it was the next best thing to a horse. You could deploy Shermans like cavalry, drive them like cavalry, feint and thrust with them like cavalry. These goddamn machines could turn on a dime! What was more, they made cavalrymen of their crews. The Sherman's 75-mm. cannon wasn't quite heavy enough, its 80-mm. armor not quite thick enough and its 23-mph. maximum speed not quite fast enough to turn soldiers into robots. With the Sherman it was the man that rode the machine, not the machine the man.

Sure General Eisenhower had whispered to him on a tour of inspection earlier in the summer that the Russian T34 could blast the Sherman off the battlefield. What else did you say if you were a guy who insisted on taking your military intelligence from Montgomery and anyway wanted a period of peace to run for President of the United States? What Eisenhower didn't understand, what he'd never been able to understand, was that you didn't sit on your ass waiting to see how your armor measured up technically to that of the enemy. What you did was duck around the bastards, zap across their lines of communication, and go hell for leather for their undefended balls. That's how it had always been with the Sherman, no matter what weight of armor the Krauts had tried to throw at him. And look at the places it had taken him and Third Army. Patton was eyeing one squadron of Sherman tanks standing idle in a gray, messy afternoon in Germany, but in fact he was reviewing an army of them, blackened with smoke in the battle for Falaise, garlanded with tricolors in Rennes, Chartres, and Paris, *"Vive le Général Patton!" "Vive l'Amérique!,"* haloed by snow in the icy fields around Bastogne, washed by seas of Wehrmacht prisoners at the Rhine crossings, cringed to by glum Bürgermeisters on the roads into the Reich.

There had never been anything to stop the Sherman tank, except General Eisenhower. They could have taken Prague. They could still ride all the way to Moscow—take away that flabby-jowled little Kansas creep and his mean gasoline restrictions (just 650,000 gallons for the whole of Third Army!).

Patton settled down beside his driver, Pfc. Woodring. There was a murmur of relief from the staff officers who were all beginning to think maybe the Old Man had had a seizure. But as the command car drove off, Patton stole a last look at the parked Shermans. It was as if they looked back at him with the eyes of animals, rather than lifeless metal. They seemed to be saying, "It only needs a word from you, General!"

An Army Under Investigation

"Goddamnit, Major Du Camp," General Patton mused as he took his seat on the thick leather cushioning of Goering's former Mercedes, "there's some pussyfooting, lily-livered idea abroad these days that the great men of our age creep around like ordinary guys, well camouflaged by mediocrity. I suppose by these standards we must certify men like Alexander the Great, Hannibal, and Napoleon as raging nuts. So I suppose I'm just a goddamn throwback."

Private First Class Horace L. Woodring punched his feet down on the massive controls and the car swerved crazily off on the road through Berchtesgaden toward Bad Tölz.

"I hate to do this to Hermann," mused Patton as he held onto the solid aluminum bars of the chassis. "Riding in this goddamn monster is like pinching some other guy's clothes."

"I am sure, sir, you're the man Goering would prefer to have it," said Wallis Du Camp. "If I may say so, sir, you both share the same sense of style."

"Goddamnit, Du Camp," growled the General, "that's all the goddamn creeps who bum around the I.G. Farben setup want to know to complete their dossier. General Patton's got a big thing going with Nazi Germany's Number One war criminal. Crap! I'll tell you how I rate the so-called Reichsmarshal. I rate him as a great big fat bloated stinking no-talent punk, who just happened to have a nice line in cars."

Woodring had hit the mountain road that would take the touring General straight into and through Berchtesgaden. For about a thousand yards there was a series of tight bends, followed by a nifty right-hander that must mean a rapid change into second. As the Mercedes, under Woodring's joyous control, surged around these bends, Patton added, "And the tragedy is the guy never knew what the goddamn crate could do. Bet he never had it driven like a jeep by a slaphappy GI who handles her like a rodeo mule."

Around a bend and they were in Berchtesgaden itself, with its peasant crafts, its tourist shops just beginning to put on a postwar display to catch the unwary GI—colorful Bavarian clocks, tiny climber's pickaxes, dolls in local peasant costume. And no doubt about it, Berchtesgaden was out in force to cheer the Conqueror on his way. Women, children, and the occasional veteran competed with the elderly and the maimed to get a view of the man who had put the final boot into Hitler's Thousand Year Reich.

When the more perceptive ear became attuned to the cheers and the shouts and even screams of the crowd, it was possible to pick out a shape to the cheering, less ordered than many of the same people had produced at prewar Nürnberg rallies, but equally insistent. It took the form of two syllables. These overlapped each other, and only when they passed the little square in the center of the town did these two finally elide together. Then it was impossible not to understand them. Then the PAT became part of a total chant that ended in TON. Until even the dullest ear could piece it together. PAT-TON. PAT-TON. PAT-TON. The chant was clear and unmistakeable. And now it looked as if the whole population of Berchtesgaden was lining the streets.

Woodring cut the Mercedes' speed by about 50 mph. This car, and others like it, had been seen before around Berchtesgaden in the last few years. And the figure also rang bells. An eye-riveting figure rising to its feet, standing upright beside the driver in a kind of slowly moving tableau to accept that adulation of the crowd. A figure whose helmet caught the shimmering flare of the evening sun, a figure in riding boots and breeches, with a glistening of medals on its chest.

That afternoon the small Gemütlich town of Berchtesgaden was suffering from a joyous, spontaneous attack of *déjà vu.*

Confidential report from Major Lowel Packer, Third Army, to General Bedell Smith, USFET

Certain columnists back in the United States have, as widely reported, been very free to comment on the general state of General Patton's mental health and even, in once case, to use the words "paranoid behavior." Up to now, in following your original instructions to make period reports on the General's psychic make-up, I have shunned such loose, and indeed damning, conclusions— contenting myself merely with pointing out the verifiable psychological disturbances and imbalances.

After what I have today witnessed in Berchtesgaden, I feel compelled to revise my earlier, and less alarmist, conclusions and to sound urgent alarm bells with the full force of my conviction. Indeed you may even be witnessing the curious phenomenon of a Harvard professor agreeing with journalists and broadcasters, and giving academic weight to their dramatic and doubtless commerically profitable accusations. To put it succinctly, it may well be true that the General is "going nuts," if "nuts" means severe and ireversible psychotic derangement. It may also be that Bavaria, traditional breeding ground for antisocial monomaniacs, has worked its full environmental force on the recessive and female persona of the General.

Today I saw General Patton ride in triumph through the streets of Berchtesgaden. But this was no ordinary procession. Consider the circumstances: 1. Choice of venue. Berchtesgaden, cradle of the folksy Nazi movement, womb retreat of Germany's maniac Fuehrer. 2. The car. Not the simple, undemonstrative jeep which General Eisenhower uses as a "nonemotionally loaded" piece of pure transport to reach the military destinations, but a portentous Mercedes-Benz which I gather from Major Du Camp was specially built for Reichsmarshal Goering, a grandiose and oppressive toy for an anal-obsessive and mentally retarded child-man. 3. General Patton's projection. The General was clad in his normal fantasy-projection garb, to which we have become used. (In parentheses I would like to comment on his addiction to the U.S. field helmet in preference to the more normal cap. This is clearly due to a penis complex, the smooth glistening helmet representing in the patient's mind the circumcised and excited end of the male phallus, and thus compensating him for a clear area of deprivation.) Armed with this one might have been prepared for the phenomenon which followed. In full view of the German crowd and making no attempt to discourage its hero-worship, General Patton coquettishly postured before his conquered foe, as if the former owner of the car had come back to receive the homage of the place, or even his monomaniac master whose craggy lair can still be descried across the valley. Powerfully, monumentally, with full intent of purpose this man, now in full grip of his fantasy alter ego, turned around to return the salutation of the crowd. Carrying his right arm to its full extent in subconscious homage to the Nazi salute before settling for the more orthodox American military one. It will not surprise you that this symbolic Car of Evil gave up all attempt to disappear from our sight and instead calmly and slowly proceeded through throng-packed streets to the delightful and still untouched Rathaus (a charming relic of Ober-Bayerische Volk Kunst). There, you will not be surprised by now to learn he was greeted by a gathering of ex-Nazi dignitaries, personally unknown to me. Major Du Camp, again acting as my guide, informed me that they included General von Ritter, Bürgermeister Frolich from Kolb (a personal friend of Jew baiter Streicher, though not apparently an official member of the Nazi Party) and even the Bishop of Bayreuth. Drawn up outside the Rathaus was an orderly line of Germans, whose military bearing—brisk drill gave the lie to their civilian clothes—identified them as former members of the SS. What happened inside the Rathaus I cannot comment upon, since not being in General P's select circle, I was not invited. I can merely say it was over two hours before the General reappeared to accept once more the adulation of this crowd.

As a result of this day in Berchtesgaden I now opine that General Patton is a dangerous case of paranoia and should be taken under immediate observation at some suitable hospital or sanatorium.

The Inspector's office at the police station in Hof was a somber place. The furnishings were sparse and there were no pictures, although you wouldn't have needed to be an acute observer to see where a large portrait of the Fuehrer had recently been hanging. In fact the room looked as if it hadn't been painted since the Chancellorship of Hindenburg.

Colonel Bob Miller put his long arm out toward a sullen-looking thirteen-year-old boy and said, "Want a Hershey bar, sonny?"

The child seized the chocolate bar. He took apart the wrapper with suspicion. Then he wolfed the contents hungrily.

"Now let's you and I have a little talk," Miller continued, letting a reeking cloud of cigar smoke roll over the boy's tousled head. "Where is *sein papa?*"

"The father was killed on the Russian front in 1944," the German police Inspector said tonelessly.

"Und sein mama?"

"The mother was killed in air raid in the same year," the Inspector answered.

Miller turned to Eric Weber, who had been regarding the scene with a half-paternal smile. "Ask what he's been doing with himself all these years."

The police Inspector said, "The boy is a veteran of the 22nd Waffen SS."

"Look, let him answer the questions," Miller snarled. "Okay, Eric, ask him why he murdered that poor bastard Private Harrison Jacoby."

Eric Weber phrased an elaborate question in German.

"GI fucking bastard," the child said.

Miller put his hand on the boy's head as if he was going to give it a friendly pat. Then his hand closed over a tuft of hair and jerked it up tight. "Now ask him what he and his cute little chums have done with the man's uniform."

"The child says he doesn't know anything about Private Jacoby," Weber reported.

"Like hell he doesn't." Miller released the boy's hair and took a gold cigarette lighter out of his pocket. He snapped it open and held the flame out to the boy's lips. "Don't tell me you haven't seen this before," he shouted in English, "and don't tell me you don't know who you stole it from. The guy you and your wholesome little Andy Hardy gang sliced apart like a piece of meat. You made a mistake holding onto this, sonny, didn't you? Because this is how we're going to hang that murder on you so hard it's going to break your goddamn little neck."

"I do not think the child understands," Eric Weber said.

"Could he be that dumb?" Miller wondered as the child

stared at him sullenly and unblinking under the wandering threat of the lighter flame.

"There is no such thing as bad tank country. Some types of country are better than others, but tanks can operate anywhere."

The riskiness of the invasion operation lay in the fact that for thirteen miles his flank was exposed to a sudden counterthrust from the Mongol bastards manning a slice of Russian territory that stuck out like a sore thumb in the direction of Coburg.

In fact he was taking the kind of gamble Brad could never have countenanced. It would have turned poor old Brad's gray hairs shining white. Lucky for General Omar Bradley, and maybe the future of Western democracy, he was home in the States, safely wrapped up in the duties of Administrator for Veterans Affairs.

Of course there was a bonus at the end of the trail. His armor was going to collide with the Russkies on a narrow four-mile front representing a point where the high ground of the Thüringer Wald gave way to the basin of the Saal River. His Shermans and Pershings were going to come pouring down on the unsuspecting Mongol infantry with the advantage of height as well as surprise.

General George Patton, Jr., was indulging in another dream of conquest.

The smell of fir trees and damp earth, hoarded by darkness, the sound of squelching tracks, the chorus of massed 460-BHP engines; the shadows of men and machines: the eerie gleam of dawn, signaling like a fellow conspirator to that tumultuous feeling in the pit of your stomach—these were the irresistible sensations of war. And here was a paradox. Nine times out of ten the moment before an attack was wrapped in the opaque, drab colors of predawn, but it was these moments that provided the most vivid experience of living a man could feel. Some men could be half scared, half jubilant, some, himself included, would meet the moment with a sublime sense of release; others could be so damned terrified they'd shit in their pants—none of them, brave men or goddamned cowards, could deny the supreme potency of those minutes before an attack started.

Look, a galaxy of man-made star bursts up on the ridge ahead. This time no screaming, ear-splitting barrage of artillery, no racing shadows of rocket-firing Air Force Mustangs by courtesy of General "Tooey" Spaatz. They were all on their own this time. In terms of machines, not to mention leadership, they were actually mustering half the strength of Third Army that had burst into Brittany down the narrow road from Avranches. What the hell, they were still the best goddamned fighting outfit in the world!

He stood up in his jeep and watched his tanks rolling through the Russian positions like clock-work toys. He raised his binoculars and saw three of his Shermans knocking hell out of a revved-up convoy of Russian trucks. Day was breaking now. He could see men falling out of them with little bundles of flame on their backs. Goddamn it, he'd really caught those bastards with their pants down! The lousy Bolshevik sonsofbitches had been loading up for Halleck's front forty miles to the south.

"Okay," he yelled down at Pfc. Woodring, "let's go and liberate Saalfeld!"

No air cover. No Generals Wood, Walker, Irwin or Eddy. Not even any 4th Armored Division. That elite force was locked up with General Maxwell in that damned fool deathtrap Eisenhower called the "American presence in Berlin." Never mind, they'd pick them up later.

●　●　●

The General knew his military history and he was aware that Napoleon, for one, had fought some of his most brilliant campaigns with conscripts and missing marshals. The battles of 1814, and those last-ditch victories of the Aisne, had been masterpieces of improvisation against odds that never gave him a chance. If he had been beaten in the end, it was because he'd drawn on his last reserves. For Patton it was different. He had the whole of the United States behind him and, though they didn't yet know it, they'd only just begun to fight.

Right now General Keyes' Seventh Army was asleep in its barracks. The aircrews of USFET were dozing too, but later on that morning they'd wake up to find they were at war with the Soviet Union. A few minutes later "Tooey" Spaatz, commanding the Air Forces in the Pacific now, would have the news, and LeMay's Superforts would be warming up on the tarmack of their new airbases in Okinawa—bases within striking distance of Russia's industrial center, planes with the capability of dropping tons of TNT or, if necessary, one or two little A-bombs to spread total destruction. The United States was still mighty enough, given the provocation, to knock hell out of the goddamned Russians. In the meantime he was driving like a demon for their undefended rear, before some crazy sonofabitch like Eisenhower had time to ring Zhukov and make peace.

"General Patton, General Patton, sir..."

What was General Gay doing here? Hap was supposed to be back in Bad Tölz ensuring the telephone stayed dead, till Third Army's tanks were safely on the road to Jena. Then he'd be on the scrambler to Beetle Smith with the news that the Russians had pulled a goddamned Pearl Harbor on Halleck's front. He'd give Beetle a few seconds to digest the fact that the phony peace was over, then he'd demand an immediate air strike on all the Russian armor that had got itself bunched between Plauen and the Czech border.

"General Patton, please, George."

"Sorry, Hap. This is one trip you've got to sit out. Your place is back by that scrambler in Bad Tölz. Leave your commander to cook up maybe the finest piece of rock-soup campaigning of his career." Now Patton was off in a cloud of dust to catch up with his armored spearhead, which was pouring along the road to Jena. He felt the spirit of Napoleon very near. Goddamnit, His Imperial Highness was riding with him or *in* him. And there was another notable presence at his shoulder: the vital ghost of General Thomas J. Jackson of the Confederate Army, the man who one summer in the Shenandoah Valley had brushed aside two Union armies, nipped through General Banks' supply lines and chewed up his superior force when it tried to retreat. He wondered if Marshal Tolbukhin knew his Civil War history. Unlikely, since the bastard probably couldn't even read. Be that as it may, Marshal Tolbukhin was about to experience the uncomfortable fate of the Union General Banks—one helluva kick up the backside!

"General Patton," Gay repeated patiently, "your appointment with the delegation of congressmen from the Northwestern States: they're waiting for you in the main hall."

At last Patton stirred in his ornate chair behind his massive mahogany desk and pulled himself reluctantly out of his dreams.

Major Packer's eruptive conclusions reached USFET headquarters at Frankfurt two days after General Eisenhower had gone on his vacation. In his absence they aroused a riot of contradictory thoughts and emotions in that complex mechanism commonly known as the Beetle's brain. Their mixture of fantasy and fact, surmise and reportage had the General in two minds. For a moment he was seriously considering forklifting his boss straight out of his shooting lodge in the Highlands of Scotland and back into the maelstrom of yet another Patton Affair. But then he thought again of the mild-eyed Harvard egghead he had cruelly snatched from the academy pleasure into the madhouse of Third Army Hq., and a hilarious widening of the mouth passed like a ghastly rictus for a moment over the Beetle's somber, uncommunicative features. A stool pigeon to end them all. By lunch he had reached his conclusion. One copy of the Packer report was already halfway across the Atlantic for the personal perusal of General Marshall, another was safety filed, pending Ike's return. A third was marked "Top Secret" for the eyes of Colonel Robert Miller only.

"Here, you better read this." Colonel Bob Miller slid a photostat of Lowel Packer's report across the desk to Eric Weber. "It's penetrating reflections are commended to us by General Bedell Smith's staff, so maybe you don't need my opinion. But if you insist on asking for it, I'd just like to add I think it's a lot of crap."

Weber put on his unnecessary glasses and read the report with thorough concentration. Finally he said, "I am even less well acquainted with General Patton than is Major Packer, so I cannot comment on his analysis. I find the reference to the Bishop of Bayreuth interesting, if only because his name has not been mentioned before."

Miller spat out the end of another cigar. "That's typical of our absent-minded prof. Characters flit in and out of his narrative like some screwy movie where they keep firing the scriptwriters. For instance, whatever happened to the glamorous Gerda Gettler we were panting to hear more about? Not a mention, not even a credit. You know, that's the only interesting thing—in my humble opinion— in this big important junk heap of Freudian prognosticating shit. Not a whisper about Gerda. I find that interesting. Particularly since the honest Harvard prof now has all the information he needs on that cute Fräulein's humanity-loving past."

Weber cleared his throat of another Lucky Stirke inhalation. "If you will allow me to say so, Colonel, I think you may be in danger of placing too much significance, perhaps too much hope, on this one woman."

"Sure, and what we ought to be doing is grubbing around in cellars looking for more of your lousy child murderers!"

"I know the boy you saw did not talk."

Miller pushed away his chair and went to have another look at the nude statue with the golden tit by the chromium lily pond. "Well, what the hell can you do with a kid like that?" he bawled. "You can't beat it out of him because he's taken all the beatings anyone can hand out. You can't twist his balls because he hasn't fucking got any yet. You go ahead and tell me what we do..."

"The murder of Private Johnson in Regensburg of Third Army, the murder of Sergeant Clay, I believe these too have been committed by children. I believe we can establish a connection; I believe," the German added with deferential emphasis, "it is *important* to establish a connection."

"Sure: I'm sorry for Clay and Johnson and Jacoby. I'd love to get my hands around the little bastards who murdered them, but that's routine investigation for Third Army police. It's not central to our brief."

"Always they remove the uniforms," Weber mused. He added, "The Bürgermeister, Frolich, at Kolb. I think he could tell us more."

"Well, why the hell don't you dig up something on him? You've got the whole of U.S. Army Intelligence working for you."

"That is reassuring, sir," Weber sighed.

"Right," his superior said, nodding, then he abruptly shot an accusing finger at the little German detective. "Hey, are you trying to cast aspersions on the efficiency of American Army Intelligence? I've warned you before,

Weber, that your sheet isn't one hundred per cent clean. Never forget I've got it in my personal safe. I'd hate to have to take it out and try to dust it."

"Naturally," Weber said, bowing, "if we fail to establish this connection it will be my responsibility, but some of your Intelligence men are..." he met Miller's ferocious smile and shrugged, "...well, do not speak German."

Miller surprised him by walking over to him and placing a meaty hand on his shoulder. "Okay, Eric, I know it's a crazy assignment. I appreciate it's... boy, a honey. You know what I'm tempted to do? I'm tempted to endorse that crappy report—memo them back saying we suspected all the time Old Blood and Guts was nuts. All they gotta do is fire him before he gets dangerous, and the case is closed. It makes sense, doesn't it?"

Weber tore open a new pack of PX Luckies. He said, "There would still be some leads not followed. What you call I think 'loose ends.'"

"Sure," Miller groaned, "there always are those pukey loose ends. You catch a homicidal maniac in the act of sticking a bread knife into his mom. You put him in the electric chair, fry him and cremate him. And still you find there are lousy loose ends. That's how crime reporters earn a living. So what?"

"It is your investigation, Colonel Miller. If you order it, I will terminate my inquiries."

"Okay," Miller told him. "You go back to your cute kids, maybe you'll even strike gold. Me, I'm going to make another visit to Bad Tölz to find out whatever did happen to the glamorous Gerda Gettler."

"He especially wanted me to look you up. Al wanted you to know it's only a temporary embarrassment," Du Camp said, beaming in his best social manner, although it may not have been entirely appropriate to the condition of his brother officer, who was under house arrest at his quarters in Bad Tölz.

"I respect the gesture of friendship," Herr Sauber said, nodding. "I think some of your American officers are forgetting the proud country they represent—the United States, a kindhearted, generous people. Some of your officers here, not the best sort, are trying to punish us beyond what is bearable for human dignity; even your General Eisenhower, who is a German, though I suspect his family is from Prussia."

"*Prosit,* anyway!" Du Camp grinned, raising a glass of Herr Sauber's schnapps. There was an uncomfortable gurgling noise coming from the nearby bedroom, where Lisa Sauber was dying of cancer.

"Many of your officers do not understand what we are having to suffer here in Bavaria," Herr Sauber was saying. "These Slav prisoners you have liberated are roaming the country, terrorizing our people. In addition we have to accommodate thousands, perhaps millions of Prussian refugees, not only those who have been made homeless by the Communists. From the north, too, they are coming in thousands, misled by rumors that there is still food in Bavaria."

"I guess you got off easier down here than some people. You should see Cologne and Frankfurt," Wallis Du Camp sighed, helping himself to another slug of his host's schnapps.

"We can only thank the gods for General Patton," Herr Sauber decided with emphasis. "He is a true aristocrat, a man in the mold of our old Bavarian aristocrats. He is a firm ruler, but he is a just overlord. He understands what we are suffering here in Bavaria." He looked mistily in the direction of the Stars and Stripes hanging limply over the field-gray parade ground. "The people rightly salute him as a great commander, an implacable champion of their cause; and he returns their acclaim." The old man added dreamily, "It is a pity he is such a wealthy man. I would like to offer him some gift, some token that could express my profound esteem."

Du Camp considered the idea extremely thoughtfully. "Tokens of esteem can be tricky," he felt duty-bound to point out. "Our people in Frankfurt have them categorized as one of the seven deadly sins—perhaps the deadliest. Just the other day we had a bottle of schnapps from the Bürgermeister of Augsburg; the good citizen was just trying to say thank you to General Patton for saving his hygiene officer from getting hauled into the de-Nazification courts. Some nosy character from USFET found out. The thing went all the way up to Ike. You'd have thought they'd caught us taking hush money from the Mafia."

"I am not thinking of a bottle of schnapps," Martin Sauber said contemptuously. "I know my situation is modest, but I have resources. I was thinking perhaps of Von Moltke's sword, a token worthy of a great cavalry leader, or perhaps a *Schloss* of suitable elegance. To offer anything less would be an impertinence to our new Fuehrer."

"Sure," Du Camp agreed with a dawning sense of fellow feeling. "I see your point."

The old man fixed him with two penetrating and surprisingly young brown eyes.

"Most of all I would deeply appreciate the opportunity to talk with your great leader, so that we could discuss some suitable expression of a humble Bavarian's gratitude."

"I'm sure the General would love to talk to you . . . but gifts, well—he's one of the old school."

"You are a favored officer on his staff, Al has told me," Herr Sauber insisted, "you could facilitate an introduction."

Du Camp smiled boyishly. "I guess you understand the General's a pretty busy man."

Herr Sauber understood perfectly. He was, after all, a businessman of legendary success. "Of course, I would also wish to record my indebtedness to you, Herr Major."

"Oh, I don't look for favors." Du Camp waved an arm in sketchy protest.

"Naturally," Martin Sauber nodded, "an intelligent man looks for more practical benefits. Herr Major, I am no longer a wealthy man, but I still have a certain influence in this country. My informants tell me that your interests are wider than mere soldiering. You are, I understand, something of a collector."

"Anything from Dürer sketches to secondhand Mercedes," Wallis smilingly confessed. "You've sure got some informants."

"It is possible that in certain areas I could provide you with profitable introductions—you understand, as a friend of Al."

It was Du Camp's turn to understand perfectly.

Major Lowel Packer felt about her in a lot of different ways. First of all he saw and desired her as the proud captive pagan princess who refused to plead for mercy at a corrupt Caesar's feet. A lot of the thrill about making love to Gerda was to be found in this dynamic paradox. Fate had made Lowel Packer a victor and Gerda Gettler one of the vanquished, but in bed the roles could be dramatically reversed. Gerda became the imperious chieftainess whom no fetters could hold; and Lowel her captor turned captive, a man with his loyalties deranged, risking courtmartial and damnation to sweat in her service.

This was the fantasy he had built into their sexual relationship, but the reality didn't always keep in step. Increasingly, over the past few days, Lowel found that his magnificent captive captor was looking for reassurance and protection in his embraces, instead of ravaging with teeth and fingernails across his body, as if it was conquered territory.

"My darling," she would sigh, "you must hold me very tight in your strong arms because all the world is turning against your Gerda."

The sex was still sweet, but it was becoming another kind of affair. The tigress he had loved now tended to nestle up to him like a lamb, and once again Lowel was forced to feel responsible again. Terribly responsible.

This evening as the sun disappeared early as usual behind the mountains and he lay in bed with Gerda without his glasses and his detested major's uniform, his proud captive princess actually shocked him by her submissiveness. She said, "Lowel, my darling boy, your Gerda has been very stupid. She has said things which are dangerous for a German to say now. She has perhaps spoken about herself truly—I know you admire that—but I do not think it has been wise. Do you realize how much your Gerda must beg for your friendship and kindness?"

Up to a point he realized what was happening. Until two weeks ago she had been enjoying the protection of Major Al Kopp. In fact she seemed to have taken the gallant Major's support so much for granted that she hadn't bothered to disguise her contempt for her conquerors and all that they stood for. Now Major Kopp was confined to his quarters. At the same time she had heard about the messy attempt to arrest Obergruppen-fuehrer Ernst Hart and she seemed somehow to be aware of the increasingly tough demands USFET Hq. was making for a real crackdown on Nazis in the Third Army zone. Lowel didn't know where Gerda got her information from, a lot of him didn't want to know, but he knew that Gerda's future was going to place heavy demands on himself.

"Darling," she murmured, turning away her lips to prevent him from engaging them in an intimate kiss. "You must promise never to write about me in your reports."

"I told you, honey, I don't write any reports."

"I think you have orders to report to General Eisenhower about everything here in Bad Tölz."

"Listen, beautiful, I want to screw you."

She gently blocked his hand, which was moving eagerly south from her naked navel.

"Or if you must mention me, you must say I am a friend of America—it is true, isn't it?" She kissed him on the forehead. "I am a good friend of America. You cannot want them to put your own Gerda in a cage."

"I dunno," he grinned lasciviously, "if it could be a golden cage and I could be in it too. Just us. I dunno."

"You must promise," she told him as he pleaded with her to thaw.

He was a Harvard professor, who, although he occasionally could direct a soft glance in a promising girl student's direction, led a quiet life with his family and his civilized neighbors. He had never desired any woman as he desired Gerda now. Of course he promised.

It was almost dark when Lowel Packer stepped into the narrow Bad Tölz street. He heard behind him the familiar patter of not so childish children's feet and then the stridently whispered demands. "Hey, Mister Yank, you have gum!"; "Hi, soldier, you give me Lucky Strike, please!"; "Mister, you have good screw with Fräulein, now you give us cigarettes!" Packer pressed on toward Third Army Hq. He knew from experience that to stop and attempt to distribute largesse was to ask to be practically stripped by these ravenous children of total war. Then he heard heavier footsteps behind him; someone growled savagely. Not at himself, Packer thought, but at the kids who were hounding him. Of course he should have looked around then, but he thought he'd turn the corner first only a few yards away now and offering at least a street light. If he was being followed, Lowel reasoned, it would be useful to know by whom. But suddenly the footsteps were so close behind him he had to turn around, and as he did so he received an explosion of clenched knuckles in his face. His hands went to his face for protection, which was another mistake, because now a tough leather boot smashed into his groin. Packer crumpled and pitched forward into his face. Luckily, his shattered glasses had already fallen off. He wasn't allowed to lie there in his blood. A hand reached down to grab his collar and pull him to his knees. Packer was twisting in agony, and this may have saved his life. The Colt that was meant to come down on his skull thumped onto the fleshier base of his neck, and another blow only tore away the flesh from behind his ear. Still Packer had taken enough punishment to imagine that the spotlight that was now switched on was the eye of God, and the whistles and shouts of the MPs were the noises of another world.

In the past two weeks Sergeant Joe Offenbach had discovered his real vocation in life; he'd gone into the civic amenities business. Put it another way—there was a whole lot of two-way bargaining that could be done to alleviate a man's lot in life. Joe had always been an unembarrassed, outgoing sort of man: he could handle a section of men, rip sizable chunks off a young officer's confidence. He could bully and inspire; play with the guys and then turn around and chastise the guys. He had led his men through a dangerous defile in the mountainous heart of Sicily into a nest of machine guns. Equally he could inspire them in the paths of peace. But now he began to perceive that he had other, and further, talents besides lacerating the butt of a reluctant recruit or dipping his head behind a rock with uncanny timing to avoid a homing bullet. His career in peace (a mere eight weeks long, so far) had started with a booty bonanza, when he'd swaggered into peaceful Bavarian homes at the drop of a hat to stick 'em up, and depart with all kinds of souvenirs. Hell, the Russians did it too, didn't they?

Then the numb aching in his loins reminded him that he was living in one huge brothel, and he could literally take his pick among the ladies of Bavaria. Great, big-bosomed brazen blondes with an appetite for Americans. At the same time he had kept his military hand in with a bit of beefing up the raw rookie recruit men who kept flooding Third Army in place of the erstwhile heroes (now crumbs) who had run for cover to the States (having falsified their points to get home quick). His tasks had been triple: to initiate the rookies as soldiers of Third Army, and as full-blooded men and as booze receptacles. But soon he lost interest and contented himself with leading them across the border on misty nights on retaliatory probes for the occasional jeep or truck hijacked by marauding bands of Soviet "allies."

It was on one of these that he discovered that two months of peace had impaired his reflexes. Having slid precipitously into a ditch with a haul of Russkie vodka, along with his unit, one starless night he had found himself still there after the other guys had cleared off like hot popcorn and made the border with a mixture of wolf calls and rebel yells. For a few seconds he was so winded he couldn't get up, then, a bottle of vodka in each hand, he kept on sliding down the muddy slope, while peremptory Russian was spat into the night, and a searchlight probed and a few distant machine-gun bullets hit the ground ten yards beyond. And with this failing in pure physique a new sensation came oozing—bowel-voiding panic.

You could say that in one giant slither Sergeant Joe Offenbach had grown out of the Army. From that moment Offenbach's active mind became increasingly devoted to matters strictly ancillary. He began to resent the military life, like the goddamn game everyone was playing that World War II wasn't over yet, or Number Three was just about to start. He hated too the adolescent drilling of his bunch of recruits. Like any good tradesman, his sympathies were being channeled more in the direction of his new customers—"some of the finest guys around." To Sergeant Offenbach the war against Hitler's Germany suddenly seemed an obscenity. He just failed to understand why everyone didn't love the Krauts like he did. He was at the moment handling his single biggest commission—the discreet handing over of a massive quota of U.S. Third Army stores to the eager hands of Bürgermeister Frolich, one of the most upstanding guys Joe had met in his life.

Lowel Packer woke up to see through the painful slits of his eyes a big, genial U.S. Army colonel looking down on him.

"Good morning, Major," Bob Miller greeted him. "It is good to see you're well, or at least alive." He paused to let a big cloud of cigar smoke roll over the bandaged Major. "Guess you're wondering what hit you. Well, I can clear up that mystery. You've been the victim of a vicious assault by Major Al Kopp, one of the toughest, fightingest officers on General Patton's staff, and also, if you want my humble opinion, just about the biggest slob in the whole outfit. Guess we made a mistake getting special permission for Major Kopp to be released from house arrest; guess he'd somehow got to hear about you and Fräulein Gettler. A guy like that would act kinda mad if you have him the chance. Anyway Kopp is back under arrest."

Another puff of cigar smoke. Lowel Packer closed his

aching eyes, wishing at the same time he could close his aching head.

"But it hasn't turned out bad for us—incidentally, my name is Colonel Miller, USFET G-2—we've got Major Kopp where we want him, and that's behind bars. At the same time . . ." Miller paused to look at the chewed end of his cheroot, "we could have you, Major, just about where we need you."

"I don't understand," Packer murmured through his pain.

"No," Miller agreed. "That's because you're not feeling too good right now—and also because no one around here seems to be too smart. They say Bad Tölz is sacred to Leonardhi, patron saint of horses, but I think it's stuffed with a lot of damned stupid mules who aren't swinging on any stars. But think it over and you'll see what we mean."

"I still don't understand."

"You're Gerda Gettler's boy friend now, an interesting chick I'd sure like to know more about." Miller's smile suddenly changed into a snarl. "You haven't got any competition—at least while we've got Major Kopp behind bars. So let's have some information about this broad. No more smart, psychological shit. No more expert, Freudian analysis calculated to impress superiors with your damned expensive college education. No more erudite hokum designed to mislead honest U.S. Army generals—you're reporting to me now, Major Packer. And I'm counting on you to tell me just what a cute wanted war criminal like Gerda Gettler is doing sleeping around Third Army Hq."

The Colonel tiptoed to the door of the ward and waved his fingers at the invalid. "Keep me posted," he called soothingly.

"I hesitate to impose again on your time, General Patton." Ex-General Klaus von Ritter bowed his handsome close-cropped gray head. "But you have been so sympathetic to an old adversary, I have dared once more to trespass on your generosity."

Patton smiled vaguely; he had received five Germans

in audience that day and his concentration on their problems was beginning to wander. A part of his mind was maneuvering with his tanks on the plains of Poland.

"The truth is, General Patton, I feel bound to bring the matter which is concerning me to your attention."

"Don't say that military governor you've got over there is still riding you. I gave express orders..."

"Oh no, in that respect the situation is much more satisfactory. You should have seen the children's faces when they received your generous gift of candy. You are the favorite of children, General—they call you 'Great Uncle Patton.'"

"Yeah?" A warmer grin appeared on the great man's face.

"No, the matter I have to report I regret concerns our own people—Germans who disgrace the name. You know how, with difficulty, we have formed a committee to work as best we can with your American authorities. General Patton, I have learned that some of these officials, good and conscientious burghers, are being threatened—they are being told their safety and their children's is at risk."

"Who's goddamn threatening them, Nazis?"

Von Ritter smiled dubiously. "Worse than Nazis—Communists, General Patton. Yes, I am ashamed to confess the Soviets have agents in our small town. They are telling certain members of our committee that it is unwise to serve the Americans. They say soon the Americans will withdraw and the Russian Army will march in. They are saying that anyone who has worked for the capitalists will be shot—their families, too."

"The hell they are!"

"Believe me, General Patton, these people are not joking. I am old enough to know what happens when the Bolsheviks take power. I remember Munich in 1919, the things those bestial people did in our Bavarian capital. I was an officer with the Reichswehr under General Ovens. It was our privilege and also our sorrow to liberate the city from the Bolshevik revolutionaries. I say our sorrow, because we saw what they had done in the city. I myself saw the corpses of the martyred hostages of the Luitpold Gymnasium."

Patton's face had suddenly purpled. "General, are you telling me that there are goddamn Communist bastards walking around threatening honest Germans in my goddamn zone?"

"The Communist rattlesnake dies hard, General."

"By God, we'll have the whole goddamn lot of them behind bars this afternoon." He had grabbed the white phone and was already hollering, "Hap, I want Koch in here right now."

"I knew that General Patton would be so good as to understand," Von Ritter murmured.

Seven monastic days in the hospital had worked its full effect on Lowel's sexual mechanism. Desire had slowly been surging up in him, prickling hard against the Professor's cerebral aloofness. The very thought of her had caused his phallus to surge joyously in stupid expectation. This same need now made Packer practice subterfuge, made him want to bite at the cherry before he spat it out.

But Lowel's stars were strictly in the brutal quarter of the id and this had its effect on his technique. Instead of fumbling his lines, in place of the fey protestations and awkward fingers trembling between the licit and the illicit, the proper and the improper, Packer rewrote the fifth act of *Othello*. He tore her nightdress off her figure. As she gasped he put one hand across her mouth to stifle her protests. When she started to scream he slapped her viciously across the face. Without a hint of preparation he then transfixed her on the bed, his phallus performing its lonely brutal act of claustrophobic masturbation. Toward the end she was with him, her body swaying in sympathy with his wild gyrations, but to no avail. He tore himself apart from her at the moment when she was approaching fulfillment and curled up selfishly on the other side of the bed.

There was a five-minute silence to be broken by Gerda's voice. "They say the Americans are great fucks, but you were incredible!"

"Shut up, damn you!" screamed Packer, splashing the rest of the Jack Daniel into his glass. "I'm a lousy awful fuck. But at least I now realize it's true what they all say about German women. They never feel anything unless they're split wide open. And that's what I'm going to do to you, honey. When I've finished with you, sweet, you'll repent those youthful hours you spent in the cornfields as a young girl, imagining your goddamn Fuehrer was groping around on top of you. Those prissy little out-of-the-corner-of-the-eye looks you flitted at Reichsmarshal Goering. Your hours on the ski slopes with Germany's most athletic Nazis. Those cozy cups of tea on alpine balconies with Eva Braun while that evil little photographic toady Hoffman adjusted his lenses to capture the high tide of German blond womanhood."

Gerda swallowed the rest of Packer's whiskey. "Darling," she said, "did you know you are really very sweet? In fact, hysterically so. I love you so much tonight."

"Then take this," said Packer swinging her a blow across the face less violent than that which her former protector had doled out to him a week ago, but yet enough to knock her backward across the bed. "And this," he continued, crunching his knee into her groin.

"That is not nice, *liebchen*," she stated flatly between clenched teeth. He went at her again, his tactic to drive a wedge between those two long and shapely legs, a change of tone intended—brutality phasing out into eroticism.

"I know how you saw me," he shouted, vainly trying to open the road to her blond-fringed secret CP. "You thought that just because I had brains and a great IQ I hadn't got the guts to beat the shit out of you. Well, baby, here's another think coming."

Her muscular legs resisted the advance, stopping his tank assault in full rush, and a thought blinked through his brain, something else about her. A piece of history, of reportage. Something he had known before he had ever met her. He drew back *pour mieux sauter*. The change of direction got the enemy in two minds. Her legs momentarily flicked further open as he pounded in again with double reinforcements. He pushed aside her thighs to open the way through. She went with his hands, opening and then sliding up. As he rushed toward his objective they closed in a vise about his neck and held him in a lethal leg-scissors. For a second the thighs, white and quite unmarked, yet with little spare flesh about them, threatened to snap his windpipe. Tears started from his eyes as she lay back, her eyes smiling, to savor her Cannae. In a split second the facts intertwined. Gerda Gettler being congratulated by her Fuehrer as she carried off her Bronze Medal in the Berlin Olympics. For sure those rippling legs had lost none of their drive.

They they slackened.

Lowel came out of it, his head a medley of cacophonic multicolored sparks, his quiet gray professorial eyes uncharacteristically close to popping. "Must remember next time which side of the tracks I was born," he said, trying to smile. "A short-sighted intellectual should never swap punches with an Olympic Bronze Medalist."

"Sorry, *liebchen*." She was refilling his glass, splashing in a new slug of Jack Daniel, sending it crazy with soda. "Did I hurt you?"

"No," he deprecated. "It's just that I've fallen a little behind in my physical training exercises."

"*Liebchen,*" said Gerda, lying back on the bed, her legs wide askew. "You know when I felt your face between my legs, I really liked you there."

"The sensation was mutual," gulped Lowel. "I assure you I too was having a ball."

"Why don't you put it back?"

"Jesus," he exploded. "You want a repeat perform-ance?"

"But this time so gently," she insisted. "And then, when we both feel relaxed, we will talk."

It was a considerably pacified Major Packer who poured himself out the final drips of Jack Daniel a half hour later. In the subtle half light Gerda gave him what could be a grin or a smile or a wink.

"You've thought I've been meeting all the wrong people," she confessed. "And in a way you're right. I have been, as a young virgin of seventeen to the final champagne party Goebbels threw at the Propaganda Ministry, just before the war. And yes, I did once allow Reichsmarshal Goering to slide his podgy little hand a few centimeters up my knee. Hitler has given me little Austrian cakes in his Eagle's Nest, and Eva Braun and myself have swapped schoolgirl jokes and giggled behind his back at Heydrich. But that's all a matter of the past, *liebchen*. Now as you see I am trying to turn over a new leaf."

"Go on," he urged.

"But how can you cut off your past life? So still I meet people, crazy people, who hark back to the Nazi period. Even the certifiably insane who think that we can somehow return there. These people are friends. You understand I cannot quite cut them out of my life."

"Yeah, I see your predicament," concurred Lowel. "In a way it's kind of a crisis of loyalties."

"There are others, Lowel, who are bad people. As bad as Major Kopp. For you too have, even in the American Army, men without honor. These men would betray their friends, even America itself."

"Can you swap me just one or two names?" inquired Packer coolly.

"Because you have been such a nice lover, I will give you one gratis. Darling, how well do you know Major Du Camp?"

"Wallis? I suppose we do gravitate together. In our way we're both culturemongers, hangers-on for the ride. Not real soldiers, like most of the officers in the Third. We can compare notes on Thomas Mann or Cosima Wagner. It's good to know someone like that."

"Your friend Major Du Camp is a viper."

"Yeah," laughed Lowel, "you've got him. He's strictly a creep. He's selfish, he's snobbish. He's the world's most consummate name dropper. And I guess he doesn't have that much time for any other member of the human race but Wallis Du Camp. So what?"

"My poor Lowel, you are so lenient. What you've said about him makes him not nice to know. Well, I'm saying he's dangerous to know."

"He's a goddamn funk, Gerda. He's the kind who bends over backward to keep his asshole clean."

"Major Du Camp is a very bored man. He likes danger, particularly for his friends and colleagues. Kopp gave you a black eye, but it's Major Du Camp who will get you into greater trouble—with Colonel Miller."

Miller! Oh God, he wished she hadn't mentioned that name. It forced him to remember he was a man with a mission: to spy on the woman he desired and slept with, and if possible bring her to trial. "Keep me posted" Colonel Bob Miller had said in the hospital doorway in a manner that suggested it would be suicide to disobey.

"It started with a bit of this [she held up the bottle of Jack Daniel] a few hundreds of these [she tossed some Camels over to him], but then he found these were small things for a man with his position and influence..."

"I don't think I want to know anymore," Lowel groaned.

"It is for you I am telling you, *liebchen*. It is to warn you."

"I don't want to know anything about what you know—do you understand!" Lowel shouted at her. "If you've got to give me information you shouldn't have, we better not do any talking, we better just screw."

She blinked at him. "You are not interested in who is selling information about your general, about his troop movements, about his plans?"

"Not from you, not from you! I don't want to have to find out anything from you," Lowel pleaded. As if to make sure, he closed her mouth with a long, old-fashioned kiss.

It was three in the morning before Miller's call finally tracked his most brilliant assistant down to a small Gasthaus some fifteen kilometers west of Kolb.

"Listen, I'm getting nothing from that little creep Professor Packer. Just the same intellectual crap he deals the top brass," the Colonel's harsh voice crackled down the wire.

"Indeed, sir," Eric Weber said, yawning.

"The punk has orders to get back into bed with that woman Gettler and get me a rap on her. He's back in bed with her, but he's not saying anything. Just helping himself. Are you listening, Weber? Or has this got to be a one-way dialogue?"

"It's three in the morning," his assistant reminded him. "I never claimed to be a superman, Colonel. I am certainly these days capable of feeling very tired."

"Okay, I guess a little relaxation is sometimes permissible, even for a member of the master race. But I tell you what I'm gonna do: I'm gonna have that chick in for intensive questioning, and pronto. Do you get me, Weber, or are you flaking out or something?"

"Do not worry, Colonel Miller," came back Inspector Eric Weber's dry voice, "I'm receiving you loud and clear."

"I'm gonna run a fine-tooth comb all over her gorgeous physique. I'm gonna give her the full treatment, till she gives the lot. Then I'll set her up in the U.S. officers' brothel where she belongs, with the slogan "Security Risk" etched across her tits for everybody to see. And to make the whole thing swing, I want you there, on special rack-and-thumbscrew duty. Okay, Weber?"

The Inspector grunted into the phone.

"Say," Miller signed off, "you beautiful, lovable sleuth you, I'm not keeping you up by any chance, am I?"

Weber put down the phone, but it was a minute or two before he turned off the light. His cold eyes took a rapid look around the room with its pine paneling and cozy solid folk furniture. They took in his one spare suit hanging neatly from a peg in the door and his briefcase parked beside the bed, and a rummage of clothes—shirt, lederhosen, and Bavarian green jacket—on the chair on the other side. The hardness of his gaze softened only as he twisted it around to fall on the fair-haired soft-shouldered slumbering form on the double bed beside him, a sheet ruffled across his tousled head. The detective allowed his hard calloused hand to touch the young boy's face before he turned out the light.

The boy snored and Eric Weber discreetly kissed the point on his smooth face where, if the war had gone on for another ten years, he might have worn a mustache.

How could he justify himself to either God or Colonel Miller? whoever turned on him first. The boy talked. In their intimate conversations he had gradually introduced the detective to a savage world ruled over and peopled by young boys with the hearts and souls of rocks. He had learned that there were no adults in this world. They had been eliminated by logic, the premise being that if they were real Germans they would or should, have died in the defense of the Fatherland. Those who occupied their country now were not adults because they were not human—they were the *Untermenschen* of all their childhoods' Goebbels broadcasts. Weber had also discovered that this was a world that accepted no adult frontiers, moral or geographical.

"You ask about these murders," the adorable boy had said. "You are concerned because *Soldaten* of your masters die, and you look here in Bavaria to find their killers. But Eric, you must not be too worried. Russian pigs are dying too. Yes, on the other side of the hills the same mysterious killings. And I tell you something, Eric—they cannot find the murderers, either."

"Do they find the bodies in the same way, too?" Weber had asked with deliberate casualness.

The boy had pouted, but Weber had checked through Frankfurt with the Russian Fourth Guards Army. The answer was that in the past week four Russian enlisted men had been found murdered and stripped of their uniforms.

Weber had seen him first standing outside the police station in Hof, as he had followed a swearing Miller into the street.

The Colonel had brushed past him toward his jeep, spitting out his frustration at the small prisoner they had left behind bars, bloody but unbroken by his thorough interrogation. Weber's emotional boss hadn't paused to wonder what this blond boy was doing outside the police station; it seemed he could only concentrate on one problem at a time, a serious deficiency in a detective. But Weber had wondered, and paused to look twice. His second glance had been met by a gaze of incredible destructiveness.

The next day Weber had returned to Hof on his own. He told Miller he was anxious to widen his investigations, which happened to be true.

In every sense it had been a rewarding return journey. He had left his Army driver back at Kolb and himself taken the wheel of the jeep. By that evening he and the boy were on first name terms.

In the meantime he had discovered a number of interesting facts. First that the child Johan was the most beautiful thing he had ever touched. Second, that he was a friend of the boy Karl, whom they were holding in the police station at Hof on the charge of being in possession of a cigarette lighter belonging to Private Jacoby. Third, he discovered in the course of a rambling, teasing conversation that this Karl had a young friend called Frolich—the same name as the Bürgermeister of Kolb at whose house a certain Private Jacoby had died. That had been enough detective work for one day. The rest had been a dialogue of bodies, one old, tired, and government weary; the other young, sweet, and ruthless.

"These feet," he said to the boy who was no longer sleeping, "they are hard and calloused, as if they are always walking."

"You should make me a present of your jeep, Eric. Didn't you know I haven't got an automobile?"

Weber smiled tenderly. "All the same, my dearest Johan, there are I believe restrictions on travel. A boy cannot walk far in Germany now without the necessary permit."

The boy looked at him with level blue eyes. "Some of the American pigs have soft hearts. For a little tickle you can sometimes get a permit, or a lift in an Army truck."

Weber wagged a stubby finger. "Be careful—I work for the Americans."

Johan snarled, "I said what a boy could do. Myself, I don't go anywhere," then he grinned. "Now is different, isn't it? I am here with you."

Weber lit a Lucky Strike and passed it to Johan.

"Have you ever been to Bayreath, Johan? You would like Bayreuth."

"I have been through it in a troop train in the war, but that is different, isn't it?"

"Or Nürnberg or Regensburg . . . Ingolstadt? That is a nice town too." It was also the location of the last reported murder. Another GI found in a bomb site without his clothes.

"I don't go anywhere," the boy told him without blinking.

Eric squeezed his hand and smiled. "I tell you what. Tomorrow will be your treat. We shall go to Ingolstadt together in my jeep."

Outside the Gasthaus, shaded from the creeping light of dawn, were three youths who were not sleeping. One of them, at the age of fifteen, was a veteran who had helped to hold off the Russians from the Oder bridgehead for forty-eight vital hours in late April that year.

"The swine-traitor is awake," his companion whispered, a lad on whose young shoulders the Fuehrer's trembling grasp had rested as he had pinned the Iron Cross Second Class to his ill-fitting uniform in one of his last recorded forays from the Bunker. "We should not have waited to kill him."

"He makes a good target," another young voice murmured. "Look at the filthy old queer smoking his American cigarette: the bedside lamp shows him up like a searchlight." The boy was stroking a steel point against his smooth cheek, like some cupid toying with the contents of his amorous quiver.

The Iron Cross holder stabbed the earth with an SS ceremonial stiletto. "We could pick the animal off from here, then we could move in and finish him off as we wish.

Johan too will want to have his turn."

Their leader dreamily shook his head. "The beast is not ready for sacrifice," whispered Rudi Frolich, the missing son of the good Bürgermeister of Kolb and author, among other atrocities, of the murder of Private Harrison Jacoby.

The Patton Bomb

The news came through officially in the form of a stirring command broadcast from General Eisenhower, but all morning the radio had been carrying reports that Emperor Hirohito's new government had applied to General MacArthur for an armistice. For any American, patriotic or war weary, sober or drunk, at home or abroad it had to be good news. Those photographs of Corregidor's gaunt defenders marching into captivity before the bayonets of grinning pygmies had etched themselves too far into the national mind for victory to be anything else than a cause for celebration. Similarly there had been the picture of one of Doolittle's captured Tokyo bomber pilots kneeling blindfolded while the camera caught his Japanese executioner in the act of bringing an obscene medieval sword down on his neck. And there had also been the film of the attack of the kamikaze pilots on Halsey's fleet, an enemy so vindictive that he was prepared to sacrifice untrained airmen to delay his defeat.

"Fellas," Major Wallis Du Camp called out in the officers' bar at Bad Tölz that historic morning, "I don't think I ever heard of a better occasion to blow the last of old Herman Goering's wine cellar!" He whispered instructions to the bartender, and soon the Bourbons and beers were being rapidly replaced by beakers of priceless bubbly.

"Gentlemen," a G-4 colonel announced, "I give you Hiroshima and Nagasaki—and that other mighty atom bomb those bastards were just too yellow to let us drop on Tokyo!"

Major Lowel Packer appeared blinking in the bar at the moment that more than twenty lusty voices shouted their approval of this toast.

"Lowel, you poor old home-living professor!" Du Camp shouted. "Do you realize you could even see Cambridge, Mass., again? The war's over—*kaput!* There's no more shooting anywhere in the world, because we beat the whole goddamned world!"

"Except perhaps nineteen million Bolsheviks," Commandant Philippe de Forceville, the senior French liaison officer with Third Army said, smiling to himself.

"Everyone can go home," another major shouted, "except the headquarters staff, officers and men of Third Army. The way things are in this army, we're gonna be here till they start World War III!"

"Maybe you'd like to stand up and drink a toast to General MacArthur," the caustic Major was told by a newly promoted brigadier, and someone else shouted, "Hey, we really licked those yellow bastards!"

Lowel Packer accepted a tumbler of champagne with mixed feelings. A few weeks ago his heart would have leaped at any news that promised a return to his lecture room, his home and family, and the small dinner parties with good conversation. Now there was Gerda, and Lowel wasn't so sure.

An old colonel who had seen service in World War I was trying without much support to sing a bawdy version of "When Johnny Comes Marching Home" and a captain had climbed up on the bar and with fingers tugging at the corner of his eyes was doing an imitation of General Tojo.

Someone shouted, "Hey, what we need is some

Fräuleins. You can't have an armistice without Fräuleins!" And the G-4 Colonel said he wouldn't mind being
the occupying power with a few of those Japanese geishas.
He said that although Jap men looked like monkeys and
acted like them, their ladies could be one helluva
revelation in bed. He added with a chuckle that judging by
the lambasting LeMay's Superforts had given them, there
wouldn't be too many Jap men around to compete for
their women's attentions.

"Guess I'm putting in for a transfer to Tokyo," Wallis
Du Camp giggled with a flushing face. "Guess a guy could
get in on some great old oriental rackets over there!" His
eyes didn't mean to catch Lowel Packer's but they did,
and a funny smile came over both men's faces. Du Camp
wondered just who had been talking to the Harvard
professor about him. Gerda Gettler? "Well one thing you
gotta admit," he said, gesticulating nervously, "old
Hermann's Perrier Jouvet must be preferable to sake!"

The Colonel who had been in World War I was having
better luck with a revival of "How Ya Gonna Keep 'Em
Down on the Farm?" Several younger officers were
joining in with blue or obscene versions of the old lyric,
and others were interposing tunes of their own choosing.
Strains of "Paper Doll," "You'd Be So Nice to Come
Home To," and a few more of the devastatingly
sentimental tunes which had somehow helped the
American Army to fight its way into the heart of Europe
started to get mixed up in the drunken cacophony. Then
someone shouted an anguished warning, and suddenly
General Patton was standing in the doorway of the
officers' bar.

The General was literally dressed to kill. He was
wearing a soft green leather cadet jacket, set aglow by two
rows of golden buttons, a four-tier display of campaign
and medal ribbons and eight bright service chevrons, not
to mention the gleaming stars of a four-star general, and
the brass-trimmed general officer's belt. In a shoulder
holster under his left arm he carried a revolver that had
helped to win the West, an 1873 model Colt .45 with ivory
stocks. Tight riding breeches curved stylishly into a pair

of soft leather boots, but the ultimate effect was in the General's headgear: a dazzling, gold-painted plastic helmet that, combined with the ferocious scowl he was wearing underneath it, was calculated to convince the beholder he was witnessing a visitation from the god of war.

"What the hell's going on in here?" the awesome figure demanded in his eerie falsetto.

Everybody's eyes turned to Major Wallis Du Camp. It semeed a long time before the aide finally found the courage to reach for an empty glass. "General, it would be a deep privilege if you'd join our celebrations."

"Celebrations? What have you goddamn got to celebrate?" Patton made no effort to accept the proffered champagne glass.

"The victory, I guess—I mean, against Japan, sir," Du Camp murmured.

"Victory!" Patton flung the word back at the trembling aide. "What kind of goddamn victory is it when you've got to hire a lot of sonofabitch, lousy scientists to smash a proud enemy with their goddamn unholy chemistry? Hiroshima, Nagasaki—do you call these 'victories,' gentlemen? I tell you what I call them, I call them cold-blooded massacres. And I'll tell you another thing, if I may be permitted to argue with the fine words our Supreme Commander addressed to us over the radio this morning. I consider this so-called victory is a stain on the honor of the United States of America!"

"Sir, I guess a lot of us are worried by the implications of those two A-bomb strikes," the newly promoted Brigadier General was foolish enough to intervene, "but don't you feel we owe a salute to the men of General MacArthur's army—the guys who slugged their way up from Guadalcanal to Okinawa?"

The mention of the man who had finally dashed Patton's hopes of a Pacific command had a disastrous effect on what remained of the General's self-control.

"I have nothing but praise for those brave men," he began calmly, although tears were already sprouting in the corners of his gray-blue eyes. "I salute their sacrifice, I

weep for the blood those heroic fighters had to spill—
especially since most of it was goddamn unnecessary.
Sure it made good headlines—all those lousy beaches
where those poor bastards got shot to hell. But I'd like to
know what military textbook says you've got to throw
away brave men on every goddamn, stinking little island
where the enemy happens to have set up a machine-gun
nest! You know what I would have done, gentlemen? I'd
have left those stinking little islands to rot and gone hell
for leather for the nest all these goddamn yellow termites
crept out of. I wouldn't have wasted a piss drop of blood
mopping up in all those lousy atolls nobody's ever heard
of anyway. I'd have grabbed Tojo by his slimy little nose
and kicked the bum till he squealed for me to stop. I'd
have slipped an army through China and another through
the Pacific and wrung that little shit's neck right in his
own backyard. You wouldn't have found me swishing
around the Philippines like some sodomite opera singer in
a funny cap. I'd have concentrated on murdering the
enemy—instead of my own men! But you're right,"
General Patton nearly sobbed, "they didn't ask Patton,
did they? They wanted that dashing, Napoleonic leader
General Hodges. Boy, they sure picked the right fella to
serve in that bastard MacArthur's outfit!"

General Patton turned his back on his silenced
audience. He would have swept from the room if the idiot
Brigadier hadn't dared to call after him. "At least the
shooting's over, General Patton, we've done what we got
into this war to do."

"How long have you been serving in Europe, General?"
The Third Army commander wheeled around to scream
at him.

An agonizing pause. Finally, "I guess about a month,
sir."

"Then you may not have had the opportunity to
appreciate that there are four million Russians under
arms right here in Germany. Maybe you're also unaware
that though we've given those bastards half of this
goddamn country on a plate, they still reckon they've had
a raw deal. They'd like to overrun the whole goddamn

Continent and you want to know who's stopping them? Less than a million raw rookies that our Supreme Commander likes to call the U.S. Third and Seventh Armies, and all the time General Marshall is telling him that's a darn sight too many. You say the shooting's over, General?" Patton snarled with his unshining teeth. "You ought to listen to the shooting in Poland, there's a helluva lot of it going on because those Commie bastards are shooting every poor sonofabitch they didn't manage to murder in Katyn. They're shooting all the guys the two-faced goddamn British started fighting the second goddamn war for, and whatever those British think, I don't consider that's a cause for celebration. I think it's a warning, a warning which sooner or later with God's almighty grace some bastard in Washington's going to get it into his flea brain we've got to heed. Don't tell me the shooting's over, General." The General's eyes scorched into the new arrival's ribbonless uniform. "As far as you're concerned, it could just have begun."

The door slammed. It seemed like minutes before the staff officers dared to stand at ease.

"Well, so much for World War II," Major Du Camp tried to quip over a glass of champagne that had suddenly turned flat.

He had it all written down: he had it all rehearsed. He stood there on a couple of packing cases: the mikes stood on just one packing case before him. His helmet blazed in the hot California sun, before him stretched detachments of Third Army, the hand-picked advance guard of that elite group which was now, by virtue of the Mighty Dollar, being swung on a long loping half-arc over the Atlantic and back past their grass roots to embarkation points on the Pacific, from there to be fed like a dose of high fever into the heart of Japan.

His hands hooked jauntily on his hips, he addressed the assembled troops, every man jack of them a veteran. "Up to now I've been using you for one purpose and one purpose only. To kill, murder, maim or mutilate Krauts. Forget it. You're now on vacation. I'm asking you to do just about the pleasantest thing known to man; I'm asking you to kick the piss out of the purple-pissing Japs. I'm requiring you, as Army Commander, to screw the balls off the slimy Yellow Peril, to decontaminate the stinking Nippon. I'm offering ten dollars per Nippon scalp, out of the taxpayers' money, goddamn them. And I'm not that particular how you do it. Some guys may prefer to throw a few bombs and add up their score in Nippon entrails hanging from banana trees, like yellow spaghetti. Others may prefer to beat the shit out of our slit-eyed friends with the butt of a Garand. Others may choose to use Jap backsides for bayonet practice. Uncle Sam doesn't give that much, just so long as those purple-pissing corpses come rolling in, hell-bent for the morgue. I want you to kill Japs like your forebears killed buffalo, 'cept buffalo are almost human in comparison. And when you're tired of killing, I just want you to slay just a few more for Old Blood and Guts' sake. Whatever, it's better than shoveling shit in Louisiana."

But today he wiped the text of the speech on his hips and threw it into the wastebasket.

In the cool of the Church of St. Ludmilla, Eric Weber put his arm around Johan and said, "Come, let me show you a picture that may instruct you if it does not move you."

He led the boy to a large dark canvas at the end of the early baroque nave. "We are familiar with the torment, but some of us in Germany have forgotten the figure," he murmured, watching Johan's stony blue eyes suddenly gleam with interest as they took in the details of this ancient atrocity picture—the hands punctured by crude nails, the scalp bleeding from a thong of ugly thorns. "The local people are convinced that this crucifixion is by our great German painter Grünewald, an early work in his progress toward his supreme achievement, the Isenheim altarpiece at Colmar. Pedantic art historians prefer to think it was largely executed by an apprentice in his studio, but that does not diminish the agony of this Christ, does it, my Johan?"

The boy's eyes were concentrated on the details of the figure's suffering, not on the sublime face.

"Of course they would not have told you much about this man in the Hitlerjugend, would they, Johan? They would have pointed you toward the examples of other martyrs—the street hooligan Horstwessel, the elegant torturer Heydrich. You may say what is particular about this man? And the answer is nothing in particular, except that he was innocent, innocent of any hatred. That, incidentally, is what so enraged his torturers. You could call him 'the Christ,' but he could be anyone innocent enough to believe that innocence will not be punished in this world. He could be any young German soldier dying of wounds in a country he had never even heard of until the troop train put him there. He could be your uncle, your grandfather, your mother mutilated by English bomb fragments—or Johan, he could be the stupid young American soldier who allowed himself to be horribly stabbed to death, here in Ingolstadt, only last week."

The boy kept his eyes on the bleeding hands. He said, "I told you I have never been to Ingolstadt."

"Let me draw your attention to another feature of this remarkable painting—this group of Roman soldiers at the man's feet. As you will see, they have stripped him of his clothes. Now they are throwing dice for them. Yes, right under his dying eyes. Could you believe people could be so cruel? Of course you could. Even if you have not been to Ingolstadt, you have been to Hof, you have been to Kolb where they also murder Americans for their clothes. I wonder, don't you, if they cast lots for them? Or did they have some other use for them in mind?"

"I am hungry," Johan said. "You promised me you'd give me a good meal today."

"My dear boy," Eric Weber said, smiling, suddenly hating the professional in him which forced him to interrogate this beautiful creature in the sanctity of a church, "you shall have everything you ask."

He had not noticed there was a third spectator of the picture. As they turned to leave, he found there was a little old priest looking up at them benevolently through steel-rimmed glasses.

"I am glad, sir, you have found the time to observe some of the cultural riches that God has preserved for us here in Ingolstadt," the priest said in English as if from the depths of an airless vault. "Not all your countrymen, *mein Herr,* have time to appreciate that our past is not all wars."

Weber, in his insignialess zipper jacket, had been mistaken for an American serviceman. "I am a Berliner, Father," Weber murmured in German, "and also a Lutheran."

The old priest seemed not to have heard him. "Our friend here does good service to our town. He has shown you the peerless Grünewald Passion—but has he shown you the St. Sebastian martyrdom, almost certainly by the same masterly hand? No, then you must see the St. Sebastian martyrdom, in its way quite as fine a painting as our crucifixion."

"I told you, I am hungry," the boy hissed.

"My dear boy. This is a discovery. I did not know there was another Grünewald in St. Ludmilla. We must allow the good father to enlighten us."

"You will agree, will you not, sir, this is a masterly portrayal of suffering?" the old priest said. Weber looked at Johan first instead of the saintly human target. This time the young eyes were not drinking in the details of the inflicted pain. For some reason his face had turned white.

"The sublime features could have been by no other hand than the master, do you not agree?" The old priest was still insisting on speaking in sepulchral English. "Only the authentic Grünewald could have combined such suffering with such sublimity. You know, sir, I will tell you a military secret, you might say an 'enemy' secret which perhaps may be safely revealed now. We owe the preservation of these rare paintings to a local gentleman and soldier, General Klaus von Ritter. Yes, he has a *Schloss* here in addition to his house in the Alps. Throughout the hostilities they were stored in the good General's wine cellars. 'There will be many heartbreaks for Germany, Father,' he has told me, 'but to lose our Grünewalds would be to break our souls.' General von Ritter is a great friend of our poor town. Is it not true, Axel?"

Weber looked around for a fourth person. Nobody had joined them.

The priest accompanied them back to the door of the church talking like subdued Bach organ music. Johan started to push his way out first into the sunlight, but the priest's gnarled hand closed on his sleeve. "This is a good boy you have as your guide, *mein Herr*. He has not, poor child, much education in the benevolence of our blessed mother and son. But he loves the divine beauty he sees in our Grünewalds. Is that not so, Axel," the old man smiled, patting Johan affectionately on the head.

"So the old fart thinks I am called Axel." Johan turned on Weber back in the Gasthaus near Kolb that night. "Couldn't you see he was half blind, half stupid. The old bugger thought I was somebody else!"

Weber put a slug of Bourbon into two tumblers and walked over to the boy. (Was it debauching a child of this age to give him whiskey? the detective had asked his conscience. Not this child, in this age, he had been able to answer.)

He soothed, "Do not think I am trying to play the grand inquisitor. I am only curious..."

"You'd better stop being curious," the boy snarled, snatching the tumbler from the detective. "You could be sorry."

"Sorry? Exactly what do you mean by that?"

The boy smiled slyly. "Well, I could save myself a lot of sweat for you in bed tonight."

"Johan, you must understand I love you. I want to help you. But, you must see, I cannot help if you tell lies."

Johan tore a Lucky Strike from the pack that Weber had left by the bed, and lit it savagely with Weber's lighter.

"I told you why I tell lies—it is against the American laws to go anyplace. I would get into trouble if I told the truth."

"So you admit, you have been in Ingolstadt."

"I promise you I am not called Axel."

"The priest recognized you."

"Listen, you are a German—you call yourself a German—why should a German want to stop me from going where the hell I like?"

Weber too lit a cigarette, hating himself, hating his job, hating everything around him except this beautiful young criminal. "You have to go to a lot of towns, don't you?" he sighed. "It's your job, isn't it, Johan, Axel—it doesn't matter. As you say, why shouldn't you go where you like? You are young, it is great for a boy to be free to wander. What is sad is that such a lovely boy should be engaged on such terrible errands." It was only supposition, but he was becoming more certain about it than any Miller hunch. "In Hof, Kolb, Ingolstadt, and perhaps other towns in other zones, you have been the messenger of death."

The boy tried to blow a smoke ring.

"Who sends you? Is it Bürgermeister Frolich here at Kolb? Are you his courier?"

"Why don't you screw yourself," the boy said, grinning, "if you *can* screw yourself?"

"Who sends you on these errands?"

"I told you I go where I like."

"Very well, who do you go to see? For example, in Ingolstadt where did you make your call? At the church?"

"Bugger that church."

"The brothel, the parents of friends, the house of General von Ritter?" Now he knew he was clutching at straws.

"That old queen!" The boy grinned before he remembered he had never heard of General Klaus von Ritter.

"Now you do interest me," Weber goaned. He put another slug of Bourbon into the boy's empty tumbler. "Von Ritter likes boys?"

"Don't you, Eric? Don't you like boys?"

"Listen please, there need be no trouble for you if you

tell me the truth. You cannot be punished," Weber pleaded, "if you are an innocent accomplice, and that I am sure is what you are, and what I am prepared to swear in any court. But you must tell me now who gives you your orders, and who you take them to."

Johan sprang off the bed and screamed into Weber's face. "You are a filthy, perverted traitor! Yes, you are a revolting, toadying, criminal traitor to the Third Reich! Why should you care if some American vermin die? It's no business of yours—you filthy old queer. It is no business of a German!"

Weber tugged deeply at his Lucky Strike. He said, "I beg your pardon, Johan, it *is* the business of a German— crimes committed on German soil *are* the business of a German. You must realize there can be no recovery for Germany without laws."

"Anyway," the boy raged, "you don't need to worry too much about a few American corpses. Soon, very soon, they will be at war with Russia. Then there will be thousands of corpses—Americans and Ivans too."

"Who told you this?"

"Yes, they will bleed like pigs and they will have to come on bended knee to Germany to help them fight the Bolsheviks. They will have to give us back our panzer tanks, our machine guns, and rifles. They will have to help us build a new Luftwaffe. You talk about the recovery of Germany—I tell you, we will not be waiting long."

"How long?" Weber demanded.

"Perhaps a month, perhaps even . . ." The boy suddenly became a suspicious urchin again. "I don't know, I'm just saying what I think."

"Come now, Johan," Weber said grimly, "these are sophisticated thoughts for a young boy like you. Who has told you all this?"

"I am just saying what I think."

The detective grabbed the boy's thin arm in a total reverse of tenderness. "My God, I'm going to make you tell me."

Then the telephone rang. It was Colonel Bob Miller. "What the hell are you doing answering this phone?

You're supposed to be in Bad Tölz. I couldn't wait to go
through Third Army. I've got the Supreme Commander's
authority to call on that cutie Gerda Gettler tonight. You
and I are going to have a talk with that sultry sexpot."

"I would like to ring you later. There are interesting
developments here."

"Yeah, I know, those kids!" Miller sneered. "You
better tuck him up in bed and get into that jeep you've
hijacked, if you're gonna make Bad Tölz tonight."

He leaned over his desk for a moment, pen poised in
hand, attitude clam, studied and contemplative, like a
vice-president of some major investment company posing
for his retirement portrait. Then a hot flush suffused his
cheeks, followed almost instantly by a pixyish smile. His
pen started to splutter with ink-spattering haste over the
ruled lines of his notebook.

> August 13. Must try to put this all down in some
> semblance of order. Been going through a heavy
> leaning on Du Camp phase, simply because I judge
> he's the kind of officer who needs a powerful leather
> projectile up his ass just about once a day or he'll
> start thinking he's as smart as Codman was. In fact I
> have every intention of finally busting him for the
> shit-pumping creep he is. Anyway today he came up
> with what looked like a clever schedule. That is, he
> decided on a trip to Rosenheim and the area just
> south of the Austrian border. That was shrewd
> thinking because it enabled me to wear all my three
> hats just about at once. I mean my governor of
> Bavaria's hat in taking a sharp look at how to get
> production going again in the industrial site of
> Rosenheim; and my four-star general's hat in taking
> a look at how the military detachments in that area
> were keeping their peacetime muscles in trim. And
> finally my newfound feathered Bavarian jaeger's
> hat, because they say there's some good shooting up
> there in the forests.

Found the chemical works at Rosenheim nicely

in trim. That is, they weren't in actual working order but they weren't blasted into kingdom come, either. And with goodwill and a touch of encouragement from us, they could be working again.

The man who owns them was introduced to me by Du Camp, and I was eager to have a few words with him in his office. That turned out to be a pretty disused kind of place, with one giant mahogany table and no chairs. So both being fairly elderly men we just leaned on the edge of the table and conversed.

This man whose name was Krauter, or Stauber or something like that, struck me first as being just pathetic, his face serried by lines of resignation. He spoke appreciatively of my efforts to back the best guy they had for the job of running Bavaria—i.e. our friend Minister-President Schaeffer. Then he told me that there was a real ground swell of enthusiasm going for me in the province. I told him straight that if they wanted to get me fired all they had to do was get out in the streets of Munich and start cheerleading. That there were people around just waiting for that kind of thing! He then floored me by quoting exact chapter and verse of the current George S. Patton Gospel on the need to let bygones be bygones with the Germans because the real threat was coming from the Mongols. He even spoke regretfully of the demise of our friend Obergruppenfuehrer Hart. I told him that whereas the SS were very special sonsofbitches at first, later some SS were no worse than Democrats or Republicans. He then cited instances of Jews creeping back into positions of power in Germany and doing a kind of carpetbagger job in reverse. I tersely reminded him that "it simply isn't politic to be anti-Semitic." He agreed but started to hint that despite the fact that the Nazi gold hoards had been traced there was still a lot of money around in Germany, and it could be easily channeled in the direction of any top-ranking American general who started to see things from his point of view.

I told him that if he wasn't clear in five minutes
I'd make history (and headlines) by actually using
one of my pearl-handled pistols.

She was awakened at precisely six in the morning by a
tap on her bedroom door. "Come right in, Lowel," she
muttered sleepily. "I think I must have been dreaming
about you."

"Is that Fräulein Gettler?" a brisk voice inquired from
her living room. "Gee, I sure hate to interrupt your beauty
sleep, but I guess I'm one of those restless guys. I don't
sleep that easy at night."

"Who are you?" She was slipping on a black silk gown
with gold trim. "You Americans seem to think you've got
the right of entry anywhere."

"Yeah," purred Colonel Bob Miller, peeping around
the door, "I guess that's one of our national vices. Back in
Los Angeles they call it lizard prowling." The Colonel
made an uninvited tour of the room. "Gee, that's a nice
Sherman." He took from her mantelpiece a heavy object,
an ornamental tank. "Pretty impressive piece of hard-
ware, the old Sherman. I guess it's just about run out of
gas by now. I wouldn't care that much to pitch it against
the T34. Still, it's a strange kind of thing to find in a
German lady's boudoir."

"It was given to me by one of my dearest and best
friends."

"Which one?" asked Miller in his bright-eyed kind of
way. "By the way, Bavaria seems in danger of running dry
these days, so I thought I'd bring along a little liquid
reinforcement."

He proffered a bottle of Haig whiskey and a bouquet of
flowers. "And somewhere in my pockets I've stashed a few
cigarettes. Most German ladies these days seem to prefer
them to perfume."

"Am I supposed to offer you a drink?"

"Sure. Just neat, if you don't mind, unless you've got a
chunk or two of ice hidden away." The Colonel settled
himself on the divan which had featured so much in
Gerda's recent life.

"You are American Military Police, aren't you?"

"Not at six in the morning, I ain't," said Miller, grinning. "I'm more a kind of inarticulate Don Juan, who's suddenly run dry of broads and happened to have picked up some nifty addresses from his comrades in arms. I'm here strictly on pleasure, Fräulein."

"Needless to say, Colonel, I don't believe you," said Gerda with her most enigmatic smile.

"Getting back to this romantic little souvenir," remarked Bob Miller, running his stubby fingers over the model Sherman, "I was just trying to think up what kind of sentimental American jerk would leave a lady this kind of memento. Matter of fact, I think I've got just the man. I visit him in his cell when I get the time. A mean, violent guy name of Al Kopp."

"He was a brave man," commented Gerda.

"Sure, sure. You don't get a Congressional award for flunking it in the field. Trouble about heroes, though, is they can never quite get it out of their bones. So no sooner has the enemy hoisted the white flag than you get them burning down alpine hotels. Or smashing up peaceful nonmilitary types like Major Lowel Packer. All in the line of duty, of course. Know him too, don't you?"

"Not that much, really," said Gerda with flickering eyelids.

"Funny. Thought you did. That's him up there, isn't it? Quite a memorable face really, if you like eggheads." He motioned to a framed photograph on the mantelpiece. Two officers and one woman were grouped around a Mercedes-Benz having what looked like a picnic. Lowel Packer had an arm around Gerda, who in turn had stuffed a huge four-decker sandwich into her mouth. Major Du Camp was in the process of uncorking a bottle of champagne.

"Great guy, Packer. He's quite a psychiatrist. You know, inkblot tests, facial twitches, mother fixations, you name them—Lowel will pin them on you. Half an hour with old Lowel and you'd swear you were a nut case. What's he like in bed?"

"I do not understand you," Gerda said with a cold voice.

"Help yourself to some more Haig, Fräulein Gettler, and you will."

All her defenses were shrieking urgent warnings inside Gerda Gettler's intuitive female system as she prepared to play it out.

"You know, Fräulein," Miller was saying, "one of the truly great things about my job is people. Fantastic people. You read about them, take them apart from afar, indulge in your private fantasies. And then—you meet them. I suppose I'm a simple guy who's just in love with living."

"You might come to the point, Colonel. I am very tired. I have only had two hours sleep."

"Great place you've got here," mused Miller, kicking off his shoes and lying full length on Gerda's sofa. "Doesn't look like poor, downtrodden Germany to me. By the way, does General Patton ever call here?"

"Why don't you ask him?" Gerda directed a cool eye toward the intelligence officer.

"Anyway, it sure is a nice apartment. How do you pay for it? Who exactly donates the dough? We know you were picked up in Czechoslovakia with nothing to bless you but your Luftwaffe boots and a winning smile. Obviously that was enough."

Gerda was beginning to see her way through. The amiable Colonel was simply passing his time of day (or night) on a point of order—to be specific, the most laughable order to come out of Frankfurt yet, and the most relentlessly disregarded—de-Nazification. In that case her course was clear. The gallant Major Kopp was already in a U.S. military jail in Munich on a few charges, including arson and assault. Setting her up in Bad Tölz couldn't add to these charges.

"Major Kopp was very generous. I think he was in love with me," she told him.

"Boy, he sure must have been," said Miller. "And he did you proud." His eyes rakishly slid up her figure. "I can see what he was shooting at. Not bad for four years near-starvation on ersatz butter and German pickle."

"So?" Her eyes were fixed expectantly on him, with

just a touch of the vamp about them.

"There's this goddamn piece of paper that's burning a hole in my pocket. It's a kind of rundown on you, Fräulein. It shows when you were born, what color eyes you've got. Your hip measurements, waist measurements, and what size shoes you take. It shows where you were educated. Reminds us that you won a Bronze in the Olympics. Shows what kind of company you kept—Hitler, Goering, Goebbels, Braun, Heydrich. Also contains interesting information on experimental work you put in with the Messerschmitt jet, and the cute way you handled your slave laborers. It kinda made me think you might be quite a girl, Gerda—for a dedicated anti-Nazi, that is."

"What are you going to do, Colonel? Put me on trial in Nürnberg? I did not think I was so important in the eyes of the American Army."

Bob Miller giggled in his most affectionate way. "Know something, Gerda? I haven't enjoyed an evening, or do I mean morning, so much for years. The scenario's top Hollywood. It's got the lot. Great apartment, great broad. Great scotch. Handsome hero with a kind of craggy John Garfield charm to him. And just that gentle whiff of espionage under the rug. The only trouble is I'm being a bit of a jerk. I mean, cutting my best buddies out a slice of the action. Do you realize, Gerda, there are three honest upright guys shivering to death in the lobby downstairs. And not a drop of scotch to warm the cockles of their hearts. Mind if I ask them in? They're quiet guys, with excellent manners."

Bob Miller lazily arose from the sofa and stretched his limbs in slow-motion style. He wandered over to Gerda's door and gave a very low whistle. "I want you to meet Sergeant Crane, who's a sensitive student of the subtleties of third degree. And this here is Sergeant Angelo—ex-free-style champion of the most harum-scarum part of the Bronx. A guy with just one desire in the world—to live in peace with his fellow men. And this man here you should make particularly at home. He's probably the greatest cop in the history of Germany. Maybe you never heard of him, but he's sure been making a detailed study of you. His name's Weber, and I guess he's intending to add to its luster."

Major Al Kopp had been getting pretty bored in his psychiatric ward in a Munich military hospital. He had the uneasy feeling that life was passing him by: and life was there to be lived and wrenched apart in Bavaria that cataclysmic fall. Unlike his commanding officer, for Kopp that difficult transition from a state of war to a state of peace had been painless, and almost unnoticeable. The pistol-packing Texan who could open up six cans of Army issue beer at a distance of fifty yards in five seconds with one fully loaded Colt .45 had pitched into the dizzy, zany business of peace with all the zest he had employed in shooting up Krauts.

Not that he loathed Krauts: it was just that they made nice snappy little targets. And Kopp discovered that far from trying to tan the asses off the whole Kraut race, he should be shaking their hands. They were great guys, who were as much concerned about the continuing purity of their racial stock as he himself and his hero Colonel Lindbergh were. Hadn't Kopp supported Lindbergh in his famous America First campaign? Now that he saw the Bolsheviks at close quarters, Kopp's trigger finger was becoming as itchy as Doc Holliday's. He had one dazzling and repeated dream, where he bespattered Zhukov's broad bemedalled chest with five neatly spurting blood fountains. On two such occasions when he woke up he found that he'd ejaculated.

At a time when many American soldiers were experiencing that "Johnny Come Marching Home" élan, Kopp found that he was achieving the same kind of hero's welcome right here in Germany, scene of his greatest exploits. Because he had his pals here, his kith and kin, he had a kind of ready-made *Brüderschaft,* swapping tales with the simple unpretentious Bavarian folk who'd stayed behind when Great-Aunt Gretchen had immigrated to Houston two generations ago. When he went to visit his friendly old Uncle Sauber he got that lovely feeling that

HERE WAS HOME. It was just that they were trying to foul it up all over again. Like that guy Kellerman running back to his hotel as soon as the war was over, like some Yankee carpetbagger. Meanwhile he'd found himself a lovely Gretchen all of his own, a girl so close to him it was like screwing his sister. With Gerda nicely installed in an apartment, life simmered merrily along. And the best thing was it was clear as a stampede to Buffalo Bill that the Old Man had seen the light. What the old General was concocting right there in that star-studded brain box of his was likely to do the Russkies no good at all. So though it was a pity it was peace, it was still almost as good as war.

Then his guard had slipped. Some crappy smart-aleck brain screwer had arrived on the scene with a load of scary shit about psychoanalysis and somehow inserted his diminutive scraggy member into Kopp's fair Sieglinde. When Kopp tried to knock him into kingdom come, that sonofabitch Miller had fallen on him from Mount Sinai and taken him off to jail. When he spent his day turning one wall into a vast blazing Stars and Stripes, and another into a Nazi emblem, the headshrinkers had moved in and carted him off to a psychiatric ward. All Kopp could do then was spend the day handling himself, till one beautiful morning a spurt of his semen actually hit the ceiling, eight feet up.

Maybe it was those getaway stories he'd read as a boy, maybe it was sheer spontaneous inspiration, but a plan was forming in Kopp's mind. He was reverting. America became now like a kind of cruel stepparent and he was seized by an urge to defecate on the Stars and Stripes. When an Army psychiatrist came to visit him in his private ward, Kopp found his features Semitic. When he started to question him about his German relatives, Kopp held his cool. He wouldn't give up. He went on and on, and as he persevered Kopp found that he'd developed a bad attack of asthma. His words became more indistinct, even huskier.

Then when the headshrinker bent over to get it, Kopp gave it to him with interest. A massive ox-like blow over the back of the neck rendered him insensitive. Five minutes later the orderly sergeant saw a bulky figure in white overalls leave the ward.

Four hours had gone by, although in Gerda Gettler's third-floor luxury flat, as sponsored by the big-thinking Major Kopp, it was difficult to chart the exact passage of time. The heavy velure drapes had been drawn to keep out the bright autumn sunlight and the deepening twilight. A few other minor adjustments had been made in the room. The roomy, voluptuous sofa had been pushed to one side; in its place in the center of the room stood a more spartan upright cane chair to which Gerda was tied. The overhead chandelier lights had been dimmed. Just one light upturned at an angle and masked by black carpet stood in for a flash. Gerda Gettler herself had divested herself of her black and gold dressing gown. She was now virtually naked, save for a scanty underskirt that covered her lower limbs, though even this had unfortunately been ripped to open up vistas of her long, sturdy athlete's legs.

In the shadows on the sofa sat Bob Miller, still toying with his glass of scotch, though it could be noted that the level of the spirit in the bottle hadn't dropped by an inch in the last few hours. Whatever this party was devoted to, it certainly wasn't to boozing. The center was held by Miller's two henchmen, now missing their jackets and with rolled-up sleeves; both were freely and unpleasantly perspiring. Eric Weber hadn't changed since he first entered Gerda Gettler's apartment. He still had on his neat American officer's jacket and well-tailored trousers, without so much as a badge or any kind of insignia.

"You have told mostly things we already know," Eric Weber sighed. "Your friendship with Eva Braun, the criminal Hitler's admiration of you and your achievements. Your work on the Messerschmitt 262 project. The unfortunate accident by which the slave laborers died. You have told us only what is on record about your friendship with Major Al Kopp—except that he has aged relatives in Rosenheim called Sauber, whom he occasionally visited. This, I agree, is fresh information—but it

hardly justifies four hours of painfully intensive questioning. Can it be we are wasting our time?" The question was
fired at the prisoner, but it was to Colonel Bob Miller that
Weber appealed with his eyes. Would the American ox
never understand that the answers to their inquiries were
two hundred twenty-five miles away at a Gasthaus
outside Kolb? And how did you convince him that every
second lost on this futile investigation was time gained for
Johan to disappear into the shifting populations of
defeated Germany?

"Who had the cute idea of burning down the Hotel
Edelweiss?" Miller wanted to know. "What did you want
from Major Kopp? And how come a luscious frail like
you falls for a short-sighted egghead like Major Lowel
Packer? Are you telling me it was his sex appeal? Or was it
his assignment that interested you? How come, in spite of
all the evidence we've presented to Third Army here in
Bad Tölz you're still the toast of this one-horse town? Just
how many staff officers here are slipping you their PX
rations—and how many of them are talking in their sleep?
I'm telling you, baby," the Colonel said, grinning, "we've
just begun to get acquainted."

"You ask so many questions," Gerda moaned.

"All you've gotta do is answer them," Miller told her,
rolling a meaningful glance at Weber. The German
detective motioned sadly to Sergeant Angelo, who took
his thin cheroot and slowly advanced it in the general
region of Gerda's silk underskirt.

"Come, Fräulein," murmured Weber, "we do not like
this kind of work." The red-hot tip of the cigar made shy
contact with the silky texture. A small but pungent smell
of burning was in the air. The Sergeant began to push the
cigar through the opening it had made toward bare flesh.
He paused to look around at Weber. Weber took in the
face of Gerda and then gave a quick nod. The cheroot
went further and suddenly Gerda was screaming.

Quickly Sergeant Angelo twisted a knotted kerchief
into Gerda's mouth. Again a nod from Weber. Again the
Sergeant poked forward with the red-hot end. This time
Gerda's body fought and twisted within its corded strait

jacket, held in position only by Crane's huge biceps, who at this moment resembled a yachtsman trying to hoist sail in a gale. Then Weber touched Angelo on the shoulder and he took back his cigar. Pulling it in front of Gerda's face, he took an enormous puff from it so that the tip smoldered and took fire. He deeply inhaled the smoke, then bent over Gerda again and blew it all in her face. At a sign from Weber, Angelo now removed the knotted gag. "You see, Fräulein. No policeman is good. Not us Germans, and not even the Americans. They are hard men, and in this case hard men who cannot think. When a policeman is puzzled, he can be very dangerous."

Yeah, thought Miller, I guess it's quits between us and the Gestapo. Love-all, or hate-all. In the exploitation of human weakness and fear the Gestapo could give his crew a few tips and the homicide boys could return the compliment. Each could add a few creative tweaks in the dossier of sadism and brutality. Those were the irreversible facts behind the human condition, the significant small type behind the regime of cliché and hypocritical soap opera that the Allies had set up in conquered Rermany—the mocking truth behind the United Nations Charter and the Nürnberg trials. And when it came down to it they were all thugs. He, Bob Miller, was a thug. And Heydrich had been a thug. And even the cultivated Eric Weber, with his Old World courtesy and love of culture, was a butcher treading knee deep in blood and tears.

But shit, who cared. This kind of thing went with the furniture. Because behind it all was justice, justice of a kind. And for Bob Miller it was a curiously personal justice. Bob Miller was not a man to theorize. He was a man of instant mental (and physical) reflexes. A hunch merchant, moving by gut feel, and in twenty-seven years' duty with the force, those guts had never let him down.

And his guts had already accused Gerda Gettler of being a prima-facie type of Nazi criminal, the crucial lady vamp. His guts told him that somehow Gerda was at the very heart of all the things—strange, menacing, brutal, and bizarre—that had been occuring in the Third Army sector in the past six weeks. He felt her criminality like a dog noses shit, and dimly he guessed the cause. Somehow to degrade the status and reputation and inner pure, glowing honor of the most brilliant, the most full-hearted American general to appear since Stonewall copped it at Chancellorsville in 1863. Somehow Gerda was trying to machinate Bob Miller's hero (the ticker-tape idol of America). Besmirch his glory so that the crummy Quisling elements of the Third Reich could again be raised to a life of privilege.

The very thought made the Colonel's bile rise swiftly within his throat and threatened his slow, laconic Jimmy Stewart smile. Weber was motioning again to his henchmen to resume the questioning, when Bob Miller rose easily from the sofa and strode into the spotlight glare.

"You Krauts are all the same," he spat out, "the finesse of torture. You take so goddamn long to get anywhere. It's all holes in the tongue and burned fingernails. Stretching out the agony for the sake of it. Get the hell out of here, Weber, and produce some results somewhere for your pay. Because I'm warning you if you don't..."

Bob Miller's arm was wrapped around Weber's throat in a kind of friendly bear hug. "Go on," said Miller, "get lost. And take Abbott and Costello with you. Leave Gerda to me. I'll make her spill the beans California-style." Miller went over to Gerda and undid the ropes that bound her to her chair.

"Okay, baby," he whispered, "for me you're going to talk. Because if you don't I'm gonna pummel you to death. Like this, for openers."

His clenched fist smote Gerda a glancing blow on the forehead and sent her reeling against the window. As she turned Miller caught her and thrust his face right into hers. "Okay, baby. Here are the rules of the game. I'm gonna smash you into little bits. But the rules say this. When you tell me something interesting I stop. If it's real bonanza stuff, maybe I stop for cocktails for two. If it's the ultimate mind-bending truth behind life, I put you to bed and kiss you good night, all right?"

As Gerda turned to answer him, he gave a quick short-armed rabbit punch in the groin. The vomit started to her lips. She turned to him beseechingly. "Here goes," said Miller, and she was cascading over his shoulder to land in a heap in a corner. "That was jujitsu, baby," said Miller. "Every L.A. cop has a smattering."

Gerda didn't get up and Miller came in for the kill.

"I told you this was going to be short and sweet, honey," he panted. "But I haven't heard anything from you yet to make an honest cop stop and think." His arms were set in a loose handlock around her throat. With one arm as pivot he began to bring gradual pressure straight onto her jugular vein. "Spill, baby, spill," he crooned. "Spill like you've never spilled before."

He did not hear the door open behind him. He didn't appreciate the comedy of Lowel Packer's startled face as his precise bespectacled academic eyes began to read the writhing human puzzle on the carpet.

"Hold it, Buffalo Bill," guffawed Miller as he nonchalantly fended off Lowel Packer. "Don't you know what you're doing? Obstructing a cop in pursuit of his duty. Assaulting a superior officer. Or just putting your jaw on the line. Whichever way it won't look good for you, Packer."

"You're a monster," screamed the psychologist. "A sadistic killer, worse than the Gestapo bullies you've displaced."

"Look," said Miller, "this ain't your kind of game, Packer. If I'd been real ratty I could have laid you out cold any number of times. But seeing as how I'm a decent God-fearing kind of guy I guess I'd prefer to settle our differences more amicably. Over a glass of Haig, for instance."

Together the two men took the unconscious body of Gerda and put it to rest on the bed in the next room. Then they returned to the living room. Miller rolled the sofa back into place and slumped down on it, easing his tie and kicking off his shoes.

"Okay, Lowel," he challenged, "the ball's in your court. See if you can advance it."

Lowel Packer was beginning to simmer down, to

recover from the trauma of finding Gerda laid out cold on
the floor and in the process of being methodically choked
by Colonel Miller. He now began to muster his arguments.

"I take it there's no point in trying to arouse any sense
of conscience in a man like you." He too was now sipping
his scotch, letting the mellow liquid glide slowly down his
throat. "And I suppose as far as you're concerned the age
of chivalry is dead. But can't you understand that what
you've done isn't just brutal and horrific? It's useless.
Utterly without point."

"I don't quite get you," drawled Miller.

"Well, isn't it obvious, even to a suspicious moron like
you, that Gerda's no spy? Come to that, there's no
conspiracy either. Just a few Nazis trying to survive. A
lunatic general trying to forget that the war's over. A
handful of black-marketeers, and a small band of
infantile fanatics bumping off GIs. Take it all together
and you haven't got a row of beans."

"Jeez don't say that," sighed Miller. "It's my job you're
attacking."

"I'd say there wasn't as much going on in the whole of
Bavaria as in Los Angeles on a normal-to-quiet night.
And I'll tell you another thing. You know it."

"I don't quite get you, or maybe I do. Are you
suggesting that the little floor show you've gate-crashed in
on was a kind of charade?"

"Yes, that's exactly what I'm saying." Lowel snatched
the bottle of scotch and splashed the rest of the contents
into his glass. "And what's more I'm saying you're
professional enough to know it. So what do we have?"

"You tell me, Doctor," sighed Miller.

"I will. You're doing it for kicks."

Miller languidly got up and strolled over to where an
Army bag had been placed in the corner of the room.
From it he took another bottle of scotch and proceeded to
pour himself a slug.

"And if I am, why the hell not?" he lucidly asked.
"Everyone else here is out for himself one way or another.
You've climbed in with the juiciest bit of Kraut horsflesh

around for miles. And no doubt are sanctimoniously, humorlessly, and do I dare say it, unimaginatively screwing her night after night. Kopp burns down hotels. Du Camp passes the time of day licking famous asses and picking up cultural bric-a-brac for a hundredth of its real worth. Ike sneaks his way into the slimy political rat race. The Beetle hangs like a spider waiting to suck our blood. The whole goddamn shit shop is on a crash course of self-indulgence."

"So you think that lets you out," sneered Lowel Packer. "Leaves you a clear way to behave like a San Francisco hoodlum cop."

"You're right," Miller agreed crisply. "I'm a cop, a hoodlum cop, maybe, but a cop all the same. And a good cop has hunches. So until something else comes along, that's about the only sure lead we've got."

The Russian bastards knew there was no hope of stopping him taking Jena. His tanks were moving too fast and they'd gotten themselves too far off balance. What they didn't expect was that like General Jackson and General Lee in their fabled offensives up the Shenandoah Valley, he'd split his outnumbered force in front of the enemy and sent two thirds of his armor racing southward to seize the heart of Tolbukhin's communications artery.

He had allowed himself just ten minutes to savor his Napoleonic victory at Jena, then he and Woodring were off to catch up with the action in the south. There was a lot of noise going on that morning, but the old warrior could identify in the noise of destruction the specific sound of a massive rocket air strike. Hobart Gay had done his job, he'd called down all hell on that tight mass of T34s that had crowded like rush-hour automobiles onto Halleck's front.

Right now they were in the outskirts of a one-street town. What the hell were these white-helmeted MPs doing standing across his route, telling him that Commie snipers were still active, imploring him to take cover? Goddamn it, hadn't they served with him before? Didn't they know that taking cover was something Old Blood and Guts left to other generals?

He tapped Woodring on the shoulder and swore at the MPs to get out of his way. Then he reached for his pearl-handled Colt .45, the same firing piece that had brought down two notorious Mexican bandits in Pershing's campaign of 1913, and rode into town with a loud YAHOO and an exploding six-shooter.

He personally picked off a rooftop Mongol, brought the bastard and his 7.62-mm. submachine gun crashing into the street, an ugly mess. But his track-borne infantry were doing all right without him. He watched three tough-looking fighters in GI helmets flush a whole nest of fur-capped heathens out of a basement and smiled as they shoved them down the street with the encouragement of a few well-aimed kicks in the backside!

"Nice work, fellas," he called encouragingly. "You can tell those Commie bastards that what hit them was the Lucky Third."

The GIs looked at him proudly but without comprehension, the reason being that they didn't speak English. Patton realized he'd stumbled on the veterans of the 25th Waffen SS, now re-equipped and rearing to go under the big "A" shoulder patch of Third Army! These crack Kraut fighters were clearly giving a good account of themselves. There wasn't much these tough guys needed to learn about fighting the Russians—they hated the bastards!

"General Patton," General Hobart Gay said patiently, "your appointment with Major Bogamov."

"I told you, Hap, I'm not talking to that bastard. I told you it's your job to keep the sonofabitch out of my sight."

"You will remember, sir, you agreed to see him now, if only to stop the guy from going over your head to Eisenhower."

At last Patton got out of his chair behind his big mahogany desk. Every time it hurt to have to leave his dream.

Later that day they were drinking Third Army ration coffee from Major Kopp's collection of genuine eighteenth-century Dresden coffee cups. A little late summer sun struggled through the windows into the living room where Gerda was sitting wearing dark glasses. Packer wasn't feeling that great either. A few hours' fitful sleep on Gerda's sofa had failed to settle his moral dilemma. Had he not been, as an officer, a scholar and a gentleman, almost honor-bound to slug Miller? Now, he was in a gray mood of self-doubt, bordering on self-disgust. Gerda, on the contrary, was beginning to feel better.

"Seriously, Lowel *liebchen,* there is a funny side to it. I mean Colonel Miller knocking me clean unconscious and then you, with your beautiful sense of timing, just coming in."

"What's not so funny is the kind of license we give our guys over here. A ticket to roam around, plunder and maim at the drop of a hat. I'm sure Miller was merely satisfying the brute within his psyche. He's a self-confessed sadist, not to mention voyeur. Getting his kicks out of watching others doing it, crunching in himself for the grand finale. And we call ourselves the Conquering Heroes. But don't worry, I nailed the guy. I showed him in a mirror the kind of monster he was."

Gerda lay back on Major Kopp's luxurious sofa (pillaged from a villa close by) and let her pale face extract the final atoms of warmth from the setting sun. Pensively she inhaled a Lucky, stubbed it out, and lit another. Finally she said, "In a sense, Miller was right about me. I am embroiled. I can't help being embroiled. With my kind of record, what would you do? But I really do hate war, Lowel. And believe me, I really have seen the error of my ways. I've seen those pictures of Belsen, I have visited Dachau—just after the war I was taken there by force by some American MPs. And yes, I had guessed at the horrors even before the war was over. And in a sense Miller is right. I am guilty. And he made sense in other ways. Madmen are trying to repeat their madness. Blind men who do not understand that what has happened, and last night too, is a judgment."

"Sure we're guilty," was Packer's quiet comment as he puffed on his pipe. "Mass guilt, individual guilt. That's my territory you're on, baby, and I can assure you as of now, all your trauma are very obvious ones. A kind of first steps in rehabilitation. But you personally didn't chuck that gas down the vents."

But Gerda was already up from the couch and her arms were right around Lowel and what she was saying was yet another jolt to the Professor's systematized method of thought.

"Can't you see it makes no difference if I'm guilty or not, because others are. I know it's crazy but what Miller and Weber were saying made a kind of pattern. The things they were trying to connect really *do* connect. In a different kind of way."

"What do you mean? You're not making sense."

"Yes, because there's an atomic bomb right here in Bavaria. It wasn't dropped at Hiroshima or Nagasaki, but it's a thousand times more deadly. It's worse because it's an atomic bomb made out of human flesh and blood. It's got a warhead that can penetrate all the way to Moscow and blow sky high all your hopes of peace. A bomb with a shiny helmet and a lethal brain. And its name is Patton. What if they succeed in detonating him, Lowel?"

"This is crap," tersely commented Packer. "Pure, unadulterated crap."

"There was something Al Kopp was saying the night before he was arrested. He was talking about Herr Sauber, you know, the uncle Colonel Miller and his thugs found so uninteresting. Well, of course he is a little old man you might think is not so interesting. But he has many friends—bishops, industrialists, great soldiers like General von Ritter, and not so great soldiers like your Major Wallis Du Camp. He knows how to use people. To mold them. Like putty in his hands. He was among the first to spot the talent in Hitler. The first to back him. And to build a huge fortune on him. A hidden fortune, because this man is just a simple Bavarian, as cautious with his money as a peasant. And Kopp was seeing him, and he said there was a tie-up. Somehow to ignite Patton, somehow to hurl him, like a high-explosive truck, straight at the Russians. That was what Al was saying and I know, I know, I know he was telling the truth."

But Packer was already running. Running from the room, running, down the stairs and out into the street to where his jeep was parked. His getaway would have done credit to a racing driver.

Major Bogamov had been sitting in the outer office for twenty minutes refusing all suggestions of coffee or Coke from the friendly WAC clerical staff. Now suddenly he was being patted warmly on the shoulder by a balding elderly man he recognized as General Patton without a helmet.

"Why, I'm sorry to have kept you, Major. I certainly hope they've been looking after you. What can we do for you, Comrade Major?"

Behind Patton, General Hobart Gay blinked. Was the old man going completely nuts? He'd never known him to be so polite to a Russian in five months of inter-Allied exchanges.

"Sir, I carry a message of portest from Minister Tolbukhin of the Fourth Guards Army."

"Yeah," Patton said, smiling broadly with his gray teeth, "what's worrying the old bastard?"

"The operations of General Halleck at the camp for fascist revisionists at Fogelheim. Marshal Tolbukhin wishes strongly to protest that they were not carried out in accordance with the Yalta Agreement."

"We couldn't stop all those poor sonsofbitches from hanging themselves," Patton replied, again with surprising bonhomie. "Maybe we even saved you from getting your own hands dirty there. From what I hear, those poor bastards get strung up anyway the moment they cross your frontier." Patton continued to smile.

"Our list takes into account the fascist suicides." The Russian drew a dog-eared clutch of papers from his jacket pocket. "It is still not complete, General. Five Coassack fascists who were particularly requested from you by the Soviet Government for crimes against the Soviet peoples have not been returned."

"Look, Major," General Gay said, tight-lipped, "I wouldn't press General Patton too far on this thing. He was there at Fogelheim. He didn't actually throw up, but a lot of his boys did. You understand. What you asked us to do made us vomit."

"Easy, Hap," Patton purred. "Major Bogamov is only obeying orders like you and I have to do. Only difference is that if he disobeys them, he ends up with a goddamn noose around his neck. Isn't that true, Comrade Major?"

A look of suspicious gratitude crept into the Russian's small eyes. Hobart Gay seemed stunned. Patton said, "Tell you what, Major, you've got to take a drink with us. Goddamnit we're allies, aren't we? Least that's what they tell us back at Frankfurt."

An exquisitely tailored sleeve slid around the Russian's big prickly shoulders. General Gay followed them with disbelief into the map room.

"Major, you've got to join me in a Patton 75." A white-coated Army bartender had already appeared and was mixing the notorious highball that had sent generals, Allied commanders, senators, and Lieutenant Summersby reeling from Third Army CPs. "We'll drink a toast—maybe to victory."

"The question of these five criminals, General."

"It's always possible one or two of those poor bastards managed to get away into the woods," General Gay said.

"Don't spoil the party, Hap. We're having a little drink here to solidarity. Hey!" Patton's bright eyes had caught the Russian sipping tentatively at the lethal cocktail of champagne, brandy, and nobody knew what else. "That's not the way you guys drink back on the Steppes. Down the hatch, Major, as the goddamn British say. *Prosit!* And now, why don't we have another one?"

Bogamov downed his Patton 75 and put out his glass

for a refill. He clicked his heels and said dutifully "To the solidarity of the victorious peoples of the Soviet Union and the United States of America!"

"An agreeable sentiment, Major." Patton smiled without raising his glass. "Now I'd like to propose another toast—a toast to war!"

The Russian had already been looking uncomfortable in the plushy inner sanctum from which until now he had been rigorously barred. Now he looked even more uneasy.

"What's the matter, Major? Don't tell me you're another of these goddamn modern soldiers. I can tell you we've too many S.O.B.s who are ashamed of their goddamned profession—ashamed of the honorable profession of arms. You ought to read the classics, Major. In Athens and in Rome war was regarded as an art, a field worthy of the highest achievements of man. It was even sanctified by its own god. Major, I give you the mighty divinity of Mars!"

"I must report to General Tolbukhin tonight, General."

"But first, sir, you are going to do me the honor of joining me in another Patton 75. Let's agree on one thing, Major Bogamov. We've got no goddamn business wearing the uniforms of our countries if we're not goddamn willing and able to protect its interests with arms. If we're not willing to do that, by Jesus we've got no right to call ourselves soldiers. Let's take yourself for example, Major. You say you're here in my CP as a friend. I note you are wearing the uniform of a foreign power and you're also a soldier. Now who's kidding who? I'll tell you one thing, you're not kidding me into thinking you're here for the sake of the grand alliance. I would pay you the compliment of supposing that as a patriot and a soldier, you're here to spy out the military resources and depositions, or do I mean dispositions, of Third Army."

General Hobart Gay had been with Patton since Sicily. He didn't believe he'd ever seen the General get stewed quite so fast. In fact he'd never seen him get stewed at all in front of a foreigner.

"General, Major Bogamov is anxious to return to his headquarters tonight."

"He can inform Tolbukhin he is drinking with the commander of Third Army." Patton turned on his second-in-command with the first sign of irritation he'd betrayed in the interview. "Now refill your glass, Major, and I'll come clean with you. I'm doing everything within my power to make sure you bastards never get a chance to see what we've really got here in Bavaria, because, goddamnit, you know as well as I do we're not sitting on that frontier holding hands. We're facing each other with goddamn machine guns!"

"Prosit," Major Bogamov said feebly. He added, "Concerning the fascist criminals, what am I to report to Marshal Tolbukhin?"

"You can have another drink and tell Marshal Tolbukhin to go to hell," Patton said, smiling graciously. "Another thing you can tell him. I know where he's hiding every one of his goddamn T34s. Would you like me to enlighten you?"

"I guess Major Bogamov hasn't got much time," General Gay protested, as his commander swerved with jutting forehead toward Koch's sacred maps.

"Sure he's got time," Patton chuckled. "He's a goddamn Russian spy, isn't he? Well, take a look at this, Major. We're down here at Coburg and Hof and here are you and our gallant allies up here in Thuringia. Those red circles correspond to ten of your T34 tanks. And this is where they're distributed. Correct me if I'm wrong. Quite rightly your Marshal Tolbukhin is keeping his armor concentrated, and this is where he's concentrating it— right here between Jena and Saalfeld. I don't blame the sonofabitch; your Marshal Tolbukhin is keeping his options open. He can push his tanks down to Plauen and maybe cut through the Czech border and come around our backside. He can shove straight down to the road to Bamberg, or he can throw his punch through the Thüringer Wald. He can suit himself. Only trouble is, thanks to Koch and his G-5 goddamn clairvoyants, we're not missing a trick. In fact we're thinking that's an awful lot of goddamn tanks to keep in one place."

Patton smilingly accepted another 75 cocktail. Bogamov, however, pushed the waiter aside.

"General Patton, if I am understanding you, you are making offensive statements. You are suggesting hostile intentions to the Soviet armies."

"I think General Patton is joking," Gay said hopefully.

"Hell, I'm not joking; nor is Marshal Tolbukhin. He's got his goddamn army on a war footing. I'd have to be crazy to overlook that fact."

Bogamov clicked his surprisingly small heels. "I must protest at your provocative statements, General Patton."

"Same goes for me," Patton chuckled like a guest who's stayed a long time at a cocktail party. "I too protest at your provocative statements concerning the conduct of my men in executing your goddamned unholy requirements at Fogelheim. There's two things we can do about it, Major. We can draw our revolvers and shoot it out like gentlemen or, like gentlemen, we can have another drink. Major, don't tell me your armor plating is too goddamn fragile for another Patton 75."

The Russian broodingly accepted another refill and General Gay whispered, "George, why don't you let me see this guy out. He's small fry. You don't have to worry about him."

"I'm enjoying our conversation, Hap. So I venture is Ivan, here. Aren't you, Ivan? I mean Major Bogamov?"

Major Bogamov was at last beginning to look a little stewed too. He raised his glass unsteadily and tried to put on a reasonably pleasant smile.

"General Patton, sir. I would like to be able to report to Marshal Tolbukhin that you are carefully investigating the matter of the five fascist criminal revisionists. I do not ask more. Only to be able to report to Marshal Tolbukhin you are making serious investigations."

It was a reasonable request, at least as Russian requests tended to go in postwar Germany. In his bad English, slurred now by the chemical shrapnel of the Patton 75s, he was in fact asking the Third Army commander to help save his face with Marshal Tolbukhin and the Marshal's political commissar. But now a faraway look had come into Patton's eyes. He wasn't listening. George Patton himself was a long way off.

It was still only twenty-four hours since they'd left their starting line in the Thüringer Wald, and consider what they'd done in a day's work. Jena was taken at three times the speed of Napoleon, so was Tolbukhin's line of communications. Those Russian T34s that had not been smashed by the Air Corps strike had been set blazing by his Pershings and Shermans. Now refueled with good Caucasian gasoline, his two columns had linked up at Zeitz. By breakfast time they could be in Leipzig, except Leipzig wasn't where they were heading. He was going to push his tanks to within four miles of the town, close enough to make sure the garrison of Bolshevik bastards stayed bottled up in the place, then he'd swing across country to jump the Elbe at Dessau. Providing he could beg, borrow, or capture enough gasoline, he could reckon on being across Poland in three to four days, and then . . .

"If I can have your solemn word, that is all I am asking at this time," Major Bogamov was repeating boorishly. "That is what I require to be able to report to Marshal Tolbukhin."

Patton's eyes, which had been staring through the dawn of his fantasy toward the Elbe, suddenly swiveled around to fix this single Russian standing sloppily in his map room.

"You can report to Marshal Tolbukhin that Fogelheim was the last time I'm going to let my boys do any of his goddamn dirty work. You can tell him for his private information that that goddamn slaughter of goddamn innocents was carried out only at the direct instigation of General Eisenhower, and in spite of my own personal protests. You can tell that bastard Tolbukhin that next time he tries to lay a hand on any individual enjoying the protection of the United States Third Army, I'll kick that lousy sonofabitch back to goddamn Siberia ..."

Hobart Gay could see that his commander was in the grip of one of those terrible passions that had so often nearly wrecked his military career. As Patton's right-hand man since Sicily, he knew them only too well; he also knew there wasn't anything he could do but watch the destructive impulse rip. Since that terrible afternoon in Troina when he had assaulted shell-shocked GIs in two separate field hospitals, Gay knew he was helpless to intervene when George Patton was seized by this demonic fury. He could no more stop Patton's shrieking indiscretions now than three years ago in Sicily he could have saved A.S.N. 70000001 Private Paul G. Bennett from a slap across the face.

"You think I'm kidding, don't you?" Patton was screaming at the Russian. "Well, you better take a look at this!"

Hap Gay saw the General's hand go to the red cord that brought down the details of his cherished paln.

"General, you're doing something you're going to regret," he shouted, although he knew it was useless.

The map came down. Gay watched Bogamov's little eyes bulge as they tried to take in the mass of U.S. and Russian dispositions on the outsize representation of the Bavarian-Thuringian border. He saw Patton pick up a pointer and indicate the blue arrows that designated the planned armored maneuver behind Halleck's rear up into the Thüringer Wald, and again he watched the Russian trying to turn his liquor-blurred eyes into a camera. Then suddenly Patton tweaked the map and it shot out of view.

"Guess maybe after all that map is kind of confidential." George was unexpectedly smiling again. "Even though, Major, you're a gallant ally. Sure, why don't you tell Marshal Tolbukhin we're investigating the matter? We don't have to argue about what the hell the matter is. But before you go Major, I'm going to insist you do me the honor of joining in another Patton 75."

General Hobart Gay, thought, What can you do about a guy like George Patton when you never know what he is going to say next?

"Kick Their Hind End Back into Russia"

Just about a mile past Ingolstadt the jeep did a crunching semi-circle in the mud and came to a stop. A slim figure emerged from behind a group of fir trees. "Luckies, mister? Chewing gum? Coca-Cola?" trilled a pure soprano voice.

Weber allowed a small smile to pass his lips as Johan climbed in beside him, then he threw the jeep back onto the road and soon they were climbing high into the mountains. The boy said very little; once or twice he gave a shudder as the mountain air blasted through the open sides of the jeep. Keeping one hand on the wheel, Weber reached behind and threw a spare Army jacket around his shoulders.

"The usual place?" Weber was thinking of the frightened lady who would ask no questions, the big creaky Bavarian oak bedstead, the shutters that opened out onto a sublime expanse of the Aubergensee and those hot crunchy pastries in the morning.

"I'm bored with it," the boy told him. "I've found someplace new. It's like camping out in the mountains."

"Okay," commented Weber. "You direct me."

Weber drove carefully and fast, the jeep taking the bends sharp and tight with minimum deceleration as it waltzed its way up the mountainside. Eric Weber had taken to the American jeep like he had taken to the uniform, the lingo, the coffee—with a mocking courtesy. And the driving made him forget that shambles of an interrogation with himself cast in the Heydrich role. Gerda Gettler's only mistake was that she looked an easy lay, and in fact was remarkably prudish—and somehow in the process she had challenged Miller's self-image, his virility. Weber's examination of her had blown a sexual fuse in his brain, induced a kind of nausea. He thought again of the "new place," some lonely Gasthaus among the fir trees, with its warm, soft bed, the windows open, and outside the wind murmuring through the fir branches and the sharp scent of pines gently permeating their tired bodies. His foot banged down again on the accelerator. He had not slept, really slept, for forty-eight hours.

Weber lay beside the boy and felt a mountain breeze breathe across the room in regular bursts, like a dynamo. It was three in the morning: beside him Johan was curled up in a characteristic attitude like a fetus in its mother's womb. The silence was total, and Weber's need to sleep was an overwhelming physical fact, yet the Inspector had never been more awake—his brain clicking like a high-speed camera, his whole body alert and taut. His whole policeman's sixth sense, and Weber had one even stronger, even more infallible than Miller's, was signaling danger in deep-etched scarlets, oranges, and reds. Quickly, silently he got up from beside the sleeping boy and put his U.S. Army overcoat on his shoulders. He went down the stairs of this empty Gasthaus with the slightly mincing stride of the homosexual that he only revealed in certain movements. It was a great shambling kind of place which Johan had taken him to. Only just taking guests for the past week or so, and managed solely by a large-bosomed fifty-five-year-old Fräulein, whose brother was missing somewhere east of Königsberg. In its prewar heyday it must have been a sizable hotel. Today only a very few rooms had been opened. The Inspector switched on his flashlight and began to give the place a going-over. He smiled grimly to himself: Miller would call it "casing the joint."

From the main building a corridor with worn-out floor boards creaked him through to an annex. In each room his technique was the same: a quick flash of light onto the china doorknobs. He would bother to enter a room only if the layer of dust on top of the knob had been disturbed.

He came up against a brown door across which the word *"Warterraum"* had been painted in Gothic script. Weber's flashlight at first picked up a lot of metal racks from which dusty old clothes were hanging. It took seconds before the light picked out the details—the Third Army patches, the U.S. campaign medals. Hanging from another rack was a less familiar collection of clothes. But they roused even more jarring notes in Weber than the American ones. There were the baggy trousers, the jackets fastened tight around the neck, the caps with their narrow peaks from which the Red Star glinted. And suddenly he was away from reality. He was in a children's toyshop in prewar Berlin, buying Christmas presents one traditional snowy winter. These uniforms weren't serious: they were kiddies' outfits, fancy dress costumes, things for make-believe and carnival.

On the floor were U.S. rifles (boys again) and two amazingly accurate life-size models of American machine guns. There was a pile of grenades and a connoisseur's collection of Russian World War II firepower.

He took up a Russian rifle and opened the bolt. A bright metallic bullet sped out onto the floor with an uncanny rattle. And the American M-1 was real enough and in good working order. The whole *Warterraum* gently reeked of metal and gun oil. There was enough live ammo here to knock out a battalion.

Weber had on arrival verified there was only one phone in the Gasthaus and that, inconveniently enough, was in the Fräulein's bedroom—a large unfurnished reception room in which the Fräulein lived and slept with her tatters of the past. Weber took out his Mauser and squeezed open her door. In a few strides he had made the phone by the window. Weber lifted the phone and dialed a number in Munich. He heard the phone beside Miller's bed ringing and ringing. And then the ringing went dead. Weber spun the dial around, but now there was no response. Weber, in anger, crashed the phone mouthpiece down on its rest. Then twisted sharply toward the sleeping form of the Fräulein. Still she didn't stir. In a second Weber was over beside her, had found the light switch beside her bed. He shook her to wake her. "This is vital," he whispered sibilantly, "where's the nearest phone from here? How far?"

The Fräulein's head rolled over the neck in response. Her neck had been twisted around and broken like a three-year-old child might have screwed up a doll.

The arrow caught him as he was running full stretch out of the house and into the thick fir tree cover. As the steel point shattered his right elbow joint, his first reaction was one of disbelief—a total blank about the nature of the projectile. The second was to accelerate—the arrow shaft flapping against his wrist, as he just made the tree fringe. The next shot was a beauty. It was shot low and on an upward trajectory. It was still rising and going like a bomb when it pierced his flesh just under the rib cage, passed through his body and literally pinioned him to a tree, with not a millimeter of space between flesh and bark.

He now knew what it was like. The searing figure of St. Sebastian in the church at Ingolstadt, and somewhere awaiting him a crown of glory or of thorns. Then a final shaft penetrated his forehead and split his cranium in two. The brain that had tracked down many a criminal, and a few innocent men, began to spill out and over his forehead.

The casualty rate of psychiatrists and other such phenomena attached with mutual reluctance to the U.S. Army had always been on the high side, and from the day Lowel Packer had been shot out of his monastic retreat and into the brawling, demonic world of Third Army politics, he had been aware that the ride would be rough. It would be an obstacle course, where the sensitive go to the wall, and the finer manifestations of the superego are snared and trampled on in this Kingdom of the Id.

But now, at the moment that the first damp, hazy glimmerings of dawn began to twitch on his oversensitive retinas, and a slight breeze blew up bearing the mingled scent of a million pine trees into the main platz of the Gemütlich health resort that Third Army Hq. had fixed on to make its very own, Lowel became aware that more was now involved than corruption or sheer bloody-mindedness. That the path along which Bedell Smith had directed his reluctant feet was more than mind-bruising, spirit-scarring, and self-defeating. It actually had unseen perils along its odor of treachery. And somewhere along that path he had effected a change of roles, from amiably tolerant, softly observant Harvard professor to fall guy in a B-movie. (He hadn't *had* to go wild on Gerda, he hadn't had to lay himself open to Major Kopp's vicious right hooks, he hadn't had to beat up an amazon and end up in a vicious leg scissors.) Or maybe he had. Lowel Packer's system of psychology had scant time for the simplistic notions of blame or guilt.

For some half hour he now realized he had literally been walking around in circles or, if not circles, at least tracing the outer lines of a parrallelogram of streets that kept on returning him to Bad Tölz's deserted main platz, while the wafting pines in the mountains above became more and more apparent. Even so, the walk had not been in vain. As a glittering autumn sun rose above the Arlberg, a circle of names, like a diadem of enigma, spanned fitfully around Packer's demented mind. Bedell Smith, Patton, Du Camp, Gerda Gettler, Kopp, Du Camp, Patton, Gerda, Miller, Miller, Miller. Where did that kind of guy hide himself? Then Packer had his first real flash of intuition of the night. Miller just had to be the inveterate bar crawler to end them all.

It was a little dive called Tony's off Kaiserstrasse, so-called because it was run by a Negro ex-staff sergeant of that name who, after discharge, had decided to stay on as a more useful adjunct to Third Army than he had ever been as a fighting member.

People met at Tony's. They met to find a screw. Or pour a bottle of scotch down their throats, or listen to Tony's cool jazz or bass or piano, or put down a cup of real strong gutsy black coffee that somehow had the aroma of Manhattan still about it. Or to pick a fight, or do a bit of gambling. Or meet a contact.

When Lowel burst down the basement stairs and into the gloom of the club proper, it took him several seconds to adjust from the feast of sun outside. He gave a nod to Tony across the bar and asked for some coffee. He took in an enlisted man whose head was buried deep in the skirts of a German lady. He took in a major snoring in a corner and still grasping a bottle of scotch by the neck. Finally he took in Wallis Du Camp. He had a figure beside him.

"Howdy, pardner," Wallis said as he saw his fellow alumnus through the gloom. "I gather you're joining the Triumphal Procession today. Should be some ball. But you'd better be all bright-eyed and bushy-tailed. Old Patsy hates a jarring note on these festive occasions. By the way, you probably wouldn't know my friend." From the black chasm beside Wallis a sprightly, neatly turned military figure stood up, saluted, and bowed. It was Major Bogamov.

"Dimitri, meet Lowel, Lowel meet Dimitri. We've just been doing some hard bargaining. Dimitri here has undertaken to get Tolbukhin to award patsyboy the Order of Catherine First Class. Apparently it weighs a ton and is covered with spangles and fake rubies. Only catch is, Patsyboy has to nose his way across the border again to collect same, and he doesn't quite share my liking and tolerance for our brave Russian allies. So it's no collect, no Cluster of Catherine. Right, Dimitri? The other trouble is coming up with something wide enough to hang round Tolbukhin's ox-like neck in return. It has to clear all his double chins."

Bogamov didn't smile. "Any testimony would be appreciated by the Marshal," he said quietly.

"Come on, Packer," continued Du Camp, "any suggestions from one of the more heroic and decorated members of Third Army? Would you rate the Congressional Award for Valor?"

Somewhere, somehow an echo crept into Packer's mind, a quote from a recent news conference that had somehow lingered in Packer's memory.

"Know what Patton said? 'Brave men died for them. All we can do is wear them.' I think that's an accurate quote, and I'd say it reflects the saner, nobler side of a paranoid personality."

After Bogamov had left them, Packer ordered two more coffees. Du Camp wasn't Miller, but he could be a lucky find. Echoes of Hollywood, words that were untypical, crept into his conversation. "Your cover's blown, Major," he said. "You may as well know it."

"Which one in particular?" smirked the Major, "I seem to have so much going on."

"Shall I tell you?"

"Go right ahead. I'll be straight with you. Whenever you hit a homer, I'll award you a point."

"Well, there's a matter of cigarettes."

"One point. But doesn't all the world love a Lucky?"

"Booze, scotch and stuff."

"Not forgetting vodka from Holy Mother Russia. Bogamov's been very co-operative, for an ally, that is. Two points."

"Hospital supplies."

"I'll argue that in the Assembly of the United Nations, and also give you three immaculate points."

"Uniforms."

"I give you a double score there, Lowel. Real nifty sleuth work."

"Plus arms."

"Heck, Lowel. This isn't a ball game, it's a walkover."

"And information, leaked to the potential enemies of America by a spy in the uniform of the U.S. Third Army. A man pretty close to General Patton and his inner circle. Information sold to Nazis, fascists, Communists, Trotskyites, anarchists, or any other interested party."

Du Camp's cherubic face was seen to glint in the half-light, as if enjoying a private joke. He then put a friendly arm on Packer's jacket. "You know the trouble about you, Lowel. You look grown up, you talk grown up, but you're still a college boy at heart. You believe in America—oh yes, America! You think the Stars and Stripes counts for more than just wallpaper. You still tip your hat to the Statue of Liberty. And you even think that Harry S. Truman's something nobler than a haberdasher's creep. You probably even rate Ike another Napoleon. Do me a favor, smoochie. You're still suffering from mental blackout. Turn on the floodlights and dance."

"Of course, you're right," answered Packer with due weight. "But I'm arguing on a strictly selfish basis. Maybe the war's over. Maybe it's time we all did ourselves a service. Maybe we should all remember we're private citizens, even though we still wear uniform. But Colonel Bob Miller doesn't quite see it that way. He reckons there's some slob at work, breaking the law and betraying his country. And Miller may be a roughneck, but he's honest about one thing. He'll deliver what he's paid to deliver."

"You mean me," twinkled Wallis. "I suppose you're right. But you know one thing, Packer—he won't unless you tell him to. Did you ever consider I can have you killed before you're even a hundred yards away from here? Come to that, I could drop you here and now."

"Yeah, I've considered that too," admitted Packer. "And I may as well tell you I'm not armed. So what's stopping you, Wallis?"

"I'll tell you what, Major Packer. I'll make you a proposition, okay?"

The visitor looked out of the apartment window at a fresh draft of GIs drilling on the parade ground. He said, "I would feel sorry for the Americans if they were not invaders of our Fatherland. They are such stupid pigs!"

Martin Sauber did not nod agreement from his armchair. "Herr Frolich," he wheezed, "you must not be so critical of our American visitors. We need them here in Bavaria. They are important to our security."

The Bürgermeister of Kolb clicked his heels. "I defer to your superior judgment, Herr Sauber: I meant only to say that in their habits these American soldiers are pigs. My daughter..."

Herr Sauber raised a white chalky hand which was sufficient to stop Frolich in midsentence. "I have been informed about your daughter, Herr Frolich. I don't wish to hear anymore of her unfortunate adventures."

Frolich's square head bowed in total acquiescence. "Now," Herr Sauber continued in a master's voice, albeit with the cracks and distortions of a pre-electric recording, "had you observed that our American friends had the mentality of children, you would have been talking better sense. The Americans have many valuable qualities, but they are children. Children whom we can help to guide and direct. But I did not invite you here this morning to listen to your observations on the American Army." The old man's eyelids flickered like a lizard's. "I am anxious only for your impressions of the American corps commander in your area. I mean General Regis Halleck."

"He is a fool, *mein Herr*."

Sauber shook his head sadly. "I see you are another victim of Herr Goebbels' propaganda machine—you are still seeing only black and white. You must try to be more subtle in your assessments. In what way and to what degree is General Halleck a fool?"

Apologetically the Bürgermeister tried to summarize what he had seen and heard of Regis Halleck's conduct since he had taken over at Kolb. He described the chaotic operations at the Coassack camp and reported General Patton's devastating reprimand. He told Herr Sauber about Halleck's sensitivity regarding the amount of U.S. equipment and vehicles that seemed to be getting lost.

A gentle gleam stole into Herr Sauber's misty eyes. "He is sensitive about his jeeps, is he? Yes, and naturally he blames the Russians. One is entitled to lay all crimes at the door of those savages. Well, Herr Frolich, we must arrange for the General to lose more jeeps—apparently to the Russians. I would like an immediate intensification in that department."

Frolich scratched his neck, a fat, creased neck

belonging to a German who for once approximated the Allied image of the typical Teutonic bully. "Herr Sauber, our resources are seriously strained. We have still to establish sufficient trading contacts in the American forces in our area. We need time and money to perfect our operation."

"Money is not a problem," the old man snapped. "But we have a shortage of time. I understand from sources who are close to the great General Patton that he is confident he could achieve victory this month, but less confident about October. You will have seen that General Marshall has announced a substantial reduction of U.S. troops in Germany. Soon our great General will be commanding only a skeleton army. You understand me, Herr Frolich. The tensions on the frontier must be increased at once."

Herr Frolich bowed and prepared to take his leave. Although he had a U.S. Army pass, it would be a long hitchhiking journey back to Kolb.

"I would like if it is possible to spare our children," Martin Sauber called to him in his reedy voice when he was at the door. "I am hopeful that it will not require the blood of our children to compel General Patton and his panzers to strike eastward."

"But our *Jugend* are still to strip the pigs of their uniforms—on both sides of the frontier?"

Herr Sauber mumbled his assent. You never knew when the uniforms of dead Allied soldiers were going to come in handy. Particularly when you were planning to provoke a third world war.

"What kind of screw is the lovely Gerda, you lucky punk?" asked Wallis Du Camp of Lowel Packer as his Mercedes eased its way out of Bad Tölz on the mountainous route to Berchtesgaden. "You know, at first I thought you just an ordinary kind of boring Harvard product. Boyo, Lowel, how wrong can you get. You seem to spend your life hitting sevens. What have you got? A great big cock?"

The difference between a staff officer and other mere

mortals was a thing of metabolism: the power to drink or whore all night, snatch a two-hour beauty sleep and come up all bright-eyed and bushy-tailed. Major Du Camp's bright chubby glowing face bore no telltale marks from the night before. His eyes sparkled with no black smudges beneath the sockets, his bland forehead had a clean, smoothed-out babyish glow to it. His white teeth and breath gave not one hint of stale Jack Daniel: his hand was steady, his pulse alarmingly normal.

Lowel felt a surge of bile in his throat, a bad rancid taste deep in his mouth, the taste of Gerda, but ten hours after the event. "What the hell are you so chirpy about?" he countered to Du Camp. "Your cover's blown sky high. I'm not an expert on military law, but I wouldn't be surprised if you'll be spending your next few years in the penitentiary."

Wallis sighed and took from his overcoat pocket an elegant silver flask. "Know what's better than cafe cognac for breakfast?" he cracked. "Cognac without the cafe. Open your eyes, Lowel. You're missing one of God's grandest production numbers. Just get that mountain greenery."

"You have two hours to start talking. This afternoon I have made an appointment with Colonel Koch. Or would you prefer me to take you straight to the tender mercies of Colonel Bob Miller?"

"Ever studied the Civil War in detail, Lowel?" said Du Camp. "It has some enlightening guidelines about the great American Character. During that war I guess there was more dedication to the duty of beating the shit out of the enemy than in any other war in history. And what happened when Johnny came marching home? I'll tell you. He reverted. He became a pioneer once more. He shed his uniform and bought himself a carpetbag. He became the most admirable of American types—the bounty hunter, desert rat, mule skinner, the redskin torturer, buffalo butcher. And that's where we stand today, Lowel. We are God's own creatures, bringing rape and ravage and the sword to the Promised Land. How does it feel, Lowel, to be an American in 1945—the year in which the great American ego got license to hunt and shoot and kill? As a man who was never in the war, how exactly are you reconciling yourself to the fleshy challenges of peace?"

"It isn't that easy," muttered Packer. "Whatever kind of soldiers we may be, we're both still subject to the military code."

"Sure. General Patton would argue that. But then he's bananas. He aims to become the first six-star general in history. But then we always knew, didn't we Packer, that Patton was plain stupid? Stupid as cowshit. Not like the slinky guys. Not like Ike, our glorious Supreme Commander. He's already hung up his uniform and put it into mothballs. His baleful eyes are fixed on Capitol Hill. He's pondering taking out a lease on the White House. And I'm aiming to follow him all the way up. Just a tip of the hat to his lovely lady Kay, and you're on the bandwagon, boy. But first I aim to fill my purse with a few ingots. Just so I can afford to make a contribution to party funds."

"I'm going to nail you for what you're doing, no matter how you argue it."

"And if you do," purred Du Camp, "I might feel tempted to alert General Patton to the fact that you've been sending confidential reports on his mental health to the Beetle. It's a nice question what he'll do to you, when he finds that out."

"What are you doing around here, Packer?" snarled Colonel Miller from his cups in Berchtesgaden's latest-closing bar. "Digging up a whole load more of that headshrinker's shit about how our gallant General is a raving psychotic?"

"I came here to tell you that you were right, or rather that famous L.A. cop's sixth sense of yours. Gerda Gettler as much as confessed it after you left. I've even got the name of the lead guy. A nice little peaceful Bavarian called Sauber, the kind who wouldn't say boo to a goose."

"Look, Packer. I've taken a good deal of crap from you in the past week or so. What are you trying to tell me now?"

"Just that Sauber's the man you want. Just that if you were figuring on paying him a friendly call, it could prove interesting. But the offer's conditional. I come too."

"And why would I need a myopic professor?"

Lowel Packer managed the next best thing to a genial grin. He said, "Seems as if you need *someone* to do your figuring for you."

Colonel Bob Miller inserted a knife into the lock of the mahogany desk and yanked it open. He systematically pulled out the little drawers, depositing their few valueless contents—elastic bands, paper clips, and pieces of sealing wax—on the carpet. Then finding nothing worthy of his interest, he tore the desk flap from its hinges. You have to break some wings when the bird has flown.

Now he sauntered moodily across the small study to look at a grandfather clock.

"Nice antique," he decided tonelessly.

"That's one constructive lesson the Bavarians learned from their Swiss neighbors," Lowel Packer said. "How to make clocks."

"Guess they did," Miller nodded. He put his hand up to the cherub-framed dial, as if to reassure himself of its value. Then he swung his boot through the glass panel that protected the weights and gilded pendulum and like a prizefighter finishing off a punch-drunk opponent sent the whole piece crashing over on its side. Another kick took care of the elaborate mechanism.

"Boy! When Herr Sauber leaves suddenly on vacation, he really cleans up," Bob Miller smiled humorlessly.

"You would have thought an old man with so much dough could have afforded some new wallpaper," Lowel Packer said. He was looking at a faded damask flower pattern with a lot of dark squares where Herr Sauber's picture gallery had hung; the picture of himself playing deck quoits on the *S.S. Bremen*, the picture of himself with Lisa as happy as peasants on a Bavarian mountain pass; the picture of Herr Sauber wearing the white armband of an anti-Red militiaman in 1919; the picture of his protégé Adolf Hitler staring luminously at the camera out of the gloom of a Munich beer cellar.

"Tear it off," Miller told him. "Tear all that damn wallpaper off!"

It came away easily, giving out an acrid smell like the smell of cat's pee. Miller joined Packer in his effortless work. At first they tore casually at the seedy décor, then a kind of frenzy took hold of them. After a few minutes they were standing panting in the middle of a totally demolished room, their feet buried in swathes of yesteryear's wallpaper.

"Maybe we've got the wrong Uncle Sauber," Packer said, grinning. "I guess I was trying to be funny," he added.

They moved back into the small living room that had a view of a parade ground with a U.S. flag hanging limply from it. Miller's assistants were working through a bookshelf like two men with a deep grudge against German literature. Right now they were studying the works of Goethe; the floor was littered with leather bindings with their spines broken.

"You know something," Miller said, sinking a pocketknife into Sauber's brown velvet armchair, "this old Kraut is not even registered as a member of the Nazi Party. And he's not using an alias, either. I'd like Bedell Smith to tell us how the hell we were supposed to pick him up when he's not on anybody's wanted list." He tugged the knife down savagely across the back of the chair, then sliced into the arms and flayed them of their covering.

"It's too bad armchairs don't talk," Packer said.

"I'm not crazy about your sense of humor, Professor," Miller reminded him.

"Or the walls, either."

"True, but you can still strip that goddamn wallpaper off!"

In the next room a corporal was butchering Lisa Sauber's bed. The place looked like a chicken farm, a heap of feathers and cotton mattress stuffing. Somewhere underneath was the mattress cover with the sweat and bloodstains of her suffering. Meanwhile a Negro GI was dredging gobs of paper out of the adjacent toilet.

Back in the living room, Miller had got hold of an

ornamental table by the legs and was smashing it against the wall. The thing split apart on the third impact and nothing fell out, but Miller went on swinging till there was only a table leg in his hand. He was beating hell out of a wall that was still saying nothing.

There remained a set of corner shelves with a number of ornaments still on them. Lowell Packer had got tired of messing up his uniform with plaster dust and had moved across to it to inspect an exquisite Dresden shepherdess.

"Oh no you don't!" Miller was on him like a panther. "This collection's my baby!" The Colonel's large hand closed around the delicate shepherdess from Dresden; his left forefinger stroked its head. Then he let the priceless piece fall and pulverized it with his foot, like the town of Dresden itself. A softly gleaming figure of Pan was he next object to be gripped by his Gulliver-sized hand. Then it was lying on a carpet without a head. A sweep of the same hand did for a Limousin plate and a collection of gold medals, prizes perhaps from some pre-1914 war exhibition. And that was the first shelf. The shelf below was a review of ceramic art over the past two centuries. Miller picked out a Bavarian lancer of the Napoleonic period and used it as a projectile to shatter a display of cupids, dogs, military figures, and children. Those that survived were broken by hand. Soon there was nothing left to break or smash, except a souvenir calendar—the kind that could be kept up to date by shuffling the month plaque and the numerals that went underneath. Miller gave it a quizzical look, then slipped it into his pocket.

"Boy, you've certainly got taste. You certainly recognize a work of art when you see one!" Lowel Packer shouted at him.

"What's eating you now, Professor?" Miller grinned. He seemed to feel he had earned another foul-smelling cigar.

"What's eating me? You mean what's eating *you!* I've just watched you destroy one of the finest collections of china I've personally ever seen. I've watched your mean, spooky, life-hating little sadistic streak cut loose on works of art that can never be replaced, and you want to know

why they can never be replaced? Because they come from
Dresden, another place we've blasted off the face of the
earth! I've watched you wreck a collection of a lifetime—I
don't care whose lifetime—for no better reason than you
like smashing pretty things up. Okay, okay, I can take
that for the sake of Uncle Sam and because I know you're
a bastard cop, but you're not going to stop me throwing
up at the last thing you did. It isn't enough for you to
wreck a collection of treasures, you've got to keep the *one*
item that happens to be worthless. A cheap, tawdry,
hideous souvenir. You're not just a barbarian, Miller—
you're a fucking pervert!"

Colonel Miller took a puff at his long cheroot, while
everybody else in the apartment stopped their work of
destruction and turned around or jammed the doorway to
watch.

"I'm sorry, Professor, but I happen to collect
souvenirs." He took the calendar from his uniform
pocket. "If you don't mind, I think it's cute." He pointed
to a painted Fräulein in Bavarian costume who was
smiling woodenly down and at the month and the date. "I
know it's not as old as the other stuff, maybe that's why I
took a liking to it. This cute little calendar is practically
brand new, just about the only thing here that is. And it's
kind of nice to know you're welcome to Weiden—that's
what the writing says, in case you can't read German,
Professor. Even if we never get to take up the offer, we can
always spend a few hours wondering why Uncle Sauber
wants to be welcomed at some two-bit town that's just
about within yodeling distance of the Russians."

"Oh sure, sure," Packer nodded without unclenching
his fists. "Obviously a vital clue; a vital clue excuses
everything, doesn't it, Colonel?"

"Another thing interested me about this cute little
calendar. Maybe you've noticed it too," Miller continued
as if there had been no interruption. "It says it's
September 22, when it happens to be the eighteenth."

"So what, he probably hasn't touched it in years."

Miller shrugged his massive shoulders. "Professor,
you've still got a lot to learn about *objets d'art*. This cute

piece of rural home craft is fresh out of Weiden. Like I said it's practically brand new. Maybe that's why I kind of took a fancy to it—that's kind of a crazy date, September 22—considering it's not today, or even yesterday. Maybe Eric Weber can tell us what goes on that's so special on September 22 in Weiden."

Eric Weber was not alive to tell them, as they learned when they got back to Munich that evening, but Colonel Miller found out a little more about the kind of things that went on in Weiden. He learned that Eric Weber's naked and punctured body had been discovered that morning on a bomb site on the outskirts of the town.

Lieutenant Luria was a kind of Audie Murphy of the air. In 243 combat missions he had blasted 126 enemy planes out of the skies, knocked some seven or eight trains clean off the rails, reduced a number of road convoys to a squelching obscenity, and slaughtered an SS panzer general as he sat smoking in his staff car.

Now an umbilical cord of pure nostalgia kept him attached to his old Mustang. It was his obsessive custom to sit brooding in the cockpit for hours on end, his fingers running over the controls, a look of vague menace sharpening the soft contours of his rabbity face.

Luria was a reflex guy pure and simple: nobody had told him, but his IQ wasn't really that hot. So he saw nothing unusual when a genial crew-cut major wandered out one afternoon to join him in his lonely vigil on the tarmac of the old civil airport of Munich.

"You must be Lucky Luria," Kopp told him as he ran his eyes appraisingly over the seemingly endless rows of Swastikas on the side of the Mustang. "No other guy around here has a score like that. Used to be a flyer myself, 'seat of the pants' kind, till they turned me into a staff creep. Sure would welcome the chance to get the feel of a kite like yours. Just to sit in her."

"She's all yours, staff creep!" Luria said as he swung out of the cockpit to let Major Kopp in. "Just so long as you don't get any screwy notion of taking her up," he smirked.

"Wouldn't be sure which knob to flick, son," drawled Kopp as his lazy, crazy eyes started to read the Mustang's baffling gadgetry.

"That's a mighty fine vehicle," General Halleck said, eying the rust-colored Russian M-26 truck. "I have no compunction about claiming it as VII Corps property. Specially since it happens to have been made in America—we gave it to the bastards on Lend Lease."

Captain Hartman's young face reddened with pleasure. It had taken nerve to sneak that raiding party over the hill into Russian-occupied Germany, even though they'd found the truck empty, parked outside what passed for a house of pleasure in Commie country.

"You know what the *good book* says," Halleck said, grinning at the blackened faces of Hartman's hand-picked raiding party, "it's gonna be an eye for an eye, or should I say truck for a jeep, from now on. I trust our so-called gallant Allies are going to think twice before they again help themselves to a jeep from my own personal CP. Right, Sergeant?" A gleaming, blood-shot eye swiveled toward Sergeant Offenbach.

Offenbach blushed like Captain Hartman, but for a different reason. Sergeant Offenbach had a friend, who had a friend in the Frolich-Sauber organization, who'd told him a jeep could earn a lot of dough provided you didn't ask where it was going. He'd never thought General Halleck was going to miss it.

In the first week of September, General Eisenhower took off with his secretary Kay Summersby on a tour of Austria and Bavaria. There was no trouble about protocol when they called on Patton's area. Unlike the skirt-hating Montgomery, George Patton had a soft spot for Kay, and always asked his chief to bring her along. This was notwithstanding the fact that on a previous visit, Summersby's Scotty, Telex, had tangled with Patton's bull terrier Willie under the dinner table.

Eisenhower was in a relaxed and friendly mood. He had just spent a few days fishing with Mark Clark in Austria. Two men quietly considering how far they'd come since they'd landed in blacked-out England in '42.

Patton, as was his custom when attractive women were present, was swearing amiably and apologizing gallantly in the same breath, and Ike was saying how nice it had been to meet up with Mark Clark again.

It was true that as they roared up to the base of the Fuehrer's aerie Ike momentarily turned pink with anger. He had seen a big sign which read "Eagle's Nest—Officers Only." But his abrupt order to pull down the snooty injunction got such a mighty cheer from the crowds of sightseeing GIs that the grin was rapidly back on his face again.

There wasn't any doubt about it. Ike was the hero of the homesick GIs who were moodily occupying Germany that summer. The anonymous letters that were daily heaped on Kay Summersby's in-tray were proof of the unique position he held in the hearts of his men. They saw him as a man apart from the officers who were desperately trying to maintain discipline with "spit and polish" and close-order drill. In fact, many saw him as a benevolent demigod who could and did intervene powerfully on their behalf from the Olympus of Frankfurt. "Please take care of yourself and General Ike," one pathetic letter to Kay had ended, "for we would all suffer in our future dilemmas should anything happen to either of you."

Meanwhile as the Supreme Commander acknowledged the cheering GIs, George Patton thought to himself, Goddamnit, the sonofabitch *is* running for President of the United States.

A few minutes later they were standing on top of the world in Hitler's former living room. While Du Camp gallantly chipped away a souvenir segment of the mantelpiece for Kay and she smilingly added her name to the mass of American graffiti on the huge oak table where Chamberlain had once sat in terrified audience, the two generals strode out onto the terrace.

"That's some view," General Eisenhower said, whistling.

"You could see how it could have turned that sonofabitch crazy," George Patton agreed.

Ike looked at the mountain peaks and said seriously,

"You know, George, it's kind of weird. We spent three years fighting this guy, hitting him with all we had. We never got to see him, alive or dead."

Patton grinned. "I always told my boys I was going to kick that bastard through every street in Berlin."

Ike said, "I always wondered what I'd do if I had to accept the surrender from *him*—I mean if I could let him sit down in the same room with me, even to sign a piece of paper."

"Well, that's one problem the sonofabitch solved for you," Patton said, grinning with his bad teeth.

"That's true." Ike grinned back. "Boy, though, he certainly had some view. I want Kay to come out here and see this."

Patton said, "A pity we only got one of the bastards."

"I don't think I follow you, George."

"You know who I mean, Ike. I mean that slit-eyed goddamned Mongol who's sitting in the Kremlin right now. I mean our loyal friend and ally, Joseph..."

Ike turned to his old friend with a look of appeal. "Please, George, don't let's talk politics now. This is a kind of—well, a vacation."

"I'm sorry, Ike, but Joseph Stalin isn't taking a vacation. That bastard never takes a vacation, never will till..."

"George, it's been a nice day—don't let's spoil it."

"Listen, Ike. I've got Oscar Koch and his boys keeping me filled in on the situation over there. Did you know, for instance, there's been an actual military buildup in the Russian sector? Across in Czechoslovakia they're crawling with T34s. And what do we do? Send eighty divisions of trained men out east to fight the Japs, and leave the defense of Europe to a batch of newly enlisted greenhorns."

"Look, George, how can I say it?" Eisenhower grimaced back. "You spent so much of your life dealing out Blood and Guts to all and sundry, you've become awkward in the ways of peace. Have you ever talked to the Russians, George? I mean really talked? To guys like Zhukov. Guys as straight as you. And then did you ever sit back and consider the twenty millions the Russians have lost in this war, the devastation of two thirds of their industry? Sorry, George, but you've almost got to be a kind of psychopath seriously to believe those guys are in any mood to pick a fight with anybody. And they're certainly not going to start a scrap with an atomic bomb. So go easy, George. A guy who's fought as hard as you has earned the right to a little peace."

"Okay, Ike," Patton said, smiling. "You've just about wheeled me onto a sonofabitch couch as some kind of nut, and that's where some people are convinced I belong. But I would like to give you a bit of vacation reading." Patton pressed a slim pink file into Eisenhower's hands. "It's just a kind of rundown on the military situation, as seen by us guys on the ramparts and outposts. It's goddamned terse, lucid, and well presented. If the argument doesn't swing you, at least it will reacquaint you with some of the hottest staff brains this side of the Pentagon."

Ike wearily took the paper and found a quick occasion to put it into the hands of Brigadier General Davis, his personal aide.

They took the zigzag corkscrew bend road down from Hitler's Eagle's Nest (the elevator that the Fuehrer had had built through two hundred feet of sheer rock face in 1938 being out of action). Ike was perched at the back of his jeep. He held on tightly as Staff Sergeant Berge swung around the bends, crashing through the gears on the eerie ride. Just in front rode Kay Summersby, Wac. Then they were past the Fuehrer's main abode, the Berghof, with a huge black gaping hole where Hitler's main first-floor stateroom had been with its twelve-foot window onto the Obersalzberg. Finally the laden jeep braked sharply to a halt in a courtyard, flanked by the concrete-structured SS barracks (the Platterhof).

The party explored Hitler's second hideaway, the Fuehrer bunker of the Bavarian Redoubt. The whole concrete rabbit warren was an almost exact copy of the Berlin prototype. Major Wallis Du Camp buttonholed Kay Summersby in the cellar earmarked for Eva Braun, as the main party trundled its way up the dank corridor, which smelled of fresh concrete and decay at the same time.

"Thanks, Wallis," she said, "for that bit of mantelpiece. It was a gallant gesture."

"Nothing, really," Wallis said, smoothly. "Just trying to ensure the Fuehrer's fireplace ended up in all the right hands before those Visigothic barbarians of our citizen army hacked the whole lot off."

"I'm keeping it here," Kay Summersby giggled, pointing to a significant bulge in the lower pocket of her Wac blouse. "It's right next to my heart, Wallis."

"Don't bluff me, kiddo," he taunted her nonchalantly, "and don't keep on flashing me that winsome side profile of yours. Sure, it's delectable, sure it's irresistible—but you're the only lady I know who keeps on twisting her neck."

Kay Summersby froze momentarily. "That's just not too gentlemanly," she hissed at him. "You come from an old family, Major Du Camp. You should know better."

"Nothing personal, honey," smoothly lisped Patton's chief aide. "It's just that I get that old balls-aching feeling deep in the night about you. And I kind of resent the way you keep looking at Big Brother. Boy, I know he's got a smile in a million, but his genius does fall a bit short of Napoleon. And come to think of it," he mused, "he's just a bit thin on top these days."

A few days after the trip to Berchtesgaden, Dwight Eisenhower and George Patton were to meet again in Berlin for Marshal Georgi Zhukov's prestigious VJ-Day parade, which was in fact a carefully staged demonstration of Russian power. The two men hardly exchanged more than a few friendly words. Ike was getting along famously with Marshal Zhukov, just as he had with Winston Churchill and the King of England, and for most of the ceremony he was buttonholed by his ebullient Russian opposite number.

Patton and Lucius Clay were meanwhile allotted subsidiary places at the fringe of the rostrum, crowded with Soviet brass who Patton, in a muttered aside to Clay, compared to "recently civilized Mongolian bandits." The only time his face showed animation was when the crack U.S. 4th Armored Division roared past. Then he stepped forward with a radiant smile and brought his hand up in a model West Point salute. He had no smile for the seemingly endless formations of Russian infantry and T34 armor. But his eyes missed no detail of equipment, training, or discipline.

Immediately afterward Eisenhower flew out for another round of triumphal receptions in the U.S. "So long, George, see you when I get back from the States. Any problems, ring Joe McNarney. He'll be minding the shop while I'm away!" Ike called cheerily to Patton on the gray airstrip of Tempelhof.

The two men were not to meet again until their grim interview of October 2, 1945.

Major Al Kopp's Mustang gained height at the rate of feet a second. The hands that had taken many a crazy crate through and beyond its paces to land in a crumpled mess of papier-mâché fuselage on the edge of some rodeo out West—these same brawny, powerful hands now took the Mustang screaming into the air like an eagle with a cartridge full of buckshot up its rear end.

Soon the U.S. Military Airport at Munich was no more than a handkerchief-sized Monopoly board thousands of feet below the daredevil Major. Kopp lit himself a Lucky and made a deep communion with the clouds, a warrior returned to his own private Valhalla. His face then registered a gawky grin as he slipped the earphones over his crew-cut quarter-of-an-inch-long sprouting blond hair. The voice he was getting was neither loud nor clear. It was positively cracking with atmosphere and static, gabbling shrilly like a speeded-up record and yet still beautifully decipherable.

"Hey, you up there," Lieutenant Luria shrilled out from ground control, "I dunno what kind of nut you are, but I'm telling you for sure man you've just hijacked yourself a gunpowder trail. Your twin rocket chambers are loaded man, repeat LOADED. You're carrying twin bombs—so watch that little yellow lever over on your left-hand side. An you've got just about enough gasoline to keep you up there for thirty minutes. CORRECTION, the way you're blasting her around, twenty minutes maximum. The only thing is that you seem to be handling her like a crack pilot, so bring back my Mustang, you bum!"

Major Kopp's expressionless Texas drawl was already answering. "Sorry, Luria. My name is Major Kopp," came the voice as low as Gregory Peck's. "If that doesn't make sense to you, I'll explain. I'm General Patton's senior military aide. And the old guy's sure sensitive about the kind of expletives some guys use against Third Army personnel. Having said that, a word of compliment. This kite handles like a desert vulture. She's sure got an interesting kind of kick. Warnings about the firearms and heavy stuff duly noted. But this is a peaceful mission. Anyway I figure you'll be keeping in touch."

It was a fine autumn afternoon. Kopp took his plane down to ten thousand feet, and there was Bavaria suddenly spread beneath him, his eagle's shadow hovering over the peaceful country. And there plumb in front of him, just discernible through the fast-scudding clouds, was Augsburg. It was a perfect day for flying, but behind the Major's grimly heroic profile, with earphones loosely bouncing against his cheek, all was not well. Up there in the gentle luminous air Major Kopp's confused, if simple, brain was working overtime to reach a final resolution of his life's work.

A kind of compass reading on the tangled phenomenon of his career. Up to now the Good Guys were the guys people had told him were the Good Guys, and ditto the Bad Guys. But now he was suddenly picking them out for himself, going beyond race, color, or creed. Like the jerk with the crackling voice, whose static-riddled ravings were still trying to interrupt the Major's simple broad chain of thought and confuse him. Like those other jerks at the sanatorium who thought that one was a nut merely because one believed that America was still a country fit for coon-capped pioneers. Like those punks from

USFET, the rodent smiling decadents from Frankfurt who were busy selling out four years of heroism to the Public Enemy Number One. Punks like Du Camp, crooked Indian settlement agents like Beetle and Ike, selling the Gatling guns to the redskins, leading the 7th Cavalry to its martyrdom at Little Big Horn.

And there were the heroes, and one especially. The biggest, the bestest for all time. A guy who would sort them out come what may. Old Glory George. With brilliant natural cavalrymen like John Wood and Bob Grow. Hadn't Uncle Martin told him these guys were greater than Guderian or Rommel? And behind Old Glory an army of simple good guys, what matter if they were aviators, Marines or SS? That was what Lindbergh had said, what Patton wanted, and what Kopp now for the first time KNEW.

And he knew one other thing: the reason why Almighty Providence had given him this weapon, this Mustang.

Twisting his plane sharp left Kopp set the Mustang on an axis that would take it past Stuttgart, hit the autobahn at Mannheim, and follow it right up past Darmstadt—the Main now a crimson snake in the hot autumn sun, beaming him into Frankfurt. Major Kopp disconnected the earphone system and started the long run in. Carefully one by one he checked the controls. This would be a classic.

America's first and last kamikaze pilot wanted to be sure he landed on target—the massive I.G. Farben building, and its population of creeps, which was now just a smudge on the onrushing horizon. He had to lose altitude fast now if he was going to make a nice tidy entrance through the front portico of Ike's palace. Boy that was close! The Army Air Corps was supposed to have flattened Frankfurt. What the hell was that building doing in his flight path? Good as he was, Al Kopp was no circus flyer, but the sharp correction he made to get back on target demanded a circus flyer's dexterity. The Mustang's angled wing tip knifed into another office block they hadn't quite managed to flatten. The plane did a cartwheel and then exploded like any crashing airplane that has failed to unload its bombs.

Al Kopp came down to earth in a wilderness of rubble on the outskirts of Frankfurt and, as a result, didn't kill anyone except himself. It wasn't exactly the epitaph he had wanted.

Captain Hartman's truck raid on the Russian Fourth Guards Army amounted to little more than a desperate Halloween prank, but its repercussions were soon spreading up the Russian chain of command. By midday a report of the incident had reached the Russian corps commander. He phoned Marshal Tolbukhin, who in turn contacted Zhukov. By late that afternoon General Bedell Smith was standing in Eisenhower's vast Farben building office, fingering a menacing note of protest from Marshal Zhukov to his American opposite number. It didn't make things any easier that Eisenhower happened to be away accepting a few more welcome homes from the grateful citizens of the United States. General Joseph T. McNarvey, Ike's deputy and eventual successor, was sitting behind his desk and feeling it was awfully big.

"So what do we do about it?" McNarney wondered.

Beetle's pale face looked grimmer than usual, and that was pretty grim. He said, "If the boss was here, I would seriously recommend that he fire George. This isn't the first incident we've had down there on that border."

"Look, Beetle, George couldn't have had anything to do with this. This is a corps responsibility. Halleck's responsibility. How's Regis making out down there, incidentally?"

Bedell Smith sighed inwardly. "In my personal view, sir, General Halleck is trouble. Maybe he's not personally to blame, but that's how it's always been. You could say he was accident prone. And that is what has been concerning the Boss and myself; we're getting the feeling that Patton is looking for an accident down that border."

"Beetle, I know George," General McNarvey pleaded. "I know what he can be like, one helluva bastard if he wants to be—but underneath he's a good soldier who obeys orders. I remember when we were planning Torch; he tried to kid me he'd screw up the whole operation if we didn't give him exactly what he wanted. Next day he was on the telephone sweet as honey."

Bedell Smith looked skeptically at the broad, honest face of General Marshall's trusted right-hand man. He said, "With respect, this isn't an isolated incident, sir, and this isn't the first legitimate protest we've had from the Russians. Just before the Boss left for the States, we got a call from Minister Vishinsky himself. Apparently the Russian Military Mission in Bavaria has evidence that George has got a Wehrmacht division at full strength down there, guys who ought to be home plowing their fields or facing a war crimes court. Minister Vishinsky wants to know what George means to do with this division, and so does Ike."

"I better talk to George," McNarvey sighed. He picked up Eisenhower's ivory colored phone and asked Kay Summersby to put him through to Patton at Bad Tölz.

"Oh, oh, more trouble," Kay's Anglo-American voice commented smilingly, "or hopefully maybe it's just a social call. Every time I connect Ike with General Patton I have to put my fingers in my ears, just in case the phone explodes."

"Yeah, maybe that's what you better do," McNarvey told her. He made a mental note that when he took over Eisenhower's job this pert and blatantly overfamiliar secretary would have to go.

"Hi, George, this is Joe. That's right, I'm minding the store while Ike's over in the States. Look, George, I was hoping to get down there to Bad Tölz to have a look at your operation; but I don't think I'm gonna make it before Ike gets back. In the meantime, I've got a pretty disturbing complaint from no less a dignitary than Marshal Zhukov."

Patton said, "Joe, I don't see what some goddamn brawl over a Mongol truck has to do with an army commander; but I'll tell you one thing—those bastards have been giving us a helluva lot of trouble up there around Kolb. Every time those peasants get stewed, which seems to me to be every goddamn night, they come rip-roaring over into our zone raping the German women and helping themselves to our military stores. Hell, Joe, it's we who should be writing the goddamn notes of protest and addressing them to the highest level!"

McNarney started to smile. He couldn't help feeling after a week in the Byzantine court of Eisenhower's Frankfurt Hq. it was good to hear the authentic no-nonsense tones of Old Blood and Guts again. Then he looked up and saw Beetle's steel-tight lips.

"I'm afraid, George, that incident isn't the only real gripe the Russians have got."

"I'm damned sure it isn't," Patton rapped back. It was noticeable that his voice had climbed a dangerous octave higher.

"They're alleging you've got a Wehrmacht division down there you haven't demobilized yet. Now if that is true, George, what you're doing down there is in direct contravention of agreed Allied policy. Every Wehrmacht unit was due to be disbanded by July. You can see how the Russians could think..."

Patton suddenly hit boiling point. "Hell, why do you care what those goddamn Russians think?" he screamed. "We're going to have to fight 'em sooner or later; within the next generation. Why not do it now while our Army is intact and the damn Russians can have their hind end kicked back into Russia in three months? We can do it ourselves easily with the help of the German troops we have, if we just arm them and take them with us. They hate those bastards!"

McNarvey thought about Kay Summersby not putting her fingers in her ears and anybody else who happened to be listening in on the unscrambled line. "Shut up, George, you fool. This line may be tapped. You could start a war with the Russians the way you're talking."

"Sure, I'd like to get it started some way," the unrepentant answer shot back, "that'd be the best thing we could do now. You don't have to get mixed up in it, Joe, if you're so damned soft about it and scared of your rank—just let me handle it down here. In ten days I can have enough incidents happen to have us at war with those sonsofbitches and make it look like it was their fault!"

It was a terrifying voice now. Superficially it was unmistakable as the voice of General George S. Patton, Jr., but underneath welled another eerie note, a chilling, pitiless cadence calculated to put any listener, or eavesdropper, in mind of all the demonic voices that had ever called down death and destruction on the world. General McNarvey hung up fast, a man stuffing back the cork in a forbidden bottle.

"Beetle, there's something screwy going on down there. We ought to get someone to look into it."

"I've got our G-2 people down there looking into it."

McNarvey forgot about his nervousness, and the sense of inferiority he felt in the presence of Eisenhower's vastly experienced Chief of Staff. "Well, you better put a rocket up their pants," he said.

"That guy's sure itching for a fight," reflected Halleck to his G-3. "What's eating him, anyway?"

"A pernicious disease called peace," dryly reflected the G-3. "Men have been known to die of it."

"That guy sure hates the Russkies," reflected Halleck as he nervelessly arranged the transfer of a glass of whiskey and soda from hand to lip.

"Yeah," agreed the G-3, bored with the conversation.

"That guy's sure breathing down my neck," reflected Halleck as he sloshed the whiskey around his mouth.

The G-3 grunted.

"What do I do? Push aggressive patrols right across the border? He wants the entire VII Corps on the alert. He's sure sore about those Russkies. And another thing, Colonel, when Georgie Patton says aggression, he means aggression. And aggression means casualties. Unless you rustle up those, he doesn't even believe you're trying."

"Wouldn't be surprised if he didn't come to see for himself," dryly mused the G-3, stirring it up.

"Jumpin' Jehosaphat," growled the General, "he'll sure be sore if he gets no corpses."

"I'll see what I can do for you, sir," said the G-3. "I'll make it all figure. Whoever Patton bawls out this time, I guarantee it won't be you."

"Hope you're right," slurred Halleck despondently, as a now familiar sensation of nausea rose in his throat.

"Alas, poor Eric, I knew him well," Bob Miller said, nodding, blowing a cloud of cigar smoke over the waxen face of his ex-assistant. "Now tell me, who's that other stiff?"

Beside him Lowel Packer shuddered, not only because of the look of the body and because it was cold in the mortuary; he was again ehocked at Miller's vulgar heartlessness, and also surprised by the fact that this Neanderthal seemed to be quoting from Shakespeare.

"That is Fräulein Huhnein," the German policeman reported with an involuntary click of the heels. "She is keeping the Gasthaus a few kilometers outside the town. We have found her this morning with her neck broken. Terrible. It is a day of shame for all of us in Weiden."

"Particularly when you're usually so *welcoming*," Miller said, grinning. "You know, I'd like to see that *Schloss*. Guess you could get a nice welcome there too."

"But you are investigating the death of your friend," the policeman reminded him with German obviousness.

"How did you guess, Inspector?"

"He is found in a bomb site, the other side of the town. You should perhaps investigate there."

"Have you examined the body, Inspector?"

"Yes, it is terrible."

"Pretty as St. Sebastian, isn't he?" Miller agreed. "But I'm not looking at those sensational arrow wounds; I'm looking at the bruising on the face and the chest. Maybe I never saw a corpse with wounds like this back in Los Angeles, but I've seen bruises like these bruises and you know what they mean, naturally, Inspector. They mean the corpse has been dumped. Maybe you'd be so welcoming as to conduct us to the Gasthaus."

They saw the bedroom where Fräulein Huhnein had died and then they made a slow tour of the carpetless dormitories. There weren't even curtains to muzzle the echoing sound of their footsteps on the bleached floor boards.

"What do we do now, Colonel," Lowel Packer asked.

"Why don't you quit following me around?" Miller didn't smile. "Nobody appointed you to my personal staff."

"You're forgetting I'm on a mission from Frankfurt too."

"You're a G-5 guy, Major. Strictly administrative. Did I ask to have you switched to a G-2?"

"You know why I'm here, Colonel, just to see your Intelligence finds out what all this killing is about, without breaking too many unnecessary things, or people."

"You know they killed my last assistant," Miller said. "Why don't you . . . ?"

"I know what you're going to say. You're going to say why don't I start tearing that lousy wallpaper off those lousy walls. And when I'm through doing that, why don't I start slicing up a few curtains or maybe smashing a collection of priceless china. Frankly it's going to be harder here, Colonel, because, no kidding, I can't see anything to smash."

"I told you they killed Eric Weber, and he was a hell of a lot better detective than you, Prof."

"I agree this institutional wallpaper doesn't really do anything to me. And who knows, it could hide the vital clue that seems to be eluding us, my dear Watson, I mean Colonel. So why don't you just let me strip it off!"

It was no good, he could stop hating Miller for five or ten minutes, then his mind would swing around to look at Gerda, sitting in that chair, and Miller bending over her.

"Am I doing all right?" he cried, surprised at the speed the institutional wallpaper came away. He helped himself to another curling edge and opened a vicious horizontal tear. "Am I demonstrating that I've got that essential streak of insensate destructiveness that earns a man the proud title of Intelligence officer? Am I proving once and for all that no patriotic American cares a fart for private property as long as it belongs to some goddamn foreigner? Am I doing all right, Colonel?"

"Christ," Miller said, "you're doing fine!"

Packer's long tear had exposed a plasterboard surface. A little more tearing showed it was a door that pushed on its hinges.

Miller struck his cigarette lighter and crawled in, a bear entering a mousehole. "Kid stuff," he said.

"Guess what?" his voice called back a few seconds later. "This hotel has more accommodations than we thought."

When Packer reached him he was holding his lighter to a clothes rack, in particular to the smock-like jacket of a Russian infantryman.

"What do you make of that, Prof?" Miller purred. "Before you tell me we've stepped on a nest of Reds, you better take a look at Exhibit B." He moved his lighter along the clothes rack. Now Packer was examining the dress jacket of a U.S. corporal with a big "A" shoulder patch. "And this is what we came for, Prof." The lighter flame moved on to another U.S. uniform. This one had no insignia. "You never met my last assistant, did you, Prof, apart from just now in the morgue? A nice guy, a good German, and not a bad detective—except he had this fixation about kids. My god, did I say kids?"

In the end there had been no shortage of suitable uniforms. In fact there had been more uniforms than kids to wear them. What Miller and Packer were looking at were only the leftovers. If they had had any kind of break, it was simply that kids tended to cover their tracks like kids.

The Shermans Are Rolling

A lonely fly was staggering across the cream-colored ceiling of the four-star General's own bathroom, the sole survivor of a private's regular DDT raid. Although he was staring at the ceiling, General Patton didn't see the fly. He saw instead the minarets of Moscow, bathed in the rosy light of morning.

Mentally he raised his binoculars and the Kremlin came into close-up. He turned to General Guderian, who was sitting beside him—not actually on the lavatory seat, but in the dust-coated jeep of his imagination. "Take a look at it, Heinz." Patton grinned to himself. "Goddamnit, you and your panzers never got this far."

"*Ja,* but will you take it and hold it?" the great German panzer General's disembodied voice boomed.

Patton writhed on the wooden seat. He had written in an unpublished poem, "in war as in

225

loving, you've got to keep on shoving." A decent crap could present the same problems.

"Take a look at the eastern suburbs, Heinz." Patton grinned painfully at his imaginary companion. "See those puffs of smoke, that's the 4th Armored Division coming in from the rear. I told you I was going to take those Russian bastards by the nose and kick 'em in the ass!"

Another shove. A whining fart. Not quite there yet.

But what was this sound? Not farts, not guns, but bells. They were ringing clearly in the General's brain. He shook his balding head; they were still ringing. Goddamnit, it was the bells of Moscow! Those ancient shrines, so long muzzled by the brutal atheists of the Kremlin, had suddenly thrown off their shackles and found their voice. The ancient bells of Moscow were ringing to acclaim their Christian liberator.

"*Mon général*, I congratulate you," Patton's French liaison officer Philippe de Forceville murmured out of nowhere, "*devants les yeux de tout le monde vous avez frappé le monstre du communisme.*"

"For us there were only 45-mm. antitank guns," Guderian murmured, twisting his neat little mustache.

"Even for Napoleon," De Forceville enthused, "*les cloches de Moscou n'avaient sonné qu'en défi.*"

The fly had made it to a corner of the four-star General's only bathroom. But Patton was looking at a lovely lady's face.

"I can pay you no higher tribute than to say you are our new St. George," Kay Summersby breathed with wide open eyes from which any shade of reserve had vanished. "Sir, you are far more worthy to wear our patron saint's sacred cross than the poor stuttering little George who sits on our throne!"

The General's tool had been lying wanly on the

lavatory seat, the one part of his body that did not respond to rigid parade-ground discipline. Now it twitched. Yes, goddamnit, even Ike would have to salute this victory, notwithstanding it had cost the poor sucker Kay!"

"Madam," George Patton muttered aloud, "my sword is pledged to your service, and to all ladies of Christendom..."

"What the hell's he doing in there?" Major Wallis Du Camp asked himself outside in the passageway. "Does he realize he's keeping the world's press waiting?"

He need not have worried. The General's final push achieved results. The whoosh of a flushing toilet signaled that George Patton was ready to meet the media, the evening after Eisenhower had lifted his ban on informal press conferences.

Captain Hartman's jeep crunched to a halt beside the U.S. infantry compound near Kolb. The bright headlights caught and played with the swaying fir trees in the evening murk, the jagged edging of barbed wire around the compound, the low rounded silhouettes of the huts. Then Hartman viciously twisted around in his seat and with one almight push of his well-polished boot, dispatched the massive recumbent figure beside him onto the dusty tarmac below. Sergeant Offenbach had been found drunk again when he was supposed to be on duty. As far as Captain Hartman was concerned, this was the last time he pulled him out of the local brothel bar without preferring charges.

Even as Offenbach hit the ground another figure caught the corner of the Captain's eye. A figure careering out of the bushes as if a grizzly was snarling up his behind. Then the Captain's cap left the Captain's head and took off on a parabola in the rough direction of the parked jeeps. As he tried to follow its progress through the gloomy air, his left elbow took a light knock, like a polite jab against the funny bone. His jacket instantly became warm and soggy. "Jesus," he mused, "if it wasn't peacetime I'd swear I'd been hit."

Then a pointed tornado of fire rushed from the adjacent line of bushes and seared its way through the intervening feet, homing straight in on his jeep like a twisting snake. As it hit the vehicle and all hell exploded in blazing pyrotechnic, Hartman found himself bent double in a ditch five yards or so from the fast-dying jeep. "Instinct," he murmured, "soldier's instinct."

"Leave those babies to me, Captain," the blurred voice of Sergeant Offenbach reassured from a fold in the ground where by a fuddled soldierly instinct he had managed to crawl. "Just give me a Thompson sub and I'll pump the shit out of them."

"I haven't got a Thompson submachine gun," Hartman howled, groping for a handkerchief to bandage his wound.

"You got a Colt, haven't you, Captain?" Offenbach suggested as the evening exploded in small-arms fire. "You give those goddamn Russkies hell!"

"Russians? You sure of that?"

"Concentrate your eyes, Captain. Focus on the darkest part of those bushes. Then raise your sights about twenty degrees," came the ghost of a professional's wisdom. "You might just see furry little Russkie heads popping up and down."

Pursued by random spurts of fire, Hartman walloped backward toward the low group of command buildings, in which he had spent an idle hour compiling a thesis on Grant in the Wilderness. As he slammed his body against the bolted door, the rifle fire started in and was soon joined by tracers from the compound area.

Hartman dived low beneath a window as a bullet exploded in his eardrum. "Chrissake shove off, Captain," pleaded Brewer's whiny voice from the window slit just above him. "This wasn't such a bad hole till you started drawing their fire."

Captain Hartman of Lafayette Military Academy lay flat on his back, his head delving into the grassy verge, and delivered his commands to a contingent behind him that he couldn't see but only sense. "These are your orders," he yelled. "When you see me go I want you out of that hut in single file and behind me. I'm heading straight for the car compound. I aim to knock out those Russkies before they knock out our trucks. Okay. Now."

Johan's narrow and effeminate shoulders were taking a battering as the Russian submachine gun cut into his flesh. He felt miserable and uncomfortable in his Soviet button-up-at-the-neck jacket. A belt with the insignia of the Red Star on the buckle only fitted around his narrow waist by virtue of a couple of standard Soviet hand grenades thrust in at the side, and digging into his stomach. Behind him Heinz and young Frolich were having the time of their lives in the U.S. convoy compound. They were grenading literally every jeep in sight.

General Patton had not responded to his emissaries: never mind. Herr Sauber had always had an alternative means of exploding his Patton bomb. He would have liked the means to have been more elegant and business-like. A Ludwig castle, a stable of Arab horses, a stipend for life or even a crown; it was a pity that ultimately the trigger had had to be a collection of grubby children in borrowed uniforms. But, of course, the end more than justified the means. The children would have to be sacrificed to General Patton's refusal to be purchased, but their sacrifice would obtain the results Herr Sauber's bribes could not buy. The opening of the prison camps, the rearming of the Wehrmacht and the Waffen SS. The liberation of the factories and the mineral wealth and the loved ones in the East. Although there was now a frontier's distance between them (for a time Herr Sauber had found it advisable to take up residence in Switzerland), he knew his general. Here was a fighter who could not fail to respond to a "Russian" attack on his border outposts.

Across the barracks area Johan saw a single figure

detach itself and run swervingly toward them. A short burst of 7.62-mm. bullets from Johan's tommy gun made him swerve and crash behind a burning truck. Then he was on his feet again. In quick dashes the U.S. officer came on, narrowing the gap between them. Each time Johan fired the sub pulled his arms with it, erratically and yet inevitably blasting off some two feet above the Captain's shoulder. Then with a final spring the man was on him. Johan choked as Hartman's Colt crashed across the back of his neck. Then he was down on the ground and the American was jabbing his forehead with the nose of the pistol.

Hartman's first instinct was to shoot him, to plug him right through the skull. But as his finger tightened on the trigger and the "Russian" flailed hopelessly beneath his knees, Hartman felt the whole of the back section of his head disappear, as if it was papier-mâché. From then on it was slow motion. Hartman noticed the crazy way he went into a head spin and finally belly-flopped his dovetail way to the earth. The way the three Russians looked at him with predatory innocence. And he also took with him to the grave the curious solemn youthful innocence with which the leader of the three took out his Tokarev TT automatic and presented it with graceful nonchalance to the bone matter guarding his brain. And the smile of this blond boy-man, as if he was shyly asking permission of his victim to pull the trigger. That was the final sensual touch, the warm eyes of the soldier, the cold touch of the snub end of the Tokarev, and the curiosity of all three or four of them as to what might happen when he pulled that trigger. All this, before the carefully set scene collapsed, and the young Captain lost all connection with that dry, ambiguous joke called "life."

"Gentlemen," General Patton ended, "if you'd care to join me in the next room, I'd be happy to answer any further questions you have over a glass of liquor. Guess I could take a drink after all this gabbing I've been doing."

There was a rush, but not in the direction of the refreshment room that had been prepared for the doyens of the U.S. press. General Patton was looking down on an audience that was making hell for leather for the nearest phone booths.

"Boy, I never saw a pack of journalists run away from the offer of a drink before," Patton quipped to General Gay, who had been sitting silent and helpless beside his chief throughout the proceedings.

"George, you've done more than offer those guys a drink," Hobart Gay sighed, "you've given them your head on a plate!"

Making for the telephone booths the newspapermen jostled and yelled to each other.

"Talk about cooking his goose—the old bastard's positively cooked it in gasoline—*en flambé,* hey!"

"What the hell did I say, anyway, Hap?" Patton was asking his wan-faced subordinate.

"This evening, September 22, at his Bavarian Hq. at Bad Tölz," Slim Allen of the Sodersheim Syndicate dictated, "General Patton issued what must be the most provocative statement in a career that has been marked, and often *marred,* by provocative statements. The General claimed to see, quote bold type, no difference between Germany's Nazi Party and our Republicans and Democrats, unquote. This amazing confession was elicited by me in a conversation with the General during which I questioned him frankly on his much-criticized soft treatment of former Nazis, notably his continued retention in office of Bavarian Minister-President Friedrich Schaeffer, a recognized Nazi Party member. New para. From the outset of our interview, General Patton showed that he remains unrepentant under the mounting criticisms that have directed against his pro-Nazi Bavarian administration, both in the United States and here among people at General Eisenhower's Frankfurt Hq. A man who perhaps among all our wartime military leaders had struck the deepest terror in the hearts of our Hitlerite enemies is now tragically revealed as the friend and protector of SS criminals and thugs..."

"Well, guess I'm gonna have a drink if nobody else is,"

Patton tried to smile with a lot of gray teeth.

General Hobart Gay and press officer Major Ernest C. Deane followed Patton to a table at the end of the gymnasium conference room. Two GIs in white coats waited in front of a linen-covered table loaded with bottles, ice buckets, and glasses to cater to the traditionally powerful thirst of the U.S. press.

"To absent friends," Patton said, grimacing as he raised a triple Bourbon to his lips.

"Friends?" Hobart Gay echoed tonelessly.

"Hell, Hap, they've gotta learn the facts. And that's all I did; told them the facts. Sooner or later people back home have got to realize they're gonna have to build up Germany unless they want to see the goddamn Russians fishing in Long Island Sound. And I'd say sooner rather than later. We haven't got a lot of time."

"...when I politely asked General Patton about the progress he was making in implementing the de-Nazification program in his area," Slim Allen continued, "his reaction was frankly contemptuous quote you must appreciate he told me quote that practically every able administrator and technician in this country was a member of the Nazi Party. Dr. Schaeffer has administrative abilities I just cannot spare and the same goes for the other so-called Nazis I am accused of harboring. Back home you don't fire a good sewage officer just becaue he happens to be a Democrat. Unquote. It was then that General Patton produced his amazing statement, certain to shock Americans of every political complexion. Quote what you are saying General unquote I challenged him quote is that most ordinary Nazis joined their party in about the same way that Americans become Republicans or Democrats. Unquote. The General agreed that these were exactly his sentiments."

"Okay, so Ike's going to have kittens." Patton was scowling into his Bourbon. "That guy is always having goddamn kittens. They should have put him in charge of a cats' home instead of goddamn armies!"

"He's called Supreme Commander, but he isn't

anymore," General Gay reflected. "These days he's got to take orders from the whole United States Congress."

Patton smacked his glass down on the table, a signal that he wanted it instantly refilled. He said, "You know, Hap, the more I see of liberal, subversive S.O.B.s like those press people, the more I regret I survived the goddamn war."

"George, you mustn't talk like that."

Very suddenly General Patton was looking like a very old man. Perhaps that tough warrior's expression had always been a conscious effort. In any case, the granite jaw was sagging badly now. The most feared Allied commander sank wearily into a chair and sat there sucking his Bourbon, like a pensioner or a baby.

"Hell, Hap," he sighed, "they're just a bunch of yellow little shits. Who's going to care what the hell they write?"

General Gay could have said, "Remember Knutsford." He meant the village where a careless word about the Russians to a few English matrons had nearly cost Patton his place in the invasion of Europe. A lot of people could care what a bunch of yellow little shits wrote. Hap Gay decided not to state the obvious.

"Guess tomorrow every goddamn paper in the United States will be howling for my blood," the four-star General finally admitted. "Tell you another thing. Nobody's going to lift a finger to help me. They don't need me anymore."

A few minutes later at the nearby Bad Wiessee press camp the press were celebrating.

"I give you George Patton, Jr.!" Slim Allen toasted. "A gallant general who died with his boots on this evening at a press conference at Bad Tölz!"

As they were drinking, the General received an urgent summons to the war room. Reports were coming in of an attack by Russian infantry on a U.S. Army compound in the Kolb district. Some officers on the Third Army staff could hardly believe their ears. But to the General himself, it sounded like the intervention of heaven, the final justification of his lonely crusade. A defeated old man was abruptly transformed into an icily decisive commander. It didn't matter that his trusted G-2 chief, Colonel Oscar Koch, happened to be on vacation in the States, or that certain key officers were absent with or without leave, with girl friends or drinking companions in the town. The plan had been ready for two months. It only needed a series of curt telephone calls to set the beautiful thing in motion. Then General Patton's personal jeep rode away into the alpine night to make news that would knock his press conference off every front page in the world.

"What the heck's going on, Kay?" clipped Eisenhower.

"Some guy Beetle's planted at Bad Tölz says George has just stage-managed the press conference to end them all—straight into the ears of those left-wing special correspondents."

Kay Summersby gave her boss a fleeting glimpse of her best (left) profile as the breeze from the fan bounced the dark curls up and down against her fine high cheekbones. "Oh dear...oh my...oh Georgie..." she droned.

"Seems he blurted out something about Nazi Party members being no worse than good Democrats or Republicans."

"Impetuous boy," she mocked.

"Why can't he follow my directives?"

"A tame Patton wouldn't be so lovable," she mused.

"Lovable or not, I guess he's hanged himself now," said Ike brutally. "Marshall's bound to want his scalp for this and Truman's going to hit the roof. I've got to do it this time, Kay," he added grimly.

"Oh dear," she sighed, "you are serious today."

Her boss drummed his hands for a moment on the huge boardroom table. His face puckered as if he was trying to overcome a difficult bit of mathematical calculating. "The only trouble is, he's still got a big following in the States. A lot of folks still think he's our finest general. It's not that easy to rub the aspirations of millions of Americans in the mud..."

Colonel Bob Miller and his team rode onto the scene too late to save Captain Hartman, but then they were aiming to save something bigger than the life of an individual U.S. officer. They were only hoping they were in time to stop the world from going to another war.

The last couple of miles of their odyssey had been the easiest. They had the sound of gunfire to guide them to their destination. They roared into the compound while it was still lit up like a fireworks display. Miller and Co. had an advantage over the defenders, scuttling about like the victims of a second Pearl Harbor; they had a shrewd idea what was hitting them. The G-2 Colonel took a quick look around him, then hurled the jeep and its blazing headlights at the line of bushes where all hell was coming from. It was suicidal, but it was also completely unexpected. The crouching figures behind the bushes started to run, and Miller was on them like some giant dockside brawler. One hammering jab to the groin put in question any further perpetuation of the ancient house of Frolich. A Joe Baksi type sucker punch, followed by a crack on the spinal cord from the butt of his automatic, came next. And trusty Heinz, Rudi Frolich's companion at the Oder bridgehead, collapsed in a sickly mess on the ground, his mouth mixing blood and vomit as his eyes flicked up to get a final sharply angled view of his despoiler. Johan had made another five yards before he fell to a breathtaking all-American football tackle performed by the scholarly Lowel Packer. "Yahoo!" shouted the Professor as he brought his Russian to the ground.

"Hold him up," commanded Miller. Spitting on his handkerchief with explosive venom, the Colonel began to polish the face of his captive. "Boy, how he cleans! Notice something, Packer," he asked grimly as the freckles and dimples emerged through the camouflage of bootblack. "No, this cutie ain't Soviet. He's genuine Kraut. All the way from those blondie kiss curls to those frozen blue peepers of his. He's one of Baldur von Schirach's blue-eyed whizz kids. Know anything about third degree,

Fritzy?" Bob Miller casually delivered an artistic karate to the nerve ends around the back of the neck. "Up in Michigan that's the way they're solving the Rabbit Problem. And just in case you ever crossed swords with an old German friend of mine called Eric Weber, here's a thought for the future." The Colonel's kneecap crunched succinctly into Johan's groin as the boy juddered to the ground.

"You're murdering him," yelled Lowel Packer. "Stop it, you screaming sadist."

"Don't worry, Major," Miller remarked grimly. "This lad's gonna live. In fact I'm going to spruce him up nice and dandy. He's going to meet some mighty classy people before the night's much older. C'mon, kid."

"Look, George, I want you up here right away. But just to hot you up en route I want to tell you here and now that I've virtually decided to put you straight on a plane home. In fact, you can take that decision as virtually final..."

He had it fine and dandy. The right words, the cold clipped voice, the brusque man-to-man tone with just a well-controlled hint of outraged friendship.

"Are you getting me that call to Bad Tölz?" he urged down the mouthpiece. "Heck, I've been hanging on here for fifteen minutes."

"Sorry, sir, there seems to be an abnormality somewhere on the line."

"Abnormality..." Ike's voice echoed.

"You see, the line's been cut, sir. It looks like Third Army Hq. is technically uncontactable..."

You might have thought it was the rumble of a distant train except for the fact that on this side of Erlangen there was no railway track. You might have said you'd never heard anything like it before, except that once you had. One spring evening you'd been shocked to see your own invincible army hurrying down from the Franconian heights, little specks at first scampering from the cotton puffs of enemy gunfire, but later, as they hurried furtively through the town, revealed to be pale-faced boys in outsize helmets, many of them staggering under the weight of adult MG-42 machine guns. Then half an hour or so later you'd heard this roar, like an express train approaching where there was no railroad track, and afterward you'd seen a vista of tanks such as you'd never witnessed outside of a Goebbels propaganda film. Once in a lifetime, you'd thought, but now here was this sound again.

You hurried to the window of what was left of your home. Could it be the Tigers roaring back in the counterattack you'd expected five months ago? Could it be the Russian's T34s you'd prayed would never come? Look, and listen again! What could you think as a burgher of Erlangen on the night of September 22, 1945, except that you were listening to the combined roar of a whole division of Pershings, Shermans, and their accompannying infantry half-tracks, and that as far as you could deduce they were heading due north to Bamberg, where they could fork left for Schweinfurt, the city flattened for the crime of manufacturing Luftwaffe ball bearings, or take the right-hand turn for Saalfeld in the Russian zone. Most of the inhabitants kept their thoughts to themselves, but some people ran out into the unlit streets with the aim of cheering and kissing the crews of this land-locked armada; they didn't have any bread or wine to offer. There was also a handful of citizens who hurried home to their transmitters to tell Marshal Tolbukhin's headquarters in Zeitz that Patton's armor was moving toward the Thüringer Wald.

No one in Erlangen could know the orders that were lodged in the fifth Pershing, where Major General Irvin Caulfield, successor to the mantles of the legendary Generals Wood, Walker, Grow and Haislip, was riding. "Irvin," Patton had squeaked at him over the scrambler, "you take the road to Saalfeld, and make all the goddamn noise you can, because that's where the Mongol bastards have got it figured I'll strike. Leave a screen up there and then creep back down to Kolb, and stand by for orders to capture Plauen for breakfast—pancakes and maple syrup courtesy of Third Army Hq.!"

Patton's armor was on the move, but as always not in the direction the enemy was anticipating.

● ● ●

Miller and Packer had no trouble finding General Halleck. The noisy comings and goings of vehicles, the cacophony of commands and countercommands made it about the best advertised headquarters in Germany that night. Miller pulled his captive straight before Halleck. The General's eyes were glowing beneath his two-star helmet.

"The Commies have dug their grave sky high," the General informed him. "I've reported back to General Patton. I've got every shred of evidence I need. I've even got eyewitnesses that can even personally tell you what regiment and division these Red marauders hark from. So now I'm personally leading a posse of vigilantes right into Russian territory with license to burn, rape, and despoil in turn."

Before Miller could reply, Lowel Packer was in front of him. "I know what it looks like, General Halleck. But you can't judge everything by appearance. Sure, you want to belive they're Russian—but they happen to be Germans. They're not even soldiers or grown men. What your eyewitnesses weren't cute enough to figure was that they were just a bunch of kids with deadly live peashooters."

"Easy, Packer," Miller interjected. "Let's unfold this one in order. You're getting my pieces jumbled. A man like the General prefers systematized thinking and presentation. You want the evidence, General? Here's one of your 'Russkies,' General Halleck. If you don't like the stink of him, it may be because he brings back old scores. And smells. Come on, Fritzie, show us how the crack Jugenders do the Hitler salute."

Halleck stood there, gaping at the boy called Johan, whom Miller had pushed before him. Veins stood out on his neck and forehead. His gray misty eyes clouded over.

"Well, sir," Miller finally prompted, "guess you'll be calling General Patton again to tell him there's been one helluva misunderstanding."

Halleck tugged at the chin strap of his helmet. He said,

"I can't go back on my report now."

"What do you mean you can't go back on that report?" Packer shrilled, regardless of the two stars on the General's metal head.

There was a long silence while Halleck wondered if he dared help himself to a slug of liquor in front of two junior officers. "The evidence is inconclusive," he stalled.

"Sir, the evidence is in front of your eyes."

The General licked his lips. Boy, how he needed that drink! "What do you think General Patton would say if I told him I'd made an incorrect assessment?" he finally snapped. "He'd tear me apart. He'd crucify me!"

"You'd be stopping a war, General," Miller told him.

"You don't know General Patton," Third Army's unluckiest general complained.

By a ferocious internal effort Colonel Bob Miller managed to retain his deference to rank. "In that case, sir, maybe you'll allow me to call General Patton myself. It's important someone calls him."

"Yeah," General Halleck mused. "Only trouble is, you won't reach him now. General Patton left Bad Tölz fifteen minutes ago . . . for the battlefield."

At 11 P.M. on the night of September 22, Third Army Hq. at Bad Tölz finally broke silence.

> *Message from General George Patton to Supreme Commander USFET* This is it. The bastards have got through our lines and are shooting up Halleck's corps Hof-Kolb area. Third Army positioned to kick the sonsofbitches back into Plauen and beyond, but demand release gasoline to minimum 15,000 gals. Enemy armor is wrong-footed Saalfield-Ilmenau-Jena triangle, but essential order USTAF strike down to clear my flank. See you in Warsaw! George.

The message reached Eisenhower and Bedell Smith with the sixth cup of coffee Kay had brought in that night.

Ike had kicked the cigarette habit a few months previously, but now he was looking into a heaped ashtray.

"What do we do now?" Ike asked the ashtray.

"That's got to be your decision, sir," Beetle said.

"Maybe I better call the President."

Bedell Smith stubbed out a Lucky Strike. "And have him call up LeMay's Superforts in Japan? You realize what that could mean?"

"Yeah—atomic bombs on Russia. Thank God that's his decision, Beetle."

"Calling the President would make it your decision, too," USFET's Chief of Staff said unhelpfully.

"Kay," Eisenhower shouted at the retreating back of his aide, "are we crazy, or is George crazy? Are we at war? Or is this just some nutty nightmare George is dreaming?"

Kay didn't answer. He realized things had got beyond the point where Kay could come up with a smiling, reassuring answer. Kay could smooth away any number of day-to-day problems, but it was beyond the ability even of this amazing woman to smooth away a Third World War.

"George may have gone nuts," Bedell Smith said, "but the fact is he's shooting at real live Russians, and Russians usually hit back."

"So what do we do, for Chrissake?"

"There's one thing you've got to do, with respect, sir." Beetle lit another Lucky Strike. "You've got to put Vandenberg's Air Force on alert and pray for divine intervention before 4 A.M. this morning."

It had lasted a heck of a long time. Now he had a feeling, as he had hinted in letters to friends in the States, that his luck was running out—at last. Luck was important to George Patton; it was the outward meaningful manifestation of the will of fate. That still small voice. That was why he was where he was now, perched high atop an M-20 command car, his hand restlessly rotating its machine gun, his face scowling beneath the sheen of his four-star helmet. Personally

eading the flurrying onslaught of Shermans on that deft
eft hook that could carry them through wooded terrain
o debauch finally in the area of Plauen. Here he
lismounted to help release a Sherman that was stuck in
he mud, there he gave a bawling out to a colonel whose
nen were behind schedule. If this was to be his last battle,
ne would lead it personally himself—as ferocious, as
vulnerable as Murat. Prepared at any moment to unleash
a hail of bullets into any Mongol or slit-eyed Caucasian
who was fated to cross his path.

Third Army was on the move again, but it was not the
irresistible torrent it had been in the spring. In April 1945,
when it had stood at the gates of Prague, halted only by
Eisenhower's orders, it had numbered no fewer than
twelve infantry divisions, six armored divisions, and three
cavalry groups representing a grand total of nearly half a
million men. Five months had sapped a mighty force to
half its strength. Only three weeks ago the General had
had to bid a fond farewell to his beloved Sixth Armored
Division. The Shermans and Pershings and half-tracks
that were squeaking through the night toward Plauen
belonged to the Lucky Third's remaining three under-
strength armored divisions. In Patton's own words, Third
Army was now "rather a group of soldiers, mostly
recruits, rejoicing in a historic name."

If Patton's armored spearhead had been heading
straight for Tolbukhin's T34s, it could only have been
blasted to fragments, but on the night of September 22,
1945, Marshal Tolbukhin's armor was concentrated fifty
miles to the north in the Jena-Saalfeld-Ilmenau triangle.

Exactly what was going on in Marshal Tolbukhin's
mind is still a matter for speculation, but two factors were
obviously influencing him. One was Major Bogamov's
confidential report on the dispositions he had spied in
Patton's map room. The other was the series of reports
now reaching him that Patton was moving north along
the Erlangen-Bamberg road.

General Patton had gone back to school to study his
heroes of the always outnumbered but always outsmart-

ing Confederacy, and as a result he had bought himsel
four precious hours—maybe more, if Vandenberg put i
his rocket strike—to smash through the Russian infantr
and hook around to Jena to shoot off Tolbukhin's ass

The wooded mountainous country was not ideal fo
tank deployment; but neither had been the Ardennes
where Patton had raced to the rescue of Bastogne. Fo
four hours at least there could be nothing to stop Ol
Blood and Guts. Not even General Eisenhower himsel

The Longest Night

"Major Wallis Du Camp of Third Army Hq.," General Bedell Smith announced without getting up. "He's just flown in on his own initiative from Bavaria."

In the doorway of Ike's boardroom office Du Camp gave his Supreme Commander the snazziest salute he'd thrown since the end of the war in Europe.

"I know what you're going to ask me, sir." His eyes were as bright as a West Point cadet's on graduation day. "You're going to ask what the hell's going on in Third Army. I wish I could be more precise, sir, but briefly the situation is that the Archduke Ferdinand has been assassinated, and the Emperor Franz Josef is howling for Slavic blood."

"What's this guy talking about," Ike snapped at the Beetle.

"I was using a historical allusion, sir," Du Camp said, smiling tolerantly. "I was referring to the causes of World War I and suggesting that history could be about to repeat itself. I was comparing the reported attack by Russian forces on a U.S. camp near Kolb—drunken scavengers, if

I know our heroic ally—to the Sarajevo assassination. By the Emperor Franz Josef I meant, of course, the gifted but wayward commander it's been my privilege to serve."

Ike looked at the staff officer with an expression that, if photographed, would never have been released by his press office. "Major, if you've got any factual information to report, I want to hear it. Otherwise you better scram."

Du Camp flushed. He had often thought that his urbane style would be even better appreciated in the sophisticated Frankfurt "Court" than it was at the harder swearing throne of King Patton. In fact, as he had watched his boss gleefully unleashing the thunderbolts of war, it had occurred to him that it was high time he switched allegiance, preferably before anybody found out about his commercial relationship with Martin Sauber. As he figured it, his midnight flight could only be seen as an impulsive gesture of loyalty to his Supreme Commander. He had reasonably expected to be welcomed with open arms if not highballs.

"Facts are vital, sir," Du Camp said, smiling a little less confidently, "but there is also the background. I'd like to try and fill you in on that. For three months now, General Eisenhower, we've been sitting on an emotional powder keg down there in Bad Tölz. It's been our sad responsibility to watch a great general gradually losing contact with reality. We've watched the dangerous sycophants breed, and we've seen the men of integrity and sense progressively banished from the counsel chamber. We've..."

"I asked for information, not self-justification," Ike cut him short. "You'll appreciate we're pretty busy here right now. You are dismissed, Major!"

"You know something, Kay," Du Camp brazened when the door had been closed on the desperate decision makers, "your boss doesn't seem to like me." He put a chummy hand over Kay's brand-new silver captain's bars. "Considering I've blown the whole Mad Hatter's tea party, at least twenty-four hours ahead of that Keystone cop Colonel Bob Miller and the absent-minded professor

Major Lowel Packer, I think that's pretty ungrateful. But then, honey, I guess your boss is human like the rest of us. He can't forget catching you and me together that afternoon in Berchtesgaden." An after-shave-scented cheek cozyed up to the Wac Captain. "Tell you something, my beautiful British baby, your boss isn't going to be around much longer to get pink with jealousy around those cute bulldog jowls. Your boss is paid to keep George Patton on a leash. And look what's happened—the mad dog is loose and biting."

With the polite firmness of a former female chauffeur, trained to handle lecherous staff officers as easily as a wheel, Kay removed the comradely hand from her shoulder. "Major Du Camp," she said, smiling elusively, "your trip to Frankfurt tonight could just have saved you from a court-martial. Or maybe you didn't know you were under investigation for mismanagement of U.S. Army property. I wouldn't push my luck if I were you, soldier.'

The armored group, which had just suddenly ground to a halt thirty miles north of Kolb, stretched back some twelve miles. It comprised upward of a thousand tanks—gleaming new Pershings, battle-scarred Shermans that had undergone a new peacetime coat of paint. It was the rear end of this long column that Miller and Packer were now busily engaged in circumnavigating.

"It's a moment in history," commented Lowel as Miller took the jeep into the ditches in a frenetic attempt to outflank the snake of armor that had somehow gone to sleep on the road. "And if we live through this, we can say we were there. The moment when the whole world went haywire."

But Miller didn't reply. Under his hands the jeep became an exercise in hairy driving skills, egged on by the GIs in the tanks who wisecracked and the tank commanders who swore. Looking for a general in a haystack of armor.

● ● ●

General Mauder, senior German officer in Detention Camp 23 at Landshut, saluted the U.S. Camp Commandant with minimum deference. This was not only because the Camp Commandant was a mere colonel, nor just because he happened to be a Jew called Gluckstein; information had reached the General which indicated he could safely begin to resume his old arrogance.

"Colonel Gluckstein," he said, smiling thinly, "I understand you may shortly have more important work for us than cultivating vegetables."

Gluckstein hadn't swung his feet off his desk or stubbed out his cheroot for the German general. "I don't know what you're referring to," he said, trying to look as bored as he usually looked when he was receiving high-ranking German officers.

"I think perhaps you do, Colonel," General Mauder told him confidently. "As I understand it, your orders can have left you in no doubt."

"I'd be fascinated to know where you get your information from," Gluckstein said, trying to look as bored as hell. In fact he was looking miserable.

"Colonel Gluckstein," the German deliberately avoided pronouncing the name with a sneer, "you must know that relationships between Third Army Hq. and the German authorities are rather more cordial than they are in this camp. There is an atmosphere of sincere harmony at Bad Tölz. Victors and vanquished are beginning to work in profitable partnership for the sake of Germany and Western democracy. As a senior officer of the Wehrmacht I should be informed of orders that will shortly place me at the head of my men in the field of battle."

"Okay," the Camp Commandant drawled, "security may be lousy in this camp, and there may be a limit to the kind of discipline I personally would like to see enforced. But my orders are my orders; and I'm not going to have any sonofagun in jackboots tell me what they are."

"You misunderstand me, Colonel."

General Mauder gestured toward the canvas chair in

front of Gluckstein's desk. He wasn't invited to sit down. "My point in seeking this interview was simply to state that since by 10 A.M. tomorrow morning we shall be mobilizing, you may wish to discuss details of the arming of my troops."

"You're not getting your hands on one peashooter till I get the green light," Gluckstein sighed.

"So, Colonel, at least we agree that you have orders to begin arming my division at 10 A.M. tomorrow morning."

"And not a moment before, General. What's more, they are subject to confirmation by Bad Tölz later tonight."

"Colonel Gluckstein," General Mauder said, deciding to be seated anyway, "isn't it a pity at a time like this to quibble about matters of detail? You must be aware that your great General has long foreseen the remobilization of my division. My understanding is that it is for this reason we have been detained, or should I say maintained, as a complete unit, whereas of course the normal custom is to accommodate officers separately from the men. In fact, if General Patton needs the 43rd Infantry Division, isn't it advisable to waste no time in placing us at his service?"

"Listen, General," Gluckstein said, "I've seen what you guys do with firearms. I'm also familiar with the kinds of targets you like to choose—helpless Jewish kids from Warsaw, old ladies, cripples—and so help me, babies. I'm not going to put one gun into your bloodthirsty hands one moment before I'm ordered to. Is that clear?"

General Mauder smiled glassily. He said, "It is a pity you should take this attitude, Colonel Gluckstein, when by the morning we shall be allies."

In life there is usually a fall guy, and if there was one in Patton's masterstroke, it was the intrepid General Karels, halted to await further orders outside Bamberg, and about to be elected by destiny for an imperishable place in the scrolls of patriotism.

Destiny approached in the shape of a command car

with its headlights on bright. "Are you a cavalryman?" the ghostly outline of Old Blood and Guts himself was suddenly piping at him.

"Sure am," the Minnesotan General volunteered, "from the day I entered West Point."

"To be more specific, are you a horseman, I mean the kind that doesn't run on gasoline? Have you actually got your butt atop a saddle? Or are you one of those so-called Ford-mounted horsemen?"

Karels assured him that he had even played polo.

"Karels," Patton said, grinning, "you've just grabbed yourself the finest cavalry assignment in history. Last year I ordered General John Wood to go like a bomb for Brest. This year I'm ordering you to liberate Germany."

The plan sounded simple. While the full weight of Patton's armor headed south to throw the main punch through Hof-Plauen, Karels' force would head straight on up the road to Saalfeld, where Tolbukhin was massing to meet him. All he had to do was to swing around the Russian left, give a tip of the hat to Jena, crash through Naumburg and link up with the main force to take in the rear of the Russians trapped in the Plauen triangle.

"See you guys in Zeitz," Patton called cheerily as he sped away to a rendezvous with his private reconnaissance aircraft.

Karels didn't see the tears that were welling up in the Old Man's eyes. The truth was that this gallant young officer would need to be a superman to reach Zeitz alive. But someone had to keep Tolbukhin busy around the Saalfeld area while Patton cut off his ass.

The darkness was shattered with cries of officers issuing nervously confident orders. There was an incoherent burble of radio sets in the night air. Around the compound flitted the shadowy figures of U.S. infantrymen, pulling on combat jackets, cramming steel helmets onto their peacetime helmet liners. Sergeant Offenbach decided he could afford to ignore it all. He had already seen all he wanted of the Third World War;

besides, his officer was dead, and he had had too much to drink for heroics. Danziger, Brewer, and the rest were crowding around looking to him for orders now.

"Okay, you guys," he muttered, "you've had your first taste of real combat and if you're the yellow, stinking, pants-shitting lot of bastards I think you are, you won't be looking for any more. Christ knows what's going on around here, but I'll tell you one thing—this goddamn army has got itself into a shooting war, and we're in the lousy front line."

He didn't have to emphasize the point. The medical corpsmen had finally got around to collecting the casualties of the brief encounter with Hitler's *Jugend*. As Sergeant Offenbach was speaking, Ned Cohn was passing on a stretcher screaming as if his face had been shot off, which in fact it had.

"So, who's volunteering for the privilege of being the first goddamn outfit to get shot to hell by the Russians?"

Nobody said anything.

"Okay, who's volunteering to get the hell out of here?"

There was a murmur of approval. Pfc. Perry Brewer said, "Wouldn't that be deserting, Sergeant?"

"Who's talking about deserting?" Offenbach asked, grimacing. "I'm just suggesting we do a reconnaissance backward. If you weren't such a green rookie, you'd know the first rule of war is make goddamn sure you're not in the first wave."

As Halleck's corps began to move forward, Sergeant Offenbach and company began a slow retreat.

Moving ahead of the mass of his infantry, General Regis Halleck had now set up his headquarters in the main square of Hof. This way he could keep an eye on the enemy from whichever way they came. In fact, Hof would soon be an armored fort, protected from attacks on all sides. Now that these dispositions were made a curious sense of security began to creep over the old warrior. It was comforting to watch the battalions of puzzled-looking GIs tramping into town. He hadn't fully appreciated just how many bayonets he'd gotten to protect him from the Russians, General Patton, Colonel Bob Miller or any other troublemaker. He was pouring himself a deserved slug of Bourbon when some fool aide came rushing in to inform him that General Patton had managed to make contact on the field telephone.

"Regis, what the hell are you doing in Hof?"

"Guess I'm poised to lick hell out of those Russian bastards, sir," Halleck sighed.

"You're not reading my orders, Regis. You better get your goddamn map and explain what the hell you're doing in there."

In fact, it was Patton who did all the explaining. "So you see what I mean, Regis, the sooner you get off the main road and into the goddamn woods, the sooner I can pass my armor through Hof, and rid the world of Mongol bastards!"

Regis Halleck pondered the map his commander had so considerately explained to him. Then he saw it all with blinding clarity. He bent over it with a twinkle in his bloodstained eye and opened his mouth. The most succinct campaign since Vicksburg disappeared beneath an onslaught of vomit.

Lieutenant Clive Greenfield of General Harrison's armored division had missed the war in Europe by two months. The nearest he had come to commanding a Pershing tank in battle had been the armored maneuvers at Fort Benning in March 1945, when Greenfield and his command had been called upon to attack an artillery position using live ammo to simulate the real thing.

He had been unlucky, or perhaps lucky, not to get transferred to the Pacific, where there was still a fanatical enemy to fight. In fact, the War Department in its wisdom had dispatched Greenfield's outfit to a vanquished Germany. For three months Clive Greenfield had been adjusting himself to the long, boring peace his training had hardly prepared him for. Then suddenly, less than a day ago, Greenfield and his pals had returned from a coach tour of Berchtesgaden to find the whole division on a war footing.

Now burbling at him over the Pershing's intercom was a stream of tensely worded orders. Some of them emanated from his divisional commander, others from Third Army Hq. itself, others were the strictly tactical instructions of his own unit commander.

Where exactly they were heading and who precisely they were going to fight was still uncertain, but Lietuenant Greenfield had clear orders on one point. Any units coming in the opposite direction down this road would be hostile forces and were to be treated as such.

Sergeant Offenbach and his men had bowed out too early to be aware of the corps's orders—namely to advance across open country, leaving the roads clear for the tanks. To Sergeant Offenbach's practical mind, the simplest way backward was down the nearest road, and this is where he was leading his battle-weary flock.

Pfc. Brewer was uneasy. He kept asking Offenbach if he was sure they were doing the right thing, whether some brass hat wasn't going to come suddenly roaring around a corner and have them all shot for desertion in the face of the enemy—he had heard what happened to GIs who'd chickened out of the Battle of the Bulge. Sergeant Offenbach ignored him. His mind was on other things and other places. In spirit at least, Sergeant Offenbach was going home. Funny thing, for four hard years he'd hardly missed his fat, frumpy wife home in Indiana or his two teenage boys. Now he saw himself stepping off the bus by that old tin mailbox and walking up the dusty path that led to a clapboard bungalow called home. *Kiss me once and kiss me twice, and kiss me once again, It's been a long, long time.* Yes, it was time to go home. Now while you still had two legs to walk on, and your duffle bags were still stuffed with all the greenbacks you'd earned with Uncle Sam—and Bürgermeister Frolich's gray market in military supplies.

They knew they were vacating a battlefield, and that's how they were moving; not straight down the center of the road, but hugging the side of it. The furtive way they seemed to be advancing was a key reason that led Lieutenant Greenfield to grab his turret-mounted machine gun; this and the fact that in the darkness American steel helmets can look awfully like Russian steel helmets. The best thing Offenbach and his men could have done was probably to keep on walking. What Offenbach did was nothing for a vital fifteen seconds as the tank column closed on him and then he shouted, "O-kay, you bums, take cover!" This semeed to clinch it in Lieutenant Greenfield's agitated mind. Infantrymen hurrying for cover from American tanks had to be Russians. Suddenly Offenbach's bulky body was a magnet to a load of hot metal. Then the tracer stream switched to Pfc. Brewer, who was shouting at Greenfield to stop, and turned his unheard mouthings into a scream of agony. Another burst tore off Private Larsen's nose. He reached out for it in an absurd gesture, then doubled up as the rest of the burst ended the possibility that he would have to go through life with a grotesque disfigure-ment. A few rookies managed to make it into the pines. Others found that a fringe of bracken was insufficient protection from the arcs of flaming machine-gun fire that were now sprouting from three Pershing tanks. Corporal Danziger managed to roll into a fold in the tormented earth, even though he had taken three slugs in the stomach. From here he had a fine view of the scudding clouds and the pine tree tops. He thought it was a pity he was dying, especially since he couldn't understand why.

"Where is the crazy old bastard?" asked a red-faced Ike. "Isn't he contactable anywhere? And why the heck didn't I bust him months ago?"

Silence. Just silence.

"There's nothing for it, Beetle. I've got to press the alarm switch."

"That'll be Marshall, Secretary Patterson and Tru-man, in that order."

"Yeah," answered his Supreme Commander. "And

you'd better throw in Tolbukhin and Zhukov for good measure, or we'll be getting a Soviet air strike around Frankfurt."

"Rather you than me, Ike," said the Beetle with one of his rare and menacing essays toward the art of humor. But six minutes later he had some better news—the chance of a phone call in which his boss could return to the more genial role of predator, rather than tight-lipped suppliant.

"We've just hit on a weak link," he excitedly told Ike. "I've kept G-3 hot on it all night, and they've actually got an answer. Some guy in the Third sent hello back to us. If you lift that phone now, sir, you'll be straight through to Halleck in Hof." He turned to offer his general the instrument with a deprecating smile, but Ike's big hand was already gripping the phone. The hand at the other end of the line was by now in an advanced state of rictus tremulens.

"He'd bust me for this," an incoherent voice rasped into the Supreme Commander's right ear. "But how can a general refuse to speak to his superior general? I mean . . ."

"Look, Halleck," came Ike's voice, now grim and purposeful. "This is General Eisenhower, Halleck. This is your Supreme Commander talking to you from Frankfurt. Your Supreme Commander, Halleck." The old Ike was back in control, the voice clipped and charged with quiet purpose, friendly and yet somehow not. "And I'm personally taking active operational command over the Third Army."

"Old Blood and Guts . . ." trailed Halleck's voice. "He'll crucify me unless . . ."

"General Patton, for the moment, is also under my command," Ike reassured him. "But here are my orders, Halleck, and they're irreversible. First, you keep in constant fifteen-minute contact with my personal G-3 here at USFET, Frankfurt. Failure to obey this command will result in instant dismissal. Second, you place your corps along your assigned section of the frontier in full battle order, prepared to oppose any frontier infringement from wherever it comes. From either side, is what I mean, Halleck. That means the Russian side, or the U.S. side. Your force will intervene itself, like some kind of peace-keeping force."

"But General," slurred Halleck's Bourbon-heavy voice as he puffed noxious fumes down the telephone mouthpiece. "My men are in full action order..."

"Great," cut in Ike.

"Very enthusiastic. And very keen to get a few Russkie scalps. But if you order me different..." The voice came to a halt and then the line went dead on the Supreme Commander as, for the first time in ten years, someone put a phone down on him.

"Someone's got to get down there fast and take immediate tactical command," snapped the leader.

"There's only one man with the personality to do that," theorized the Beetle.

"So I want you to grab one of Vandenberg's planes and take over first Halleck's corps, then full operational control of any Third Army units that haven't yet gone around the bend. And hold the line, Beetle. If you fail, there may well be no future for any of us."

The Beetle's immaculately filed nails for a second drummed against the desk top, then he spoke up. "Normally you'd be right, Ike. But as you say, this is literally a critical moment in the world's history, and I'm not that sure I've personally got what it takes to ride this particular situation. And George, it's well known, hates my guts. He'd probably shoot me."

There was a minute's silence as thoughts speeded with computerized logic and speed behind Eisenhower's genial puckered brow. Then he put an arm on his loyal staff man's shoulder. "I know what you're trying to say, Beetle. And gee, yes, I'm complimented, but," the voice started to gain a harder edge, "there are good reasons, historical reasons, why you've got to be the man of the hour. Besides," he flicked across a boyish smile, "I've got a little fighting to do on my own account, back here in Frankfurt. In fact, by the look on her face Captain Summersby seems to have gotten that call through to

George Marshall, who may just be wondering how come my armies are busily engaged in starting off a Third World War."

In the immediate foreground a posse of Shermans had cut an aperture into an ancient Bavarian pine forest and cauterized a covey of tender saplings. A tortuous maze of tracks had bitten deep into that rich dark soil. Now the support vehicles were following the virgin track—trucks, jeeps, troop carriers, half-tracks, tank destroyers, antitank guns, howitzers. The noise was like some kind of syncopated, never-ending racing meet, but to Captain Hank Holliday's trained ear, there was still one vital internal-combustion clue missing. On this clear autumn dawn, with just a thin ground mist that the Austerlitz sun was busily dissipating, there was one comforting element lacking. The high altitude hum of the Fortress engines, the low daredevil swoops of the Mustangs with their slaphappy pilots hopping the fences, brushing the tips of the trees, and shooting the shit out of anything that moved below. To an experienced man like Holliday there was just this one jarring thing to mar the élan of the dawn, and his gray eyes lazily scanned the sky and wondered when the Nineteenth Tactical Command would be swooping on its way.

But high above the tanks' murmurings and reverberations there was another, higher, purrier sound. First he saw it flashing behind some fir tops, then turning above them in the sky, height about eight hundred feet and fast gaining alitude. It was a gray, metallic, graceful thing, a civilian plane with U.S. Army Air Force markings—a millionaire's plaything from Long Island, callously drafted for military service. The plane went east to take one final look at the pullulating anthill of tanks in that primeval Teutonic forest, then turned reluctantly southwest to begin an ascent toward the distant outline of the Erz Mountains. General Patton was now airborne, watching his columns advance from clouds of pink morning glory.

Miller and Packer caught up with Holliday five minutes later.

"For Chrissake, someone lead us to General Patton."

"I'm getting the notion Old Blood and Guts is busy," drawled the Alabama Captain.

"Don't you understand?" yelled Packer. "If you cross the frontier, it will be a direct violation of Yalta and Potsdam!"

"One thing's for sure," said the Captain, "it ain't another vodka binge. I saw Old Blood and Guts an hour ago. Looked like his old self—real mean."

"We've got to find him," yelped Packer. "It's literally a matter of life and death—for the whole world, maybe. Which way did he go?"

"Know something," drawled Hank Holliday, "he's floating on air. He's communin' with the stars." And his gray eyes trailed nonchalantly upward toward the opaque blue sky.

"I'm gonna shatter you, limb from limb," yelled Miller. "And then I'll put the pieces together and have you dismissed for insubordination. I'm not joking, Captain."

"And I'll have you arrested and shot, Colonel," gently riposted the Alabaman, "as a Red spy."

"Say," the Captain had caught sight of the boy Johan, still in Soviet uniform, pinned between two burly MPs in the back of the jeep, "that's a Russkie you've got there, isn't it?" A Colt automatic leaped from his holster. "Always wanted to shoot myself a real live Russian skunk."

"Don't kill him, or we haven't got a hope in hell!" Packer cried.

"Like Russkies, do you?" the Alabaman said, grinning on his chewing gum. "Nigger-lovers, Russkie-lovers—guess you're all the same." The Colt muzzle switched to Packer's stomach. "You gonna stop me drawin' a bead on that stinking Commie punk?"

Miller's express-train fist put an abrupt end to this menacing dialogue. As Holliday rolled about in the grass swearing through his splintered teeth, two of his men came forward with probing rifles. Luckily there was enough light for them to take note of Miller's insignia and slink back again.

"Now I'm gonna ask you nice and polite where General Patton is," Miller bellowed down at the writhing officer. "If I don't get a courteous answer, I'm gonna kick out your guts."

"Like I said, he's up there in the bright blue yonder."

"He's got to come down to earth somewhere."

Then Holliday yelled. Colonel Bob Miller had never had any scruples about kicking a man when he was down. A lot of four-letter words poured out of the agonized Captain, but there was one with three leters—the place name of Hof.

The jeep did a raucous turnaround in the forest clearing and hit the road again in search of a General Patton who was here, there, everywhere, and nowhere.

In the back of the jeep the boy Johan fainted again as blood ozzed from his roughly bandaged forehead.

A G-2 captain was standing at the door of the pulsating scout plane, trying to salute in the slipstream. "Something screwy's going on at Hof, sir," he shouted.

"What kind of screwy?" Patton wanted to know, tugging himself out of the Piper cub.

"It's Halleck's corps. My reports are that they've moved back onto the three main roads out of Hof."

"How many times do I have to tell those sonsofbitches their job in this thing?" thundered Patton. "I want them out there on their hands and knees in the forest. Foraging, cleaning out the position, digging out Ivans from their foxholes and getting their goddamn butts out of the real action."

"I know, sir," the Captain apologized, "but they're there all the same. Since the last half hour, that is; the 3rd Armored can only be a couple of miles away. There's gonna be the most godalmighty fuck-up."

●　　●　　●

General Harrison's crack armoured division was pounding up the surface of the windy road that led from Kolb to the frontier village of Hof. The incoherent roar of their Pershing T25, the supertank that had almost missed World War II—heavier, more thickly armored than the ubiquitous Sherman—was bracing itself for an encounter, often imagined but never before realized. The crump of U.S. armor against the crack Russian T34s, that Armageddon of men and material to end them all. And now there were just a few miles to go—then the rapid plunge over the border.

Then over a summit the leading Pershing saw the folksy silhouette of Hof's church, sending out sharp pinpoints of refracted light in the shimmering autumn sun.

"Remember orders, you guys," the leading tank commander reminded his men. "Don't loiter around Hof. We're going straight through. And out the other side. No Fräuleins. No fraternization. We've got a war to fight."

The roadblock when they came to it was a makeshift affair. A few busted-out jeeps and trucks, upended along the road, covered by barbed wire, from which an occasional M-1 peeped. Behind them were groups of troops drawn up—American troops.

The leading Pershing crunched to a halt. Other tanks came up beside it, their guns swiveling around to bear on the roadblock.

"Obstruction fifty yards ahead," the leading Pershing commander informed his divisional general. "And soldiers in American uniform. They could be okay—and then they could just as well be Russians. Seems a lot of funny guys have been changing uniform around Hof."

Back came the orders. "If they're Russians, shoot 'em. If they're genuine Americans—clear them out. That road's meant to be clean as a fairy's asshole!"

Patton's binoculars were resting on a distant line of fir trees. These were Russian-held fir trees. And thinly held at that. No tank guns were sprouting from this neck of the woods. There was just a little smoke over to the left, which designated the field kitchen of a single Soviet infantry battalion.

This was the promised land. So close you could almost reach out and touch it. Then the binoculars traveled downward to focus on a far more strongly manned line of defenses: Halleck's corps with orders not to let anybody pass.

General Harrison said, "Of course, we could rush through and out. It wouldn't take much to elbow this bunch of rookies aside."

"Sure we could," Patton said, "except I've never in my life given orders to fire on my own men."

"Why don't you talk to them, sir? They'd listen to you."

"Maybe in time they would," Old Blood and Guts sighed. "But time is what we're running out of."

"Short of shooting, what else can you do, sir?"

"Lord Jesus give me strength," General Patton prayed.

They got into the scout car and drove down the narrow road toward the upturned truck that represented the nearest strongpoint in Halleck's defensive system. George Patton got out under the muzzles of a dozen or more trembling Garands and walked with swinging riding crop toward the barricade.

"Know who I am, Sergeant?" he said, smiling fiercely at a young man from Iowa.

"Yes, sir, you're General Patton."

"Know who your commanding officer is?"

"General Halleck, sir."

"Wrong, soldier—it's me. In case nobody told you, I happen to be the commander of Third Army."

"Yes, sir."

"In that case, Sergeant, you may care to tell me why the hell you're facing the wrong way?"

"Sir?"

"And not only that, goddamn you. I'd like to know what traitorous sonofabitch gave you orders to get in the way of history!"

If looks or vocal chords could kill, the Sergeant from

Iowa would have been dead. He survived to murmur, "General Halleck, sir."

Patton consulted his watch. In his book, time equaled men. He knew that every precious minute lost meant extra casualties, and, if time continued to run out on him, ultimately ruinous defeat.

"Sergeant, let's do a little simple arithmetic," he tried again. "How many stars does General Halleck wear?"

"Two, sir."

"Now maybe you can count how many I have—*four,* damn your hide, you blind bastard!"

"Yes, sir." The Sergeant smiled politely without making any effort to sling his rifle.

A jeep had detached itself from the tank armada at the top of the hill and was approaching them in a cloud of dust made radiant by the early morning sun.

Two bedraggled U.S. Army officers, supporting the semiconscious Johan between them, looked at first sight like a trio of late night roisterers. But Patton's eyes gleamed with an ecstatic kind of tolerance.

"Look!" He turned to the terrified Sergeant. "Can you recognize a Russian uniform when you see one? Good. Now maybe you'll believe your army commander when I say this is one of the punks who've been shooting up your comrades, killing and maiming your pals. If you call yourself an American citizen, soldier, you'll get the hell out of my way and let me smite the slit-eyed heathen S.O.B.s who've done this thing to my boys!"

"General, he's a kid. Just a kid in Russian uniform," Major Lowel Packer panted.

"I can see he's a kid, thank you, Major!"

Old Blood and Guts marched across to take a savage tug at the coarse Russian infantryman's uniform. "A goddamn, stinking little Mongol bastard who's been killing and maiming Third Army heroes. I told Ike these Mongol S.O.B.s had been bled white by the Germans. They're having to fill out their hordes with goddamn awful-looking women—and kids. Kids—that's all we've got in front of us! Do you hear me, Sergeant?" Patton turned snarling on the barricade. "There's nothing but kids between us and Moscow!"

"General, you don't get the point," Lowel Packer protested. For an educated man he was making a poor job of assembling his facts. At the same time, the Sergeant from Iowa had put his rifle down and was asking his men how you got an upturned Chevrolet truck off a road.

"General Patton," Colonel Bob Miller said calmly, "there's something more you should know about this kid."

"I'd have the little runt shot if it wasn't for the Geneva Convention, which these heathen rapists don't observe anyway!"

The tough Los Angeles cop suddenly became soothingly charming. "All I'm asking, General, is that you listen to what he's got to say." Almost lovingly Miller cradled the boy in his left arm, then swung a ferocious right into his face. "Tell the General who you are," he suggested coaxingly. A silence. Then two more appalling blows.

"*Bitte, bitte, mein Herr,*" Johan pleaded from a shattered mouth.

"My God, a lousy Kraut!" General Harrison whistled.

"They were just kidding, General," Miller explained, grinning sourly at his terrible pun. "A little old Bavarian billionaire named Martin Sauber—a onetime patron of Adolf Hitler, incidentally—had the screwy idea he could kid you into thinking you were being Pearl Harbored by the Russians."

"The crazy thing was it nearly worked," Lowel Packer insisted. "A few kids dressed up in outsize Russian uniforms nearly scared us into the ultimate *Götterdämmerung*. And this is only the half of it . . ."

Lowel Packer had a lot more to say. He wanted to tell Patton about the similar strike that Sauber had been planning against the Russians. How another detachment of pint-sized soldiers dressed in "appropriated" GI gear was scheduled to hit the Reds northeast of Hof to further Herr Sauber's plan for international misunderstanding.

Perhaps he expected commendation for the way in which they'd ripped open the Sauber operation, rounded up his associates, General von Ritter and Frolich, and alerted Tolbukhin's headquarters to the danger. But General Patton was in no mood to listen—let alone hand out medals. He walked past Packer looking straight ahead of him and climbed stiffly into his scout car. "Someone better tell Karels to get his outfit into reverse," was all he said.

Two hours later George Patton and General Bedell Smith emerged into the autumn sunlight from a small cafe in the main square of Hof to address an informal gathering of Third Army officers.

"I've just flown down here," the Beetle announced with an elusive smile, "to congratulate George on the most original and vivid peacetime exercise he's pulled off since his Fort Benning days. By the way, I've asked our Russian allies to overlook the fact that here and there, in its enthusiasm, Third Army may have accidentally taken a snip or two out of that cartographical frontier we drew up a few months ago, and I have their assurance there isn't going to be a Third World War. At least not this year. Well, I guess we've all had quite a night. You have your general's permission to dismiss."

Out of the corner of that ambiguous mouth the Beetle added, "Ike would like to see you up at Frankfurt, George, the first flyable day you can fix. Well, today looks pretty blue to me. But what about tomorrow? If you drove, you'd have plenty of time to clarify your mind. Incidentally, George, last night's little escapade is forgotten. It's got to be for diplomatic reasons. Anyway, you've got quite enough explaining to do about that press conference you gave yesterday in Bad Tölz."

"I just want you to tell me one thing," Patton said hoarsely. "What are you going to do about that stinking Judas called Regis Halleck?"

"Why, promote him to three-star general," the Beetle seemed about to chuckle. "After all, he saved your bacon, didn't he, George—or at least your reputation as a soldier? There's sure to be some nice, plush job somewhere in the Pentagon that would suit old Regis to a T."

Postmortem

Transcript of a telephone conversation between the Supreme Comamnder of USFET and his Russian opposite number in East Berlin:

> Georgi, I guess I owe you an apology, but you know how it is when you've got an underemployed army. You've got to keep them on their toes. Sorry if we got carried away here and there. But you know where I stand, Marshal Zhukhov, and ultimately they're answering to me. For your private information, you don't need to worry about George Patton. He's reporting here tomorrow, if flying conditions permit.

A crackle over the three-hundred-mile wire.

> Listen, Georgi, you can reassure Generalissimo Stalin here and now there'll be no repeats. That's positive. Thank God, I mean for Allied solidarity, our George blabbed to the press before he set out on

his reconnaissance in strength last night. As Supreme Commander from this end, I've gotten all the provocation I need to remove George Patton from effective command of fighting troops.

"I think I ought to introduce myself," said the tall, handsome, gray-haired General. "My name's Lucian Truscott, and it looks as if I'm your new Army Commander. Well, over the past week or two I've been trying to tidy up a few loose ends. And wherever I burrow, your name keeps on cropping up..."

Major Packer stood at attention in that same room at Bad Tölz where Patton had administered so many grillings.

"Take a seat, Major Packer," said the kindly General, "and try to unwind. Look, I don't know how you came to be placed in the Army, but in the strict sense you're not a military man. I took the liberty of prying into some of your academic work, and confidentially, some of that psychological group therapy stuff is fascinating. So I thought the very least we could do would be to return you to the peaceful cloisters of Cambridge, Mass.—and I imagine in time your Army career will just be a distant, if slightly painful, memory."

"Please, sir," volunteered Lowel Packer. "It sounds great to be going home, but I hope you'll give me time to wind up a few things here."

"I think for your good, you ought to go," urged General Truscott. "Honestly, it would be in your best interests to whip straight out of Bavaria today. I mean—now. You see, Major, the hard fact is that the longer you stay in Bavaria, the tougher it's going to get for you. Already your presence here has been misconstrued. Some people have said you're a Nazi sympathizer, because of your known association with Fräulein Gettler. Well, you'll be glad to know that in my opinion they can't make that stick. It was just a little loneliness—we all have that problem, Mr. Packer. No, the charge that could embarrass you comes from a different source altogether.

Some hysterical people are now saying that George Patton was overthrown by an international Communist plot to create a soft-option regime in Bavaria—ripe for the Russians to pluck. And because you're a campus man, they assume you too must be a crypto-Communist. If not, why did you send those damning psychological reports on the mental health of the General through to USFET?"

"General Bedell Smith ordered me to do that, sir!"

"Yes," agreed Lucian Truscott, "and that's why it looks worse. You see, when the whole thing comes out into the open, his role won't look that clean either. No, my worry is that some mud-slinging could develop, and to use a military term—you'd be caught in the crossfire, Mr. Packer. That's why I'm putting you on a plane out of Munich today."

"But sir," pleaded Lowel Packer. "Give me something. I just about stopped the Third World War. Singlehanded, or almost."

"I like to think that's what we all were aiming for, Mr.—sorry, Major—Packer." General Truscott smiled back.

Later that morning General Lucian Truscott had another visitor. The General went straight to the point.

"I was sent down to Bad Tölz to sort things out, Colonel," he told Bob Miller. "Well, I have to admit things have gotten into an even greater wrangle down here than I first thought. I mean, there's the undoubted fact of negative progress on de-Nazification throughout Bavaria. I mean, whether Minister-President Schaeffer was ex-Nazi, neo-Nazi, Muss-Nazi or whatever, his record isn't exactly democratic... in the broad sense, that is," Truscott added smilingly.

"Patton was my hero. I worshiped the ground he spat on," stated Miller. "But there's no doubt whatever, he was soft on Nazis. Soft, did I say? He positively rejoiced in the bastards, that's why Sauber and Co. thought they might have a lever on him. He also hated Jews, niggers, Bolivians, Creoles and other kinds of *Untermenschen*. In his lovable way he was more racialist than Hermann Goering. Christ, he had everything going for him to become the new Messiah of the Bavaria Bierkellers."

"Maybe," said Truscott, "but let's get back to facts, Colonel. And the fact is I've applied to USFET to hang onto you and your services for some time more. I first want a complete rundown on neo-Nazi activities— prepared, collated, and filed—for the consideration of myself, General Smith, General Eisenhower, General Marshall, Secretary Patterson and maybe the President, too. I want the whole case, Colonel, wrapped up and cleaned up."

"I'm already hotly engaged, sir, on precisely that."

"As for that absent-minded Professor from Cambridge, well, I've sent him back to his alma mater."

"He had guts," recalled the Colonel. "He looked like a jerk, but he could act like a hero at times."

For the second time in her life Gerda Gettler was rudely, even crudely, awakened in the early hours of the morning by an eruptive, boyish, impressionable character called Bob Miller.

"Guess I've been here before," he muttered as he toyed with the late Major Al Kopp's solid silver presentation Sherman tank. "But can't quite figure when."

"I knew you were a sadist," Gerda hissed back, "but I didn't know you were also a drunken slob."

"Check. It's the second time around," concurred Miller blearily. "I'm chasing my own tail. That kind of thing is likely to occur when you're on the Sauber trail. We picked up a lot of little people. General Klaus von Ritter, the Bürgermeister Frolich and a few, lousy murdering kids. But this guy Sauber's as elusive as a clap-free Fräulein."

"Maybe you shouldn't drink so much," Gerda suggested icily. "You have to run fast to catch a man like Martin Sauber, even though he is, maybe, forty years older than you."

"How was I to know the guy had so many friends south of the border in quaint, old, neutral Switzerland? Seems he's persona grata in the land of the cuckoo clocks, and there's nothing Uncle Sam can do to get the bum extradited."

"Perhaps, after all, Colonel Miller, you are not so tough. Didn't Wallis Du Camp get away too?"

That mean look started to show in Miller's eyes. Then it gave up in exhaustion.

"He won't get far. He's never going to get to be a general or even a colonel. That's some kind of consolation considering this is a guy you're never going to be able to pin anything on anyway. But heck, let's forget absent friends. You're missing out on the champagne."

A cork popped. Herda looked at the Colonel flatly.

"Do you and I have anything to celebrate?"

"Guess I've decided it's time I had a vacation."

"You are so disgustingly arrogant," Gerda told him with the thinnest semblance of a smile starting on her face.

"Sure. Even a cop gets one from time to time. And where better than schmaltzy Bad Tölz? Home of lederhosen and the alpenhorn."

"What are you doing?"

"I guess I'm climbing into bed," said Miller, unbuttoning his trousers. "Sure looks that way, anyway."

"Look, Colonel, this is a violation of nonfraternization. I can have you arrested."

"Know one thing," said Miller as a snapping of buttons bared a chest worthy of King Kong. "After all those months with Lowel Packer, you could use a good lover."

Gerda Gettler sipped her glass of champagne, but her eyes had a gleam of interest.

The French military band struck up *The Star-Spangled Banner* and the brass of seven Western armies came smartly to the salute. Light blue kepis, red gorgets, golden lanyards, subtle variations of khaki and navy blue, quite a colorful picture on what was otherwise a bleak, cold day in the outskirts of Paris in January 1951.

The man they were welcoming at Marly that afternoon was perhaps the only military leader in the Western world with the personality and prestige to command the hodgepodge of undersized armies hopefully entitled the NATO Alliance.

He was plumper around the face now, and his new uniform couldn't disguise the fact that his figure had filled out as well. What hadn't changed was that smile, the smile that had and would weld all manner of unlikely allies together. This time against the growing threat of Russia. Ike was back.

The band had completed the U.S. national anthem with a typical French flourish, and now the ceremony was all smiles. After all, it was a reunion for old warriors.

First in line for General Eisenhower's inspection, beaming like a benevolent schoolmaster under the unmistakable tank corps beret, was Field Marshal Lord Montgomery of Alamein. Who would have thought, as they engaged in animated conversation, that they had ever exchanged a bitter word? Possibly General Juin of France couldn't have been described as one of Ike's closest wartime associates, but the new Supreme Comamnder greeted him like one. In fact, all the way along the line of senior European commanders it was a case of "Great to see you again."

Ike was a democratic general, or at least a Republican with a strong sense of the Democrat. Another commander might have limited the pleasantries to the top brass, but as Eisenhower and his Chief of Staff, the diminutive Al Gruenther, moved on to the more junior officers, the first-name greetings were kept up. After all, a lot of these brigadiers and colonels had been majors and captains on his SHAEF staff.

There was only one moment in an agreeable afternoon when Ike's cherubic face dropped its grin. This was curiously enough when the Supreme Commander of NATO paused in front of a glintingly smart U.S. colonel.

"It's a pleasure to serve under you again, sir," Colonel Wallis Du Camp beamed. In the crowd his exquisite new French wife (formerly the Comtesse de la Panne) was angling with her camera to immortalize the scene. Thoughtfully Du Camp produced a pretty turn of phrase to keep the great man in his wife's viewfinder. "Lafayette must be turning happily in his grave this afternoon, sir," he said.

It was at this point that Ike managed to place the face—this was the posturing, cynical major who'd arrived at his headquarters on the cathartic night of September 1945. The world's friendliest countenance clouded into a scowl, and General Eisenhower moved on.

Perhaps he just didn't want to be reminded of the night. Or perhaps his mind had tracked back to an earlier incident when he had caught this flashy colonel in earnest conversation with Kay Summersby in the cellars of Berchtesgaden. Kay had to be one of his most sensitive memories, especially as Marshall and Truman had decreed he must never see her again. There could have been yet a third reason for likable Ike's unexpected hostility toward Colonel Wallis Du Camp this January afternoon. It could just have crossed his mind that If Du Camp hadn't ratted on his commanding officer, George Patton might just have made it to Moscow. No Czechoslovakia. No Berlin airlift. No Korean War. No need to leave the golf links of upstate New York. No necessity for NATO. Such could have been the course of history if Patton had slipped the leash on the night of September 22 in 1945. It was a thought to make the friendlist Western leader frown.

Incidentally, George Patton himself was not present, in body at least, at this significant parade of Allied power. He was lying some two hundred and fifty miles to the east in the American Cemetery at Hamm in Luxembourg.

Dismissed for tactlessness in the face of the U.S. press from command of his beloved Third Army, and kicked upstairs to a position of impotency under the Beetle's watchful eye, he had planned to return to the United States to campaign vigorously for a tougher line against Communism. But accidents will happen. A few weeks before his departure he died as a result of a motor accident on the Frankfurt–Mannheim road.

Sit down, relax and read a good book...

CURRENT BESTSELLERS FROM BERKLEY